RIGORMORTIE

Death by Sex Puppet

DICK BOUVIER AND DECEMBER BOUVIER

RIGORMORTIE
DEATH BY SEX PUPPET

Published by RigorMortie LLC
www.rigormortie.com

Published in the United States of America
ISBN-13: 9780997174618
ISBN-10: 0997174617

Edited by Karin Kohlmeier, Ph.D.
kkohlmeier@gmail.com

For Eddie.

"...the vision in his right eye had been blurry for years, the result of a fellatio mishap that left his Indian girlfriend toothless and hard of hearing."

About The Authors

Dick and December Bouvier hooked up at a criminal career symposium in Boston where they later founded and operated a lucrative insurance fraud business. They currently live on the campus of Florida Union Collegiate University where Dick is an adjunct professor of body waxing and December runs a numbers game from the backroom of a laundromat. In their spare time, the Bouviers raise non-GMO, free-range pythons. This is their first literary effort since their failed attempt to claim copyright ownership of The Bible.

AUTHORS' NOTE

The story that follows is satire.

In the event that you slept through high school English like we did, satire is defined by the Oxford Dictionary as:

"the use of humor, irony, exaggeration, or ridicule to expose and criticize people's stupidity or vices, particularly in the context of contemporary politics and other topical issues."

That means that the book makes fun of a lot people including, but by no means limited to, racists, misogynists, haters, greedy corporate executives, scammers, shady lawyers, and others in America who make up the puke-inducing gum that sticks itself to the bottom of society's shoes.

It also means that if you see yourself in some of the more disreputable characters in this book, you're probably a dick. In fact, we'd pretty much guarantee it.

On the other hand, if you're the kind of person who can distinguish between sarcasm and a slur, love to laugh, and are cool with the kind of vulgarity that your mother would label disgusting, we can pretty much guarantee that you'll like this story.

Whether you enjoy it or not, though, the important thing to remember is that there are no refunds.

Dick and December Bouvier

January 2016

Chapter 1

"...he had clearly come to love three things in life: his penis, cartoons, and vodka which he cleverly poured into his clown-face sippy cup from his mother's bedside bottle."

By the time he started fifth grade, Morton Wayne Beech had a comb-over, a 40-inch waist, and a penis that was his pride and joy.

Born in the Beech Family Wing at Boring Memorial Hospital, Mortie was unenthusiastically welcomed into the world by wealthy, heavily intoxicated parents who owned a lucrative Chinese car dealership in Oldmens, Florida. At 42 pounds and 34" long, he was too big to fit in the hospital nursery's bassinet. The problem required nurses to lay him on the floor in a see-through plastic storage box. Just to be safe, they taped a "No Basura" sign on the side so the night cleaners wouldn't mistake him for a leftover pork roast and throw him away.

Even though obesity dripped from the branches of both family trees like grease from deep fried bacon, Belvin Beech and his wife, Sandy Lynn, were inexplicably surprised by the bulkiness of their bundle of joy. This was despite the fact that Sandy Lynn's pregnancy more than doubled her weight and made her look like the broad side of Iowa.

If it seemed strange that the Beeches were flabbergasted over giving birth to a newborn the size of a four-year-old, it was stranger yet that neither could remember doing anything to cause it. To say that the couple wasn't intimate was the height of understatement. Despite working in adjacent offices, they rode to and from the showroom in separate, chauffeur-driven, American-made limousines.

Every afternoon, Sandy Lynn Beech drank her lunch in the service department with Ju-Long Garcia, a half-Chinese, half-Cuban midget with an eight-inch tongue that made him both popular with the ladies and a skilled car detailer. Belvin usually choked down a ham and cheese while his stacked, redheaded assistant, Deedee, choked him down from underneath his desk.

What kept the Beeches together, frankly, was money. As the sole heir to Clench It Up, a national chain of walk-in vaginal tightening clinics, Sandy Lynn would eventually inherit an astoundingly prosperous business empire.

Founded by her parents, who had started out in the frozen bovine semen business, Clench It Up brilliantly re-purposed the artificial vaginas that bulls enjoyed in order to catch the national tidal wave of demand for vaginal rejuvenation. From one clinic providing side-by-side bovine and human sperm collection services in Montana in 1985, the company grew to more than 500 centers serving 3,000 women a day in strip malls in all 50 states.

One promotion in particular, the Hot Pink Cookie, a mother-daughter weekend that packaged vaginal renewal, anal bleaching, a Brazilian wax and high tea for $12,000 a pop, more than quintupled the company's already behemoth revenues and helped them launch a multi-million-dollar IPO.

Just like the Clench It Up business itself, the company's catchy theme song became extremely popular across the country by way of an around-the-clock barrage of TV and radio commercials:

> "If he's floppin' his dong 'cuz he ain't no King Kong,
> Ya' gotta make it right and make ya' kitty tight!
> Clench it Up! Clench it Up!

> Ya' know a Hot Pink Cookie will get ya' smokin' nookie.
> We don't ask no cash advance 'cuz we do our own finance!
> Clench it Up! Clench it Up!

If ya' got some busted credit ya' don't nevah gotta sweat it.
We treat you fair and square so get yo' legs up in the air!
Clench it Up! Clench it Up!"

For as long as he could remember, Mortie hated his family. Virtually from the day he was potty-trained, his assholes of a mommy and daddy left him home alone from dawn to dusk without lights or air conditioning and nothing more than a box of cereal, a black-and-white TV, and a seven-inch-long Florida chameleon. Mortie's relationship with the lizard that had wandered inside the house one day and become his only buddy ended abruptly when he accidentally stepped on the little critter and squished him to death. He took the gooey remains and put them in one of his father's dress shoes.

The old man never even noticed the stench.

A highly conspicuous figure at 5'3" and 418 pounds, Belvin Beech turned a remarkably unattractive thirty years old a few days before Ronald Reagan won the 1980 presidential election. In addition to a flimsy brown mustache, tiny, fat legs that looked like pork chops with shoes, and a chronic rectal itch that forced him to take very small, careful steps when he walked, he did himself no favors by wearing ill-fitting XXXXXXXL black suits. Between four and five inches too long, his size 64 pants dragged on the floor and collected dust like a mop.

Widely known around town as a "prick's prick," Belvin was the kind of guy who was far more likely to push an old lady into the path of an oncoming bus than help her cross the street. He released dark, mind-altering farts in crowded places. At dinner parties, he'd soak his pants in his own urine and sit on his host's upholstered furniture. He accused people in wheelchairs of being lazy and kicked homeless Vietnam vets in the head.

With that kind of reputation, it wouldn't have surprised anyone who knew the bastard that the day his baby boy got his head stuck between the bars in his playpen he told his son to "fucking figure it out yourself, ass clown," closed the door and walked away. It took Mortie two days of wiggling and weight loss from dehydration to get free.

In the big picture, Mortie's mother was less conspicuous but just as nasty. Polite society would have once described her as being a healthy-looking woman, a nicer way of saying that her ass covered three time zones. In the years before Sandy Lynn Beech started inhaling a fifth of vodka twice a day, she was an attractive girl with a beautiful face, striking green eyes, raven-black hair, and an exceptionally hot body that she loved to show off in extra-clingy tops and hot pants. Unfortunately, those pluses were largely zeroed out by an unappealing thick neck and unusually large hands that were the same size as her feet.

Despite those stumbling blocks, she prospered in high school and college by readily agreeing to sex with the most popular boys and teachers. That said, she had several rules that required agreement before anybody touched anything.

First, she didn't take any of her clothes off. Ever.

Second, her paramour was required to wear a special ballistic yarn, steel-reinforced, stab-resistant condom bathed in contraceptive jelly.

Third, in exchange for "being did," the "did one" would perform special favors for her.

Last, but very far from least, was that the "did one" would never tell anyone anything about their relationship.

The punishment for failure was simple: they would never get their rocks off with her again. As every lover, male or female, appreciated after only a few minutes in Sandy Lynn's hands, banishment would be a crueler fate than death.

Making sure that everyone followed her instructions required leverage, and Sandy Lynn had plenty of it. Her extraordinary moves transformed ordinary male orgasms into mystical experiences. An aspiring professional to the core, she studied anatomy and the physics of ejaculation and developed an impressive knowledge of male arousal techniques despite only being able to read 25 words a minute with 50 percent comprehension.

When she performed what she called "supercharging" with two of her fingers, she could turn up the muscle in her lover's sexual command center from the equivalent of a push mower to an F-18 Tomcat.

Unlike that of other penis practitioners, Sandy Lynn's work didn't produce an unsatisfying dribble or the 28 mph speed researchers clocked for average male orgasms. Sandy Lynn's ejaculation rose up slowly from the testicles where it remained for what seemed like an eternity until the man felt as if he was suspended in time and space. Then the perineal muscles, prostate and shaft of the Johnson would work in concert to release a fusillade of unimaginably pleasurable contractions, eventually firing the sperm at 75 mph through the urethra in one continuous stream.

Many guys found themselves unable to talk for at least an hour afterward. Some shook from pure ecstasy, others broke into sobs of joy, and more than a few completely blacked out. One even died. A coroner concluded that faculty member Juan "Bucky" Castro, Ph.D. passed away from a subarachnoid hemorrhage moments after his ejaculate pierced the roof of the car he was seated in. Sandy Lynn's physics professor, one of her frequent flyers, suggested that NASA could learn a thing or two from her about propulsion.

A lot of boys who didn't know anything about Sandy Lynn's sexual exploits wanted to date her simply because of her hot body and seeming popularity. She went out with some, enjoyed their money and gifts, but never even kissed them goodnight. From those whose pocket rockets she touched, of course, she extracted much, much more. Among other things, Sandy Lynn had 50-yard-line football tickets, floor seats at basketball games, a time-share in Boca, free podiatry services, and guaranteed annual selection as the school's homecoming queen.

As it happened, one of the boys who summoned enough courage to ask her out was a fit and trim young man with thick sideburns and a wavy brown comb-over by the name of Belvin Morton Beech. A fellow member of the Class of 1972 at Florida Union Collegiate University, Belvin was a hardworking, if not very smart, business administration major with a solid C-minus average.

He was also a school legacy. Florida Union, whose Latin motto "Vestra Alternative Ut Opus-Liberetur" meant "Your Alternative to Work Release," was founded in 1889 by his great-great-grandfather and great-great uncle, Edward and Vinny Palomino. The Palomino Brothers, who were originally from Chelsington, Massachusetts, made their fortunes as the owners of Steed-O-Rama City, South Florida's first pre-owned, low mileage horse dealership.

Belvin's older brother, Mickey, who died from bizarre masturbation-induced injuries involving a burned Florida Union cheerleader hand puppet when he was 40, had also gone to school there.

Spread out over an impressive 800 acres in the southern Everglades near Big Hare Key Basin, the university was the primary destination for high school graduates who ranked in the bottom 3% of their class, social deviants, and felons, including a large number of mortgage bankers. While other institutions required tough, expensive admissions tests, Florida Union could boast that its entrance exam involved little more than fingerprinting.

The school took great pride in its 35,000 full-time undergraduates, a physical plant consisting of 392 buildings, accreditation by the state and the Florida Department of Corrections, and an 80,000 seat, state-of-the-art football stadium. Their Division I Fuming Sea Turtles—also known as "The Puce Wave" because of the odd, brownish-purple stripe in their otherwise flat, dark brown helmets and uniforms—had not only enjoyed 60 consecutive winning seasons but led the nation in the post-game deaths of opposing players.

Florida Union could also be proud of the size of its research grants and the school's endowment. Florida Union's president, Dr. Amerigo "Chick" Vespucci, was the single most prolific fundraiser in the school's history. Among other stunning successes, Vespucci convinced philanthropists in Columbia and Peru to donate $275 million a year to Florida Union to advance the study of agriculture and chemistry. Their generosity built the university's Pablo Escobar College of International Trade where advanced research and development was conducted around the clock related to hydroponics, methadone, methamphetamines, methyl testosterone, bufotenine, and artificial sweeteners.

Courtesy of other benefactors President Vespucci recruited in Mexico, Bolivia, Panama, and West Africa, Florida Union had an endowment that rivaled those of Ivy League colleges. Unlike other private schools that had their money in stocks and bonds, however, Florida Union's billion-dollar endowment was largely in fifties and hundreds buried in rusty metal drums in the Everglades.

The captain of both the wrestling and competitive leg waxing teams, Belvin had huge biceps, an eight-pack, a great-fitting blazer, and what appeared from the outside to be an unusually large banana that Sandy Lynn desperately wanted to peel.

Unlike the other men and women she dated, Sandy Lynn actually liked Belvin. In fact, it wasn't long before she found herself falling in love with young Mr. Beech. Their relationship grew despite an absence of sexual activity, something Sandy Lynn was very anxious about for fear that Belvin might like her more for the prospect of her touching his thang than touching his heart. That wall eventually had to come down, of course, and it did one Thursday night in the faint light of a restaurant parking lot.

Among the impossibly hot aspects of Sandy Lynn's body were porn star-grade jubblies that were so splendid that they seemed to jiggle even when they were standing still. That evening, they were more heavily on Belvin's mind than usual as he guided her into the huge, shadowy back seat of his purple 1966 Buick Wildcat. Parked near the dumpsters behind The Chubby Vulture, a popular local bistro where candied eel on a stick was a house specialty, Sandy Lynn and Belvin made out with feverish passion while relishing the aroma of sexual suspense fused with deep fried tripe.

Realizing that he truly had a shot at visiting the Grand Canyon as he kissed his way down the nape of her neck, Belvin readied himself for the move he had dreamed about making but had so far been terrified to try. Taking a deep breath, he buried his nose and mouth in Sandy Lynn's cleavage. Much to his delight, she didn't resist. Everything smelled like heaven as he kissed his way through the creamy valley separating her miraculous cantaloupes while attaching his left hand to the full-length front zipper of her red mini-dress.

Lying on her back, Sandy Lynn reached around his neck and pulled his lips tightly against hers as she moved her pelvis in a gyrating motion that made his anaconda as stiff as a baseball bat. Feeling safe from rejection, he pulled down on the zipper and exposed her blue-and-white-striped bra.

Without saying a word, Sandy Lynn released the bra's front clasp, allow-ing her dreamy pink nipples to flow into Belvin's hungry mouth. He tugged on the zipper again to expose matching panties that he quickly pulled to her knees and then, with a broad smile, pulled down again to the bottom of her white knee-length boots.

Belvin could see her full, moist lips glisten in the shadows and, as his mind raced to the image of her warm mouth closing around his throbbing member, Sandy Lynn reached forward and unbuttoned his pants. With her rich nakedness laid out before him for the taking, she reached through his boxer shorts, pulled out a wadded-up gym sock, and brushed the underside of his uncircumcised penis with her finger.

"I want you," Sandy Lynn said in a breathy, Marilyn Monroe-style voice that made Belvin's testicles tremble.

No sooner did the words leave Sandy Lynn's lips than she felt warm, sticky sperm in the palm of her hand, the irony of which was not lost on her. As it turned out, Belvin's problems were less about ejaculating prematurely than com-ing in advance. Premature ejaculation, after all, would mean that he reached a climax during sexual intercourse sooner than either he or Sandy Lynn wanted. In Belvin's case, he had an orgasm before they even started. As unfortunate as it was for their relationship, it could also be horribly embarrassing.

Sometimes merely brushing against Sandy Lynn's hand could drive him into a sexual frenzy. One Saturday, she casually touched his arm while they were picking up pork blood sausage petit fours from fast food eatery Salute to Liverwurst at the local mall.

Jerking his arms and legs uncontrollably like he was having a seizure, Belvin accidentally spilled his lunch tray on the lap of an elderly, wheelchair-bound Rastafarian draped in a Bob Marley afghan. Then, in front of a crowd of wildly cheering onlookers, Belvin dropped to all fours, made seven or eight intense pelvic thrusts, and creamed in his pants while screaming, "*Oh, God! Take it, baby! Take the big one!*"

Understandably, the mall management prepared itself for an avalanche of customer complaints about Belvin's performance. Although hundreds of com-plaints poured in, however, only a handful concerned the sexual spectacle. Even though it was many years before smoking became verboten, the vast majority criticized security for letting Belvin light up a cigarette after satisfying himself.

Despite the failure of popular remedies advertised on TV to fix the problem in their burning loins, Belvin and Sandy Lynn were married one June day in front of 25 guests, nine of whom they knew, in Oldmens' 3,000-seat Cathedral of Limited Liability. Sadly, Sandy Lynn's mother and father refused to attend because Belvin wasn't a Hassidic Jew, a particular curiosity in light of the fact that they were practicing Catholics.

So horny that they could barely function any longer, Sandy Lynn and Belvin prayed for a miracle that would bottle up Belvin long enough to take a ride in the tunnel of love. Night after night, month after month, Belvin's comatose wee-wee oozed pitifully, and Sandy Lynn's dissatisfaction with feeling great waves of nothing grew stronger. Sandy Lynn blamed all of her problems on her husband's impotence, and Belvin blamed his impotence on Sandy Lynn's complaints about his impotence.

As time passed, the couple's sexual distress fueled a boiling hostility between the two that grew as rapidly as their waistlines as they buried themselves in triple bacon cheeseburgers, fish sticks, chocolate cake, and high proof liquor.

Unbelievably, potential answers like sex toys, psychological counseling, and a call to a urologist never crossed their simple minds. Drowning needlessly in their own miserable, booze-drenched corpulence, Belvin and Sandy Lynn Beech were two dim-witted people who couldn't have seen a solution to a problem if it shit in their ears. Far worse, they turned their rage, contempt and icy cold indifference on Baby Mortie.

They mocked the poor little fellow by dubbing him "The Stump."

"Don't you love me, Mommy?" Mortie asked one morning in a tone that went from distressed to terrified in the space of only a few words. He saw mothers hugging and kissing their children on TV and desperately wanted his to do the same.

"No," Sandy Lynn replied matter-of-factly as she sucked down her second dirty martini of the day through a straw. At least she didn't belabor the matter.

With that, Baby Mortie swore as much vengeance on the man and woman who brought him into the world as a three-year-old could muster. Exceptionally smart for his age and teetering on the edge of an acute psychotic break, he watched closely for opportunities to take his parents down with as much pain-inducing violence as possible. Unfamiliar with guns, knives, and popular poisoning methods, he had to settle for adhering razor blades to sticky toilet seats and hunting down his plastered parents while they slept.

He had all of the instincts of a predator. On nights when he decided to be "active," a state of mind he would later come to associate with murderers like Jeff Dahmer and Ted Bundy, he would spy on Mommy and Daddy from a distance to observe behavior patterns that could suggest how successful he might be. If Mommy or Daddy ate a lot of dinner but didn't drink a lot from their big people bottles, he would drop back into the darkness to wait for a more favorable time. If they drank a lot from their big people bottles and started walking funny, he'd dart silently from room to room like a tiny terrorist to study them further.

If Mommy or Daddy got into bed with their big people bottle and started to snore loudly, Mortie would move close and stand virtually motionless, carefully syncing his breathing with theirs to blend seamlessly into the setting. Sometimes he would wait an hour or more until the house was very dark and still. Then, when the moment felt right, he would raise his chubby little fists and start hitting Mommy or Daddy in the mouth, nose, eyes, throat and cheeks as hard and fast as he could. Sometimes he would feel something in their face give way as he hit it or get their blood on his hands, both of which he found satisfying.

When Mommy or Daddy woke up, Mortie would vanish like a ghost by squeezing his tonnage under the bed and waiting soundlessly until the coast was clear to go back to his room. Depending on how much fury was brewing inside him, he would attack his parents as many as two or three nights in a row. On Christmas Eves, he made it a tradition to hit them twice in a single night while wearing a Santa hat.

Entirely too wasted to realize what was going on, Belvin and Sandy Lynn never suspected Mortie as the culprit. Foolishly, they assumed that their cuts and bruises were the result of falling on the floor during booze-powered blackouts. Even more, Mortie would sometimes give his unconscious mother a haircut. Incredibly, she never noticed that the left side of her head looked like she had mange.

As much as Mortie wanted to see both of his parents slowly buried alive in cement, he was surprisingly rational in recognizing the advantages he enjoyed by having parents that ignored him. Over time, he taught himself to turn on the lights and the air conditioning, change the TV channels, order out from restaurants, and use the broiler to grill steaks and chicken. By the ripe old age of five, he could sit back with satisfaction and say that he had clearly come to love three things in life: his penis, cartoons, and vodka which he cleverly poured into his clown-face sippy cup from his mother's bedside bottle. Vodka and a splash of apple juice tended to smooth out the edges of everything from loneliness to the painful rectal itch he inherited from his father. Relaxed and half in the bag himself, Mortie rarely bothered to change out of the cowboy pajamas, leather slippers, and red silk smoking jacket that made him look like a pint-sized porno king.

He loved it when his perpetually sloshed mother came home in the evenings and praised him for being ready for bed. Except for the nights he went "hunting," he would stand silently in his mother's room, expressionless, eyes cold and empty, hands clutching the slowly-leaking bag of flour he used as a Teddy Bear, watching for the inevitable moment when she would pass out. When she did, he'd grab ten bucks from her purse and call in a peanut butter and jelly pizza, leaving him free to watch TV or grease the basement stairs in hopes that his father would take a tragic tumble.

Although mostly barren and emotionless, life for Mortie was not entirely without joy.

Like most children, Mortie wanted a pet, and his first and only choice was a dog. He asked his father for one, but after the old man told him "the only dog we're going to have in this house is your mother," Mortie fell into a lengthy depression. Disappointed with the decision, he shaved off his sleeping father's eyebrows and replaced them with round yellow candies that he attached with industrial-strength glue.

Still determined to have a little pal, Mortie eventually found companionship surprisingly close to home in the person of his penis, a happy, sensitive soul with an independent mind and an exceptionally strong will. They soon became fast friends, and Mortie named him "Mr. Pup-Pup" in honor of the warm, fluffy, puppy he would never have. They had play dates, overnighters, and sometimes even arm wrestled.

Occasionally, the lad would borrow clothes from his father's collection of vintage action figures and dress "Mr. Pup-Pup" from top to bottom as a cowboy, a king, or a soldier. He even decked out "Mr. Pup-Pup" as a scuba diver complete with a mask and flippers. At least a few times a week, Mortie would let "Mr. Pup-Pup" out for some fresh air, sunshine, and conversation. The boy would prop up his head on a mountain of pillows so that he and his pal could look each other in the eye. The hours simply flew by as they talked about the adventures they would have, the people they would meet, and the exciting places they would go.

Far more than just a comrade in arms, "Mr. Pup-Pup's" good looks probably did more than anything to boost Mortie's self-image. "Mr. Pup-Pup" also stood by his man.

When they finally lost their virginity together at the age of 25, "Mr. Pup-Pup" courageously led the way inside the dark grotto of red-haired, 38-year-old Kelly "Minimal Symptoms" Herpeliman who worked in Mortie's office. Also known as "Kelly the Jelly" because of her persistent runny nose and fondness for spermicides, she was as easy to get into as a junior college. It was twice as easy if her date had a five dollar bottle of champagne.

Trembling with apprehension and scared that he might ejaculate before he reached the end zone, young Mortie told "Mr. Pup-Pup" to take a deep breath as he pulled a thick, stimulation-resistant "Nunca Orgasmo" Mexican brand condom over his head. Not entirely sure what they were doing, Mortie and "Mr. Pup-Pup" tried the missionary position first but found the stream of mucous exiting Kelly's nostrils more than they could stomach.

Remembering the diagrams in the "Doin' It Doggy Style" chapter of his high school sex-ed book, *Tap That Ass!*, the boys gently turned Kelly face down on the pillow and lifted her snow-white booty to just the right height.

After getting a good look inside her cave with the tiny flashlight he kept for such situations, "Mr. Pup-Pup" gave Mortie a thumbs-up sign, saluted, and plunged into the abyss like a commando. Kelly relished four unbelievable orgasms before she felt the boys go limp. Not unexpectedly, she insisted that they come back for another "threesie" anytime they liked. "Mr. Pup-Pup" wiped the sweat off of his brow and Mortie gave her a wink and a nod. The boys liked the fact that everybody left a winner.

When he recovered an hour or so later, "Mr. Pup-Pup" couldn't help but swell with pride. Whenever Mortie wanted to put a bag over his head, shove him in a dark hole, and make him do pushups until he hurled, it was more than okay with him. "Pup-Pup's the name, horizontal refreshment's the game" he would often say to himself smugly.

To him sex, far more than urination, defined his purpose in life.

And he was damn good at it.

Tick, Tock. Friday, 5:07 p.m.

She was beautiful in a chaotic sort of way.

Catching his first glimpse of her from behind the sneeze shield at Uncle Deng's All You Can Eat (Not Sit on Your Fat Ass and Eat 4Ever) Chinese Super Buffet, Mortie nearly choked on the Tung Ting shrimp he was inhaling. She was 25 or possibly 43 with an oval face, pouting, glossy, nude lips, and perfectly-shaped breasts that were nearly spilling out of her tight black tube top. Her drowsy, light blue eyes and brown eye shadow were framed by straight, shoulder-length, dirty blonde hair with long sweeping bangs and large, gold hoop earrings. At 5'7" and 127 pounds with long, alluring legs and an ass like mortal sin, she was midway between being crowned prom queen and joining the ranks of sad-eyed women in dirty bathrobes that spend their days huffing glue.

The sight of her spray-tanned cleavage engorged Mortie with excitement, generating more than enough saliva to cleanse his mouth of his third second helping of Moo Goo Gai Pan. As she rounded the buffet table, he blocked her way with his bloated belly, a public eyesore that drooped over his belt so far that it nearly touched his knees.

"May I fill it?" he asked, using his favorite double entendre as he reached out to take her plate.

"Yes, you may," she said as she handed it to him, making sure that their fingertips touched in a way that made it clear that she understood what he wanted for dessert.

"Make it something *big ... and hot*" she said licking her silky lips and flaunting a tongue that hinted that she might know her way around a penis.

Then she turned, purposely brushing the back of her tight, extra short denim skirt against the front of his pants. The movement surprisingly penetrated the multiple layers of moist flesh and knotted pubic hair that covered his throbbing pink oboe.

"What's your name, Beautiful?" Mortie asked, gasping for breath while every inch of his 389-pound, 5'1" frame jiggled like jelly with anticipation.

"My name's Constance Anne," she purred, sliding her top down just enough to push him to the wafer-thin edge of sanity. She was the kind of woman who left the promise of unforgettable everything in her wake wherever she went.

"What's yours?" she asked to be sure that his name matched the one on the plastic in his wallet.

"Mortie. Mortie Beech," he responded in a high-pitched, excited voice as he embraced himself through a large hole he'd worn in his pants pocket. His unconcealed enthusiasm nailed him as an easy mark.

Constance Anne smiled broadly to show that she didn't have meth mouth, a condition that makes tweakers' teeth turn dark and crumble in the most fuckingly repulsive way possible. It was a not-so-subtle signal that she'd be far more expensive than standard street cuisine. She uttered a sad, world-weary sigh that Mortie paid no attention to, a resignation of sorts to the fact that she had no way to make more than the minimum wage other than going to bed with the chubosaurus standing in front of her.

A few minutes later, Mortie and Constance Anne walked out of the Super Buffet's red and gold front door hand-in-hand into the wilting Florida humidity.

Morbidly obese at 40 years old with a greasy brown comb-over, a thin, sweaty mustache, and 4XL man hooters, Mortie could count the satisfying sexual experiences he'd had in recent years on one hand. Having already inherited more of his old man's nightmarish genes than he could stand, he'd also recently developed another hereditary misfortune from his mother's side called EED.

An offshoot of Delayed Ejaculation Syndrome, Eventual Ejaculation Disorder sufferers could wait seven to ten days to climax after a single sexual encounter.

As Mortie and Constance Anne approached his pastel blue car, he prayed that he'd hit it out of the ballpark with her and, if not, that at least she wouldn't run away like the last one. As she hopped into Mortie's car, Constance Anne ran her hands over the vehicle's plush purple seat covers.

She liked the idea that her date drove an expensive car. In her mind it reduced the possibility that he was an undercover cop. She'd learned that the answer to the question, "How much for sex?" asked by a man in a black Crown Victoria with flashing lights and a cage between the front and back seats was "leave me alone," not "a hundred bucks."

"How much? How much?" Mortie asked her excitedly as he landed in the driver's side with a thud that flattened the tires like pancakes. As he spoke, she noticed nervous sweat dripping unpleasantly from his mustache all the way down to his third chin.

"Easy, Godzilla," Constance Anne said, touching up her lip gloss in the courtesy mirror. Rubbing her lips side to side, she pulled a brochure and her smart phone out of the $40 "Cooch" purse she bought from an Indian guy who reeked of spoiled ghee and operated out of the trunk of a rusted-out Yugo. The bag was a constant reminder of how much better her life would be if she could spell.

"Five hundred for the evening," she said as she handed him a pencil and a four-page "Menyou of Survisis" written in English, Spanish, Russian, and Ebonics. Customers could check off what they wanted from a list starting with anal sex and continuing through the alphabet to ziganka, a Russian country dance Constance Anne said she would perform in nothing but a beanie.

"Credit, debit, or EBT?" she asked, affixing a credit card reader to a "borrowed" smartphone after checking his driver's license. When the card-issuer approved the charge, she asked Mortie to sign the screen with his fingertip.

A few minutes later they pulled into La Cama Cheapo, a filthy, two-story, aqua-colored, 1950's-style motel that had its last paint job when Michael Jackson was a black kid.

The landscape featured a muck-filled swimming pool, a dead palm tree, two broken lawn chairs, and a hulking woman whose thick assmeat hung over the sides of her limited mobility scooter. A family-size bucket of greasy fried chicken was tied to the steering column with twine, and she was shoving wings and thighs into her mouth with one hand while lighting a cigarette inches above her leaky oxygen tank with the other.

Wherever she went, a distinctive stench of ass and onions preceded her by a city block.

CHAPTER 2

*"That went twice for Geronimo, a shirtless Jalapeno Indian who
sniffed gasoline in a zip lock bag and occasionally terrorized her by
swapping out his glass eye for a Brussels sprout."*

onstance Anne Madonna Dominica O'Leary of Chelsington, Massachusetts was
the product of a Catholic convent school that left her knees red, her knuck-
les swollen, and her morals negotiable.

Nearly 18, she had only rarely been outside of the ivy-covered walls of
The Church of St. Woodrow of the Holy Cross since the age of five. That was
the year her mother, BritNee, a burgundy-haired stripper with black roots
and a ketamine addiction, curiously left her on the front steps with literally
nothing more than a raw onion in a paper bag.

Founded in 1897 by the Sisters of the General Ledger, a fringe group
devoted to "putting the Jesus back in Christ," the church was better known
in the community by a different, less reverent name. According to newspaper
reports from 1901, construction of St. Woodrow's was wrapping up when the
man engraving the church's name on its breathtaking 80-foot marble archway
died suddenly from complications related to athlete's foot. The good news
was that he'd finished the job through the word "Holy." The bad news was
that the archbishop was coming the next day with a check and expected to
see the work completed.

Behind schedule and desperately in need of cash, the contractor hired the engraver's youthful assistant to carve the final word. Had the contractor known that the young man was a paregoric junkie who slammed down three slugs of lightly-diluted opium every morning, he wouldn't have been as surprised that "Crotch" had been chiseled into the marble instead of "Cross."

Although the error was corrected at enormous cost in 1913 with funds diverted from the Poor Box, the name stuck like glue.

Unusual for a place of worship, the distinguished tan brick buildings and beautifully-landscaped grounds of the "Crotch" were locked inside a 20-foot-tall, electrified, barbed-wire fence. A moat said to contain carnivorous fish with legs surrounded the entire facility. Behind the moat was an arsenal of deadly landmines nicknamed "Josés" because they often exploded under the feet of grass-cutting crews who couldn't read the warning signs in English. The mines were the last line of defense before an intruder would come face-to-face with acne-splattered teenage acolytes armed with assault weapons.

In 2010, a town council member called for an inquiry into a series of potentially illegal activities going on behind the church walls. The investigation ended abruptly when the lawmaker, a respected family man, was found in a public toilet with five bullet holes in the back of his head. At the time of his death, he was cradled in the arms of a sobbing Armenian prostitute named Marshmallow.

The coroner, whose wife worked as a highly-paid cleavage stylist for the archdiocese, said the death was the worst suicide he'd ever seen.

Compared to living with her mother, Constance Anne considered the Crotch a great joy. Even though she shared a room with eight other girls, Constance Anne was simply grateful that she wouldn't be bumping into her mother's crack-ass boyfriends in the dark anymore. That went twice for Geronimo, a shirtless Jalapeno Indian who sniffed gasoline in a zip lock bag and occasionally terrorized her by swapping out his glass eye for a Brussels sprout.

Speaking of food, that was much better at the Crotch, too. There was fancy fare like eggs with spam gravy, haddock juice, and chicken sushi, a far cry from the morning when all she could find at home was a half-empty box of crackers and a fifth of Scotch.

Constance Anne also loved the cute factor of the school uniform: a blue plaid pleated skirtini that barely covered her thighs, white leather bustier, white ankle socks, and black platform pumps with five-inch heels.

Even more, she had her own bed most of the time. Because there were only eight beds for nine girls, Constance Anne would occasionally, and be-grudgingly, have a bed buddy. Begrudgingly, that is, unless the bed buddy was Mary Margaret Gionfriddo, a gorgeous blonde with emerald eyes and stunning everything who at 15 was three or four years older than the other roommates. Constance Anne loved spooning with her, smelling her freshly shampooed hair, and gazing at the faultlessness of her lips when Mary was asleep. Sometimes they would nod off together in their regulation black mo-nokini sleepwear after a giggly kiss and wake in the morning like mother and child with Constance Anne curled up under Mary's arm. A few years later, particularly when she was living in a cardboard box in Cambridge, Constance Anne would remember those nights as the happiest of her life.

Along with the splendid comforts it provided, there was a dark side to the Crotch that students and local residents alike were reluctant to discuss. Much of the fear originated with Sister Juan, St. Woody's Mother Superior.

An imposing figure with a long face, raven-black hair, five o'clock shad-ow, and glossy pink lips, Sister Juan stood six feet tall with large feet, large hands, and a bodacious rack that she said came from soaking in "Tetas Muy Grande," her own brand of holy water. Available online for $49.95 an ounce plus shipping, "Tetas" came in used pill bottles with a picture of the Mother Superior's Golden Bozos on one side and an old, partially peeled-off, pre-scription label on the other.

Flaunting her distaste for Catholic couture, Sister Juan wore a yellow and white striped seersucker habit with cargo shorts and penny loafers during the summer. After Labor Day, she donned a navy pinstripe habit with gray flannel riding chaps and lizard-skin stiletto boots. Her beauty regimen in-cluded having her plush eyebrows regularly sheared and the hairs on her toes plucked every Tuesday by a three-fingered Korean woman with a wet cough.

Among other things, it was rumored that Sister Juan had done a dime at the Federal Correctional Institution in Danbury, Connecticut under the name

Ernesto Rosita Gomez. According to the six-lawyer defense team, Gomez's run-in with the FBI was no more than their client's misinterpretation of laws pertaining to kidnapping, extortion, bribery, embezzlement, fraud, obstruction of justice, and racketeering.

The trial revealed a year-long operation financed by Gomez's employer, the business development unit of the Nigerian email industry.

The objective of the scheme was to drive existing cruise ship lines into bankruptcy and open the way for a new "100% Risk Free, Guaranteed Money Back" internet-based, pre-paid cruise line run by Nigerian princes sailing under the Iranian flag.

The illicit activity began by enticing thousands of perimenopausal women in Wisconsin to apply for work as professional bratwurst tasters. Five mass interviews were held in different parts of the state during the winter for five separate criminal missions, according to the federal prosecutor. Each session produced at least 200 women in their forties and fifties with "suitable processing capacity" who were abducted by muscular young men in loincloths. Loaded onto buses with comfortable seats, clean bathrooms, catered meals, wine, and a masseuse, they were driven 1,500 miles to the Port of Miami.

In Florida, the women were forced to board seven-day, six-night, Caribbean cruises and eat as much as possible every day from "all-you-can-eat" buffets, plated meals, and 24-hour free room service. On all five voyages, the women overwhelmed the ships' multi-million dollar sewage systems to the point that they literally had to be torn from the hulls at a cost of millions of dollars. "Had this continued," claimed prosecutors, "the cruise industry would have sunk."

Despite having more than 500 of the women involved willing to travel a thousand miles to testify that Gomez was "a saint" and that they had the best time of their lives, the jury voted to convict on all 1,389 criminal counts.

Sister Juan's right-hand girl, Cracka Jack-sin, had also been in trouble with the law. An unclean, unpleasant-looking woman who smelled like the shit house door on a tuna boat, Cracka had been charged with 27 counts of extortion and attempted murder during June 2007 alone. As the cases came to trial, every one of the key prosecution witnesses slipped in their showers, hit their heads on blunt objects, and died. When questioned by the FBI about the bizarre coincidence, defense attorney Sammy Frescaloni, who had won 613 felony cases without ever going to court, explained it simply: "You know, you drop the soap and the next thing, *boom fuckin' boom, baby!* you wake up dead. You've got to put the fuckin' blame where it belongs here. Showers are dangerous. That's hardly my client's fault. These people knew they were involved in risky behavior but went ahead and did it anyway."

Criminal backgrounds or not, Catholic Church officials were delighted by Sister Juan's and Cracka's abilities to generate cash flow, run high-margin businesses, and acquire lucrative assets. The duo's launch of church-sponsored, online dating service www.domenow4godssake.com was spectacular. Designed to help men 50 and older lose their virginity, the site was not only successful but received a certificate of merit from the Vatican's elite paramilitary fundraising unit.

The Crotch also bought a chain of cheap motor inns and turned them into highly-profitable, rent-by-the-hour motels dedicated to customers whose lifestyles required the utmost in privacy. At the same time, they expanded into the mushrooming Furry lifestyle market with an ad campaign featuring somebody in a rabbit suit holding hands with a Furry lion under the headline, "Get Pelted!" It was so successful that the motels' rooms had eight-month, paid-in-advance, non-refundable waiting lists. Not resting on their laurels, Sister Juan spearheaded investments in coin-operated laundries in high-crime neighborhoods, offering free 9mm handguns and 100 rounds of ammo with every 30 wash-and-dries.

Last, but far from least, they eased the suffering of a cancer-stricken Jewish urologist buried in debt and misery by buying his 15,000 square foot mansion on Martha's Vineyard for five cents on the dollar. With compassion in her heart, Cracka helped him sign the contract by pointing a gun at his terrified wife's head.

With an array of Spanish Inquisition-style programs aimed at enriching the lives of the 175 girls and 50 boys who lived in the convent school, Constance Anne was stimulated to participate in a variety of extra-curricular activities. She loved field hockey, basketball, and softball and proved to be a talented athlete; however, she found sports increasingly difficult to play as she blossomed into an exquisitely stacked young woman. That, along with the school's strict prohibition against wearing bras and panties because of their established link to drug abuse, a fact noted by Sister Juan herself in the student handbook, pushed Constance Anne towards work-study programs. She gravitated towards car washes and parties in New Hampshire's Franconia Mountains for members of St. Woody's exclusive "Holy Crotch Club".

The "Holy Crotch Boys," as they were known, were a group of men 70 and older who willed their assets to the church in return for getting to touch the school's hot girls once a month. As far as Constance Anne was concerned, working at the club was easy and profitable. In exchange for standing still and letting 10 or 15 geezers squeeze their way around her body, she'd usually find special rewards like $20 and $50 bills waiting for her deep down in their front pants pockets. At least that was the case during the first two weeks of the month. If they held a party right before the Social Security checks came out, her tips would drop like a rock from a few hundred bucks to a roll of quarters and a couple of fast food coupons.

The only member who paid a prearranged gratuity was a 72-year-old from Maine who wanted hot bleu cheese enemas. He was a flat $350, plus the cost of rubber gloves, a spatula, and a clean bedpan. Sister Juan brokered the deal personally. Not everything, however, was acceptable at a price. Cracka bounced a rich guy with vorarephilia, a desire to be swallowed whole by another person or to swallow someone else whole. Cracka said she be damned if she was going to lose any of the girls to some asshole's digestive tract.

Although the Holy Crotch Club was great, Constance Anne's favorite activity was washing cars. Different from the car wash fundraisers cute high school girls advertise with homemade signs on Saturdays, St. Woody's washes were held for private patrons who didn't necessarily even have a car. Dressed in liquid red vinyl halter tops, hot pants, and matching vinyl boots, the super-hot girls who regularly worked the washes started by spraying each other with cold water until their nipples were erect enough to be seen from space. Then the client could climb into a wading pool with the girls and soap up their bodies by hand, starting with their boots and working all the way up to their magnificent young cream pies.

From late spring through early fall, St. Woody's had a long list of car wash customers from all over the Greater Boston area. Constance Anne's favorite, however, was Dickie's Funeral Home right down the street in Chelsington.

Dickie's was founded in 1701 by Colonel Ebenezer Beech Dickie, a French and Indian War deserter, who died at the age of 40 soon after hundreds of bodies that he was to have buried in coffins surfaced during a sudden flood and floated into the town square. The grief-stricken townspeople arrested Dickie, marched him down to an area near the current-day location of Schmendrik Memorial Cemetery, and threw him into a hole that had recently served as a latrine.

As the crowd hung around to debate what to do with the bastard, a tattered, ashen-looking woman named Bridget Bishop from Salem curtly stepped forward. She raised what looked like a wad of rags with a face above her head and rattled off one unintelligible word after the next in a bizarre, sing-songy voice. The rags, which oddly turned out to be a hand puppet of Pilgrim hottie Priscilla Alden, had been burned. The face, such as it was, was sunken, and the mouth was perverted. Worse, it appeared that the eyes had been purposely and angrily blacked out.

"You used this for self-indulgence, did you not?" Bishop shouted down at Dickie, accusing him of the sin of using the puppet to milk his chicken. Dickie didn't understand why the old bag was freaking out over a stupid puppet or jerking off for that matter, and didn't respond. He simply looked down at the dirt people had been kicking into the hole. It was now almost up to his knees.

"Die, Satan! Die, Satan!" Bishop screamed as she dragged her sharp fingernails down her face and drew her own blood. At some point during the festivities, petite 14-year-old Prudence Shaw, a shy girl with raging hormones and a surplus of pent-up anger about everything, quietly slid into the hole behind Dickie and broke his neck with an ax handle.

The crowd quickly joined in on the catchy *"Die Satan!"* shtick and proceeded to completely cover Dickie with dirt. Fortunately, he lived long enough to enjoy the full experience of being buried alive in a shit hole. He could be heard trying to dig himself out for almost a day and a half.

Many months later, the people of Chelsington had the story and their sentiments carved on Dickie's headstone:

COL. EBENEEZER BEECH DICKIE

Born November 5th, 1681
Suffocated, November 4th and 5th, 1721

Here Lies the Body of Ebeneezer Dickie
He buried our dead, but the process was tricky.
He laid them in a coffin and dug a deep hole
And waited 'til midnight when the sky was like coal.
When none were around beyond even faint doubt
He returned to the casket and dumped them right out.
He used the same boxes again and again
'Til a heavy flood raised the corpse of John Penn.
No box was John in as he bobbed through the town
And scores more followed face up and face down.
The old bastard Dickie harmed those whom we loved
So into a grave he was pushed and was shoved.
A puppet of Priscilla Alden with a bouncy chest
Was thrown in the hole on top of the pest.
Then we covered him over with dirt and green sod
Now he lies here forever, a soul shunned by God.

FUCK YOU, EBENEEZER.
Respectfully written by the good and kind people of Chelsington, Massachusetts

Despite the scandal, Dickie's survived and prospered over the next two hundred years through a combination of murdering their competitors in cold blood and making smart business investments. By the 21st Century, Dickie's offered their own patented procedure called "Clip and Dip" involving cosmetic surgery, embalming, and papier mâché that made their clients look astonishingly better in death than they could have ever hoped to in life. Because Clip and Dip made it possible to enlarge or reduce any part of the body, Dickie's regularly received inquiries from women wanting to know if they had to be dead to reduce their cankles, back fat, and muffin tops.

Although the answer was always "yes", more than a few women said they'd "think it over and call back."

Dickie's could also boast that they had more modern bereavement conveniences than anyone in the funeral industry: 24-hour street-facing viewing rooms for drive-thru mourners, web cams for out-of-towners and shut-ins, free Wi-Fi, a well-stocked premium bar, clean restrooms, and casual dining. The Angel of Death Brasserie, a full-service eatery with a relaxed, yet mournful, setting, was the first death-themed restaurant in the country. Its signature dishes, among them Rigor Ravioli, Pallbearer Pork Chops, and Chicken-in-a-Casket, all came with free desserts served in mausoleum-shaped souvenir dishes with spoons shaped like shovels.

Last, but not least, was Mitzi Jo's Memorable Memories, a three-story, 5,000-square-foot retail shop named after Mr. Dickie's wife that, along with the café, breathed life into the company's motto, "Come see us for an afternoon ... or an eternity!" With more than 800 different items, Mitzi Jo's offered an incredible selection of gifts for every member of the family. Shameless marketers, they took 360-degree photographs and the thumbprints of every deceased "guest" as soon as they were ready for display. Then, they shrewdly turned the photos into holograms suitable for framing and etched the fingerprints onto 14K gold necklaces and earrings.

With a tip of the hat to theme parks that take photos of screaming rollercoaster riders, the staff at Mitzi Jo's displayed the 3D images and jewelry at a booth that nearly blocked the entrance to the softly-illuminated Gateway to Eternity, the funeral home's 40-foot-wide main hallway. The location and warm, sincere smiles of the salespeople made it ever so much harder for Mommy to say no to little Susie's pleas for a $499.99 hologram of Grammy that would eventually give her nuclear-powered nightmares. Some kids preferred a $159.99 gold charm bracelet with one of Grandpa's teeth hanging from it.

The items inside the store were as fun as they were creepy. Stacked on shelves that stretched from floor to ceiling, the merchandise ran the gamut from dog toys shaped like cadavers and salt and pepper shakers inside miniature crypts, to crocheted tea pot covers that could have Grandma's face laser-cut into the wool. On a massive, 12-foot-diameter circular rack in the middle of the first floor were men's designer half-suits and women's half-dresses and off-the-shoulder formal half-gowns for families interested in giving the deceased one last makeover. On the second floor was a similar size rack with a line of Bulgarian-made clothing called "De-CeaSe-D."

Created exclusively for human decomposition enthusiasts, "De-CeaSe-D" long sleeve tees had "skin" that could be peeled off in sections to show what the wearer would look like if he was gradually rotting. "De-CeaSe-D" ball caps and short sleeve tees said "Yes, I Know I'm Putrefying" on the front and "Worm Wagon" on the back. On the third floor, adjacent to hundreds of other death-related items from coffee mugs, smart phone covers, and backpacks to sweatshirts and placemats, was a section filled with copies of *Who the Fuck Took Grampy?*, a children's book.

Who the Fuck Took Grampy? led boys and girls ages 8 to13 on a science-centered, illustrated adventure through "the return of Grampy's body to the earth." A $59.95 companion game, *Exhume My Ass!*, helped kids take things a step further by digging up a nine-inch Grampy doll from an easy-to-assemble, battery-operated grave site to see what shape the old geezer was in after a decade.

To the absolute horror of the local community, the items in Mitzi Jo's Memorable Memories sold like glue in a leper colony. Dickie's parking lot overflowed with tour buses seven days a week. Passengers poured into The Angel of Death Brasserie for a quick bite and then moved like a herd of rhinos through the front door of Mitzi Jo's to shop and gawk at the latest mortuary innovations.

In 2013, when Dickie's installed Eternal Rest Cams in selected casket models, security had to be called in to manage the spellbound crowds. Built with the idea of "bringing the majesty of death to your tablet or phone" Eternal Rest Cams provided live video of loved ones in repose six feet underground. The camera was activated by a $20 credit card swipe that gave customers a five minute look inside. Although it wasn't for everyone, some viewers were so mesmerized by what they saw that they would spend as much as $1,000 a sitting, leading one national news service to label the Eternal Rest Cam "the new cocaine."

Within a year, Mitzi Jo's had become the second most popular tourist attraction in Massachusetts. Within two years, it had its own 24-hour cable shopping channel, *Mitzi Jo's Mausoleum.* The show developed the largest female TV audience in the western hemisphere by featuring handsome young men with chiseled bodies, inexpensive jewelry, and a line of stunning, moderately-priced pumps and platform heels. Sold under the label "Foot Rest in Peace," the heels felt like fluffy slippers and could be worn all day, every day. While beautifully-dressed women entertained the viewers with chitchat and sold dreamy shoes, the men rubbed their feet, washed dishes, fixed small electronics, and lightly perspired.

Frickman "Frickey" Dickie, the funeral home's current owner and president, was a direct descendant of Dickie's much-reviled founder. A tall, 40-year-old man with a full head of chestnut brown hair, a thick-waist, a long nose, and meaty cheeks, he was never seen in anything other than a somber black suit that concealed the women's nylon granny-panties he wore underneath.

Although he looked physically well on the outside, he had what his doctors called "jumpy bowels," a condition caused by years of doing exceptionally stupid things with embalming fluid. His condition made him shake uncontrollably whenever he shit, sometimes so violently that he would literally vibrate off of the toilet seat and onto the floor. Despite that, Constance Anne adored Mr. Dickie's warm personality and looked forward to seeing him with all the enthusiasm of a Jersey girl getting her first toke on a crack pipe.

Constance Anne also loved it when Mr. Dickie climbed in the back of his shiny black hearse, wriggled into a hand-polished natural cherry coffin, and played dead while she and the other girls washed the car with their firm booties and half-exposed love muffins. She always smiled at the happy expression on his face when he ejaculated into the casket's elegant eggshell crepe interior.

The best part of the whole adventure, though, was when they finished their work. As soon as Mr. Dickie got out of the hearse, he would help each of the girls dry themselves off with small towels that required him to go over every inch of their anatomy again and again and again. Then, one-by-one, the ladies would give Mr. Dickie a "really good snuggle," a special hug in which they'd each try to burrow as deeply as possible inside his oversized navy blazer and try to find his "dickie," a silly joke that made everybody giggle.

The girl who did the best job earned $10 a minute. Not only was Constance Anne the most frequent winner, she usually made $400 or more for her persistence. As far as Frickey Dickie's dickie was concerned, she regularly worked longer and harder to find it and got more out of it, so to speak, than anyone else.

Considering the circumstances, Constance Anne was understandably bereft when the car washes abruptly ended one day with the news of Frickey Dickie's untimely death. According to news reports, Dickie tripped over a deranged-looking child's puppet that was left on the floor in the funeral home's garage, spun around, and freakishly hit the back of his head and neck on a tire iron that was hanging on a steel pegboard. Various sources claimed that he wasn't found until early the next morning when Mitzi Jo realized that her husband of 15 years had never come to bed.

People being what they are, rumors spread quickly through town. The most popular, and only true, story alleged that Mitzi Jo murdered her husband after finding his penis inside a puppet and the puppet in the capable right hand of Calegra "Picky" Hickey, a well-known local syphilis incubator. Calegra's ability to use her assets to provide overwhelming sexual pleasure had pushed more than one man into throwing away everything that was dear to him. Her signature move, fluttering her tongue on the frenulum of prepuce of penis, had generated more marriage proposals than she could count.

That day, Frickey told Calegra that he wanted to try something new, handed her a puppet made in the image of a steamy, hot Indian princess, and asked her to stroke his bayonet with it. In addition to a beautiful face, an open mouth, and long black hair with a feather in it, the puppet was dressed in a brown fringed tie-back bikini top and a matching miniskirt with a fringed bottom. The little outfit exposed so much of her perfectly-shaped breasts, taut midsection, and long legs that she might just as well have had nothing on at all.

Made of vinyl and smelling like Chinese sneakers, she was about nine inches from head to foot, or three times the length of Frickey's dick. She was also hollow inside except for a removable handkerchief with a small hole cut in the top.

Just as Frickey reached the point of no return for what promised to be the best orgasm he'd ever had, Mitzi Jo came up from behind and broke his neck with a tire iron. The shock of the assault caused Calegra to pull the puppet off of his still-throbbing ferret and drop it on the floor. When she looked down, her heart nearly stopped. The puppet had turned into something monstrous: badly burned with blackened eyes, a cadaverous face, and a horribly distorted, wide-open mouth.

With that, young Miss Hickey took off running, doing her best to get control over the multitude of dead presidents Frickey had stuffed in her thong.

Try as they might, local reporters couldn't get a statement from police about the very out-of-place puppet Dickie allegedly stumbled over and the "biological material" purportedly found on the floor. Neither would the cops confirm any other parts of the story of Dickie's death. That, of course, didn't stop a local scandal sheet from posing the question on everybody's mind on its front page.

The big, bold headline asked, "Did 'Picky' Hickey Give Frickey Dickie a Quickie?"

Tick, Tock. Friday, 5:43 p.m.

Mortie already had a key to one of the rooms and, considering his size, Constance Anne was impressed that it only took him 10 minutes to walk up the 16 stairs to the second floor.

Their destination, Room 209, was marked with cheap, vinyl peel-and-stick numbers. Inside, grimy turquoise walls surrounded a large, sagging waterbed with frayed yellow polyester sheets and two purple pillows with brown stains. Near the door, a rattling window air conditioner lazily dripped water into an overflowing green bucket.

On the side of the bed facing the bathroom was a desiccated raspberry air freshener on top of a small table covered with pink contact paper. On the side closest to the door was a tarnished brass floor lamp with a heavy-looking, broken brass shade that was very out of step with the décor. The only objects in the room that weren't smeared, broken, or shriveled were a tall metal thing and a black velvet painting of a nude woman whose nipples had been replaced by flashing lights. Both items were on the opposite side of the bed. Constance Anne found the place homey. Even the gooey stuff that made her shoes stick to the filthy brown carpet wasn't the worst thing in the world.

While Constance Anne stood silently in front of the painting, mesmerized by the rhythmic right, left, right, left illuminations of the subject's flesh melons, Mortie went to the bathroom where yellow crime scene tape had only recently been torn down and the chalk outline of a body was slowly fading. A few minutes later, Mortie's sirloin-colored face popped in front of hers.

"It's time," he said with a saliva-heavy grin on his face as he gently belly-bumped her onto the bed.

As she fell backwards, Constance Anne caught a glimpse of something she had certainly never seen before. Mortie was wearing orange suspenders over a sleeveless white tee shirt and a pair of see-through undies. The suspenders, which were clearly under immense strain, hoisted his stomach up enough so that he could reach his Hairy Houdini.

"Relax," Mortie said softly as he rolled her top down over her stunning blouse bunnies and pulled her skirt and panties over her white five-inch heels.

"*Oh, Baby!*" he said as he looked over her soft, pink, mouthwatering nakedness.

After taking in an eyeful, he waddled over to the tall metal thing and moved it towards her, stopping at the foot of the bed to place its legs on either side of the torn, filth-rich mattress. At first, Constance Anne thought it looked like exercise equipment. Also, although she couldn't recall seeing one exactly like it before, she was pretty sure that she'd seen something similar at a slaughterhouse where she'd applied for a job in the head removal department. It wasn't exactly a cheerful memory, and she got a lump in her throat remembering how the contraption was used to butcher hogs and cattle. The thought that it might be meant for her sent icy chills up and down her spine.

"Well, Mortie, I sure didn't figure you for a machine kind of guy," Constance Anne said in the thick Boston accent she'd been trying to lose since moving to Florida. She wanted to sound Indian so she could work in a call center.

Mortie chuckled but didn't say a word. His silence made her even more nervous.

"Where are you from?" he asked in hopes of keeping her calm by making small talk. Facing her, he reached up and attached something to the cross-bar at the top of the tall metal thing.

"Chelsington, Assachusetts. It's on the way to the Cape," Constance Anne replied, delighting in the wittiness of her remark. She'd picked up a bunch of zingers like that from her pal, Arf, a pale, dog-faced entrepreneur in a bolo tie and a Panama hat who sold hot pizza, doobie, and light firearms to kindergarten teachers.

"Oh, I know Chelsington. I'm related to the Palomino family. Ever hear of them?"

"Of course I have. Small world, isn't it?" she said, biting her tongue. She thought of the Palomino clan the same way she thought about having her gums infected with maggots. They made her want to yack up her breakfast.

Busy tinkering with the gantry, Mortie turned his back, giving Constance Anne an unobstructed view of his overwhelmingly large buttocks and thick, revolting tufts of black ass hair that were clearly visible through his creepy, translucent shorts. Constance Anne was pretty sure that he had ass sideburns on his hips, too. She was also more than just pretty sure that if he bent over and put the weird, bushy hair on his ass next to the comb-over on his head, you wouldn't be able to tell which end of him was supposed to be up.

Becoming increasingly anxious about what he planned to do with the tall metal thing, Constance Anne kept her eyes on Mortie as she inched across the bed to get as close as possible to the door. Naked or not, she was going to make a run for freedom just as soon as he was too busy with his work to stop her. The distance between the foot of the bed and the outside world was no more than eight or nine feet, and the only things she had to be careful not to trip over were the tall metal thing and a stepstool near the lamp.

She had a rare talent for vomiting pretty much at will, and she planned to put it to good use if she ended up in a struggle with him. There was nothing quite like smacking someone right in the face with warm puke to change their day.

When she reached the end of the bed, she stood up and lunged for the doorknob.

At the same moment, Mortie turned around to pick up a screwdriver. The look on his face wasn't happy.

"*Oh, no! No! No!*" he shouted as her world went dark.

Chapter 3

"With all the fury of a hellfire and brimstone preacher, he said, 'The answer is obvious: If they don't know shit, you must acquit!'"

As far as Constance Anne was concerned, the loveliest aspect of life in the Crotch was the peace and quiet that enveloped the campus.

The beautiful, leafy trees, sweet-smelling flowers, and manicured lawns gave her a sense of serenity and security that she never knew existed. It was also light years away from the grimy world of white girl junkies, creepers, and cross-species sexual predators that she'd lived in with her mother. The tiny 8"x10" window in their one-bedroom, half-bath apartment overlooked the growling steam vent of a Chinese laundry and the garbage-strewn perch of a scraggy Peruvian whose street-made barbeque business was quickly reducing the local cat population.

They also had a view of a bus stop that was a testament to the importance of "location, location, location." Standing between a dumpster and a liquor store, the bus stop had become such a popular place for robbery and murder that a guy opened a small bar directly across the street called "No Witnesses." With armed parking attendants and a bullet-proof window for watching the action, it did as much as 10 grand a day during the height of murder season, usually the warmer months from May to September. In fact, No Witnesses became such a trendy place to "shoot and be shot" that criminals and their victims would often travel across town to the bus stop so that their robbery or murder could be committed in front of an appreciative audience.

By the time she was five, Constance Anne scarcely noticed the screams, explosions and sirens that were a staple of life in her neighborhood. In fact, what most people would see as a real-life horror show was nothing more than the background music to her life. Wherever she went she was no more than a few feet away from rabid dogs, syringes, perverts, rapists, and personal injury lawyers.

Even though she was too young to understand everything that went on around her, she learned three important lessons from what she saw.

The first was that you shouldn't hurt others, a concept she picked up from hearing people shriek in pain when they got shot or when a needle broke off sideways in a junkie's vein.

The second was that you had to brush your teeth every day if you didn't want to look like Mr. Brooks, a toothless drunk. Although he claimed that he lost his teeth saving people in a plane crash, the truth was that they were carved out with a screwdriver by a loan shark who forgot to bring painkillers.

The third was that it was important to share with your friends, something that her neighbors were great at doing.

Every week or so, Constance Anne would see Mrs. Rivera, the nice next-door neighbor who sold "to-go" bags of dust blunt at the bus stop, bring someone who was being bad into her apartment for a time-out. As Constance Anne's tiny tot mind understood it, it was usually a person who made Mrs. Rivera mad because they wouldn't take their medicine. If the person still wouldn't listen to her after a time-out, Mrs. Rivera would wash out their ears with "sufyuricksasid" to help them hear better. Afterward, Mrs. Rivera would have her sons carry the naughty person across the hall to nice old Mr. Bill's apartment. Then, Mr. Bill would give the boys fresh-baked cookies and pull the naughty person inside so that he could get him to listen with what he called "a little lovin'."

Next door to Mr. Bill was a man who wore a big black hat, a big black shirt, big black socks, but no pants. Constance Anne didn't know his name, but she was pretty sure that if Mr. Bill couldn't get the naughty person to behave, the man in black would put him in the dumpster for recycling.

In later years, Constance Anne would be proud that her neighbors were among the first in town to "Go Green."

Although she was ordinarily indifferent to the hell around her, Constance Anne didn't like loud noises and the screams that usually came with it. When a careless public masturbator confused lube with nitroglycerin and blasted his howdy dog and the park bench he was sitting on into orbit, she couldn't sleep for a week. Oddly, the only exception to her noise aversion was the sound of breaking glass. When that happened, Constance Anne would burst out into a big smile; in her world, breaking glass meant looting, and looting meant free stuff like a TV to watch cartoons on, an actual bed, and a pink tricycle with white streamers on the handlebars.

With those happy childhood memories anchored in the back of her mind, it wasn't odd that she smiled when she heard a series of loud popping noises and saw grenades shatter windows throughout the Crotch at sunrise one morning.

Peeking out of her second floor window in her school-issued pink fishnet corset, she saw 50 or more heavily armed men and women with FBI printed in big letters on their shirts swarming over the campus. The smile dropped from her face within seconds as the God-awful irritation of tear gas swept into her nose, eyes, mouth, and lungs. A few moments later, canisters carrying the stomach-turning stench of rotten eggs crashed through the windows. Fortunately, the stink bombs had less effect on Constance Anne than they did on others. In her old neighborhood, the virtually identical odor of intestinal gas was so pervasive that regular air just didn't smell right.

The circumstances that brought federal agents to the Crotch that morning were what St. Woody's attorneys characterized as one of several misunderstandings between the church and the U.S. Department of Justice. Moreover, they vociferously complained that the Feds had destroyed their clients' chance of a fair trial by suggesting in a press conference that "something smells fishy in the Crotch."

The particular felonies in question concerned violations of the RICO stat-ute, otherwise known as the Racketeer Influenced and Corrupt Organizations Act. According to the grand jury, St. Woody's operatives shook down some two hundred churches, synagogues, and mosques in Massachusetts, New Hampshire, and Connecticut for more than ten million dollars as part of an ongoing criminal operation over a two year period. The charges specifically fingered the Crotch's three highest-ranking officials: Ernesto Rosita Gomez, aka Sister Juan, Rolester Octavian Ramos, aka Cracka Jack-sin, and Susan "Ham" Manichevitz, aka Sister Gracia of the Holy Sepulcher.

The government's case included 791 counts of extortion in which min-isters, priests, and rabbis were threatened with having their colons removed with needle-nose pliers if they didn't hand over 75% of each week's income.

The trial was scheduled to involve 34 prosecution witnesses and 53 char-acter witnesses for the defense. Unfortunately, almost none of the defense witnesses could testify because they were either on Death Row or had been recently executed. The sole exception was His Holiness, the Pope, who re-spectfully declined to appear in an American court.

As the Holy Father reportedly told the College of Cardinals at the Vatican, "I'll be damned if I'm going there. We've been in enough crotches as it is."

The legal defense team, which consisted of identical triplet attorneys Ray-Bob, Joe-Bob, and Bob-Bob Clinton, knew that their clients were far guiltier than even the Feds realized.

After a two-day strategy session in the Spitting Cobra Room at Madame Dong's Rublicated Massage Parace, which RRC paid for with a St. Woody's credit card, they came to conclusions on three critical matters.

First, not even Jesus Christ could get their clients out of the mess they were in.

Second, because the triplets had spent large amounts of their clients' money on sex, booze, and drugs without their knowledge, it was in the broth-ers' best interests to see the defendants off to prison for as long as possible.

Third, the only important thing was that the "Bobs" became instant ce-lebrities and got their own reality TV show.

Later that evening, in between simultaneous hoovers from Madame Dong's Vietnamese sex slaves, the Bobs came up with an imaginative, yet senseless, legal argument they were willing to throw against the wall. If their clients couldn't remember committing the crimes they were charged with, then they shouldn't be held responsible for them. That approach, they thought, was surely irrational enough get them worldwide publicity.

The next day in front of a cluster of television cameras and microphones, Ray-Bob said that they would sue the government for $1 trillion on the grounds that the embarrassment his clients suffered as a result of their arrests had caused them irreparable psychological harm.

"No amount of compassion is too small, nor is any amount of money too large to save these poor, broken souls," he told reporters. "Let the healing begin."

On the opening day of the trial, Ray-Bob, whose nickname, "Tuggy," nailed his weird habit of fondling his cyclops whenever he was nervous, walked into the courtroom with a mullet and a neon pink handkerchief poking out of the pocket of his wide-striped, black-and-white suit.

In order to keep their family brand easily recognizable in the public eye, Joe-Bob and Bob-Bob wore suits that were identical in design and cut, but in different colors. Joe-Bob wore a wide-striped, baby blue and white version. Bob-Bob's suit had wide red and white stripes that made him look like a barber pole with a beer belly.

As cool and fashion-forward as they saw themselves, they were always curious why no one ever asked where they bought their clothes.

"Ladies and gentlemen of the jury, this is the United States of America, the greatest nation on earth, by God," Ray-Bob said in his opening remarks with passion in his voice and an American flag draped over his shoulders. "This is not Nazi Germany or the Soviet Union or even Canada. And in this nation, the greatest nation on earth, no one can be held responsible for doing things they didn't do."

"Whatever you do," he continued, "don't let the government lawyers tell you that it's okay for us to be like Al Qaida and the Taliban and throw righteous Christians in jail. Don't let them tell you that it's okay to throw Christians to the lions."

"Because in our country," Ray-Bob said, feeling like he was on a roll, "God-fearing American Christians believe that only the guilty should go to jail. And to be guilty means that you have to remember doing something to be guilty about. One thing is very clear: if my clients don't know what they did, then they can't be guilty and, if they're not guilty, they should be set free."

"Who among you can remember doing something you didn't do?" he continued, pointing his finger at each of the jurors. "You can't remember what you didn't do, can you?"

"Don't let the government's lawyers, particularly Mr. Kapoor over there who sure doesn't look like an American or a Christian to me, lie to you," Ray-Bob said pointing at the man of Indian heritage at the prosecution table who was born in Vermont and grew up in Connecticut. "Remember that Jesus started America. Don't let people who aren't Christian Americans confuse you about what's right and wrong. They may be the devil in disguise."

"*Hallelujah! Praise Jesus!*" Joe-Bob and Bob-Bob shouted in sync until the judge threatened them with contempt of court.

The following day, Ray-Bob questioned Sister Juan on the witness stand.

"Do you remember committing the crimes you're wrongfully charged with?"

"No," Sister Juan, Cracka, and Sister Gracia replied in unison.

"Ladies and gentleman," Ray-Bob said to the jury, "I rest my case. It is evident that these are innocent lambs."

Holding a Bible and a crucifix in one hand and a portrait of George Washington in the other, Ray-Bob Clinton took a deep breath and looked squarely into the jurors' eyes.

With all the fury of a hellfire and brimstone preacher, he said, "The answer is obvious: *If they don't know shit, you must acquit!*"

Some one hundred courtroom observers, most of whom had been hired by the "Bobs," broke into thunderous applause in front of the jury. One guy blasted an air horn as the rest rhythmically stood up, raised their arms and sat back down in a continuous "wave" while shouting *"Don't know shit, must acquit! Don't know shit, must acquit!"*

Finally, court deputies cleared the gallery with spiked billy clubs and cans of sun-dried possum spray, a non-lethal crowd control gas that delivered the overpowering stench of summer-baked road kill in larger-than-necessary quantities. A request for a mistrial due to the demonstration was denied by the judge as quickly as the words came out of Ray-Bob's mouth.

In the end, the twelve-member jury found the defendants guilty after a three-minute deliberation that included a restroom break.

A judge later sentenced them to no fewer than five and no more than 20 years in federal prisons.

Because the Vatican wouldn't touch the now-exposed Crotch with a ten foot pole much less take over its operation, the school had no option other than to close its doors. After 13 years at St. Woody's, a teary-eyed Constance Anne had to find a new place to live.

The week after the trial, authorities began fingerprinting, collecting DNA samples, and taking mug shots of the "Crotch Kids" as they were known on the assumption that if they hadn't committed horrific crimes yet, they certainly would in the future. When that was completed, the plan was for the state to immediately relocate the underage residents of St. Woody's to appropriate housing. Instead, the process moved as slowly as a three-toed sloth with leg cramps.

Late one night, an employee who'd had enough of the Crotch Kids and wanted to go on vacation entered St. Woody's and pulled all of the fire alarms. Once the buildings were evacuated, he chained all of the doors and left town with the keys before any of the children could be transplanted. As a result, the kids were forced to live in a city park for three days and nights without food, blankets, or restroom facilities. The situation was so bad that some of the children may have required hospitalization if it hadn't been for the help they received from local homeless citizens.

After initially offering to provide fast food coupons, tents, and a single portable toilet for the 225 Crotch Kids, officials were forced to take much larger steps in the wake of a tidal wave of public outrage. Within a few days, government authorities temporarily reopened St. Woody's, sorted everybody out, and sent about half of the school population to juvenile correctional centers whether they had done anything wrong or not. Most of the rest went to foster homes.

In the case of students who were aged-out and clean with the cops like 18-year-old Constance Anne, relocation was unfortunately to the street and the public school system.

Although she was clear about wanting to further her education at highly-respected Richard F. Blough, Jr. High School, Constance Anne had no idea where and how she was going to live. All the government gave her was a tiny goody bag stuffed with a banana, ten bucks, a pencil, and five purple Ejaculeater condoms with industrial-grade spermicide.

The day before Constance Anne had to vacate St. Woody's and move into a three-sided corrugated box on Storrow Drive, she spotted a help-wanted ad for a "Night Sitter." Even though she didn't know what a Night Sitter was, a night job sounded perfect since it would allow her to go to school during the day. She changed out of her regulation bustier and lace panties into regular street clothes and walked two miles to the address.

When she arrived, her jaw fell open.

The building was none other than Dickie's Funeral Home.

"Uh, oh," Constance Anne said under her breath. Before she had a moment more to think, she found herself sitting in front of a coldly attractive, middle-aged woman in an expensive-looking black wool dress and pearls. The nameplate on her large, mahogany desk said that she was Mitzi Jo Dickie.

"Sometimes dead people fart. They don't mean to, I suppose, but they do. Sometimes they open their eyes and mouths or sit up or move their legs and hands. They also belch. We're looking for someone willing to roll up their sleeves and get in there," she said, explaining the job to a slightly befuddled Constance Anne.

Apparently, Mrs. Dickie didn't recognize her from the St. Woody's car washes.

"Get in where to do what?" Constance Anne asked, impressed with her own quick analytical ability.

"To go into the embalming room, into the caskets, *and get … fucking … aggressive!*" Mrs. Dickie said, speaking excitedly like a football coach trying to motivate a team that knew they were going to lose. "*Mix it up! Show them who the fucking boss is! Push their dead asses back down on the table! Spray down the farts, close their fuckin' eyes!*"

"*Go, go, go!*" Mrs. Dickie said loudly, thrusting her right hand up in the air and pointing her index finger towards the ceiling in a crazy pumping motion.

More than a little concerned about what Mrs. Dickie was telling her but in desperate need of work, Constance Anne told her that she could "wrestle the farts to the ground, slap the shit out of their dead asses, and go, go, go wherever those fucking dead people are supposed to go." She said it so enthusiastically that she lost her breath.

"*Just don't let them get the drop on you! They're sick fucks. Do you hear me? Sick, farting fucks!*"

Mrs. Dickie was moving back and forth in her chair like a kid who desperately has to go to the bathroom. Her eyes were rolling around in their sockets like marbles.

A few moments later, Mrs. Dickie abruptly stood up from behind the desk, downed two fingers of Dr. Jack, and told Constance Anne she was hired as long as she stayed in school and graduated on time. No excuses would be accepted. The job came with a bed, a hundred bucks a week, and an all-day Mexican buffet that was available when the main embalming table wasn't in use. She walked Constance Anne to her new room adjacent to the Eternal Preservation Center where a seemingly non-gaseous corpse was being pumped with formaldehyde.

The room, although tiny, had character thanks to an oil painting of an old, dead guy named Crockett Dick. For some reason, the work had never been finished because instead of eyes and a mouth, there were black holes.

"I think I've died and gone to heaven," Constance Anne said with a huge smile on her face.

"Tell me that again after one of these freaks blows their bowels all over the wall," Mrs. Dickie said with a twisted grin. "That'll suck a big one."

Constance Anne was excited and couldn't wait to get started at Richard F. Blough, Jr. High School. Named for a school teacher who drowned in the Great Boston Molasses Flood of 1919, Blough was well known for its academic and career programs and athletic prowess. As the first public school in the nation to require parents to tithe five percent of their income, Blough High had more money for computers, lab equipment, career training, and sports paraphernalia than many major universities. Although the tithing requirement was eventually squashed by the U.S. Supreme Court, the administration was able to continue collecting cash by changing the word "tithe" to "donation" and "Blough High School" to "Athletic Booster's Club."

Fortunately, it wasn't necessary to change the whispered threats that kept the program vibrant. As long as parents understood that their children's tests scores, transcripts, and dreams of a bright future could disappear in the bouncing of a single check, everything went smoothly.

On more than one occasion, families were asked to chip in an extra five or six hundred bucks per student to a "special project" fund. When $500,000 from that fund went to buy the East Coast distribution rights to Diet Salmon, a new soft drink that promised "The great taste of fish without the calories!" no one even blinked an eye. In fact, when the principal was suddenly able to afford a boat, a vacation home on Martha's Vineyard, and a new Escalade with super-pimped-out rims, everyone agreed that it was only a coincidence.

Blough's state-of-the-art career training was highly-regarded, not only in Massachusetts but across the nation. The most popular program was "Gateway to Wheels," a rigorous curriculum that provided students with hands-on experience in the exciting, fast-paced world of automotive hygiene.

More than just sloshing soapy water on a Chevy, Gateway to Wheels explored "the art and theory of car laundering" with no-nonsense courses like "Black and Wet: Tires the Way you Like your Lovers", "Vacuuming: You Know You Want it Deeper", "Dry 'Til You Die", and "What the Fuck is That? Cleaning Crap Out of Crevices". Students who successfully completed the prerequisites could take "Push the Big Green Button: Starting the Car Wash of the 21st Century", a Master's-level course designed for those whose career aspirations included operations management.

Blough also offered "Gateway to Chicken," a thought-provoking curriculum that was quickly becoming the gold standard for fast food training in America's flourishing minimum-wage chicken industry. With more than 50 hours of experience in making change and swiping debit cards in simulated situations, graduates were certified to work the counter, kitchen, or drive-thru window in any fried, grilled, wing, or chicken nugget franchise in the country. Even more exciting for employers was the fact that Blough alumni were fully qualified regardless of the number of side item combinations on the menu.

Unlike Gateway to Wheels, Blough's intensive chicken program assumed from the get-go that students wanted to pursue management careers. As a result, courses about food safety and portion management and scholarly subjects like "White or Dark Meat? A Study in Contrasts" and "Thigh High: The Story of Leftovers" stood shoulder-to-shoulder with practical training in tray stacking strategies and packing carry-out bags. To make sure that Blough's students appreciated the heroic role that chicken played in American history, students spent their entire first week of classes immersed in the topic, "Chicken, Burgers, or Pizza: The Choice and the Glory is Yours".

Blough's graduation exercises also set it apart from other schools. Based on a tradition that began with the Class of 1933, graduates not only had their names read aloud as they walked on stage, but had embarrassing personal information shared with the audience. In 1933, Principal Emil Krautzin wanted to brag about the success Blough graduates enjoyed by telling the hundreds of family members and friends assembled where they were going after graduation.

On the big day, Krautzin, a man who had more than a passing relationship with Scotch, picked up the wrong file.

Rather than reading that John Smith was going into his father's business or joining the Army, Krautzin blurted out, "John Smith, with distinction, chronic diarrhea and parasites." The blunder was simultaneously so horrifying and entertaining that eighty years later, the top two graduates of the Class of 2013 were announced as "Mary Margaret Markowitzstein valedictorian, chlamydia and anal yeast infection" and "Jamal Anatoly Weintraub, salutatorian, jock fungus and oozing eczema."

In sports, the Blough High Shiny Gamecocks had been a prodigious football power since they won their first state championship in 1955. In the many decades since, Blough had only lost one game, a bloody Thanksgiving Day contest in 1969 during which Mandible High took out Blough's first string backfield with high-powered rifles. Since then, Blough's sports program had followed a version of the Bush Doctrine, a policy of attacking other schools preemptively if Blough felt their security threatened. Blough's 1981 kidnappings of the mothers of Myles Standish High's offensive linemen and relentless 1996 urine bombings of Gorgonzola High School's math teachers were highly-regarded examples of the principle at work.

But as good as the faculty and students at Blough were at nipping problems in the bud, they were even better at retaliation.

Several nights before Ferrara Prep and Blough were to meet in their annual football rivalry, Ferrara students painted over the word "Game" on the eight-foot-tall Shiny Gamecock logo that dominated the entrance to Blough's campus. They also replaced the rooster's head with a penis. In retribution, Blough students broke into Ferrara during the middle of the night and dusted every locker and teacher's desk with PCP. Early the next morning, they made anonymous calls to the police. By nine o'clock, every Ferrara student and teacher was in handcuffs.

Because the entire football team was still in jail on Friday night, Ferrara had to forfeit the game, handing Blough another undefeated season.

Not everything was a bed of roses, however. A fairly hefty percentage of Booster Club funds went to hiring off-duty riot police and SWAT team members to keep order. Almost every football game turned into an angry, violent affair that ended with students, parents, and even grandparents excited by yet another Shiny Gamecock victory torching buildings, breaking windows, and urinating on and in parked cars.

Because the problems often started in the stands, a group of young security "experts" associated with the Junior Ku Klux Klan suggested that keeping people "with their own kind" would reduce hostilities. Blough's Principal, Carmine J. "Vig" Vaselino, decided to test the recommendations during a mid-season home game against North Roxbury and delegated the job of creating a plan to Assistant Vice Principal Jockey Smarls. A tiny man with a crew cut and brutally-yellowed teeth who covered his office, home, truck, chest, and back with Confederate flags, Smarls had an odd habit of jumbling his words whenever he got excited. In fact, he had become legendary for a mistake he made during the first student assembly of the year.

Instead of threatening misbehaving students with the phrase, "I will turn the screws on each of you" the words came out as "I will screw each of you in turn." For months afterward, kids would sneak up behind Smarls, act like they were doing him doggy-style, and run away laughing. Even Mr. Faller, a history teacher who never thought anything was funny, thought it was funny.

A few hours before the game started, Smarls put his plan, slyly code-named "Operation Control," into action.

First, he had areas on both the home and visitor's sides of the field cordoned off with barbed wire and marked with signs. Then, to keep people "with their own kind" once they entered the stadium, he had armed security officers direct ticketholders to the areas that best described the way they looked. White people with straight noses and expensive clothes went to the WASP (White Anglo-Saxon Protestant) seats. Irish Catholics sat with other "Micks." Black students sat in the "Colored" section, Jews joined other "Christ Killers," and Italians cozied up with one another under "Wop" and "Greaseball" signs. The list of choices went on to include "Spics", "Infidels", "Pajama Heads", "Job-Stealing Indians", "Heroes of the Confederacy", "Trailer Trash", "Krauts", "Homos", "Polacks," and "No Fuckin' Clue."

Smarls also restricted each group to its own category-appropriate refreshment centers with high prices and small portions. That was, of course, except for the WASPs and Heroes of the Confederacy. The WASP stand offered an enchanting chicken a l'orange with crispy, Parisian-style potatoes, green beans almandine, and cherries jubilee, all compliments of White American Conservative Christian Motors, an upscale automobile and yacht dealer. The Heroes of the Confederacy counter had a "Salute to American Wildlife" special featuring spit-roasted squirrel in a bewitching bacon-raisin sauce, sumptuous sides of okra-and-lima-bean mash and beer-basted baked beans, and a small chocolate pie for $5.95. It was only $2.95 if you brought your own meat, preferably microwave-ready roadkill.

On the other hand, Coloreds could buy a fried chicken, hominy, and ham hock platter for $19.95. Spics could score individual servings of burritos, cheesy nachos, and empanadas for $12.95, and Wops could dine on sausage, pepper, and onion spuckies with a side of Brioschi for $11.95.

Rather than keeping a lid on the crowd, Smarls' Operation Control not only proved disastrous but laid the foundation for previously unimagined danger. While the four people who came to support North Roxbury quietly ate fried baloney in their No Fuckin' Clue seats, Blough's side of the field was getting ready to boil over as the Shiny Gamecocks expanded their half-time lead to 36 points.

Fittingly, the first person to feel the heat was Smarls himself.

According to the story police eventually pieced together, sophomore WASP Emory "Trip" Farmsworthe III desperately wanted an order of "Pablo's Killa Hispanic Nachos." Because Farmsworthe wasn't Hispanic, he sent a text to his friend, Enrique Garcia, begging him to buy a couple of gooey, Super Nacho platters and smuggle them into the WASP seats. Far hungrier than worried about violating Smarls' stupid-ass snack rules, Farmsworthe shamelessly gobbled up the mountain of hot, cheesy goodness in front of the whole world.

So anxious to find violators that he could feel the excitement tingling in his balls, Smarls caught a glimpse of Farmsworthe's cheese-splattered face in his peripheral vision. Turning to a security officer, Smarls meant to say, *"Stop that WASP! He's got Killa Hispanic Nachos!"* Instead, the words came out as, *"Kill that WASP with the nachos! He's no Hispanic!"*

Caught up in the excitement, the security guard fired at Farmsworthe, missing his head by millimeters but blowing the shit out of 84-year-old Edna Schlatz's three-wheel walker. At the time of its demise, the walker was supporting Edna as she bought toilet wipes inside a drug store seven blocks away.

Filled with anger over the fact that the Spic window had run out of empanadas before halftime and slightly annoyed by the racial slurs, five Hispanic students grabbed Smarls and stripped him naked in front of the roaring crowd. Then, another ten men carried him kicking and screaming to the giant nacho cheese machine downstairs. Once they were in position, they tossed Smarls head first into 17 feet of thick, creamy fromage. Within minutes, Smarls' natural body fats and buttery earwax caused a chemical reaction with the boiling cheese that fired a 72-foot flume of cheese into the air that covered every man, woman, and child in the stands like volcanic ash in Pompeii.

Despite suffering first- and second-degree burns and respiratory trauma caused by cheese inhalation, everyone in the crowd miraculously survived. In fact, many victims later remarked that they never knew how good nacho cheese was as a standalone snack.

Although Smarls successfully ate his way to the surface, he died two weeks later from massive weight gain and blood cholesterol that had skyrocketed out of control. It didn't help that he was also lactose intolerant.

Tick, Tock. Friday, 8:29 p.m.

Barely within reach of Constance Anne's right index finger was something that felt like nylon. Sliding her finger up and down the surface, she could tell that it had small, widely spaced holes in the middle like a belt. It came back to her that Mortie had been wearing big orange suspenders with buckles that were each about two inches wide.

She remembered thinking that he looked like a brontosaurus in a clown suit.

Constance Anne moved her neck about an eighth of an inch to the right and felt her head explode with pain. The agony was centered just above her right ear and the pain reminded her of the time she downed two fifths of Crème de Menthe and a brewski and spewed green foam for three days. When she gently explored the area with her fingers, the lump on her head felt like Mount Everest.

If that was bad, moving her head ever so gently to the left was worse.

As her vision sharpened, she nearly screamed bloody murder when she saw someone sitting next to her on the bed and realized that it was Mortie. Convinced that he was a psycho bent on making her into a coffee table,

Constance Anne was stunned that he'd put a cold compress on her forehead and was gently stroking the back of her hand. He'd also covered her with a blanket and tucked her in.

"You hit your head on the brass lamp, poor baby," he whispered, taking a moment to suck on his sweat-soaked moustache. "I'd say pretty damn hard, too. You've been out for quite a while."

Constance Anne sat up as much as the pain would let her and looked angrily at the tall metal thing that was still at the end of the bed. She shuddered. Her heart had not only started to beat faster but harder than normal, and she felt a bizarre adrenaline rush in her chest. It jacked up her pulse to the point that the veins in her neck were visibly throbbing.

She didn't trust him worth a shit.

"*You're going to try to hurt me, aren't you?*" she said in the deepest, most aggressive voice she could muster. Constance Anne looked at him with so much hostility that it scared the hell out of him.

"*Oh, no!*" he said, sounding more than a little put out that she would even think that. "*No! Of course not!*"

"*Then what the hell is that?*" she screamed, pointing at the tall metal thing. It was 9 feet tall and 16 feet wide. It looked a little like an extra-large sawhorse with "A"-shaped legs and a motorized cable and hook that hung down from the top bar. Constance Anne was so frightened that his answer was going to be "for gutting things" that her outstretched finger shook involuntarily.

Mortie had held onto an absolutely absurd hope that no one would ever ask him that question. His face turned so red with embarrassment that Constance Anne thought his head was going to explode into little pieces.

"I have a problem," Mortie said. He stood up and made sure that he stepped just outside the range of her fist.

"Really?" Constance Anne replied with uncharacteristic sarcasm. "I'd have never fucking guessed."

"I know this looks strange, but there's really nothing to be worried about."

Mortie's voice was jittery and he came across like the character in a disaster-at-sea movie who assures passengers that everything is fine right until the ship sinks and everybody drowns. More than that, Constance Anne was sure that Mortie was only seconds away from pulling out a butcher's knife and carving her up like a turkey.

The truth, as it turned out, was less dramatic but weirder than she would have ever imagined.

A *whole lot* weirder, actually.

CHAPTER 4

"...she would sometimes daydream about severing his meat scepter,
liquefying it in a blender, and pouring it down a sink while he
watched. It was a terrific stress reliever."

Working in the back shop of Dickie's Funeral Home wasn't as bad as most
people thought.

Sometimes it was worse.

Every day after school, Constance Anne would stroll through Stiff
Central, otherwise known as the Eternal Preservation Center, to introduce
herself to the new arrivals waiting to be embalmed.

She found the dead less disturbing if she engaged them in brief, happy
conversation, even if it was one-sided. After looking at the nametags on their
toes and pulling back the sheets to see their faces, she'd ask each of the dearly
departed if they'd had a nice day and if she could get them anything to make
their stay more pleasant.

For months, the afternoon visits passed uneventfully. Then the day came
when Constance Anne visited new arrival Tolbert Goldfarb, an 86-year-
old with so much ear hair that he used it for sideburns. Within seconds of
Constance Anne uncovering his face, Mr. Goldfarb's methane-packed colon fired gas up his esophagus and out of his dead lips like steam whistling
through a tea kettle. The result was what sounded like the word "Hi!" in a
loud, chillingly deep voice that scared Constance Anne so badly that she kept
a crucifix taped between her breasts for six months.

After the Goldfarb incident, she would frequently push down on the guests' abdomens just to make sure that there wouldn't be any more surprises. Unfortunately, even that couldn't prevent a man who died while pleasing himself with a toy dinosaur from getting it up one more time. Mr. T.D. Kembelman, a bald man of about 70, sprang into action with a post-mortem erection after Constance Anne's breast accidentally rubbed against his icy cold hand. Horrified and sickened, she tried to push his small penis flat against his stomach. When that failed, she borrowed a hammer from the used coffin shop and tried pounding the little sucker down like a nail.

When that failed too, she cut and ripped Kembelman's salami off with manicure scissors.

Then things really went badly.

Just as she was trying to figure out what to do with the tiny, lifeless, one-eyed monster in her hand, Mrs. Dickie wobbled into the room through the heavy double-doors. Even worse, she wasn't alone.

Being pulled along by his belt buckle was hunky, 25-year-old Jason Frosse, a sales representative from Burning Eternity, Dickie's top urn supplier. As the horror of decapitating Kembelman's manhood turned into panic, Constance Anne shoved his badly mangled mongoose into a tool drawer. Then she hid behind the extra-large-capacity refrigerator that comfortably housed up to three corpses and the daily Mexican buffet. From a distance, she could hear Jason sliding Mr. Kembelman off of his gurney and onto the floor so that he had plenty of room to give horny Mitzi Jo Dickie an extensive view of his merchandise. Constance Anne also heard Jason recoil with disgust when he touched Kembelman below the belt and got a piece of the ragged surgery on his hands.

Jason wanted to have sex with Mitzi Jo about as much as he wanted an anteater to piss in his shoes. Unfortunately, Dickie's proposed new approach to cremation services threatened to eliminate the expensive containers his company sold. In response to a down-and-dirty cremation war started by discount chain Death Depot and cyber-undertakers www.mortality.club, Dickie's planned to launch a "value menu." The "value menu" would offer "below ground pricing" for ashes encased in acrylic snow globes, Christmas ornaments, commemorative plates, and the handles of commuter coffee mugs.

As an even lower-cost alternative, price-conscious mourners could have their loved one's ashes placed in a zippered plastic bag with a photo of the deceased glued to the front, as "a warm, loving memorial that also makes a practical paper weight for home or office." Hundreds of these "Ash Holds" were sold in the Boston area until the remains of Mrs. Imogene Quincy-Talbott of Beacon Hill were mistaken for cocaine and stolen by members of the Columbian night cleaning crew at her daughter's law office.

The two 19-year-old men who snorted the bag's contents were found dead in an alley the next morning with Mrs. Quincy-Talbott heavily crusted around their nostrils.

Because it looked like he was going to get fucked in the deal one way or another, Jason decided that he might as well go ahead and take one for the team in hopes that giving Mitzi Jo a long, lusty ride on his purple dragon might help his cause. Two hours later, every single inch of Mitzi Jo Dickie was happy and relaxed. That was the good news. Jason didn't get the bad news until after he'd done her four more times that afternoon in nine different positions. Dickie's, Mitzi Jo told him, would start offering cremation services that would cut his business in half. Worse, if Jason wanted to keep the business he had, he'd need to be prepared to give her what she wanted when she wanted it.

Jason quit the next day and took a job driving a 350-passenger bus roundtrip from Boston to Oldmens twice a week. It paid better, didn't involve death, and didn't require going balls deep with a woman who smelled like his grandfather. As he told his drinking buddy, Bobby Blacksmear, being with Mitzi Jo was less like pounding the duck and more like sexual "intercorpse."

A few days later Tiny Earl, Dickie's strapping 475-pound, neckless, hairless, used coffin refurbisher found Kembelman's magic wand in the drawer where Constance Anne had left it. Since he didn't know who it belonged to and wasn't going to look around to find out, he tossed it in the garbage disposal and turned it on.

At some point, either the motor broke or the badly battered penis jammed the machinery, because old Willy was still largely intact a week later. When the odor had progressed from bad to lethal, Tiny Earl called in a plumber.

He wrote "Fixed disposal. Clogged with black-and-blue schwanz. Uncircumcised" on the receipt.

While it wasn't easy being 18 and still in tenth grade, Constance Anne tried to make the best of her situation and the opportunities offered to her. Every night, including Fridays and Saturdays, she would spread out her books and papers on an empty embalming table and study for four or five hours. When she was done with her homework, she would read for a few more hours to build her vocabulary and try to improve her exceptionally poor spelling skills.

Her two favorite books were Louisa May Alcott's *Little Women* and Bram Stoker's *Dracula*. Dracula made her laugh because the title character reminded her of her first grade teacher, Mrs. Muratori, who had a canine tooth so long that it reached halfway down her chin. Constance Anne also liked one of Tiny Earl's paperbacks, *Camel Toe Jane*, the story of a busty, fresh-faced college girl from Illinois who picked up tiny Guatemalans in convenience stores and fucked them to death.

Although nearly all of the females at Blough hated Constance Anne because of her steamy-hot looks, the male teachers, boys, and lesbians couldn't get enough of her. Her exquisitely round butterballs, small waist, and curvy hips were like a rare earth magnet. For the most part Constance Anne ignored all of the sexes, especially her English teacher, Lilac Rosselli, whom she saw leaving the principal's office one afternoon with her coat open and a ten inch pink neon dildo and black harness poking out.

About 50 years old with a hunchback, a visible adult thong diaper, and a snarl that revealed lipstick-stained teeth, Rosselli was said to be so sex-starved that even crustaceans kept their legs crossed around her. Every day when the bell rang at the end of class, she would block Constance Anne's way, lift her face as high as it would go, and half-whisper, half-spit in a gravelly voice, "Fuck a humpy and you'll never be grumpy."

Although Constance Anne did her best to act tough and ignore the creepy bitch, the fear of being flunked if she didn't give "the Horny Hunchback of Notre Blough" what she wanted sometimes made her cry herself to sleep at night. She was intent on earning a high school diploma and she wasn't about to let the school's collection of sexual degenerates prevent that. Regrettably, there was a much bigger predator than Quasimodo's twin sister lying in wait for her.

Constance Anne had a grateful heart and rose every morning thanking her lucky stars that many things were behind her, including the Holy Crotch Club and the two hours a week she devoted to Ben Wa ball training for the nuns. Although living in a mortuary wasn't quite as glamorous as she first imagined, she was warm, clean, and well-fed even if the constant diet of Mexican food was making her retain ghastly amounts of water.

Most of the time, she liked her job. She also liked most of her teachers, even though her Bible-thumping math teacher, Mr. Flagroot, and her history teacher, Mr. Faller, tried to look down her shirt every day. According to what she'd overheard in the girls restroom, Percy Flagroot was fairly benign in the scheme of things. Sadly, that was like comparing Stalin to Hitler and calling Stalin a humanitarian because he murdered fewer people. There were more than a few stories about Flagroot and a sophomore girl who called him cute names like "Honey Buns," "Sweet Puddin'," and "Great Anal Master" in front of other students when she felt like being a bitch.

The little idiot also liked to brag that she often spent "topless time" with him in his hot tub, had a key to his apartment, and went there frequently to change the sheets on his bed. She had even taken curious friends there to prove it. That was uncomfortable for Constance Anne to hear, but what was worse was the girls' assessment that if Flagroot was a 9.9 on a 10 point creepiness scale, Faller was a 30.

A skinny, bald, 40-year-old with big ears, an abnormally thick neck, and the depressing smell of a loser, Spruce Faller was described by students as a guy who "only needed a black line on the top of his head to look exactly like a dick."

He was also as dense as concrete.

At a time during the 1980s when virtually anyone who could breathe could get into a public college, Faller was one of only ten in his 300-member high school class who couldn't make the cut. If that was embarrassing in itself, it was even worse in light of the fact that the other nine were exchange students from Zimbabwe who couldn't read or write in any language. Because at 22 Faller was already too old to continue in high school, he entered a remedial learning program at a local community college.

Bored and lonely one Saturday night, he gained notoriety for drawing eyes, a nose, and ruby-red lips on a sweet potato, dousing it with butter, sliding it up his rectum, and leaving it there long enough to sprout. It took two doctors, a nurse, and a representative from Future Farmers of America to remove it. Back on campus, enterprising students sold tee shirts that said, "How did Faller know he had a sweet potato in his ass?" on the front and "He could taste it!" on the back.

Two years later, Faller was admitted to a tiny four-year college in Louisiana where he earned a history degree after taking every course twice. Following a brief, painful career inseminating alligators with a turkey baster in Baton Rouge, he returned to Boston and landed a teaching job. For once in his life he had perfect timing. Faller applied for a job the same day that Delmo Harding, an elderly member of the history faculty, was brutally murdered in the Blough High cafeteria. The dessert lady, enraged that Harding took two tapioca puddings without asking, stabbed the 73-year-old 18 times with a rusty spatula.

A court later ruled that the homicide was "... a righteous kill and a warning to those who abuse their power."

If there was anyone who knew too much about Spruce Faller's personal life, it was Blough High senior Kristah Carnelli. A magnificently-built redhead who wore cropped halter tops and skirts that stopped only millimeters below her landing strip, Kristah (with an "h" for "hot" as she liked to say) took Constance Anne under her wing shortly after she arrived. Right after telling her how to get extra chicken from the horny steam table jockey in the cafeteria, Kristah filled Constance Anne in on Faller's secret life. As she did, it quickly became clear that the man had a lot bigger problems than looking like a male reproductive organ. For starters, he'd told Kristah that if he had a choice between fucking his wife and Saddam Hussein's rancid corpse, Hussein would win every time.

"She plays dead when Faller tries to do her," Kristah said with a smirk on her face. "She just lies there with her legs out and her tongue hanging outside of her mouth like a cooling corpse with a brain injury. She also farts so hard that she can blow out candles with her jeans on."

"The funniest thing," Kristah continued, "is that she likes to take out her false teeth and parade around the house topless. He told me that it made him so sick that he had to knock himself unconscious to make sure he wouldn't see it."

Despite trying hard to be respectful to poor, downtrodden Mrs. Faller, Constance Anne simply found it impossible not to laugh out loud.

"He also bullies girls into fucking him," she said.

Constance Anne stopped laughing.

"Spruce Faller tells every girl in his class with a half-decent rack that he needs her to be 'good' to him," Kristah said, rolling her eyes and shaking her head in disgust.

"If you don't cooperate, he'll make your life a living hell," Kristah said. You'll flunk his class and others, too. There are other teachers in on this shit."

"*Oh my God! Did you fuck him?*" Constance Anne asked, almost as afraid to say the word as she was to hear the answer.

"*Fuck, no!*" Kristah shot back with fire in her eyes. "When he tried to nail me, I waited until he had a smile on his face and his miniature fucking wiener in his hand. Then I took a bunch of pictures with my phone and told him that I'd send them to the school board and the cops. After that, he left me alone. He also gave me an A on every test."

"That's an A," she repeated with pride, "whether I took the fucking test or *not*."

"Be careful, Sweetie," Kristah said as she gave Constance Anne a hug. "You may not get the same chance I had. Faller is pure evil. I hope somebody cuts his dick off and stuffs it in his mouth."

Constance Anne, of course, had already cut a dead man's quiver bone out of his groin and wished that Faller knew it. She was pretty sure that he'd find "Constance Anne the Insane Penis Ripper" a much less appealing target than "Constance Anne the Stacked Sophomore." Not that she felt any anger about the matter, but she would sometimes daydream about severing his meat scepter, liquefying it in a blender, and pouring it down a sink while he watched. It was a terrific stress reliever.

For the next several months, Constance Anne's life was filled with good things. No unusual problems came up from the child molesters that Constance Anne and her girlfriends had dubbed the "Chomo Club." Her grades were good, her newly-arrived corpses farted less than the others, and she'd made friends with Michael Emmanuel Spacchio, better known as "The Spaz."

The only kid in town who wore a sharkskin suit, a white shirt, tie, and black wing tips to high school every day, his dark sunken eyes and thick black hair made him look like a lemur on his way to a board meeting. He was a riddle wrapped in a mystery inside an enigma.

According to a rumor that was repeated so often that it became accepted as fact, The Spaz used his mother's vegetable peeler to disembowel a boy at his old school. Infuriated that he had been picked last for basketball in P.E. class 274 consecutive times by the kid and his friends, he mounted the young man's small intestine on the trunk of his father's seafoam-green Mercury Marquis. Several ill-advised tailgaters actually stopped him to complain that the uncoiled, 20-foot-long organ had slapped their windshields and left a mess.

While other bigger, taller, tougher students at Blough were bullied, nobody messed with The Spaz. In fact, very few people even spoke to him. Teachers addressed him as "Mr. Spacchio" and he, unlike the late Mr. Harding, could take as many tapioca puddings as he liked. Although there was no evidence that he was ever involved in violence of any sort anywhere, The Spaz had a way of looking at people that not only made them believe he was a murderer but a brutal one at that. Constance Anne, whose knack for identifying bullshit was sharpened at the Crotch, could tell that he wouldn't hurt a fly.

Constance Anne also developed a warm friendship with Tiny Earl. On the weekends he would take a break from renovating coffins, and the two of them would spend hours in one of the funeral home's viewing rooms playing a college football video game that let them pick their own teams. Tiny Earl always wanted to be Nebraska, and Constance Anne, who usually won because Earl's fingers were too big for the controller, always picked perennial powerhouse Florida Union because she liked the unusual brown and puce color combination on their helmets. They'd order a half-calamari, half-scungilli pizza and laugh hysterically when the corpse they laid the box on would move it during a rigor mortis contraction.

More than thirty years apart in age, they developed the kind of warm, gentle relationship that fortunate fathers and daughters share. Constance Anne saw Earl as her best friend. Earl saw himself as her protector. Sadly, however, as much as he would have liked to, he couldn't prevent evil from forcing its way into her life.

Four months to the day after Constance Anne's chat with Kristah, Faller rudely stepped in front of her in the school hallway as she walked to her first class of the day. His cheap cologne, a scent reminiscent of tepid urine, could be picked up thirty feet away.

"You need to see me about your grades," Faller told her in a curt, disdainful tone of voice that was meant to intimidate her. "Come to my classroom today after school is dismissed."

Not surprisingly, Constance Anne felt a chest-crushing wave of anxiety come over her the moment she saw him. It gave her an unspeakably painful headache that made it impossible to focus. Worse, she couldn't shake a single one of the horrible symptoms no matter what she tried, from deep breathing exercises and positive thinking to plotting how she would lash Faller to a tree, tie his kosher pickle to the back of a bus, hit the gas and record his screams.

When she walked into the empty classroom at four o'clock, Faller was sitting behind his desk, staring at the back wall like a zombie. He motioned her towards a table that had a six-pack of Diet Salmon in cans and a plate of chocolate chip cookies.

"Enjoy," he said. Hungry and thirsty, but leery that Faller might have roofied the cookies, Constance Anne popped the top on a Salmon and knocked back the whole can in three big gulps.

Because Faller wanted Constance Anne for himself regardless of what it might cost her, it never occurred to him that there was anything wrong with injecting brew of damiana leaf, catnip, and assorted psychotropics into the

Diet Salmon with a small-gauge syringe to make her accommodating. To Faller, it was only important that she understood that he was her "Fuehrer."

"Mr. Faller," Constance Anne said. "You wanted to talk about my grades?"

"Why don't you do better in my class?" he barked, barely acknowledging her presence as if it would be beneath him.

"I don't know what you mean. I have a 97 average."

Faller's face grew red. He didn't like to be challenged, particularly by women. He didn't say a word until he was sure that the silence made her uncomfortable and easier to manipulate.

"*That's not good enough!*" he suddenly shouted in an angry, loud, vulgar voice. He slammed his fist on the desk while still looking straight ahead. "You're white trash, a worthless Crotch Kid. Don't sluts like you know that you have to be perfect? Don't you know that you'll end up back in a fucking hell hole if you don't do exactly what people like me tell you to do?"

Faller slowly turned his grayish face towards her like a monster in a horror movie and grinned. His sickly smile was accented by a decaying, brownish-yellow tooth that stood out like a Mexican at an anti-immigration rally. Grossed out but unable to take her eyes off of the hideous, tartar-rich tooth, Constance Anne simply stared at him. There wasn't any good news in this, but there was plenty of bad. Her severe anxiety had been replaced with pharmaceuticals that gave her a frightening jumble of emotions. One moment she felt like a loser, the next like a winner, and then back to a loser in rapid succession. It was dizzying and horribly upsetting.

Constance Anne started to cry.

Seeing that she was frozen in her tracks, Faller made the same underhanded, sleazy, reprehensible move he'd used on a score of other female students.

"Are you a virgin?"

Constance Anne felt sick. The question was crude and particularly revolting coming from a parasite like Faller. At the same time, it oddly brought back happy memories of sixth grade and her first taste of love. That was that year that her 12-year-old boyfriend misunderstood the meaning of a blow job, put his nose inside her vagina one afternoon, and exhaled. Bizarre as it was, she had her first orgasm, a deep rush that left her breathless and happily exhausted.

"*Well, are you?*" he said, his voice rising with as much curiosity as impatience and anger.

Despite Faller's repeated questioning, Constance Anne didn't utter a word. The dark, hairy unpleasant mole the size of a penny under Faller's lower lip began to quiver.

"I want you to do something," he said, changing his tack as his words created a long, thin string of saliva that connected his lips to the inside of his shirt pocket.

"Come be nice to me," he said.

Faller grabbed her by the shoulders and pushed her into a cramped supply closet adjacent to the classroom. She wanted to run but was too wobbly to even walk.

Having watched her fair share of porno movies in the sacristy of St. Woody's with Cracka, Constance Anne was pretty sure that Faller was supposed to say something about delivering pizza and that she was to supposed to scream with joy when he showed her his "pepperoni." To her surprise, he didn't utter a word about it.

"You need a name. A naked name," he told her. "You need a special name I can call you when we're naked."

The idea of having a "naked" name with Spruce Faller was so nightmarishly repulsive that it blasted her out of her stupor with the power of a nuclear warhead. Adrenaline started coursing through her veins and her brain synapses started firing at light speed to identify the best survival plan out of an abundance of lousy options.

One thing she had to consider was that she really didn't know how big the "Chomo Club" was. While there were three faculty child molesters that she knew of, there could be others that she didn't know about. And, if they included the principal or teachers she had for other classes, the pressure for sex could be so bad that she might have to give up her dream of a diploma.

Another concern was that even if there weren't any more "Chomos," her good grades could quickly turn bad depending on how horny Faller, Flagroot, and the Hunchback were on any given day.

Understanding that she was in a no-win situation, she decided that the only sensible move short of murder was to cooperate with Faller. By doing that, she hoped that he would stop the other two, or anyone else for that matter, from harming her. Even as modest as she was, she recognized that she was at the top of the school's "hottie" pile and that Faller probably wouldn't blink about killing an interloper to keep her.

"Give me a name, you little whore," Faller whispered in her ear. His breath smelled like an outdoor shithouse on a hot summer day.

Since they had been studying the Revolutionary War in class, she picked the name of a battle she found interesting.

"Call me Bunker Hill."

He felt around for her right hand and covered it with a cloth that was attached to something that felt slick and plastic-like.

"Put your middle two fingers inside the head now, Bunker Hill."

As she completed her mission, Faller put on a Nazi surplus helmet with a flashlight attached to the left side with packing tape. In the shadows, she could see what Father Melvin, the head of the Crotch's youth ministry, referred to as a "Tonsil Tickler", although Faller's was so small that she wondered where the rest of it was.

"Now, encircle Mr. Jumbo with our Glorious Fuehrer," he said, in a stupid-sounding German accent as he leaned back against a large gray, metal bucket filled with mops and filthy water.

Constance Anne looked down at her hand. Outfitted in brown cloth with a Nazi swastika embroidered across the middle and arms on both sides of the body was the head of Adolph Hitler. The puppet was complete with a little hat, a mustache, and a wide-open mouth.

"*Begin!*" Faller said tersely, the anticipation swelling in his voice.

Shrugging her shoulders and taking a leap of faith that her teacher wanted ed a hand job, Constance Anne wrapped Hitler around the old bastard's dicktator and started rubbing the generously pre-lubed Fuehrer up and down Faller's shaft. In the background, she could hear the faint sound of *Deutschland, Deutschland über alles* leaking from the cheap headphones Faller had connected to his cheap-ass smart phone.

No sooner than she started, Constance Anne could see Faller's hairy mole quiver like an earthquake as his liquid love flowed out of the Fuehrer's mouth. Faller turned off the flashlight and curled into a fetal position.

"*Oh, Bunker Hill, deine mutter schwizt beim kacken!*" Faller said enthusiastically in German. It meant "Your mother sweats when she shits."

He apparently intended it as a compliment.

Tick, Tock. Friday, 9:07 p.m.

As Mortie explained it, he ate several large platters of salted carp and lentils for dinner one evening and ended up with sharp stomach pains right before bedtime. Desperate to relieve his sloshing bowels and having nothing better to do anyway, he strapped himself into his home "toileting salon," switched on the wall-mounted 48" HDTV, and decided to make a night of it.

Built for people like himself who saw toileting as "a momentous part of the human experience," the salon was a self-contained unit outfitted with a heated toilet seat, cup holders, a foot rest, a snack tray, a bidet, and a refrigerator. After flipping through a couple of channels airing cartoons he'd already seen, he settled on the incredibly popular *Mitzi Jo's Mausoleum* shopping show.

That night the program featured a young, handsome, Latin host in a pair of taupe spandex capri pants, a Yankees tank top, and a jaunty fedora who was hawking a new coffee table book called *Burying the Bone*. Not illogically, Mortie expected the book to have something to do with funerals.

Instead, he was pleasantly surprised to learn that it was an illustrated history of sexual positions from across the ages. At least two were said to come from another solar system, guaranteeing it to be a monster hit with the Area 51 crowd.

No stranger to sex manuals himself, Mortie already knew a lot of popular positions like "69", the "Wheelbarrow," and the "Italian Hot Brush." He was even familiar with the enigmatic "Anal Lurch" that originated in China in 5 B.C.

The TV pitch man even made the shocking claim that he could cure Roving Genitalia Disorder, a rare condition in which both male and female reproductive organs travel from the crotch to the kneecaps and the back of the neck without warning during the sex act. According to government research conducted in 2014, males had more cases of Roving Genitalia than women by a two- to-one margin.

Most important to Mortie, however, was the man's promise of a solution to his Eventual Ejaculation Disorder problem with nothing more than some nylon and a crane.

EED was not only cruel in its excessive delay of relief and gratification, it was horrifically embarrassing. With no control over their ejaculations, sufferers could be anywhere or doing anything when it came time to come a week or more after sex. With more than a million male EED victims in the U.S. alone and no medical cure in sight, an entrepreneur invented "The Sperm Mitt," a specially-designed, non-latex condom with a hard plastic reservoir and disposal mechanism for wear all day, every day.

With The Sperm Mitt, men could kiss goodbye their days of soaking in the stickiness and odor of their own trouser gravy. The Sperm Mitt's patented "pump-and-dump" technology channeled the man chowder safely down the pants leg, through a tiny chamber where chemicals pulverized the pole milk into dust, and sprayed "New Car Smell" on the affected areas.

Unfortunately, The Sperm Mitt only addressed EED after the fact.

The sales guy went on to claim that he could help men have sex in the traditional "come and go" manner. "Come and go" lent itself to pregnancy, intimacy, and post-coital cigarette smoking that usually lasted until somebody went on the "Walk of Shame" or ran because their fuckbuddy's spouse came home early. Not everyone was happy with a "fix" for their EED lover, however. Some people preferred that their partner would "go" home and "come" somewhere else later for reasons including birth control and gross insensitivity.

With high expectations, Mortie bought the book and a gadget called the "Climax Pal" at www.climaxtoday.com for two large and 50,000 airline miles. In about a week, seven boxes of loose, unnumbered metal parts, a cheap, plastic Allen wrench, and an instruction booklet originally written in Chinese, translated into Spanish, and translated again into English arrived on his doorstep. Not surprisingly, assembling the Climax Pal turned into an epic cluster fuck.

"I'm going to kick EED's ass," he told Constance Anne. "But the only way to do it is with this baby," he said, patting the tall metal thing that was more properly called a gantry.

Mortie was excited to show Constance Anne what the Climax Pal could do, and Constance Anne was surprisingly eager to see it. Her fear of becoming a wall tapestry was slowly fading, and her compassion was gradually growing. She also needed the money really, really badly and couldn't afford to have him cancel his credit card purchase.

Holding an oversized remote control in his hand, he punched a yellow button that turned on an electric hoist attached to the center of the gantry's crossbar. The machine made a slight squeal as a large safety hook attached to a cable slowly descended about five feet.

Dressed in a white tee shirt, transparent underwear, and a body harness made of orange nylon, Mortie couldn't have looked worse if he'd been dressed by a blind Cambodian with the Clap. The harness had wide front straps that were linked across the chest, thick belts that went around the legs, and an adjustable metal "D" ring in the upper middle portion of the back.

Mortie took the hook and attempted to reach behind his back to connect it to the "D" ring, a difficult maneuver because his forearms couldn't get past his hefty underarm meat. After abandoning that approach, he tried wiggling against the hook in hopes that it would somehow snag the ring. That failed, too. Huffing, puffing, and turning various shades of purple from frustration, Mortie finally threw a "Hail Mary" by standing on a stool and falling backward in a desperate attempt to "thread the needle."

He inexplicably succeeded on the seventh try.

"OK, watch this!" Mortie said excitedly. He sounded like a five-year-old trying to get his grandmother's attention.

He pressed a yellow button on the remote. The electric motor kicked on immediately and within seconds the cable vibrated and the gantry creaked as it raised all 389 pounds of Mortie Beech off the ground. When he got up about two feet, he pressed a blue button and stopped the machine.

Dangling in mid-air with nothing to do, he decided to do a comical little dance to show her that he was a fun guy. He took a bow when he was done and Constance Anne applauded. Next, he put his arms out, leaned forward, lifted his legs to make his body horizontal, and pretended to fly like a super-hero. Constance Anne applauded again and whistled.

Then, Mortie moved his arms and kicked his legs like he was swimming.

That was a mistake for a variety of reasons, not the least of which was that his movements wound the cable dangerously tight. As it untangled with the force of a hurricane, it whipped Mortie around in a circle like the guaranteed-to-make-you-vomit ride at the county fair.

As entertaining as this was, it paled in comparison with what happened when he accidentally dropped the remote control. Insisting on picking up the device himself, he turned upside down to reach it with his hand. When he did, his mammoth, low-hanging, "Mother's Apron" belly fell in his face with a loud, moist "thwack." Luckily, he was able to lift his gut just enough to make an airway between his face and navel. Otherwise, he would have suffocated.

When Mortie got back on his feet, Constance Anne considered asking him how the Climax Today stuff would help him shoot his wad here and now instead of in line at the DMV next Tuesday. She concluded that it was best to leave that dog on the porch. Nevertheless, she wanted to know how he intended to do the horizontal mambo with her.

"Have you used this thing for sex before?" Constance Anne asked.

"No," Mortie said.

"Then how are you going to use it?"

"Well, I'll just sort of dangle over you and then lower myself on down so we can … can… *connect*. You know?"

He was panicky, perspiring, and terrified that Constance Anne would run off like the last one.

"You sure about this, big boy?"

Mortie pointed at his meat wrench.

"Don't worry. Mr. Pup-Pup and I have been practicing."

Constance Anne thought it was cute that he called his Count von Schlongstein "Mr. Pup-Pup."

"Practicing with what?" she asked.

Mortie got hungry just thinking about it.

"Glazed doughnuts. And a bagel with cream cheese."

Chapter 5

"When people thought about Florida Union Collegiate University, they thought about starting the day with a six pack and a chlamydia discharge."

Mortie hated his father's Magua car dealership almost as much as he hated his father.

Built for people who would pay almost anything for a car if the payments were low enough, Chinese-made Maguas looked like decomposing Easter eggs on wheels. Available for purchase in pastel blue or yellow with a standard black roof for $0 down and $12 a week, the company's sales campaign touted Maguas as "New wheels with chill rims and neon trims" that delivered "Kung Fu savings" at the pump. Together with ads aimed at the booty meat market like "Put in your ass what you save in gas" and "Buy some bling with what you save from Beijing," the 80-inch wheelbase Maguas sold like hotcakes.

Unfortunately, the company's ads left out a few details.

For one thing, Maguas didn't have door handles. They were also missing trunks, air conditioning, turn signals, and gas gauges. Instead of headlamps, Maguas had red bicycle reflectors that picked up the light from other cars for night driving. As for power, they could hit 25 mph with the radio on and sometimes 40 with it off.

The sales contracts had a few issues, too. To start, the fine print section was written in Biblical Hebrew and printed in light 4-point type to make it look like a decoration.

The $12 a week payments lasted for 3,640 weeks or until the customer paid $43,680, whichever came first. If the buyer died before paying it off, their grandchildren and great-grandchildren could inherit the responsibility of paying off the balance. According to auto industry research, Magua owners were three times more likely to dump burdens on people who weren't born yet than other car shoppers.

Last but not least, Magua America, Inc. could demand all $43,680 in one lump sum if a buyer's payment was more than 15 minutes late or Magua just felt like it. Rather than having the car repossessed, the buyers would agree that Magua could liquidate the assets of every member of their immediate family, extended family, and casual friends. As a result, Magua became the world's largest holder of real estate, savings accounts, 401(k)s, and large Christmas lawn ornaments.

Over time, no one with any brains would even speak to a Magua owner. The liability potential even gave way to dating sites like www.nomagua.com that only allowed people that had no Magua associations whatsoever.

Understandably, the company's sales training program strictly forbid discussing any details about anything before the salesperson had successfully pressured, embarrassed, or frightened the customer into submission. Among the more popular strategies to humiliate a man in front of his family was to say, "*You really can't afford this, can you?*"

Another, which not surprisingly won the company's prestigious "Sheer Terror" award, involved having a hot girl who looked 25 but was really 14 sit outside of the salesperson's office. If the customer balked about buying the car, the salesperson left the room, the girl came in, showed the guy her ID, and explained that if he didn't buy the car she'd call the cops and accuse him of exposing himself. A collection of penis photos that covered every race and skin color was already on her phone.

While both approaches were very effective, Magua's salesperson of the year, Frederico Calamario, preferred to exploit human emotions in a different way.

At the moment he needed to seal the deal, Calamario would bring a cute little boy into his office and introduce him to the customers. The little boy would look at the adults, start to sob, and say, "I don't feel well, Daddy" as he wrapped his arms around Calamario's leg. Then, Calamario would say sadly, "Little Timmy hasn't shit in three months. He'll die soon if he can't get a bowel transplant. Won't you help us by buying the car?" People were so distressed and anxious to buy the car that they never noticed Little Timmy skipping out of the office with a candy bar in his hand.

If Mortie hated his father and his cars, the old man's television commercials left him speechless with rage.

Dressed in a white bunny suit with tall, floppy ears, and a red tie knotted around his neck, the elder Beech started off by looking into the camera with a creepy, psychotic expression on his face. Then he would pick up a sledgehammer, climb on the hoods of competitor's cars, and smash in their windshields while yelling *"Dew ney! Ham ka chan!"* phrases that someone told him meant *"Fuck you! Death to your family!"* in Chinese. In the background, Deedee, whose gorgeous body had been exquisitely poured into a micro bikini, licked her lips and danced provocatively to the beat of Cantonese chamber music.

Then, Belvin would throw himself on the hood of a Magua, give it a long, passionate French kiss and dry hump the tail pipe. As the message *"$12 a week! No finance charges!"* flashed on the bottom of the screen frequently enough to cause seizures, Deedee would pour sex lube over her body, the car, and Belvin and join him and the car for a threesome.

At the end of the ad, Belvin would wickedly wink at the camera and say, *"Come do us!"* as Deedee shrieked with pleasure.

It was a helluva lot of action for 30 seconds and, thanks to the internet, the commercial became a global sensation.

Despite that, Magua's corporate marketing geniuses forced every franchise owner to air a commercial they made starring unknown Albanian "Super Rapper" Lzzzzrd Z.

Lzzzzrd Z wore billowing neon green pajama pants, a white shirt with the Magua logo on it, and neon green and white sneakers with bells on the toes. Around his neck was a spiked dog collar that was connected to his lips, nostrils, earlobes, and ankles with thick gold chains that were attached so tightly that most of his face would've been torn off if he'd sneezed hard. He wore four snap-back hats, one stacked on top of the other. The brim on the bottom of the first was pointed to the right, the second was pointed to the left, the third was backwards and the fourth faced straight ahead.

Flashing his two gold front teeth in front of the camera like he was a beaver, Lzzzzrd Z delivered what was officially known as the "Magua Rap of Allegiance":

> Get your booty in my car,
> You know it ain't bizarre,
> I'm feeling like a czar,
> I got a cool Magua!
>
> Come take a ride and feel the pride,
> Wheels be the game, yo!
> Magua da name, yo!
> Wheels be da game, yo!
> Magua da name, yo!
>
> I got some awesome rims,
> Big ass neon trims,
> Only twelve bucks a week,
> There's a lot of mystique.
>
> Come take a ride and feel the pride,
> Wheels be the game, yo!
> Magua da name, yo!
> Wheels be da game, yo!
> Magua da name, yo!
>
> So what it made in China, it'll heat up your vagina,
> Wheels be the game, yo!

Magua da name, yo!
Wheels be da game, yo!
Magua da name, yo!

In less than a month, Magua sold 23,000 T-shirts at $24.99 a piece that simply said "Magua da name, yo!" Not everyone was impressed, however. The kids at school made fun of the ads, taunted Mortie with chants of "Magua, Magua, a stupid fucking Chinese car," and threw rocks at his head. A nasty teacher had the audacity to ask him if he ever got in on the sex play with the car, Deedee, and his dad.

Even Mortie's friend Mun Ching, an Asian exchange student with buck teeth and a bronze-colored mullet, took a shot, asking him why his family sold such inferior cars for such high prices. Then he thought about it and realized that he had asked a question that didn't require an answer.

Unfortunately, young Mr. Beech had more problems with the kids in school than his association with awful cars.

His comb-over and weight obviously made him a target for harassment, and he particularly hated the embarrassing names his classmates called him. At Sam Giancana Elementary School, kids called him "Moron" instead of Mortie, a name that pissed him off so much that he shoved the genius who came up with it into a closet one Friday afternoon, locked the door, and left him there to munch on cockroaches, an often undervalued source of protein, until a janitor found him on Tuesday.

In middle school, another idiot started calling him "Whale," as in "beached whale," a pathetic joke about his size that made him feel ashamed. When Mortie finally couldn't take it anymore, he grabbed the kid, threw him on the ground, and released a loud, full-bodied, air biscuit in his face that made the little loudmouth lose consciousness.

At John Wilkes Booth High School, he gained the even more unfortunate name "Sperm Whale" after "Smacky" Famolare, a junior whose face looked like a single, continuous zit with a nose in the middle, caught him spooging into a handful of the school's cheap toilet paper squares in a bathroom stall and broadcast it over the school's public address system. As humiliating as

Famolare's harassment was, Mortie ironically decided not to do anything to him. With meth addicts for parents and a slutdog sister whose name and phone number graced the walls of every public shithouse in town, Mortie concluded that Smacky's life was probably worse than his own.

His guess proved deadly accurate when Famolare's bullet-ridden, partially dismembered body was discovered in a pool of acetone on the roof of a Korean nail salon. Although Mortie had nothing to do with Smacky's murder, he also didn't do anything to dispel rumors to the contrary. Not surprisingly, no one ever called Mortie anything rude or nasty again, even after the police ruled the death accidental.

Happily, not everything was dark in Mortie's life.

Clearly a bright young man, he took a heavy load of advanced placement courses and made the honor roll every semester. He had his pastel blue Magua customized with air conditioning, a tiny refrigerator, and a strap-on male urinal that allowed him to drink as much Diet Salmon as he wanted to without having to stop to take a leak.

Even more, the girls treated him well despite his reputation for cranking his shank in the boy's restroom.

Mortie's extremely thin auburn hair, baby blue eyes, and kind disposition made him seem more like a big goofy bear than a horny teenager. In fact, more than a few hot girls liked to press their breathtaking lovemobiles against his pulsating belly and give him a group hug.

His fortunes took another leap forward when he earned a spot on the Booth High Assassins football team as a senior by proving that he could be a formidable weapon in short-yardage situations. In fact, had any of the coaches known that his bowel movements were so rancid that he puked after emptying his intestines in the toilet, they would have welcomed him to the team much earlier.

Had they known that he could release "death farts" at will, they would have canonized him.

In the Florida state championship game against Miami's Abraham Lincoln High, Mortie was brought in as a nose guard in the final three seconds with the score tied at 14 and the ball in Lincoln's possession at the Booth one yard line. When the Lincoln quarterback took the snap on first and goal, Mortie released what he called "The Jellyfish," a long, wet, sauerkraut-powered discharge that delivered an initial shock wave of noxious odor to the target followed by long tendrils of secondary stinks that spread a thick curtain of methane over a 400-square-foot area.

Mortie's teammates, who had donned protective masks in the huddle, were weakened but still able to stand. The Lincoln line and backfield, however, collapsed in a heap, some losing bladder control and jerking their arms and legs involuntarily. The quarterback ripped off his helmet in a desperate, ferocious struggle for air and fumbled the ball.

The crowd went crazy as Mortie scooped up the pigskin and took a 99-yard stroll for the winning touchdown. None of the Lincoln players wanted to even get near him, much less tackle him.

Even though there wasn't a chance in hell that his teammates would hoist him on their shoulders like they did in the movies, Morton Beech still felt like a champion. It was the first time in his life that he'd ever felt such exhilaration and with it, he even started to change his thinking about his place in the world.

Rather than seeing little more than sadness and anger in his future, he began to believe that maybe, just maybe, anything was possible.

Mortie graduated from Booth High in the spring as salutatorian of his class, missing the top spot by less than one thousandth of one percent. During the year he had earned a varsity letter in football, was inducted into four academic honor societies, and had a landscape he painted put on display at a famous New York art gallery. It was truly a great and very well-deserved day of impressive recognition for Mortie, the kind that men and women of any age never forget.

In fact, the only people who weren't cheering for him among the hundreds attending the graduation that day were his own mother and father. They weren't there. It wasn't as if they had both fallen ill or had a family tragedy prevent them from attending. It was more special than that. They had simply ripped up the invitation and lit it on fire.

With brilliant grades, an SAT score of 1590, and a myriad of talents, Mortie had his heart set on attending Prinharvia, one of America's oldest and most distinguished universities, where his acceptance was packaged with four years' worth of breathtaking academic and athletic scholarships. Sadly, his father had a different plan motivated by an outright refusal to see his son go to a better college than he did.

Since Mortie was only 17 and still a minor, Belvin enrolled the boy against his will at Florida Union. As different from Prinharvia as day and night, Belvin reveled in the fact that an undergraduate degree from Florida Union was largely meaningless and would probably condemn Mortie to as miserable a life as he had.

As Belvin saw things, when people thought about Prinharvia, they imagined popped-collar polo shirts and ivy-covered buildings.

When they thought about Florida Union, they thought about starting the day with a six pack and a chlamydia discharge.

If a typical Prinharvia grad drove a Porsche, the average FUCU alum cruised around in a truck filled to the roof with damp towels and empty beer cans.

Even better, FUCU was virtually free. As a legacy, Mortie not only qualified for heavily discounted everything but received a free, all-access pass to the 24-hour All-You-Can-Cram Ham Buffet in downtown Big Hare Key. As far as Belvin Beech was concerned, the kid could play football if he wanted to and probably get paid a few bucks under the table for it. One thing the old man was quite sure of, however, was that the fart nonsense that was such a big deal in high school wasn't going to last very long in the college ranks.

In August, Mortie reluctantly moved into Pinto Hall, one of the school's oldest dormitories. Hand-carved from gigantic blocks of native limestone by Seminole Indian contractors Osceola & Sons in 1890, the large, dark, musty-smelling dorm room Mortie was assigned to featured creaking floors, flickering lights, working fireplaces, and wall coverings made of alligator and snake skins.

There were two beds located on opposite sides of the room with mattresses that felt like they were the very finest in 14th-century sleep technology. Due to an engineering error during the building's renovation in 1995, there was no air conditioning to contend with the 95-degree heat and horribly high humidity during the summer. To add to Mortie's misery, August was also the middle of the mosquito season.

Happier than shit about the whole situation, he picked out a bed, dropped his suitcase on it and crossed his fingers in hopes that he would at least get a decent roommate. Then he headed off to find the All-You-Can-Cram Ham Buffet on Clydesdale Street where he could spend the rest of the day eating barbequed ham, glazed ham, baked ham, ham and beans, ham salad, ham spread, ham and rice, ham casserole, ham kabobs, ham soup, honey ham, crockpot ham, ham loaf, pineapple ham, poached snouts, and mashed potatoes.

At one o'clock in the morning, Mortie bolted upright from his bed in a cold sweat. His eyes were wide open. His heart was pounding in his throat. He tried to scream, but nothing would come out. Somewhere near him in the pitch dark was the chilling, tormented sound of a wild animal growling and thrashing in pain.

Mortie was terrified and confused.

In quick succession, a lamp crashed and a metal trash can was knocked over, making a clanging noise on the wooden floor. His mouth went completely dry as he looked in the direction of the noise and saw something large moving in the shadows. With panic racing through his veins and the palms of his trembling hands sweating like a cat in a Korean deli, Mortie blindly reached around in the dark for a lamp. Finally bumping against one, he switched it on.

There in front of him was the hulking, six-foot-tall frame of a man with bushy eyebrows, chin whiskers, and patchy hair loss that made him almost indistinguishable from an ill Irish terrier. Once he could see what the man was doing and the intense agony on his face, the horrifying noises made perfect sense.

Twisting back and forth like a madman with his pants down around his ankles, the man was hopping on one foot, howling in pain, and desperately trying to adjust what looked like yellowed underwear held together with gray strapping tape.

Although Mortie didn't know it at the time, the poor bastard was wearing a homemade truss meant to keep part of his small intestine from wandering around. Not only did the man have a painful inguinal hernia, a hellish problem where part of the intestine breaks through a weak spot in the groin muscles, but the truss was pinching his balls. The pain was so bad that he'd have cut them off with a dull spoon if it would have stopped the agony.

In the morning light, Mortie's roommate looked significantly closer to collecting Social Security than a college diploma.

A sporadically rehabilitated crack addict, Arvid "Moon Dog" Grabowski looked somewhere between 45 and 65 years old, although if he was a meth user he could have just as easily been 18. As thin as an x-ray with thick, gray-brown hair like a wolf, his wardrobe rarely varied from cut-offs, a long sleeve shirt, dusty combat boots, and a ragged camo trucker's cap that said "Parasite" on the front and "Bitchmasta" on the back. Moon Dog said that he was a poultry science major and that all of his family members were residents in Raiford, home of Florida State Prison. Mortie found Moon Dog's use of the word "in" an oddity since he had only heard people refer to themselves as being residents "of" someplace.

As their first week together sped by, Mortie learned that "The Dog," as he liked to be called, went to bed at noon, slept motionless on his back with a sheet pulled over his head like a corpse, got up at eight o'clock in the evening, and didn't come back until about eleven o'clock in the morning the next day. When Mortie asked him if he'd like to join him one Sunday morning for a stack of pancakes, Grabowski politely turned him down. He explained without elaboration that he didn't let anyone see him eat.

As disturbing as that was to hear, it bothered Mortie more that Grabowski never showered or used the toilet. He also always had a collection of hypodermic needles and test tubes stuffed in his shirt pocket.

Adding to the intrigue, Mortie never saw him without a copy of the *Amateur's Guide to Kidney Removal* in the back pocket of his pants, a peculiarity that became more noticeable when an epidemic of security guard disappearances swept the campus. Around the same time, Grabowski moved a large Styrofoam cooler into their room that required frequent re-supply with giant bags of ice. Mortie believed that he was better off not asking questions.

Although Mortie didn't know it at the time, The Dog was a legend on the Florida Union campus and, setting aside any involvement he may have had with the black market kidney trade, was seen by many students, faculty, and alumni as the heart and soul of Florida Union Collegiate University.

His relaxed, low-maintenance wardrobe, responsibility-free lifestyle, and deft, quasi-criminal manipulation of education grants, the G.I. Bill, student loans, public aid programs, and federal bankruptcy laws was a guiding light to those who dreamed of making a college career a career in itself. An undergraduate since the fall of 1982, Grabowski had changed majors twelve times, enrolled in more than 300 courses, completed 91, but skillfully failed to collect enough credits in any single discipline to earn a degree. Even more, he had been able to live in a clean dormitory, access three meals a day from the cafeteria, use campus medical services, and enjoy 50-yard-line football tickets for more than 30 years without paying a dime.

Now in his fifties, The Dog came under intense public criticism from a corporate CEO on the school's board of trustees who referred to him as "an utterly disgraceful success at taking everything and giving nothing back." Curiously, the criticism swiftly vanished after a report in *Insider Trading Today*, a daily update on upcoming criminal activities in the stock and bond markets, revealed that the same CEO was moving her company's headquarters to Switzerland to "increase stockholder value" by evading U.S. taxes. The report was particularly well-read because it was adjacent to the paper's most popular feature, *Sentencing Roundup*, a series of interesting briefs about who was going where, and for how long, in the federal penitentiary system.

If those accomplishments alone didn't qualify The Dog for mythic status, what he did to pay cash for a $35,000 pickup truck certainly did.

One day, in one of the few business classes Grabowski actually attended, the professor casually mentioned how big companies sometimes pay invoices for up to few grand without even looking at them. Curious to see if that was true, Grabowski recruited help from his 5' 9", raven-haired, Afro-Lithuanian girlfriend, Squeaky, a stacked, twenty-something cello major suffering from low self-esteem mixed with sporadic narcissism. Together, they designed a brilliant assortment of fake invoices on an art department computer and mailed them to the 25 largest companies in the Everglades. Although the companies were charged for different items like ball caps, tee shirts, paperclips, or tape, each of the bills were for $2,011.17, an odd figure that made the invoice seem more legitimate.

Within a month, Cyst's Department Stores, the Florida Union athletic department, and all 17 Jalapeno Indian riverboat casinos anchored off of Chocha Bay had all paid in full and on time. Six more, including behemoth restaurant chain Gators, Taters 'n Snakes, sent their checks shortly after the due date and paid the $30 late fee.

Two of them even reordered paperclips.

With $50,000 in his pocket, The Dog picked out a 19-foot-long silver truck with a dark red full leather package, goat's wool floor mats, extra-large cup and chicken bucket holders, and blue interior neon lighting. He had it customized with a cool decal that designated it as "Dog One" and a ball hitch on the back big enough to tow Cuba.

Within a week, the truck was filled with moldy towels and empty beer cans. Within two weeks, he had twelve shriveled air freshener trees hanging from the rearview mirror and had slapped on a dirty bumper sticker that said "Deer Hearse". Within three, the driver's side door had the imprint of a grill where it had been T-boned by an AMC Pacer driven by an old geezer wearing a "I'm here for the Methadone" shirt and a chest-level adult "high-top" diaper.

Soon after, Grabowski put the official school decal on the back window. It had 2-inch FUCU letters with "Flrida Unin Cllegiate Universty" under it in puce, errors made by distressed Chinese workers who weren't allowed to urinate during the day. Sadly, no one in the Florida Union community except Mortie ever noticed the mistakes.

Besides killing his father and balling a freshman girl named Bridget Garbonzole, football was Mortie's favorite thing to daydream about.

Although FUCU had a main library with only 900 volumes, the school had twice come within spitting distance of national championships but had their winning records vacated when officials discovered that two of their players in three separate seasons were former pro starters who had recently been released from prison. Rather than being fired for the violations, FUCU Head Coach Marsulis "Roach Clip" Goodman was given a $500,000 "emergency bonus" from the school's boosters to help him "heal" from the governing authority's "vicious, mostly groundless attacks."

Since The Puce Wave first fielded a football team in 1892, every game had been sold out to the walls. In fact, the waiting list for season tickets was twenty years deep. FUCU football was so popular that the sale of puce-colored Fuming Sea Turtles tees and ball caps alone exceeded the university's $275 million annual tuition income. Happily, an additional $25 million in sales of "We're #1" foam finger wavers covered the university president's athletic recruitment budget.

Because of the school's commitment to the community, half of the funds were spent at The Mount Ed Club, a dining and entertainment hall the university said it used for academic and medical research. The liquor license was still under the club's previous name, The Warm Meat Pocket.

After tugging on a Florida Union helmet for the first time on the practice field, Mortie realized how fortunate he was to be a walk-on. Every man on the Fuming Sea Turtles football squad had exceptional speed, strength, size, and a lengthy criminal record that involved some combination of armed robbery, attempted murder, and assault with a deadly weapon. While this was clearly intimidating, Mortie took heart in the fact that none of them had the ability to knock down all eleven opposing players, referees, coaches, and even spectators the way he could.

Oddly, Mortie's high school success hadn't been widely publicized. Although his teammates knew that he had a unique talent, they didn't know what it was until the last ten seconds of the season opener against Sea Critter State. With Florida Union ahead by a field goal and Sea Critter with the ball on the FUCU two yard line, Mortie was sent in on defense. When the ball was snapped on first and goal, he released his lethal package. Within seconds, Sea Critter State was leveled and, minutes later, video of dazed players, many staggering, vomiting, and experiencing seizures, had gone viral. Some viewers said they could see a dark mass creeping across the field like a predator.

One spectator wearing a gray tweed do-rag, a bright red cravat, and hospital slippers could be seen covering his eyes with his hands, twisting in convulsions, and falling backwards over the railing on top of the FUCU cheerleaders.

The cheerleaders, all of whom were named Tiffany, shared the same gynecologist, Dr. Arnold Moosener. Moosener's ad promoting "Jubilant Genitals" was printed on the back of the girls' uniforms, on the scoreboard, and on the toilet paper in the boys and girls restrooms.

Although Mortie didn't know it at the time, his "flair for bad air" would send every college football coach in the nation sniffing for the next Mortie Beech. Players were routinely stuffed with broccoli, garbanzo beans, red kraut, radishes, and cauliflower. Prunes and onions were baked into every meal. Meat, poultry, and eggs were purposely left in the sun and then undercooked to whip up malodorous bowel frenzies. Students and locals who were known to be lactose intolerant or lard abusers were brought in for tryouts, sometimes against their will.

The "search for the stink" even made its way into professional sports in addition to a significant number of bowling leagues. Fans of England's national rugby union squad demanded a "blow off man." Politicians around the globe considered it as a debate tactic and rumors flew that major world governments had looked into the use of "high-velocity intestine products" for military purposes. In the end, despite spending tens of millions of dollars, no one could find or manufacture another "Death Bowel."

On the gridiron, the only thing that stopped the Fuming Sea Turtles from having a perfect season was college football's hastily installed Beech Rule, a fifteen-yard penalty, loss of down, and forfeiture of the day's beer concession revenues for "the use of human intestines in any manner that endangers the health and welfare of players, officials, or spectators." As far as Florida Union officials were concerned, the threat of the penalty was effective. Forget losing yardage and a down: Mortie was left on the bench more than once solely to protect the brewski money.

From the moment Mortie released his first blast in Miami, he could have never predicted the impact that his bowels would have on his life. A broad smile came over his face every time he saw himself on the stadium Jumbotron, on billboards, tee shirts, and even on game tickets with the words "Join the Intestine Movement!"

He loved the roar of the crowd when he lumbered onto the field. For once in his 18 years he felt appreciated, useful, and in control of his destiny.

For all he knew, his intestines might even carry him into the professional football ranks one day. All of the zany hoopla aside, one brief moment meant more to him than anything else. Looking into the crowd from the Florida Union sideline, he saw a remarkably attractive girl with blue-streaked black hair and a body to die for poured into tight shorts and a black crop top. She was waving to him with her left hand and blowing him kisses with her right. He was giddy with delight that such a beautiful woman had paid attention to him.

It was a magical moment for Mortie. It was good that he didn't know she was waving to the player behind him.

Tick, Tock. Friday, 11:54 p.m.

Constance Anne woke up in the pitch dark. Her head hurt badly again and, until she saw a sliver of moonlight push its way through the filthy motel window, she was terrified that she might be blind.

Something very big and very heavy was pushing down on her so hard that she couldn't move her arms and legs. Panic set in. Constance Anne tried to scream, but nothing came out. The harder she tried to breathe, the more difficult it became to get the air her lungs needed.

Utterly terrified, she started kicking her feet and bowing her back in a fast, savage attempt to free herself. It didn't work and, when it was clear that she was only making her situation worse, she burst into tears. To make matters worse, her hot pink stilettos punctured the waterbed's safety liner and let 187 gallons of fetid water swamp the room. Some of it splashed on the spot where a walking personality disorder named Larry had tattooed a red rose on her ankle one Christmas Eve. She was strangely relieved to breathe in the dirty, sour smell of stagnant water. Because she couldn't remember much about what happened, the stench helped to remind her where she was and, just as importantly, where she wasn't.

At the top of the list was relief in knowing that she wasn't buried alive. That was a horrifying possibility that had occurred to her in the cold darkness when she realized she couldn't move.

In second place was a strange peace of mind that came from remembering that she was in a filthy Florida motel with a guy who was the size of an SUV. His aftershave was unforgettable. Wet Membrane, a scent typically sold in gas stations, was packaged in old liquor bottles recovered from sewage plants. The label depicted a bald, middle-aged man striking a pose at a bar with the slogan, "When you need to be remembered." While other aftershaves built their fortunes on deft combinations of citrus, sage, and sandalwood, Wet Membrane cut to the fucking chase. Its distinctive blend of soft boiled eggs, asparagus, and rubbing alcohol was still there a week after you soaked your body in tomato juice and burned your clothes for the second time.

She remembered that his name was Marty or Mortie.

As her brain popped into gear, Constance Anne concluded that the crushing weight she was trapped under almost certainly had to be some or all of Marty or Mortie. Since she was buck naked and he was on top of her, it made sense that sex had probably been involved.

Struggling to understand just how big of a mess she was in, Constance Anne did the only thing she could. She started sniffing and tasting everything within the very limited reach of her nose and tongue. She quickly regretted that decision when some of Marty or Mortie's sour-smelling underarm hair attached itself to her tongue and she couldn't spit it out.

A lot of things crossed her mind at that gag-inducing moment. She was pretty sure that he was about six inches shorter than she was. If they were having sex, she thought, how the hell did he end up with his armpit on her face? Couldn't that only happen if he was taller?

And where, by the fucking way, was his dick?

She wondered if he was like a guy she'd met who had two fully functioning cocks or what he liked to call a "double-decker." One regulation-size penis was in the usual place and another, slightly smaller one protruded from an area just above his navel. He tried to be nonchalant about it, telling her that the only real downside was that he had to unbutton both his pants and shirt when he urinated. On the other hand, the upside was that he only needed one other person to have a threesome.

The bed's cheap plywood frame made a sharp cracking sound as it collapsed. The water rushed in between them and covered her diamondique belly-button ring in the blink of an eye.

The good news was that Constance Anne could feel him float off of her a little bit.

The better news was that it was still too dark for her to see him.

He was staring at her with milky, saucer-sized eyes. His mouth was wide open and frozen in a scream.

CHAPTER 6

"The unsettling thought that he had been using the Hitler puppet to extend his manhood when they had sex sprinted through her mind. It sent a silent, bloody scream through every corner of her being."

As they walked down the poorly-lit hallway of an old, musty-smelling apartment building, Faller put his hands on Constance Anne's shoulders. He maneuvered her into Apartment 19, a tiny place with peeling green paint, a high, brown-stained ceiling, and an embarrassing lack of furniture.

Sitting by the window in a dilapidated plaid recliner smoking a cigarette was a little old man with dark, sunken eyes and a wheezing cough.

"This is Mr. Reeves. He's a ventriloquist," Faller said, shoving a reluctant Constance Anne uncomfortably close to the old geezer. "I'm going to love what he can teach you to do."

Shoving her hands into the tiny pockets of her jeans to avoiding touching his nicotine-stained fingers, Constance Anne said hello in a soft voice that Reeves could barely hear over his own loud, labored breathing.

"Hello, Beautiful," someone other than Reeves said back to her very clearly, startling her.

The sound seemed to come from the other side of the apartment. She turned her head to look, but seeing no one, she shifted her eyes back on the old man.

"I can teach you how to do that, dear," Reeves said with a laugh, breaking into a smile that unveiled all 17 discolored teeth he had left in his mouth.

Then he offered her a seat on the floor and gave a terse nod to Faller, who disappeared from sight.

Constance Anne thought that ventriloquism sounded cool, even if she wasn't entirely sure what it was. Always curious even to her own detriment, she proved to be a rapt audience when the old man launched into a litany of outrageously funny stories about his days on the road "talking" his ventriloquist's dummy on stages around the world.

He loved to freak people out wherever and however he could.

On a network TV show he made a woman believe that she was hearing someone call for help from inside a kitchen sink. Another time, he talked a passerby at a rodeo into reaching into a huge pile of horse shit to rescue someone who said he was the victim of "a hit" by a Clydesdale. Every tale made Constance Anne squeal with laughter. Instead of being wholly repelled by Reeves' creepiness, she strangely found herself starting to like him. If nothing else, he was fascinating, funny and didn't seem to want anything sexual from her. "That's a first," she thought to herself. "Thank God for small favors."

Eventually, Mr. Reeves needed a few minutes to himself. As he and his walker moved slowly across the grayish-green ocean of grime between the recliner and the bathroom, Constance Anne took the opportunity to look around the room.

Displayed in various ways here, there, and everywhere were puppets, puppets, and more puppets of every size, shape and theme imaginable. On one window sill alone were a dozen or more hand-crafted hand puppets including several that resembled famous people.

One with a mustache looked like Clark Gable. Another with blonde hair and big boobs that actually bounced looked like Marilyn Monroe.

Yet another had the likeness of Vivien Leigh and was dolled up in a tiny green dress straight out of *Gone with the Wind*. Pressed up against the window on the left was a bizarre Marie Antoinette puppet holding its bloody head in its hands. The Queen sat next to a pair of lobster fishermen with unnaturally large biceps, a busty college cheerleader with an "F" on her chest and a sword-carrying Joan of Arc in a coat of armor.

On the right was an Indian chief in full ceremonial headdress, a young blonde woman dressed in Pilgrim-style clothing, a zombie girl with half a face, and a morbidly obese Santa Claus. Each head was disturbingly life-like. And just like the Hitler puppet eerie Spruce Faller had, each one had its mouth open.

Constance Anne thought that the woman in Pilgrim clothing was unusually pretty and, oddly enough, looked a lot like her. Dressed in black boots with a white apron over a black skirt, the puppet had an astonishing degree of detail on her face and hands that made her look more like a living human being than a toy. In fact, the Pilgrim girl was so immaculately made that Constance Anne couldn't see a single brushstroke, seam or imperfection of any sort. When she leaned forward to pick it up, however, a disturbing sensation came over her, one that she could only describe as "walking in pudding." Even stranger was the added perception that everything around her was moving very slowly, then very quickly and then very slowly again, a feeling that started and stopped and started and stopped like blinking Christmas lights.

Mesmerized by the Pilgrim, Constance Anne drew it closer to her face. As she narrowed her eyes to see it better, she swore that the puppet twitched its nose. A second later she was quite sure it said "Hello, Constance Anne. It's me!" and then, "Constance Anne" a few seconds after that in a freakish voice that had the same horrifically disturbing effect of a fingernail being dragged across a chalkboard. Frightened out of her wits, Constance Anne quickly put the puppet back on the shelf, keeping her eyes on it while vigorously wiping her hands on her pants as if she had just touched something gross and disgusting.

As she slowly backed away from the window, it struck her that Mr. Reeves had surely "talked" the princess as a joke and she laughed with relief. Moments later, in fact at exactly the same moment Constance Anne heard Mr. Reeves flush the toilet, she was sure that she heard the puppet clearly say, "Faller will die." She was even surer that its mouth moved.

Constance Anne shook her head and laughed again, convincing herself that the formaldehyde fumes at Dickie's were doing strange things to her. But when she saw a larger puppet in an uncovered box on the other side of the room sit up, slowly turn its head and wink at her, there wasn't an explanation in the world that was going to stop her from shaking with terror, eyes wide open, as she gasped for breath, struggling to push an earsplitting scream out of her lungs.

As if being terrified to the point of paralysis wasn't enough, Constance Anne was worried about Mr. Reeves who was still in the bathroom. She knocked on the door.

"Mr. Reeves, are you okay in there?" she shouted in a panicked voice.

There was no response.

"Mr. Reeves?" she said again, this time even louder, looking over her shoulder through the "pudding" all around her in mortal fear that the puppets might be creeping up on her while her back was turned.

"Mr. Reeves?" Constance Anne shook the door and the doorknob so hard that the cheap, crummy lock fell off, making a high-pitched, ping sound as it hit the black-and-white tile floor.

With her pulse pounding in her ears, she tried to push it open. Something large must have been lying behind it, and when whatever it was and the cheap, plywood door collided, the door rattled so ferociously that Constance Anne thought it might come off its hinges.

What she saw when the door finally opened would take her a long time to forget.

However badly Constance Anne might have wanted to find a rational explanation for it, the fact of the matter was that the bathroom was gone. In its place behind the door was a large empty room with bright white walls, a bright white ceiling and a single light bulb hanging down three or four feet from the ceiling on a bright white cord. None of it made sense. There was no Mr. Reeves behind the door. No walker. No tracks imbedded in dust. No toilet that she absolutely, positively heard flush. Nothing more than the blinding paint and a very big question about how something like a bathroom, or at least what she thought was a bathroom, could simply vanish into thin air.

Tears started to fill her eyes from emotional exhaustion and, with her blood pressure on a disastrous course, her head started to ache and her chest tightened. Her nose bled. With every inch of her body on red line overload,

Constance Anne slowly sank to her knees, half inside the room and half out, still gripping the doorknob with her right hand. Her body didn't feel like it belonged to her anymore. In fact, she wasn't even sure that her head was still bolted to her neck.

Had there been a thin stream of what looked like coagulated blood on the wall opposite her when she first looked inside the room, she had clearly missed it.

At the bottom of the wall sat a faded full-color picture of a pretty little girl, a dried rose, and a bloodstained razor blade.

Constance Anne didn't have the energy to investigate it and simply wanted to close her eyes and let the world wash away. She heard light steps come up behind her as somebody loudly whispered "Grab her!" and a cold blade sliced through her right Achilles tendon.

She screamed and went down on her side in agonizing pain. Blood spurted and spread across the floor. It was a carousel of horror. Tiny feet were all around her. Santa Claus plunged a pair of scissors into her left calf. The wall wobbled. The "pudding" was thickening. White, Black. White, Black. White, Black. The lights popped on and off like old-time flashbulbs. Barely conscious, she reached out lazily to swat something away and missed. A bald-headed puppet wearing a tie stabbed her in the ear with a sharp pencil, and the head of Marie Antoinette opened its jaws and buried its teeth in her neck.

The arm of the plaid recliner had a handful of loose threads and clumps of something white poking up through the seam. At first glance she thought there was an infestation of maggots, but as her vision sharpened she realized that whatever it was thankfully wasn't alive. Constance Anne yawned. She was in the drowsy middle ground between wanting to go back to sleep and knowing that she needed to get rid of the pins-and-needles feeling in the hand that she had apparently been sitting on. As she put her feet on the floor, she saw a cool, wrinkled hand with raised blue veins and translucent skin touch hers. Startled, she jerked a little to her right. Then her heavy eyes caught the face of old Mr. Reeves, whose smell of liverwurst, damp towels, and re-heated fish was strangely comforting.

Carefully leaning over his walker to pat her hand, Reeves whispered "Welcome back, young lady. I was afraid that you were going to turn into Sleeping Beauty."

She stood up, wrapped her arms around him, and burst into tears of relief.

"There, there. Everything's fine," he said to her, gently patting her back.

She told him the entire story of how she looked for him in the bathroom, about the bright white walls, the evil puppets, and how badly she bled.

"Well, as you can see, the bathroom's here," Reeves said, pointing to the toilet that was visible through the open door. "I'm here, you're here, and the puppets haven't moved an inch. You've been out like a light for the past nine hours."

"Where's Mr. Faller?" Constance Anne asked, leaning forward in the chair and turning her head towards the open room.

"He's not here," Reeves said curtly. He looked at Constance Anne with a rutted brow and an expression that reflected heartfelt concern.

"Did he give you anything to eat or drink?" he asked, flinching in anticipation of her answer as if he was preparing to be stung by a bee.

"Just a Diet Salmon," she said.

"*Stay far away from him!*" Reeves said loudly to make sure he had her attention.

Then he looked directly into her eyes and, speaking slowly to add dramatic emphasis, said, "You'll live a lot longer than the others."

His words terrified her.

"Believe me," he said, "that son of a bitch will try to drug you again."

Mr. Reeves escorted Constance Anne to the bathroom to assure her that it hadn't been painted bright white and that evil puppets weren't hiding inside the toilet waiting to attack her. Although she left the door open a little while she washed up just in case things weren't as quiet as they seemed, the old man's gesture made her feel considerably better.

When she came out, Reeves had already made them a simple frozen spaghetti and meatball dinner in his ancient, dust-covered microwave. Modest as it may have been, Constance Anne thought it was one of the most delicious meals she'd ever had purely because of the company. She and the old man, whose lanky frame and shocks of white hair gave him a touch of boyishness, talked for more than two hours. At points, Reeves made her laugh so hard with his seemingly unending supply of stories that her sides hurt and her mouth muscles happily ached from smiling.

When Constance Anne realized that she'd been missing in action from Dickie's all day Saturday and Sunday and had to go to school the next morning, she politely got up from where she had been sitting on the floor, collected their plastic dishes, and put them in the garbage. She was developing affection for the old man's calm, sweet, spirit and didn't want to leave. He was the grandfather figure she dreamed of. Reeves went to an area behind the recliner, picked up two of the hand puppets and handed them to her.

"Come back when you can and I'll teach you how to make these," he said.

She smiled broadly. One of the puppets was the Pilgrim girl. The other was a football player with a 1930s-style leather helmet.

"Who's this?" she asked, holding the football player.

"That was me when I was your age, a very, very long time ago," he said.

"Who's this?" she asked, pointing at the Pilgrim girl.

"Someone wonderful," he answered. "Her name was Elga."

Constance Anne gave him as big a hug as she could without breaking him in half. As she started out the door, one more question leapt to the front of her mind.

"How do you know Mr. Faller?" she asked.

"I ... well ... I teach him ventriloquism," the old man replied with an embarrassed look on his face. "Now, young lady, go home," he said with a broad, warm smile.

She smiled back, turned, and just like the woman-child she was, half-walked and half-skipped home to Dickie's as fast as she could. It struck her that the puppets were among the few gifts she had ever received without having to do something sexual in exchange. She nestled the puppets in her arms like babies, taking particular care of the one she was now going to call "G-Daddy."

Spruce Faller was a man with a mission as he left Reeves' apartment.

It was going to be a big night for him, and he headed straight home to prepare his wife, LaVelma, for the Annual Fuehrer Society dinner in Boston. He was thrilled that this year's event was being held at Joey Krabowski's, a steakhouse located in the basement of the Fallopian Motor Hotel near the airport known for its value-priced meats, 6-for-3 all-day happy hour and cabaret atmosphere. Having worked at Joey Krabowski's as the coleslaw boy in his younger years, Faller's saliva glands were working overtime as he thought about the juicy D-grade steaks that he liked so rare that they were pulsing.

He was also fond of Joey Krabowski's weekend "Nana Launching" dinner shows that benefited local senior citizens. Created by anti-Jesus Christian fundamentalists for church fundraisers, Nana Launching involved firing desperately broke seniors out of a catapult for prizes including cash, stool softeners and unlabeled food cans. The contestant who "flew" the furthest, usually across a dining room or a church basement at around 30 mph, won. Cruel beyond belief, "Nana Nightimes" had become a major revenue-generator for the restaurant and became even more popular when they went "Texas-style," meaning that they did away with the few pieces of protective gear they regularly used like football helmets, knee pads, and floor mats. That, as aficionados knew, promised evenings filled with more hilarity and an even higher potential for fatal injuries.

Faller, who had a regular front-row seat near the wall where most of the players crashed, hated the community do-gooders who had tried to have the "sport" outlawed as "a senseless, callous act exhibiting a willful disregard for human life." In the end, fans were relieved that the brouhaha never produced more than a toothless regulation calling for the use of cushions "at the establishment's option." No one complained that beer went up a buck a bottle to cover the hundred large that was pumped into local politicians' pockets to make it so. In the minds of people like Faller, no price was too high to pay for the freedom to watch old people suffer.

On the way, he stopped at the mall to pick up something for LaVelma. Disgusted by the fact that she had gained weight in recent months, he had paid special attention to a TV commercial for something called "The

Crammer," a latex-looking thing with hundreds of little fingers inside that the makers claimed could "comfortably trim" anyone into an outfit up to four sizes smaller. Promoted with the promise that "you'll never ask if your butt looks big again," "Crammers" were selling like hotcakes despite a warning on the package that they could cause permanent organ damage.

The truth of the matter was that it made most wearers look firm, fit, and fantastic between the collar bone and the top of the knees by pushing their flab down into their legs and feet under extremely high pressure. That meant that very few people in "Crammers" could walk, sparking a hysterically funny "Crammer People" site on the internet that featured women and men of all ages with svelte, sexy bodies and bulging, watermelon-sized legs that looked unbearably painful.

There were several different types of "Crammers" depending upon how much weight needed to be beaten into submission, each packaged in a cigarette-sized box with the photo of a young, boiling hot girl on one side and a cartoon of a hippo in fishnet stockings, curlers, and a threadbare bathrobe on the other. Choosing from among three available colors, flesh, chocolate and camo, Faller picked out the industrial-strength "Hindenburg" camo model for his wife who had never quite fit into the too-small Nazi Luftwaffe uniform he bought for her to wear on special occasions. He loved the black leather boots, bluish-grey jacket, and pants as ferociously as she hated them. Despite that, LaVelma usually put the suit on voluntarily. She preferred it to being persuaded at gunpoint.

LaVelma Ruth Gold had married, or more accurately, settled for, Spruce Faller after having so many God-awful dates with men she met on the popular matchmaking site www.nomorefuknlosers.com that she doubted that there was anyone left in the world with a Y chromosome, a full set of teeth, and an IQ over 20. As she constantly tried to remind herself, she was far from being a loser. With long black hair, a great figure, kissable lips and a great job, she assumed that she should be a good catch.

It appeared, however, that all of the fully functional men were married, gay, asexual, bisexual, trisexual or a new thing that was very confusing and somehow involved a garden hose and a smartphone app. If nothing else, she had stories of the weird and wicked to share with her similarly-situated friends: the guy she met for a drink that showed up in an expensive suit, diamond cufflinks and women's pumps; another who told her on their third date that he sometimes liked to sleep with his mommy; and yet another who unzipped his pants at a red light while they were driving to dinner and said that he couldn't wait to touch himself while thinking about her. Speechless, she jumped out of his car, caught a cab home, and cried in her pillow until the sun came up.

Unfortunately, becoming the bride of Spruce Faller, an awkward elf she met in the pizza line at a balloon fetish convention, simply magnified LaVelma's problems. A year into their marriage, just as she was hoping to start a family, LaVelma discovered that the man she had married also had a strong sexual attraction to Nazis.

One Saturday afternoon, she heard a loud crash in the bathroom and sprinted across the house to find Spruce collapsed in the shower with an Adolph Hitler puppet clasped around his putz. As she fought to release the puppet's frighteningly strong grip, LaVelma came face-to-face with a tiny swastika he'd had tattooed on the underside of his penis head. The swastika, which was so small that it looked like a smiley face from six inches away, was not only a major revelation in light of the fact that she was Jewish, but also because she had yet to actually see her spouse's wedding tackle. It was radically smaller than she expected and explained his insistence on marrying a virgin. It also explained why they'd only had intercourse in absolute darkness. Although she'd never been with another man, she knew that his slim, inch-and-a-half thang had much more in common with squirrel peckers than the aircraft carrier Spruce claimed he was packing. The unsettling thought that he had been using the Hitler puppet to extend his manhood when they had sex sprinted through her mind. It sent a silent, bloody scream through every corner of her being.

With his swastika-spangled micro-dick now literally out in the open, Faller told his wife in no uncertain terms that he would kill her and dismember every member of her family if she didn't keep his tiny tool a secret. He also promised to make the vile, degrading punishments he regularly meted out for "crimes against the Motherland" more severe.

Where before a slice of burned toast only cost LaVelma two hours of singing Nazi golden oldie *Es zittern die morschen Knochen* ("The rotten bones are trembling") while Faller waltzed with little Adolph, it could now get her strapped to a heavy chair all day, naked except for a Nazi helmet, to await whatever the puppet told Spruce he had a craving for. A more serious offense, like failing to make Spruce's nightly bubble bath the right temperature, used to mean a night outside without a blanket. Now, it meant Sunday afternoons at home serving beer and oatmeal sandwiches to Spruce and his Nazi buddies while they watched football. Obviously, this was a much better gig than sleeping in the yard and, after four consecutive Sundays, LaVelma started to get suspicious.

In the first place, she found it strange that anyone would eat an oatmeal sandwich.

Secondly, she found it odd that she couldn't remember anything between serving refreshments and drinking a Diet Salmon and waking up on the living room couch without her bra and panties on.

Even though she was a little slow, LaVelma eventually realized that the man she had pledged to love was drugging her and sharing her body with his homies. Every Sunday, they did what they wanted to her until they were done or the game started, whichever came first.

Not surprisingly, it didn't take much of Faller's cruelty to push LaVelma into the arms of a lover. Strong, reliable and available in handy 1.5-liter bottles, Mr. Gin not only helped her bury the nightmarish realities of having married a sick, violent freak but tamped down her growing desire to kill herself. Within a few months, LaVelma was rarely sober at any time of day. So it was unusual that on the Saturday her husband took her Luftwaffe outfit out of the closet, laid it on the bed next to "The Crammer" and told her to be ready for inspection by four, LaVelma was lucid and decisive.

Realizing that Spruce's only reason for taking her to the Annual Fuehrer Society Dinner was probably to pass her around again, she wanted to be prepared. LaVelma waited ten minutes after she heard her husband start his car and drive away. Then she put on her sneakers and a pink ball cap and started the three-mile walk to the mall in the pouring rain.

⋏

More than just an unspeakable monster, Spruce Faller was an unspeakable monster with big ambitions.

As he drove to the annual Eva Braun Look-Alike Contest and Schnitzel Soiree being held that afternoon in the lobby of the Fallopian, Spruce thought about the things he needed to do to climb the Fuehrer Society ladder. At the top of the list, not surprisingly, was making LaVelma disappear. Since he had already cut off communications between his wife and her family, nobody would miss her when he sold her to one of the city's better white slavery rings. The organization, which specialized in trafficking middle-aged women with culinary skills, had already promised him top dollar based on her delicious booty and apple strudel alone.

With his wife nothing more than a memory, he could not only move Constance Anne right into his house but into his bed as well. Her tight teenage body would clearly fit into LaVelma's Luftwaffe uniform, and her hot looks would clearly generate a larger turnout at his Sunday sports gatherings than he ever thought possible. Far more important, having the power to pass Constance Anne's sexual favors around inside the Nazi community to whomever he wished, whenever he wished, might even help ensure his selection as a Deputy Fuehrer, a powerful position that would have been unimaginable to reach on LaVelma's back. Excited about his prospects but mindful of the work ahead, he reminded himself that his first step was to make sure that he made a positive impression at the Annual Fuehrer Society Dinner. A good showing that night by LaVelma and lots of satisfied Nazi faces could give Faller the boost towards the kind of big shot status he craved.

⋏

By the time LaVelma reached the mall a little more than an hour later, she was exhausted, soaked to the skin, and so cold that her teeth were chattering.

But with determination, she made a stop at the bank then walked into the local megastore and picked up some new jeans, a jacket, some peanut butter, dishwasher detergent, laxatives, a head of lettuce, chocolate chip cookies, mustard, ketchup, paper plates, microwave popcorn, a Taser, a pair of black socks, two boxes of crackers, and a navy blue backpack.

Done with her shopping, she went home, showered, turned the burners on the stove to high and sat on the couch with her hands in her lap as the bitter taste of bile rose in her throat.

Dressed in his SS uniform with a jaunty black patch across his left eye and a long cigarette holder in his right hand, Faller sauntered into the Schnitzel Soiree like a man who had the world on a string.

The buffet was incredible. As he walked around the six-foot white plastic folding tables laid out in a Swastika design, the arrangement of epicurean delights virtually came alive. Schnitzel and sauerbraten stood shoulder-to-shoulder in the middle surrounded by the flags of the Third Reich. On the taste-tingling left side of the schnitzel was a pyramid of pork sausage with barbeque sauce, bologna triangles, and a mouthwatering sauerkraut casserole. On the right side of the sauerbraten was a monument to blood sausage, caramel-covered lima beans, fruit cocktail and a plate of carp knishes left over from the Levine bar mitzvah. Faller was as giddy as a schoolboy. In one corner of the room was a tall, handsome box of Liebfrauenmilch wine. In another was a station where women in Oktoberfest costumes mixed fudge and oyster milkshakes to the guests' specifications. In yet another corner was the piece de resistance: a stunning, 20-layer presentation of Hitler's favorite dessert, Goose Liver Meringue Pie.

Not only was this ausgezeichnet, but the Eva Braun event that had just ended had been exceptionally well done, too.

The artistry that the female contestants put into recreating Hitler's main squeeze never failed to amaze him. This year's winner, Buffy Ann Himmler, 23, of Bavaria, Illinois, even had prosthetic teeth made to perfectly replicate Eva's smile following $30,000 in plastic surgery the previous year to have the shape of her jaw match Braun's. Her victory earned her a free 16-inch Schwarzwurst, her own page on the official Fuehrer Society web site, and dinner for three at any of Bobby Lee Schlosswirtschaft's Family Restaurants in Alabama. With that kind of celebrity, Spruce put young Miss Himmler high on his radar as a future wife candidate.

Everything was going exceptionally well until a problem that would have been impossible to anticipate raised its astonishingly ugly head. A fellow Nazi, old, drunk and staggering aimlessly around the room, stumbled into Faller and looked at his name tag. When the man read, "Heil! My Name is Spruce" he started to chuckle. In just a few moments, his chuckle turned into fall-down, roll-around-on-the-floor hysterical laughter.

"Your name is Brust?" he asked, spraying a large portion of his sentence into Faller's hair. "Ha! The mole on your face looks like a nipple. *In German, we call a nipple a Brustwarze! A Breast Wart!*"

From then on, the drunk introduced him to everyone high and low as "My friend, Mr. Breast Wart." Even Faller was smart enough to realize that guys nicknamed "Breast Wart" didn't become Deputy Fuehrers.

Never good at forgiving those who trespassed against him, Faller took the serving knife for the Goose Liver Meringue Pie and plunged it into the old man's forehead. Then he stood the body upright against one of the Nazi flag poles and later extended the arms as it went into rigor mortis. Remarkably, the murder went unnoticed, although not because the partygoers were bombed out of their minds. In fact, the characteristically efficient Germans repurposed the man as a rather attractive coat stand.

As he drove home to pick up LaVelma, Spruce decided to take out as much of his anger about the Breast Wart disaster on his bride as possible. Spruce's father, a greasy, snake-handling Pentecostal minister with a penchant for saving young girls' souls in the back of his truck, had frequently reminded Spruce that he had to "take control of his wife" regardless of what it might cost her in physical pain. As the old man explained it, that was what God expected of a man and Spruce should be always be willing to kick LaVelma's ass to avoid disappointing the Holy Spirit. The fact that none of it seemed very Christian was beside the point.

LaVelma barely moved her head when Spruce finally burst into the house. Seeing that she wasn't dressed for the Annual Fuehrer Society Dinner, he slapped her across the face with the back of his hand.

"*What is this insolence?*" Faller demanded in a voice that was quickly rising into a scream.

LaVelma's head snapped back as if it was connected to a bungee cord. The expression on her face was cold and dead.

"Oh, Sprucie," she said softly, looking deeply into his rage-filled eyes as she pulled the trigger on electrodes carrying 50,000 volts of electricity.

Because of the Taser's twelve-degree-down angle she had aimed at his chest in order to deliver the shock directly into her husband's sad excuse for a scrotum.

His reaction was immediate.

Writhing in pain on his back, his muscles in violent contractions, he was unable to raise a single finger against her as LaVelma walked over to him and kicked the center of his face with every ounce of the fat that Faller had wanted her to cram inside the reprehensible Luftwaffe uniform. Then she disconnected the sharp Taser probes and shot him again in the neck, this time holding the trigger so that the electricity would cycle through his body again and again and again. Faller simply stared at her through the blood he couldn't wipe away from his eyes while his body jerked uncontrollably.

Having already moved every penny they had in the bank into the pocket of her new jeans, LaVelma picked up the car keys and made a quick stop in the kitchen. When she came out, she placed a white-hot iron Star of David in the middle of Spruce's forehead. After giving him several minutes to scream in utterly horrifying pain, LaVelma took out a vegetable-cutting utensil known as a mandoline.

"If you ever come looking for me," she said while angrily slicing a carrot, "I'll crinkle cut your tiny goddamned dick."

Amused that her husband's punishment was to live rather than die, LaVelma could triumphantly smell his burning flesh in her memory for the first three hundred miles of her new life.

Tick, Tock. Saturday, 1:07 a.m.

Constance Anne thought that Mortie was probably pretty messed up. She was fairly sure that whatever happened to him involved a "Four Buck Fuck."

Insanely excited with the prospect of "coming and going," Mortie had worked up a massive head of sexual steam. When the time came, he shouted, "*Mr. Pup-Pup, open your mouth!*" as his body served up such an intense, brain-shattering orgasm that he lost 15 pounds in a matter of minutes. It was a hell of a lot more fun than cutting carbs.

In spite of that, something inside him didn't feel quite right. It was similar to the rambling nausea and unsteadiness he felt a few hours after powering down a pound of unwashed, unpeeled shrimp. But instead of his stomach, the tremor was inside his dicktator.

Acutely distressed, Mortie looked down and screamed, "*Mr. Pup-Pup! Are you okay?*" Pup-Pup whispered something, and Mortie leaned over as close as possible to hear him.

Mortie's face turned the color of ash.

He screamed, "*Uh-oh!*"

Then he didn't say another word.

Because Mortie rarely followed the news, he may not have known that the condom he was wearing had been recalled. Advertised as "the rubber that killed the dinosaurs," the popular $3.99 "Four Buck Fuck" came with an unheard-of guarantee. If the condom failed to prevent pregnancy, genital reflux, or the transmission of any STD in a single sex act, the manufacturer would pay $50,000 to each participant with proof of purchase, a doctor's note, and appropriate videos. The company could make the offer confidently because of a tiny, invisible force field inside each condom that electrocuted anything that tried to get in or out.

After years of producing a perfect high-tech product, however, something went terribly wrong with the force field. Although no "Four Buck Fuck" deaths had been reported, thousands of injuries, ranging from ruptured condoms and electrical burns on genitals to severe nerve damage, were coming in daily from around the world.

Several weeks after Mortie's incident, the first "Four Buck Fuck"-related penis amputation was performed in Australia. When the procedure became public knowledge, the company's stock plunged from $52.19 a share to $0.03 in a matter of minutes.

Not unexpectedly, the world's top business paper carried the headline "Four-Buck-*Fucked!*"

Chapter 7

"...he promptly vomited into the open purse of horror-stricken passenger Alma Pearl Leak, a 63-year-old medical transcriptionist, who until that ill-fated moment was simply minding her own business."

By the time Spruce Faller was conscious enough to get on his knees the next day, the Annual Fuehrer Society Dinner had been over and done with for hours.

By the time he could stand without leaning on sturdy furniture, it was late Sunday afternoon.

LaVelma's Taser had ripped through him like a tornado, leaving him with a painfully twisted spermatic cord that he was sure had cut off the blood flow to his testicles and several foul quarter-inch Taser bruises on his neck. When he eventually made it into the downstairs bathroom and looked in the mirror, the swelling and bruising in his face were so bad that he barely recognized himself. In fact, he couldn't even see the Star of David burned into his forehead. Desperate for relief, he found the ibuprofen in the cabinet and took four pills with a big glass of water. Then, he hobbled to the living room sofa and sat down, realizing too late that his pants were soaked with bloody urine.

Although he was urgently in need of medical attention, Spruce had no choice but to go to work on Monday morning. The city's schoolteachers were paid with paper checks on the first and fifteenth of the month, and Monday was the first. Having spent entirely too much money on the Fuehrer Society festivities, he urgently needed to get his paycheck and rush it to the bank before he bounced checks all over town. He cleaned and bandaged himself as well as he could, trying unsuccessfully to cover as many of his injuries as possible with LaVelma's makeup.

With the pain intensifying, he grabbed the ibuprofen and swallowed almost half the bottle with some vodka while trying to concoct a cover story about his injuries that would make him look like a hero to the principal, the hospital, and the police who would surely poke their noses into the matter. He settled on the idea of breaking up a fight between an armed drug dealer and a ten-year-old with "ground-and-pound" techniques he learned by watching mixed martial arts on TV.

Then he picked up his Hitler puppet, put it in his back pocket, and went out to get his car. Violently angry when he realized that LaVelma had taken his truck, he added to the already searing pain in his balls by kicking the garage door until he knocked a hole in it.

Without other options and looking like a pale, ragged zombie, he limped down the street to the city bus, got on board, and promptly vomited into the open purse of horror-stricken passenger Alma Pearl Leak, a 63-year-old medical transcriptionist, who until that ill-fated moment was simply minding her own business. Without making the slightest effort to apologize, Faller continued to leave a trail of semi-digested schnitzel and lima beans on violently upset riders all the way to the back of the bus where he tumbled into a seat and cracked the window with the back of his head.

As if the events of the past twelve hours hadn't been enough, he started feeling angry cramps rise up in his abdomen. He was in a cold sweat, shaking like a leaf.

It was a few minutes before nine o'clock when Faller finally staggered up the front steps of Blough High, stopping briefly to realize that he was disintegrating as he spit out a mouthful of blood-flecked mucus.

The bell rang a second or two before he was able to pull himself together and walk through the door. The hall was mobbed with noisy kids in the middle of changing classes. As Faller turned right in front of the school's giant glass trophy case on the way to his classroom, he literally ran into Mimi Mapperson, a freshman girl with shiny braces, a pixie cut, and a school spirit shirt that said "Blough Me!", who was on her way to second-period English. Virtually nose-to-nose with his scary, twisted, swollen face, she screamed *"Mutha-fuck-a!"* at the top of her lungs, causing every student and teacher in earshot to turn and look directly at Faller, who was in the process of banging little Mimi's head into a locker.

As Mimi crumpled in pain and Faller shuffled down the hall looking like a trailer park version of The Mummy, kids started laughing hysterically. One wiseass sporting a yamaka with a Red Sox logo saw the Star of David burned into Faller's forehead and yelled, "Spruce, I didn't know you were Jewish" as five of his crazier classmates walked behind Faller imitating his limp to the overwhelming approval of the crowd.

The excitement continued when Faller slipped on something filthy that oozed out of his own pants leg, fell, landed flat on his back, got up and fell down again. When he reached his feet on the second try, he realized that he wouldn't make it to his classroom and instead made a panicked beeline to the boy's restroom. He paid no attention to the fact that when he hit the door with enough force to knock it off its hinges he took sophomores Parno DeVito and Bootsy Fishbinder, the school's poster children for genital herpes, crashing into the electric pissatorium with him.

Faller knew that he had a far bigger problem than diarrhea on his hands by the time he got his pants down. His arms and legs were weak, he was having trouble breathing, and it was unbearably painful to urinate.

He might have been able to put it all together in his head if he had thought to make sure that the ibuprofen he swallowed was actually ibuprofen.

Knowing that she would have the opportunity to kick the shit out of Spruce and make his face swell like a pumpkin after shooting him with the Taser, LaVelma emptied out the ibuprofen and replaced it with a powerful laxative that the label touted as "the nuclear warhead in the fight against constipation." Sadly for Faller, he had consumed about 11 doses. At that level, his body's solid waste matter took on the personality of an irate elephant, giving it the capability to tear his bowels and pretty much anything else it wanted apart. It was LaVelma's last "fuck you" to her sick, abusive husband and, although she was far from Chelsington at the moment he sat down on the toilet, she laughed out loud that she would probably be able to hear his bowels explode from the other side of the Mississippi River. As it was, even sputtering releases from his intestines had enough power to momentarily lift him off the toilet seat. As the amount of fecal material pouring out of him increased, he wasn't so sure that he wouldn't be blasted into the ceiling.

His groans were tortured and savage, and every time his bowels moved, all of the stalls in the boy's bathroom shook. It was as if someone was hitting the thin metal walls with a pile driver. At the same time, the sickening odor wafting through Blough High was nearly paralyzing.

Until they heard about Faller, however, most of the students simply thought that the stench was Meatloaf Monday in the cafeteria.

Eloni Running Bear Johnson-Gonzalez, a Black-Hispanic-American Indian-Pacific Islander who was his own minority group, remained standing inside the bathroom door after helping drag Parno and Bootsy out of the restroom and into the hallway to await the EMTs. An aspiring sports announcer, he provided an enthralled student body with play-by-play commentary and a live video feed to a local TV station.

By this point, Faller's plight had become so interesting that the teachers didn't even try to send the students, who were chanting *"Fall-er! Fall-er! Fall-er!"*, back to their classrooms. Attracted by the near-deafening hubbub, Constance Anne came down the stairs from the second floor and stood behind the crowd of onlookers straining to get a glimpse of what the excitement was all about. Suddenly, the painful, animal-like thrashing stopped and the scene became unnervingly silent.

At first there was nothing to see except an empty boy's bathroom with blue painted toilet stalls lined up on the left and sinks and urinals across a very narrow aisle from them on the right.

Then, the door to the middle stall opened out lazily to the left, its hinges creaking like an old, unlocked gate being blown in the wind. On the brink of blacking out from a loss of fluids due to his massive diarrhea, Faller stood up in the stall and, with his pants still down around his ankles, took a step forward.

The events of the next several seconds would become as much a part of Americana as the Fourth of July, fried chicken and Alabama threeways as people around the world replayed Eloni Gonzalez- Johnson's video on the internet an astounding four million times in the first 12 hours after it was posted.

The action was almost graceful.

Like a tree being toppled, Faller's six-foot frame fell straight forward, first hitting his head at the hairline on the hard ceramic top of one of the floor-length urinals and bouncing like a ball from the impact. As it did, his body bowed and his left hand rose slightly above his shoulder, tilted slightly back and came down on the handle with enough force to flush the urinal as his body slid down and his face came to rest at the bottom like a ton of bricks. Oddly, the tumble also broke Faller's neck.

Eloni, ever the video artist, zoomed in to show Faller's open, dead eyes, his bloody nose stuck in the mothball-smelling pink urinal cake, and his mouth submerged under four inches of swirling toilet water. Next to him was an Adolph Hitler puppet. It was severely burned. Its mouth was open and menacing. The puppet's eyes were blackened, and it was burned to the point that parts of it were crisp.

The ruling on Faller's death by the coroner's office was as ironic as it was bizarre, in part because no one could determine a single cause of death. While it was true that electrical impulses from the Taser had caused his heart to beat abnormally, and that he had a traumatic brain injury from hitting his head on the urinal and a broken neck, Faller also died from dehydration while he was drowning.

Not wanting to fool around with this mystery any longer, the coroner simply wrote "Suicide" on the death certificate, signed it, and brushed off a speck of egg salad that had fallen out of his sandwich. Since no one had yet claimed the body, he called Dickie's for a pick-up, suggesting that they'd need every rubber sheet they had to protect their hearse from the deceased's unstable intestinal tract which was degrading into a pool of slush that occasionally spit steam like a geyser.

Constance Anne was a little ashamed that she didn't feel badly about Mr. Faller's demise. Although he was clearly the biggest shit she'd ever met, she was too sweet to wish death at the bottom of a swirling basin of urine, pubic hair, and chewing gum on anyone.

As Constance Anne and her fellow students watched the EMTs carry Faller out of the school in an orange cadaver bag, she heard little Tim Gophy, a freakishly-short freshman whose parents occasionally used his head as a cocktail table, imitate the sound of a flushing urinal over and over again with "kashuush, kashuush, kashuush". Not surprisingly, it caught on with the crowd. Within thirty seconds most people couldn't hear themselves think over the roar of seven hundred kids mimicking a toilet flush in unison.

By Tuesday morning, Eloni, ever the entrepreneur as well, was wearing a black tee shirt with white print he made at home that said, "The Faller Flush" on the front and "Kashuush!" on the back.

By Tuesday afternoon, the Booster Club had decided to switch from selling candy bars to death-themed Faller merchandise.

By Wednesday morning, 30% of the students and teachers had purchased black cotton tees, backpack stickers and black-and-yellow lanyards saying, "The Faller Flush" or "Go Flush Yourself."

By Thursday, it was 90%. The principal bought a dozen shirts and a copy of the death certificate autographed by Eloni Johnson-Gonzalez. Within three days she had sold them online, making enough of a profit to buy a vacation home in Fall River.

By Friday, Eloni's video rap had gone viral:

> Spruce Faller was a teacher at the local school
> He thought he was the bomb but he nuthin' but a tool
> Bastard blew his bowels out after takin' bogus meds
> He went from bein' livin' to be bein' frickin' dead.

Spruce Faller's dead, hear that y'all?
Laughed my ass off when he took the fall
Drowned in a urinal built in a wall
Flush me!

A Nazi bastard who tried to nail young chicks
Gave them A's and B's in exchange for turning tricks
Tried to mess up Constance Anne with a can of Diet
Salmon
Thought he'd use a Hitler puppet to get her hot to slam him.

Spruce Faller's dead, hear that y'all?
Laughed my ass off when he took the fall
Drowned in a urinal built in a wall
Flush me!

He shit on blacks and women, Injuns, Gays, and Jews
Mean was how he treated folks, that weren't no frickin' news
He made his wife do other guys, all he did she hated
She shot a Taser in his balls and burned a sizzlin' Star of
David.

Spruce Faller's dead, hear that y'all?
Laughed my ass off when he took the fall
Drowned in a urinal built in a wall
Flush me!

It would be difficult to say that Spruce Faller's fellow faculty members were unhappy about his death. As the details of his twisted life came out, more than a few found fame on radio and television news programs around the world, including the Blough High football coach who took things up a notch by claiming that he knew everything about the Faller disaster and would provide all the sordid details in his upcoming book, *Going Down on Hitler*, which he hoped would also become a major motion picture.

The only teacher who seemed even to remotely like Faller was "Licker Store" Clark, the nasty, pint-sized, stringy-gray-haired girl's field hockey coach who darted around campus like an anxiety-ridden Chihuahua with a sugar rush.

Famous for advertising her sexual tastes with an upright, ten-inch Christmas-themed dildo glued on the trunk of her car, Clark was fond of more than just a few distressing things. One was emulating celebrity CEOs and their capacity for boundless self-indulgence at the brutal expense of others. Licker Store admired their lack of conscience and, translating their thinking to her world, saw how she could quickly improve her lifestyle by robbing others of theirs.

Within a month after moving her cancer-wracked mother from a nursing home to a grimy roadside motel to cut expenses, Clark had more than enough cash to pay for an all-girl cruise to Yemen she had dreamed of for decades. Selling all of the old lady's painkillers on the street also paved the way for a new, fully-loaded, $90,000 giant-ass truck with a larger dildo.

Not surprisingly, Licker Store also had a taste for buxom young women, which gave her more in common with Faller than anyone imagined. Like Pavlov's dog, she would show up the moment she heard the shower in the girls locker room start, running her wet tongue over the hair on her upper lip with her eyes fixed on Constance Anne's bountiful bosoms. In fact, Clark and Faller had enjoyed a long, reprehensible business arrangement. When one found a tasty girl to fulfill their sexual wants, they'd terrorize the child into having sex with the other under the threat of planting cocaine in her locker and calling the cops. Curiously, each of the twelve girls they'd shared over the past nine years had not only dropped out of school, but left the state.

Constance Anne couldn't wait to tell Mr. Reeves the news about Faller and bolted out the door the minute school let out for the day. Walking as fast as she could past police, reporters, and a hundred or more inquisitive onlookers, she stopped by a bakery to buy two fancy cupcakes for a quick celebration and then nearly sprinted to Reeves' nearby apartment.

She knocked. There was no answer. She knocked again louder, putting her ear to the door to try to hear any signs of life inside.

Nothing.

Then she knocked a third time. Concerned that there was still no answer but mindful that she had to go to work, Constance Anne left the old man a note decorated with hearts and smiley faces along with the box containing the cupcakes. She took a deep breath, shrugged her shoulders in a cute, "Oh, well" kind of way, turned around and headed home.

As she approached Dickie's, Constance Anne nearly ran headlong into a surprised Licker Store Clark and two Nazis in colorful, tie-died swastika tees at the funeral home's front door. Clark said that they had come to pay for Faller's funeral.

"Oh," Constance Anne said in a voice that was only slightly above a whisper. "Please wait here while I find Mrs. Dickie for you."

After a few minutes and a series of brief, awkward introductions during which the Nazis responded with "Heil Hitler" and extended right arms instead of handshakes, Licker Store presented Mitzi Jo Dickie with an American Fuehrer Society check for $7,000.

"This is for the Oktoberfest special" Clark said, referring to Dickie's internet coupon that offered a free holiday festival theme party with every full funeral or cremation package.

Mitzi Jo smothered a laugh.

"I'm terribly sorry," she said, pointing to the fine print with a long, shiny red fingernail. "Seven large is our all-inclusive price for customers who just need a little freshening up. 'Shovel-ready' we like to say. Mr. Faller arrived here in a slightly different condition. It looked like his guts had been scraped up with a spatula. I'll need another five hundred dollars."

"We don't have the money," Clark replied, her eyes as sad as if every woman on earth had just turned straight.

"In that case he rots until you do, bitch," Mitzi Jo growled, her voice becoming significantly and frighteningly deeper when she reached the last word in the sentence. Then she curtly walked away, her high heels clicking loudly on the marble floor of the funeral home's vaulted, shiny white Hallway to Eternity as she returned to her office.

Not unpredictably, it took more than a little effort to come up with anything for Spruce Faller, much less five hundred bucks. Licker Store spent the evening and the entirety of the next day calling and visiting everyone she could imagine who might be talked into helping. The Nazis went out, too, telling their colleagues that their purchase of a swastika-shaped candy bar would go to preserve the glory of the Reich. Although their pleas were largely met with laughter, a few of Faller's acquaintances were willing to contribute, although everyone who pulled out a five wanted $4.75 back. Even Bouncing Blubber Boys, Faller's favorite restaurant where they were selling 4 and 5XL black "Faller Flush" tees like hot cakes, wouldn't do more than give them a handful of 2-for-1 coupons good on Tuesday nights. A collection at the bar only produced $3.82, most of which was change that had fallen between the stools and come to rest on a disgusting, sticky piece of something that smelled exceptionally bad. Running out of time, patience and places to find change, Licker Store finally went to a pawn shop and hocked her aunt's new Medicare-supplied wheel chair to get the last two hundred bucks.

"Get your goddamn hands off it, you whore!" Clark screamed at her mother's sister. Terrified, the 92-year-old widow held onto the chair for dear life as Clark heartlessly dragged her down the street.

Now, with $201.00 in bills and another $299.12 in dimes, nickels and sticky pennies in a plastic grocery bag, Clark and the Nazi boys walked back to Dickie's and rang the bell. When Mitzi Jo and Constance Anne answered the door, Mitzi Jo quickly reached out and jerked the bag out of Licker Store's hand.

"If it all adds up to five hundred, you can have the funeral as soon as you settle on the party," Mitzi Jo told them. "Constance Anne will write down all the details," she added, gently pushing the girl forward and locking the door behind her.

Standing in front of Clark and the Nazis as they stared and visibly licked their lips over her generous cleavage made Constance Anne feel a little like Daniel in the lion's den. Nevertheless, she proceeded to do her job. She began by reviewing the standard Dickie's checklist to make sure everything would be in order.

"As I understand it," Constance Anne said in as professional a voice as she could muster while choking back vomit, "you want the deceased buried and his life celebrated with the Oktoberfest package. Is that correct?"

"Yes," piped up one of the Nazis who Constance Anne noticed had his nasal hair cut in a mullet. "We'd like a selection of hot and cold sausages, schnitzel, zwiebelkuchen, prinzregententorte, breads, cheeses, pickles, Bavarian chocolates, and a foot-tall Goose Liver Meringue pie." Both Nazis could feel their saliva rise with the mere mention of the pie.

"And beer brought directly from the Fatherland. We'll need several very large barrels. And ten-foot swastika flags with floor stands, bunting to wrap each of the tables, and red and black roses on each table," said the other Nazi whose nose hair was so dense that it looked like he had to cut a hole in it to breathe.

Apparently, Constance Anne thought, there was some connection between Hitler and thick nostril hair that she clearly didn't get.

"As for costumes, black dirndl dresses with white aprons for the ladies and black goat bundhosen for the men."

"Including the servers?" Constance Anne continued.

"The waiters will wear bundhosen. The male guests will be in full dress uniform," the other Nazi said, followed by an inappropriately loud "Heil" and a thoroughly overdone Nazi salute. "And all of the ladies' blouses must be cut very low."

"That's a shocker," Constance Anne said under her breath. "And how many mourners do you expect?"

"Three or four hundred, I think. Yes, at least 400 if not more," pronounced the Nazi with a shoe brush poking out of each side of his nose.

"That will require a very large tent near the burial site and portable toilets," Constance Anne said.

The Nazis nodded in agreement.

"Alright, then. Thank you. I'll give this to Mrs. Dickie to review," Constance Anne said, turning towards the door.

Like lightning, Licker Store's left hand shot out and clamped down on Constance Anne's right shoulder at the same moment she pressed her wet, wispy mustache hair against Constance Anne's ear. Hoping that she might get a shot at the beautiful plaything Faller left behind, Clark whispered that the two of them should go somewhere where they could be alone.

"Don't touch me, you fucking freak!" Constance Anne screamed.

Mitzi Jo Dickie and Tiny Earl, her strapping 475-pound coffin refurbisher, arrived within seconds and brought the situation under control. In a single motion, Earl grabbed the two Nazis by their throats and wedged his right foot so far up Licker Store's ass that he could wiggle her sigmoid colon. Then he threw them out onto the pavement face-first, unzipped his pants and, with stunning precision, urinated directly into their terrified eyes.

"Get the fuck out of here!" Mitzi Jo screamed at the trio rolling in pain in the middle of the sidewalk.

With that, Earl walked over to Clark and kicked her squarely in the face with the sharp toe of his cowboy boot. Blood and a hodgepodge of other things spurted out of her mouth and nose.

"You apologize to Miss Constance Anne when you see her again. You understand?" he told her, reaching inside Licker Store's mouth to pinch her tongue with his right thumb and forefinger. Then he grabbed both Nazis by the balls and squeezed them until their screams could be heard over the ear-splitting sounds of three fire trucks racing down the street with their sirens on full blast.

Meanwhile, a man named "Slosh" Rivera in knee-high muck boots was trying to deal with another nasty matter at the other end of the building. Faller's body, which smelled like a Mexican diarrhea farm in August, had just been brought over from the city morgue. Although the deceased had been rolled up in enough rubber sheets to handle a platoon of competitive bedwetters for a month, his body was oozing so many different fluids that they were seeping through gaps in the wrapping and pooling on the floor below the rusted transport gurney. At some point Faller's bowels had taken such a brutal beating from the explosive gasses and hot, burbling feces inside him that several areas simply burst, firing ragged pieces of intestinal wall through most of his other internal organs. In short, the man whose violent death in a urinal was making headlines around the world had turned syrupy, and it was Rivera's job to put him back together.

Considering Faller's condition, it was a good thing that Dickie's was one of the nation's most innovative corpse disposal practitioners. Dickie's offered several different body preparation and disposal packages based on the deceased's religious customs, personal wishes and, most importantly, their family's or estate's ability to pay. Although "Ash Holds" were now a thing of the past thanks to the unfortunate Boston incident, Mitzi Jo was more than willing to push the envelope on other fronts in search of a fast buck.

They were proud to have received a patent and state approval for the first see-through plastic caskets that offered to keep a body crisp and fresh for eternity by simply pulling up a corner on the top, squeezing out the air and snapping it shut. They had also created a painted foam rubber plug that could be inserted into a standard 9' long, 6' deep, and 40" wide grave and secured with a waterproof sealant. Called "Grave-To-Go", it was the perfect solution for families that didn't want to leave grandma behind when they moved out of state. Cemetery workers could simply pop what looked like a soda can tab on the top of the plug, listen for the "wheeze of freshness", lift the coffin out of the grave, hose it off and send it on to the next stop. Although universally unpopular with religious leaders and funeral directors, Grave-to-Go was quickly approved by the government after a legion of dead presidents found their way into the right pockets.

Reading the Faller file at her desk later that evening, Mitzi Jo was alarmed by the size and scope of the party that had been ordered.

She and her late husband had started adding theme parties to funerals several years earlier to get a bigger cut of life insurance policies, and it wasn't uncommon for family and friends to order special things they couldn't otherwise afford. The idiots in Faller's case, however, had not only overdone the menu but ordered so much that they could have fed every man, woman and child in New England and still had leftovers.

Of the $7,500 the Nazis paid for the Oktoberfest package, the party alone came to $7,100 including $200 for swastika flags and bunting and another $200 for the tent. There was also a grand to buy off a delivery guy who suggested that the Jewish Defense League might like to attend.

The bad news was that there were only four hundred bucks left to embalm, display and bury the dearly departed. On the other hand, by preparing only about ten percent of the food the Nazis had paid for and lying to them about it, Dickie's stood to make substantially more money stuffing Goose Liver Meringue into the mouths of drunken fascists than boxing up what remained of Spruce Faller.

A crisis of conscience led Mitzi Jo to the only conclusion that made sense: if need be, she'd cram the remains into a jumbo yogurt container, dump it in a storm sewer, and cry about it all the way to the fucking bank.

In the meantime "Slosh" Rivera, dressed in a yellow biohazard suit, started working on the deceased. Since the money for embalming had been poured into schnitzel, it didn't take "Slosh" long to figure out that the only way they could put Faller on display without the mourners throwing up was to shove a 2,400-watt vacuum up his rectum, suck his innards out, swap his blood for a low-sodium vegetable drink, and stuff him like a Thanksgiving turkey with pine air fresheners. Thanks to "Slosh's" tender touch, Faller's chest cavity was as clean as a newborn baby's ass after only 20 minutes. Three hours later, the dearly-departed's odor had magically been transformed from festering garbage into an Alpine forest.

At ten o'clock the night before the funeral, Tiny Earl went into his workroom to prepare a magnificent mahogany casket for Faller's burial. He took a moment to admire it. Affectionately known around Dickie's as "Earl's Girl" because of the loving care he gave it, the casket's sleek lines and burnished gold hardware were a tribute to mankind's ability to make things that are as beautiful as they are functional. Even though it was fifteen years old, it had been used less frequently than some of the caskets that had been around only a year or two, largely because Earl didn't like the idea of having any old Tom, Dick, or Harry inside her.

He smiled broadly as he donned his lime green hazmat suit and began the usual preparatory scrubbing, savoring every touch as he checked each luscious inch to ensure that no mud or grass were on her and that her white velvet interior was pristine. Earl even put his fingers deep inside to double-check that the ejection hinges below the mattress were well-lubed.

When he was done, he turned on an industrial deodorizing machine with a scent that made everything smell like nothing. Then, he unleashed two powerful carpet dryers to finish the job. Swallowing hard, he approached her from the rear. With a soft cotton cloth and a fine paste wood wax, he polished her, moving his powerful hands over her vigorously until he could feel her succumb to his will. He lit a cigarette and looked down at her. Earl was proud of what he and his colleagues could pull off. Not everyone in the business could conduct an exquisite graveside service and drop the body out of the casket and into the grave before the mourners even left. Even better, they did it with nothing more than a well-placed patch of canola oil and a trapdoor. Afterwards, they would load the empty casket into an unmarked hearse and return it safely to Dickie's. Maybe that was criminal, Earl thought to himself, but it was surely just as criminal to put such loveliness underground where no one could see it.

Earl thought about a lot of things that way, which is one of the reasons he always sided with health insurance companies in the Obamacare debate.

"Hell," Earl told his friend, Boobies, whose name came from the unfortunate results of a bad drug he had taken, "why would you want to insure sick people? They're just going to die anyway."

Earl checked to make sure he was alone. When he was satisfied that the coast was clear, he put his arms as far around the casket as they would go and pulled her close in a hug. Then he climbed inside. Even at his size, the casket had plenty of leg room and enough extra space to fit a medium size pet or two without needing someone to throw every bit of their girth on top to shut the lid.

Without a second thought, he rubbed his face on the plush white velvet interior. Then he kissed it. And kissed it again, eventually plunging his face into the soft linings that were about as useful to a corpse as bowling shoes on a fish. Earl wondered if it was legal to live in a casket, like one of the tiny houses he'd seen on the internet. He thought that would be cool and sexy.

As he unbuckled his pants and pulled out his party bus and a hand puppet made to resemble the casket, a Croatian cleaning guy with a headset that drowned out everything except the throbbing sound of the Zagreb rock scene walked in.

He carelessly let the door slam.

The reverberation made the lid on the coffin drop and lock. Earl didn't give a shit if he ever got out or not.

Tick, Tock. Saturday, 2:21 a.m.

Constance Anne was concerned that Mortie might be dead.

Although he hadn't exactly been a chatterbox to start with, she thought that he'd at least grunt occasionally. Instead, he hadn't uttered a word. More importantly, she couldn't hear him breathing.

If he was dead, she was going to cry for both of them. He was far too young to die and, for her part, spending the night with a dead guy wasn't going to look good on her permanent record.

Rather than live with uncertainty, Constance Anne decided to find out for herself.

Still trapped in the pitch dark, she felt around for something that might help her deliver enough pain to wake him up if waking up was still an option. Eventually, she came across a sharp splinter from the bed frame. With the slight movement caused by the water, Mortie's left ear was accessible and, using every bit of strength she had, she slammed the splinter into his ear canal. Although the projectile went in easily enough, Mortie didn't respond. Constance Anne tried the maneuver again with the same result, but now found it terribly difficult to pull the splinter out.

Believing from her Catholic upbringing that almost anything was possible with enough lubrication, she scooped up some of his body greases, put them in his ear, and tried to slide the item out. It didn't move.

"Maybe he's just a little dead," Constance Anne, said to herself as thirst burned a ragged hole in her throat. A lack of optimism was not her problem.

As if things weren't bad enough already, the struggling air conditioner gave up the ghost and stopped running, making a gasping sound as it passed away.

Constance Anne heard footsteps outside the motel room door. She tried to scream for help, but the continued pressure of Mortie's bloated body against her diaphragm made it come out more like a croak. As she heard the footsteps fade in the distance, she began to give up hope.

"Please, God," she begged. "Don't let me die this way."

Chapter 8

*"The plot…was adjacent to an alley and a crumbling strip mall.
It was, as one mourner said, "the perfect burial spot if your life had
been nothing but a shitbag of wasted time and opportunities."*

Meanwhile, the state chapter of the American Fuehrer Society and the school board that supervised Blough High, two groups that couldn't possibly have been more different, were facing the same nightmarish public relations issue.

In the school's case, the revelation that the Booster's Club had made a huge profit on Faller's death and spent it on 36FF breast implants for select female teachers gave them a black eye around the world.

Not surprisingly, the school board demanded corrective action and wanted it to start with a show of respect from the students and administration for a deceased teacher even if he was, as one board member said, "a Nazi shmuck."

The Fuehrer Society, which usually flew very, very low under the radar, felt compelled to bring mourners to the funeral in an attempt to show that "Nazis are people, too."

As a result, both groups had to beg, bribe, and threaten people to attend the funeral who wouldn't have pissed in Faller's mouth if his guts were on fire.

At first, Blough students were told that attendance at the funeral was mandatory. When that was met with lawsuits from a potpourri of civil rights groups, the deal was changed to a pair of free movie tickets. After that offer was met with derisive laughter, the school had no choice but to eventually sweeten the pot to include an "A" in any course of the student's choice, a free first-run movie in the gym every Monday and a public spanking of the lunch lady.

The Nazis simply spread the word that anyone who didn't show would be barred from that week's steamed-milk enema gala. That threat alone ensured that everyone would be in their places with bright, shiny faces right on time.

Spruce Faller was laid to rest on a dark, blustery afternoon with the aroma of grilled bratwurst dancing in the air. The rain, wind and the mass of black umbrellas held by the blackmailed mourners made the scene look like something from an old movie. The weather, of course, required the coffin to be closed, truly a blessing in light of the deceased's condition. It was also a blessing to Tiny Earl's assistants, Narwood Gipp and "Pappy" Gonza, who were charged with transporting the groin-ripping, massively heavy casket from Dickie's to the cemetery. Having overheard hushed conversations about Faller's remains that were followed by gagging sounds, neither man wanted to even be in the same room with the box, much less have to touch it. As if things weren't bad enough, it also looked like there weren't going to be any pallbearers. The most obvious candidates, the Nazis, had already dropped Faller like a burning venereal disease, and Tiny Earl, who was three pallbearers all by himself, was nowhere to be found.

Without Earl, in fact, Narwood and Pappy had to hunt down Faller's casket all by themselves. After searching for about an hour, they eventually found it closed and sealed and oddly out of place flat on the floor of the workroom. It should have been sitting on top of a dolly ready to roll out onto the grimy rear loading dock with rusted gray roll-up doors they flippantly called the "Pearly Gates." Looking for a better option than breaking their backs trying to carry the casket, Narwood and Pappy paid a skater kid screwing around in the parking lot ten bucks to borrow his board. Then, they put it under the box, tied the two together, hooked the whole mess to a golf cart and pulled it down the funeral home hallways. Narwood ran alongside to keep the casket from falling off while Pappy drove and made stupid choo-choo noises.

Considering the negative attention Faller's death had attracted in every corner of the world, it wasn't too surprising that not a single religious institution of any faith would even discuss the idea of hosting his funeral. With no other practical choice, the service was organized at a gravesite that had been hastily purchased by the Fuehrer Society in Chelsington's Schmendrik Memorial Cemetery. The plot, which had been on "quick clearance" for 45 years, was adjacent to an alley and a crumbling strip mall anchored by Hungarian Bail Bonds, Yo' Hair, Bitch! and Moe's Cigs-Lotto-Beer-Ammo. It was, as one mourner said, "the perfect burial spot if your life had been nothing but a shitbag of wasted time and opportunities."

To take advantage of the nearly 1,800 Blough High students in attendance, 17 food trucks featuring everything from deep-fried doughnuts and bratloaf to corn dog pizza were parked haphazardly on the cemetery grounds within spitting distance of the grave and the Fuehrer Society's Oktoberfest tent. Twelve face-painting booths and eight bounce houses were set up next to the Goldberg family's mausoleum where a sad-eyed girl with green hair and a large gold nose ring sold tickets.

Because it was nearly impossible to find a holy man to conduct Faller's service, Dickie's took fifty bucks out of the beer money to pay a defrocked priest to convey the asshole's vile soul to God. In the rush, no one had asked what the priest had been defrocked for. Consequently, it shouldn't have come as a complete shock to the Dickie's people that the man pulled up his robes during the responsorial psalm and started to sing a little ditty that was more than slightly off topic. The crowd thought it was just another Catholic ritual and started to sing with him. They stopped when he got to the line:

> "Pubes are just like forests that protect
> Our hallowed dicks,
> But sometimes you have to check yourself
> For big old thirsty ticks.

> If they bite you, you will hate it
> And you'll get a fever, too.
> So remember to always scrub your putz
> So they can't stay there and chew."

At least one girl puked at the mere notion of it all.

At the very moment that the priest said, "Unto Almighty God we commend the soul of our brother departed, and we commit his body to the ground," the bounce house girl started screaming something and a mass of about 300 people, including the only Nazi still at the side of the grave, dashed towards her. Despite the priest's appeals to their better nature by shouting, "Come back here, you Godless assholes!" the offer of "two-for-one bounces for the next 15 minutes" was way too good to ignore. Others drifted away for food or a face painting of Faller drowning in a urinal. The second the service ended, the rest of the huge crowd turned their backs on the casket and walked away as if on cue.

Having been tied up much of that day by a new urn vendor who understood the link between the happiness of her clitoris and his sales success, Mitzi Jo Dickie arrived at the funeral late and distracted. Knowing that the body removal would be in Tiny Earl's capable hands, she went directly to the Oktoberfest tent.

She was shocked.

The Fuehrer Society's "Heil! Heil! The Gang's All Here!" party had turned into a standing room only affair due to the rain. Terrified that she was going to get busted for shorting the food order 90%, Mitzi Jo chilled once she realized that only a few people even knew they were in a Nazi tent and almost no one knew there was any food. Apparently, the Nazis had started eating and drinking beer long before the funeral began and never left the tent. The good news for Mitzi Jo was that they were so shitfaced that she could have told them anything and gotten away with it.

There was even better news for the caterer, Sausage Schleppers.

Not smart enough to pick up on a single clue, none of the Nazis noticed that the sign on the truck said, "Yes! We'll Cater Your Bris!" The owner, Jesus

"Bone Crusha" Levine, had prepared a very special marinade for the event consisting of fresh English shallots, red wine and magnesium citrate and made sure that all of the meat was kept in the bags of marinade at room temperature for hours. The magnesium citrate sent every Nazi goose-stepping to the toilet within 30 minutes after their first bite of knockwurst.

Sadly, "Bone Crusha" had forgotten all about bringing the portable restrooms. The rather explicit TV news footage of Fuehrer Society members screaming in pain as they defecated on the graves of the city's revered founders didn't exactly do much to improve their image.

Some three hours later, the rain finally stopped. It had come down so hard at one point after the crowd left that the small tent over the gravesite had collapsed, and one of the poles put a long, ugly gash on the left side of the casket. Parked in Dickie's white hearse behind Hungarian Bail Bonds, Narwood and Pappy kept shaking their heads, imagining how Tiny Earl was going to go ham on them when he saw the scar on his "girl".

After drinking coffee in the car for the four hours since they'd lugged the casket to the cemetery, they finally got out and scurried to the only tree within a hundred yards. As curious passersby leaving Moe's with unusually large supplies of beer and ammo looked on, the men pissed on the tree and produced so much smoke-like steam that it looked like someone had dumped a pile of dry ice in a bucket of water.

Twenty minutes later, they went to the casket. As Narwood stood at the foot holding it steady, Pappy placed his hand on a tiny, recessed button at the head of the casket. After the button was pushed, there would be a jolt as the trap door opened, followed by a rumble when the body slid out into the grave. This time, however, was different.

There was no jolt.

In its place was a far scarier, violent rumble and the tortured squeal of wood and metal being shred into splinters. All of a sudden, the box came apart as the bottom of the casket and the corpse both plummeted into the grave. Since there was no liner, much less an expensive vault, inside the grave, the rain had filled it knee-deep with liquefied mud. Narwood and Pappy were as stunned and upset as a straight guy who just learned that he'd been blown by a tranny named Elmer. Sweat was pouring down their faces. The irony of the situation, of course, was that the demolished casket itself was actually the least of their problems. They could simply toss the top of the casket into the grave and have it all filled with dirt. The really bad problem they had to face was telling Tiny Earl that his girl wasn't just scarred but utterly disfigured. The far worse problem waiting for them involved Tiny Earl telling Mitzi Jo Dickie that she would have to buy a new casket.

There were certain things that you told Mrs. Dickie about and certain things you didn't if you wanted to keep your scrotum intact. This was one of the latter.

"Tiny Earl's Girl" had been paid for at least 50 times over and had another 200 funerals in it, if not more. It was one of Mitzi Jo's favorite profit centers.

Leaving the casket where it was, the men walked back to the tree they had just soaked with urine and sat down to plan their next move. Eventually they agreed, although not unanimously, that Narwood would go into the grave to figure out what happened. He was, after all, stronger and younger than Pappy and didn't have little mouths to feed. At 23, Pappy's three ex-fiancées and six kids under the age of four were taking him for a cool $500 a month in child support.

"Why don't we just fill up the hole and leave?" Narwood said in the whiny voice he used when he didn't want to do something that Pappy certainly didn't want to do.

It reminded him of the time the late Mr. Dickie was wiping himself in the shitter and had his expensive watch slide off his wrist into a toilet brimming with diarrhea. When they were ordered to "gently" retrieve it by hand, Narwood refused right up until the moment Pappy stunned him with a hard blow to the head, violently took control of his right arm and plunged it into the tepid darkness. For a year afterward, Pappy reminded him every day that those kinds of episodes were what the "big leagues" were all about. Even more, Pappy boasted that he had singlehandedly saved Narwood's career. Although Mr. Dickie never thanked Narwood for retrieving his watch, he did shove Narwood out of his way as he returned to his office after washing off his watch and drying it on Narwood's shirt. All Narwood got was a memory that no amount of alcohol could kill.

"Homie don't play dat," Pappy replied, trying to sound cool, even though he was as white as toilet paper. "Earl swallows his own dick over that box. Don't you think he's gonna want to know what happened? He's not just gonna say 'okay,' moron. Someone has to go in there and figure it out."

Terrified that Pappy would blame him for the casket catastrophe if he didn't do what he wanted, Narwood shrugged his shoulders, crossed himself, and walked back to the grave. Pappy slid the casket just enough for Narwood to get into the space between what was left of the casket and the straps below it that, in the case of a real burial, would be used to lower the casket into the earth.

Without warning, Pappy suddenly slid the casket back to cover the grave, a move that left Narwood in the pitch darkness, hanging onto the straps for dear life.

Letting go was really a piss-poor option. Rather than the standard grave depth of six feet, Dickie's graves were dug to 12 feet deep, to avoid having bodies float to the surface in a flood. Letting go would mean a straight drop into a filthy, smelly black hole with a dead body. It reminded him of fucking his girlfriend.

"*Jesus!*" Narwood yelled as loud as he could. "*What the fuck are you doing?*"

"Shut up, Mr. Aassweepee," Pappy said. He loved changing "asswipe" into a realistic-sounding name. "Somebody's coming."

Lurching out of Moe's like a drunken sailor was St. Dagobert of Pisa, a local kid formerly known as Denny Cordovan. Dressed in a black shirt, white clerical collar, and a black, full-length, hooded cape from Priest Warehouse, he was carrying a six-pack of Old Labia beer under his arm, a Milwaukee brew that went for six bucks a case and came with a plastic toy. Somehow, Cordova had convinced himself that he could rake in as much coin as Sunday morning TV preachers by starting his own religion. He dropped out of high school, took the name of an old dead religious guy, chucked a "St." in front of it for good measure, and proclaimed himself the "Holy Leader" of "Godvisionism."

Although not a religion in the sense that it had a deity or an organized system of beliefs, Godvisionism essentially took pieces of mainstream religious and secular celebrations and incorporated them into major party events. He declared Labor Day, Thanksgiving Day, Black Friday, Super Bowl Sunday and Valentine's Day official Godvisionism holidays that required a minimum of 72 continuous hours of drinking, sex, heavy metal, Baltimore Club and making out large checks to the Holy Leader of Godvisionism. Drugs were optional. Christmas and Hanukkah were combined into "Hanukmermas" an eight-day holiday during which followers exchanged gifts, lit candles, decorated their homes with yamaka-clad Santa Claus figures, ate fattening foods and made out large checks to the Holy Leader of Godvisionism. Better yet, "Hanukmermas" was held every month, which should have made selling prospective members a no-brainer: they could skip work or school most of the year by stating that their religion required them to strictly observe every sanctioned holiday.

Despite the obvious social benefits and a "fellowship package" that included pizza discount coupons, low-interest payment plans for tithing, a framed membership certificate and forgiveness of any other faith's sins for only $50 down and $50 a week, things weren't going well. A year into his ministry, St. Dagobert of Pisa had a congregation of only 15, none of whom had done anything more than use the coupons. He even recorded a rap song and put in on the internet.

> If you know dat you been sinnin'
> And you need your ass forgiven,
> We make it cool, y'all.
> Ain't never cruel y'all

> Fifty down will get you blessed
> Out of shit you never guessed
> Let the Catholics all confess
> Cash will rid you of distress

If you been covetin' and stealin'
There ain't no need for kneelin'
You can be a creepy lurker
Or get away with murder

Fifty down will get you blessed
Out of shit you never guessed
Let the Catholics all confess
Cash will rid you of distress

Fifty bucks every seven
Will get you into heaven
It's the promise that I make
Nothin' bout it is a fake

You can piss on Ten Commandments
And screw the whole damn planet
Put some cash in my hand,
And your sins will turn to sand

Godvisionism, men and ladies
Will keep you out of Hades
Put some cash in my hand,
And your sins will turn to sand

All it produced was nasty complaints and a not-too-veiled threat by some-body named splityoassinhaf45 who described what it would be like for St. Dagobert to wake up one morning and find his pecker sewn inside a Gila monster.

Considering that he was broke, living on a diet of pigs' feet, boiled eggs, and weak lemonade and sharing his sick grandmother's bed, it wouldn't have come as a surprise that St. Dagobert of Pisa was praying for a major miracle.

If the old bag rolled over and kissed him goodnight without her teeth in one more time he was going to kill her.

Seeing the action in the cemetery, he headed toward the casket.

"Greetings, Fellow Citizen of the Republic. What are you doing?" St. Dagobert asked Pappy as he walked up to the grave. He loved the "Fellow Citizen of the Republic" shtick. It sounded sophisticated.

"Burying somebody," Pappy said.

"He's ... dead?" St. Dagobert asked, hesitating to say the word. He had never seen a dead body and desperately wanted to.

"I hope so," Pappy replied, choking on St. Dagobert's stench as he came closer to the grave. He smelled like beer and spam wrapped in rotten onions.

"Let me perform the sacraments of Claxicuma and Posthomima to absolve him of his sins. I'm a man of the cloth," St. Dagobert said, making up the names of the rituals and the rituals themselves as he went along.

"*Fuck you!*" Pappy said, holding onto the casket firmly in case St. Dagobert made a stupid move.

"I must perform the sacraments," St. Dagobert said with disconcerting passion in his voice, his brownish saliva spitting like a geyser.

He suddenly slammed his hands on the casket, tipping it just enough to make Pappy shudder. Then he reached into his cape and produced a small plastic bottle of "holy sauce," which was actually meat gravy his grandmother had made the previous Sunday. He poured all of the "holy sauce" on the casket, where it dripped slowly down the side and hung like thick, stringy mucous.

"In the name of Godvisionism, you are forgiven for any bad shit you ever did or even thought about doing," St. Dagobert shouted in a shrill voice. "May your sins be transformed into water and spit into the universe. May you rise and live again, although you're not required to."

Although clearly a peculiar way to send off the departed, it was all the self-proclaimed saint could come up with off the cuff. The moment St. Dagobert said "not required to", he tried to rush past Pappy to unlock the casket. St. Dagobert of Pisa was intent on opening the coffin and taking a selfie with the deceased. No more than a second before he reached it, the casket rattled and the screeching, painful sound of twisting metal filled the air.

No more than a second after that, the casket suddenly jerked an inch to the right.

"*Hey, get me out of here you douchebag!*" came a voice from inside the box. "*It's dark in here. I can't see a fuckin' thing!*"

"Did you hear that?" St. Dagobert asked Pappy, shocked and turning as pale as a ghost.

"Nope."

"*You must have heard that! You must have! Are you fucking deaf?*"

"Nope."

"*Get ... me ... out ... of ... here!*" the voice said again, this time at a volume that was so loud and piercing that it hurt St. Dagobert's ears.

St. Dagobert of Pisa nearly shit a condo. This was really fucking real. It was one thing to tell a dead guy to rise and live again and quite another for him to actually fucking do it. St. Dagobert's head was spinning. Was he having a drug flashback? Maybe the hash he bought off the ice cream truck was laced with something really bad, like anti-freeze or something else that was making his brain melt.

Was the guy really alive?

Was he a zombie?

What would he do if he was a fucking zombie?

After almost wetting himself over the negative possibilities for a whole 15 seconds, his mind leapt right to what this colossal, incredible, mind-blowing gift really meant: he was going to be the richest man on the planet. Really, he thought, what would people pay to come back from the dead? He didn't know for sure, but it would probably be a lot.

More exciting, he might even lose his virginity to a woman without a mustache.

"Well," Pappy said. "That sounded funny. Maybe you should investigate. I'll open the box so you can take a look."

St. Dagobert of Pisa's throat quickly turned dry and he found himself unable to swallow in anticipation of seeing something he never dreamed possible. Black and white flecks of light started to throb in front of his eyes as his entire nervous system hit tilt.

"Okay," St. Dagobert whispered. He could feel his pulse pounding in his ears.

Pappy unlocked the casket and told him to lift the top. As he did, St. Dagobert's anxiety came to a virtually immediate stop. As he looked down and saw Narwood dangling from the casket straps, Pappy's shovel sliced through St. Dagobert's medulla oblongata. As St. Dagobert tumbled into the grave, his body hit Narwood like a ton of bricks and they both crashed into the muddy, watery hole like a nuclear warhead.

"*Get off your lazy ass and get to work!*" Pappy shouted down at Narwood who was invisible in the darkness. All that came back was a horrifying scream and a blast of methane that Pappy found surprisingly charming.

Narwood wondered if there was anyone else that had ever had a grown man's body thrown on him while dangling from the top of an open grave.

Although it didn't seem like an everyday sort of thing, he made a mental note to look it up when he got out. His mama always said that he was special, and if he was the only one in the whole world that this had ever happened to, he might even be extra special in his parents' eyes. Maybe, he thought hopefully, he would be so extra special to his parents that they would let him move out of the cardboard box in the backyard and sleep in the kitchen for the same rent.

As much as Narwood hated to admit it, winters were hard on him.

During one particularly bad storm his box collapsed from the weight of the snow with him inside. The very next year, the box was covered with so much thick ice that it took him a day and a half to punch his way out.

Had he been older than eight, it would have probably taken him less time. Nevertheless, Narwood could never figure out where his parents were coming from. Just because he'd scrawled death warrants for each of his sister's pets on the wall over her bed and murdered them one-by-one was no reason to put him out of the house.

First of all, in light of the nasty shit the animals had said about him behind his back, the little fuckers had it coming.

Second, everyone should have known he was only kidding when he invited his sister to play a game called "Mary, Queen of Scots." Jesus, he was only six years old. Where was he going to get a guillotine?

⚔

Terrifying was not a big enough word to describe what it was like inside Spruce Faller's grave.

Cold and disgusting with two feet of thick, filthy, slimy water at the bottom, it was worse than the hell Narwood had been taught about in Sunday school. Using the razor-sharp mind that had already brought him so far in life, he decided then and there that he never wanted to be buried. "If it's this bad in here when you're alive," he thought to himself, "it's got to be worse when you're dead."

Trying to look at the bright side, Narwood could be thankful that there was now some light. With the casket pulled away from the top of the grave, a slice of moonlight was able to get through, making his imagination work overtime about the horrible things he was inevitably going to see. It was bad enough to nearly have his back broken by the guy Pappy killed, much less waiting to see a couple of dead faces rise up through the mud. Above him he could hear Pappy telling him to "get his ass in gear" and to "quit fucking around." He hated that because the words made him feel like a loser.

He told himself that once he got out of the grave, took a shower and had a nice bowl of soup, he was going to pound Pappy's head with a brick.

"*What, are you playing with their balls or something? Hurry up, for Christ's sake!*" Pappy hollered as he tossed an old plastic flashlight into the hole, hitting Narwood's right shoulder.

"Okay, okay," Narwood shouted up at Pappy. "I found something."

In an odd way, seeing the left nostril of a human nose penetrate the mud was calming. Not surprisingly, every time Narwood tried to get control of the nose, he would immediately lose his grip. Finally, he had no choice but to put his hands underwater, feel around for the ears, and use them as handles to lift up the head. Out of the muck came the face of the kid Pappy murdered, his eyes wide open in shock the way a man would look if his life had ended abruptly or he'd just noticed that his penis was growing arms.

Since St. Dagobert was only a small cog in the enormous cluster fuck Narwood had on his hands, he part rolled, dragged and slid St. Dagobert's body about four feet from the middle of the grave to the foot and propped him up in a semi-upright position. Occasionally, he would fall over and make a muffled plopping sound.

"*Of course you found something, moron!*" Pappy yelled back.

"It's the kid you killed," said Narwood. Do you want the metal part of your shovel back? It's right here in the back of his neck."

Apparently, the wood handle and the shovel had each gone their merry ways after impact.

"I don't know what you're talking about," Pappy said, looking around to make sure they were alone. Among other things, Pappy wasn't very good at taking responsibility for his actions.

"*Put that damn thing under the mud!*" Pappy screamed.

"*Okay, boss!*" Narwood shouted back at the top of his lungs, confirming Pappy's worst suspicions that Narwood was a professional-grade idiot.

Pappy pondered splitting Narwood's head open with an axe, stuffing it in a blender, and hitting "liquefy." The thought took him back to the first time his mother let him throw a couple of unlucky lizards in the blender and press the puree button. Although he was only six at the time, the anticipation made him drool, and the actual sight of the little suckers whirring into pulp gave him a much warmer, happier feeling than he got from blowing up small birds in the microwave. He smiled.

Moments later, an unusually loud, squishy sound rose up from inside the grave as Narwood pulled, wiggled, and twisted the murder weapon out of the lower half of St. Dagobert's brain stem.

As Narwood tossed the shovel head out of his way, his feet slid out from under him and he fell on his ass like a ton of bricks. Humiliated, even though Pappy didn't see him go down, Narwood used his right hand for balance and slowly got to his knees. While his right hand promptly sunk into the sludge, his left came across something light and supple in the muck that felt flat on one side and bumpy on the other. As jittery as a hen at a wolf convention, he warily brought it up to the surface and peeled off the mud. "Weird," he whispered to himself. It was a shoe, specifically a large man's left wing-tip dress shoe with loosened laces.

Narwood plunged into the muck again. This time he came up with a thing that looked like a puppet.

"*Mother of God!*" Narwood bellowed.

He could feel the cold, unforgiving grip of terror actually touch his soul.

The puppet, which resembled Adolph Hitler, was more than just scary.

It was mangled and distorted in a way that would make it the centerpiece of a sweaty, heart-pounding, scream-in-your-sleep nightmare, the kind of indelible image that would torture you if your mind drifted to it, God forbid. The face and neck were burned as if someone had held up a lit match and slowly let the plastic drip, bubble and double-over on itself. The nose and right eye had sunk into the deeply-blackened skull, and the mouth had twisted and bowed so much that it had opened as if it was about to suck on a straw. Some of the plastic had turned yellowish and formed a mouthful of tiny, sickly teeth. A thin layer of red made it seem like the gums were bleeding.

If anything was clear to Narwood, it was that this was a lot more than just a fucked up toy. From the hair ripped out of the thing's scalp to the bottom of its torched, brittle shoes, its purpose was to send somebody a very unfriendly message.

Narwood crossed himself while holding back his urge to scromit, a word he made up to mean scream and vomit at the same time. Then he pulled a rosary out of his pocket. The rosary was a gift for renewing his subscription to *Exorcism Quarterly*, a Catholic webzine that featured articles like "Sex with the Possessed: Ready for a Threesome?"

For a split second the rosary and the puppet brushed against one another.

The puppet shook.

Then it groaned.

Terrified beyond the ability to speak, Narwood looked down and saw that his right foot was planted on Spruce Faller's neck. Then he saw that his left foot was pressing down on Earl's right ear so hard that blood was coming out of it.

Narwood scromited at the top of his lungs long enough for the horror to fully consume his psyche. When he finished, he sat down in the muck, stared straight ahead, and sucked his thumb.

Tick, Tock. Saturday, 2:59 a.m.

No matter how much Constance Anne wanted to believe otherwise, Mortie was dead and had probably been that way for quite a while. Accepting that as truth was vomit-inducing because it meant that she had spent the past 18 hours imprisoned under a truckload of decomposing human flesh.

Considering how much the last 18 hours or so had sucked, Constance Anne wasn't unduly surprised when Mortie's bowels fired off a loud, wet, fart heavy with the smells of eggs and garlic.

In fact, it was turning out to be the highlight of her day.

Neither was she surprised that the fart was powerful enough to shift his carcass nearly an inch to the left. Although the movement was tiny, she unexpectedly found it easier to breathe. It occurred to her that he might have also moved enough for his dead manhood to have slid out. As disgusting as it was to think about, she had to admit that Mortie was like a steel girder and had hung in there like a champ even as his equipment turned icy cold.

It crossed her mind that he might have taken one of the erection aids advertised on television that warned men to call their doctors if they had an erection that lasted more than a few hours. Of course, the manufacturers didn't say what to do if you still had an erection after death, although she figured that they probably hadn't had the deceased in mind as a market.

The thought made her laugh, and she believed she deserved at least a little credit for finding anything funny under the circumstances. She was also pleased with herself that she didn't want to rip Mortie's eyeballs out in anger. Despite everything, she saw him as a sad soul who certainly didn't die on top of her on purpose. For that matter, at least half the blame was on her shoulders for going out with him in the first place. Clearly, selling her ass for cash wasn't going to be part of her future, and buying ass for cash apparently wasn't going to be a part of his either.

Irrationally, but understandably, she started to worry that if the cops found her alive, they might charge her with involuntary manslaughter. After all, it was pretty obvious that Morton Beech didn't commit suicide.

Having spent time with stiff things other than penises in her past, Constance Anne knew something about how the human body goes into rigor mortis, a hardening of the body that usually starts in the jaw and neck within three or four hours of death.

Inside the breathlessly hot second-floor motel room where her body continued to expel fluids it couldn't afford to lose, the dearly departed's neck became rigid, and his puffy face rose from where it had settled on her right shoulder, moving almost mechanically to the right until the tip of his cold nose came close to touching hers.

Sprinting across her mind faster than a coke snort were the words "corpus delicti," a term meaning "body of the crime" that she'd heard one of the hot crime investigators on TV use. Constance Anne had laughingly twisted it into "corpus delicious." Trapped inside a real-life reality horror show, Constance Anne thought it was funny that there was nothing delicious about her bed partner.

"*Oh, God! He's fucking Rigor Mortie!*" she said to herself. The words thundered inside her head a moment before she passed out again from the unbearable combination of heat and meat.

CHAPTER 9

" ... {they} started referring to the slaughter as simply 'Woo-Woo Wednesday.' The popularity of the term spread like gonorrhea in a prison dayroom."

Perhaps it was just a coincidence that Schmendrik Memorial Cemetery stood on the site of the darkest event in Chelsington's history.

Like a soldier at his post, a ten-foot-tall stone memorial sculpted in the shape of a portly Puritan and spattered with pigeon shit stood at attention at the cemetery's decrepit entrance. Chiseled on his vest were the words, "In Memory of the Nine Noble White Men and Women Butchered Here by Jalapeno Indians on Wednesday, November 21, 1691." In the statue's left arm was a tablet that said "Site of the Great Chelsington White Folk's Massacre of 1691" across the top. Below it was an elaborately-chiseled, thee-dimensional scene of smirking Indians scalping white men, drinking whiskey, and carrying off young white girls with bodacious cleavage.

The story was so much a part of local lore that every Chelsington school child knew the story of that day's horrifying carnage when some 400 Jalapeno braves in war paint attacked the squirrel farm owned by Puritan brothers Dwaine and Laysum Pipe. The Indians, who desperately needed to restock many of the area's huge New World Wampum stores with their blockbuster maize body wash, scalped all nine members of the family and boiled their bodies in order to use their dripping fats in the soap.

While they were at it, they rustled more than a thousand head of Grade A Prime squirrels and herded them north for the menu at their five-star restaurant, Pow-Wow's, where the squirrel l'orange was without peer.

As time marched on and students grew significantly less respectful, kids tired of calling the fabled bloodbath "The Great Chelsington White Folk's Massacre of Wednesday, November 21, 1691" and started imitating the "woo-woo" noises from Indian war dances in old movies whenever the massacre came up in conversation. Eventually in 1976, sixth grader Lester "The Barbie Molester" Schmeltzman started referring to the slaughter as simply "Woo-Woo Wednesday." The popularity of the term spread like gonorrhea in a prison dayroom.

The fascination with these more than 300-year-old events would have been fine if the story of "Woo-Woo Wednesday" hadn't been twisted and turned into something that only vaguely resembled the truth. In fact, the only parts that hadn't been distorted were the incomparability of the squirrel l'orange and the tribe's robust soap sales at New World Wampum stores.

The bullshit had been made up by Magistrate Crockett Cuthbert Dick, a one-time sewage shoveler on The Preyflower, a "pay for what you want" ship that charged for every bag and sailed to America some 50 years after The Mayflower. Dick rose to power and wealth in Chelsington through an active career in fraud, assault, conspiracy, arson, extortion, shoplifting and murder. A nasty, little one-eyed shit who stood 4' 9", he wore a powdered white wig, a black robe, and fresh wolf feces behind his ears every day for good luck. When an imposter named Wyllyam Anthonye Dildoe, who looked and sounded like Dick, tried to cut in on business that Dick and his business partner, DeJon Palomino, CEO of used horse empire Steed-O-Rama City, had in Salem, the Magistrate had him thrown in a cage with a dozen rabid woodchucks.

When the woodchucks were done tearing Dildoe, the fake Dick, apart, the Magistrate lifted up the man's face for all to see and loudly proclaimed, *"This man is a Dildoe! I am the only true Dick!"*

In the end, it was more than fitting that such a miserable bastard would go down in history as the source of words like "Dickhead" and "Dickface," and the popular saying, "He's a real Dick."

On Tuesday, November 20, 1691, Dick and Palomino launched a plot to steal every squirrel the Pipe family owned and sell them to a coat factory that outsourced its work to slaves overseas in order to maximize stockholder value. Then, the factory would attach fake "Made in Plymouth Colony" labels and sell the coats to New World Wampum Stores which, in turn, would sell them to consumers at prices no one else could compete with.

Unfortunately for Dick, the scheme fell apart when the squirrelnappers were caught in the act by Dwaine Pipe's nubile 16-year-old daughter, Corncobia, who happened to be out that night checking the squirrels' nuts. Holding them at gunpoint, Corncobia blackmailed the men rather than turn them into her father, telling them that she would keep her mouth shut in exchange for a new Mustang and 50 bags of oats. Infuriated by her demands and steadfast in his refusal to pay her off, Dick hired three underemployed apple peelers to dress up as Jalapeno warriors, kill every member of the Pipe family and blame it all on the Indians.

Quite the opposite of what Dick tried to make them out to be, the Jalapeno Indians were a peaceful people that had devoted themselves to offshore gambling and the preservation of the chili pepper that bore their name. Rather than viewing tomahawks, knives and arrows as weapons of war, they saw them as big profit items in their chain of wigwam improvement and hunting equipment stores.

They weren't exactly a military power either. While it was true that they had 400 warriors in the tribe, the number included their reserve units and retirees. When they got down to the men who could actually fight, they had about 50, half of whom were over the age of 40 with prostate issues that forced them to make frequent rest stops.

Most importantly, they didn't murder or kidnap a single member of the Pipe household. At the time of the "massacre," in fact, almost every able-bodied Jalapeno was busy running the tribe's flotilla of three-masted cargo ship casinos anchored off of Juniper Cove in Salem. To get their Pilgrim, Puritan, Wampanoag, Nauset, and Massachuset Indian customers to and from the boats for the buffets, gambling and entertainment, the tribe started the first shuttle system using 60-person, double-decker "mega canoes" with fully-stocked bars to "keep the party going."

Despite Magistrate Dick's hit order on the Pipes, Dwaine, Laysum, and Laysum's son, Meerschaum, all died the next day completely by accident. The three under-employed apple peelers got lost in the thick woods and took a little over seven hours to walk a mile to the Pipe homestead. They arrived shortly after midnight, almost at the same time thunder and lightning hit and thick columns of rain began to fall. Not sure that they wanted to kill anybody but very sure that they didn't want to get wet, the apple peelers huddled together under a canopy of trees and broke out the mulled wine they'd brought with them in six "easy pour" sheep's bladders. The mixture of Cabernet, cinnamon, honey, and orange tasted so good that one drink led to another until they all passed out.

Around three o'clock in the morning, lightning struck the squirrel fence and burned a large section to the ground. In a moment of very bad timing, Dwaine, Laysum, and Meerschaum awoke and ran out of the house to see what had happened. As the men leapt off of the porch, their feet flew out from under them in the slimy mud.

With nothing to protect them, they were trampled to death under the paws of a multitude of squirrels with serious psychiatric disorders that were pouring through the gap.

Unbeknownst to the Pipes, the critters had been eating yellow mushrooms packed with hallucinogens that gave the little guys new and unusual insights into life along with heightened paranoia. It was a disorder that was rare in the squirrel community and wouldn't be seen again until the Summer of Love in 1968.

When the apple peelers came to in the wake of the lightning strike, they walked very slowly around the front of the house like tax cheats on their way to an IRS audit. By the time they reached the kill site, all of the squirrels, except one who was lying on his back contemplating his paw, were gone and the bodies of Dwaine, Laysum, and Meerschaum were flattened and half-submerged in the mud.

On the front porch, nine women ranging from babelicious to ox-faced on the Puritan hottie scale screamed, cried, and wailed over the sudden, horrible loss of their loved ones. Expecting that the grieving would go on for some time, the phony Indians stayed hidden in the woods. Much to their surprise, the women not only stopped crying after a few minutes, but soon moved onto a practical conversation about burying the bodies.

The men were even more surprised to hear them refer to Dwaine, Laysum and Meerschaum, respectively, as "Little Bone", "Ass Clown", and "Squirrel Fucker", a particular reference that was apparently meant literally. When they finished digging the graves, the women picked up each body and tossed it in a hole like it was trash. Then they bowed their heads, said a prayer and concluded the service with an odd little dance and cheers of "God has delivered us!" Even the three geniuses scratching their asses in the woods should have been able to figure out that the Pipes probably weren't the happiest family on the planet.

On the same day that local Indians were alleged to have gone ham on a bunch of white people, Crockett Dick and DeJon Palomino sat in the dark backroom of Salem's Old Mouse and Buzzard Tavern, the first trattoria with an antipasto buffet outside of Boston. They had a problem on their hands.

Over the past few months the two men had managed to lose their asses playing blackjack and keno in the Jalapeno Indian casinos. While that was bad, it was far worse that the money they lost belonged to The Massachusetts Great Big Wooden Ship Company, a firm that was gearing up to build the largest fleet of wide-body, ocean-going ships in the world. Twice the size of The Mayflower, the ships were designed to provide sumptuous first and second class accommodations for up to 200 passengers, including a waste removal system that allowed travelers to relieve themselves inside the ship rather than having to suspend themselves over the sea on a "poopee" rope. The system paid for itself quickly.

Without the "poopee" ropes, the ships were able to introduce a new, no-frills section known as water view class that offered space for yet another hundred souls. In addition to low cost, water view class also offered passengers spectacular, unobstructed views of the sea and an abundance of fresh air.

Although the accommodations were actually on the outside of the ship, each passenger had their own seat on a white cedar bench, a big cup holder and a small hook to snag a fish snack.

The money Dick and Palomino had blown was being "borrowed" by two disgruntled bookkeepers at the Great Big Wooden Ship Company, Arthur Wainscot and Ichabod Wormler, who were doing it in exchange for a quarter of the gambling profits. Pissed off by a lot of things, including having the coal supply for their office fireplace reduced 30% in a cost-cutting move, Wainscot and Wormler had managed to misappropriate almost enough money to build an entire ship.

The four crooks made very substantial profits for quite a while until Dick and Palomino hit a staggering losing streak. Now, they weren't only losing the ship company's money, but were pissing away the profits they made beforehand. Livid that Dick and Palomino were turning his badly-needed profits into warm stool, Wormler had marched onto Palomino's horse lot the previous day to give him a piece of his mind. At some point, the money was going to have to be put back in the Great Big Wooden Ship Company's coffers, Wormler told him, and it wasn't going to come out of his and Wainscot's pockets. Both of them had spent their ill-gotten gains and were nearly broke.

"You lost the money. You repay it!" Wormler said, his voice rising with rage.

"Kith my ath," Palomino said, his foamy lisp spraying slobber into his mustache. Centuries later, people would have compared the way he spoke to the sound of a sinking motor boat.

"You do not want to anger us, Master Palomino," Wormler told him in no uncertain terms outside of the service department where horses were shod and gelded. "If we are caught and sent to Salem Dungeon, you will surely go with us. We will tell the authorities all that we know."

Palomino stared at Wormler with cold, dead eyes that screamed an anti-social personality disorder. Then he turned and walked away. Wormler shuddered.

He felt as if he had looked into the eyes of Satan himself.

At their table in the Old Mouse and Buzzard, Dick and Palomino shared a bowl of baked ziti and rationally agreed that they needed to make their problem go away with as few entanglements as possible. In an abnormally charitable move, Dick and Palomino decided to pay half of the loss, but would tell Wainscot and Wormler that they would have to pay all of it just to see if they would do it.

There were too many more important things going on with the potential to screw up their incomes to mess with this too much. Chief among them was witchcraft, which got people so freaked that they quit spending money.

A few years earlier, it looked as if witchcraft hysteria had simmered down after the hanging of Anne Glover in Boston in 1688 on more than a few ridiculously bullshit charges. Instead, Cotton Mather, the famous minister and writer who would later build the foundation for the Salem Witch Trials, riled things up again, probably to build demand for a new book he was writing called *Wonders of the Invisible World*. Palomino disliked Mather because he'd returned a horse he bought from Steed-O-Rama City under questionable circumstances. After putting 200 miles on it he wanted his money back on the grounds that the horse was possessed by the Devil.

"The guy's meshugganah," Palomino had told more than a few people after the incident.

Dick wasn't exactly a big fan of Mather's either. Mather claimed to have saved the soul of a young Irish woman named Mary who had frequently given Dick such intense head that he claimed it had literally changed his life. Skilled at standing on her hands for hours at a time and a talented ventriloquist to boot, Mary could not only focus on the task in front of her but sing popular songs at the same time. Now protected from an eternity in Hell, all she would do for Dick was darn his socks.

Later that night, the three idiots in Jalapeno Indian outfits sauntered out from their hiding place in the woods. Seeing only women and mindful of the long walk home that was still ahead of them, they decided that killing the remaining Pipes should and could be done with the least amount of effort possible. After a minimal amount of thought, the idea of tying the women up inside the house and then setting the house on fire seemed like a pretty easy way to go.

"Woo, fuckin' woo," said Norville Oswald, the biggest asshole of the three, with as much enthusiasm as a teenager at a harpsichord concert as he walked through the empty squirrel pen into the clearing in front of the house. He ended his sentence with a friendly little wave and a big yawn. Caught off guard, the nine women stared at the men with a combination of shock, fright, and anger. They kept their eyes peeled on the intruders as each girl reached down to pick up her shovel.

"Pray pardon me, Mistresses," Oswald continued. "Fear not. We are not Indians. We are white men who have come to save you."

"Oh, how fortunate we are to be rescued, aren't we, sisters?" Sarah Pipe, the eldest and by far the toughest of the women said.

"Did someone send you big, handsome men here?" Sarah asked in the frailest voice she could muster. "If so, I must thank them for their kindness."

Her sarcasm was lost on Oswald who didn't even get simple jokes. When someone would say, "Knock-knock," Oswald would say "Come in."

"We are the agents of His Holiness, Crockett Dick," Oswald replied, bowing as he gave Dick the grandest title he could think of despite the fact that it was ridiculously stupid. "Now put down your shovels and let us all go into the house to talk. You are merely women. You need the protection of strong men."

The women laughed out loud. Then they pointed at the men, made inch marks between their thumbs and index fingers as if they were measuring things that were very small, and exploded with laughter again.

Realizing that the women were giggling about their tallywhackers, the men's faces filled with rage.

"*Now, I say! Or we will come get you!*" Oswald growled. A misogynist's misogynist, he didn't like women making fun of him. Ever.

"*Stop laughing!*" he yelled as the veins in his neck popped out and his face turned purplish. He looked like a child throwing a tantrum.

Far more concerned with protecting their masculinity than their perimeter, Oswald and his men were making too much of a ruckus to hear sisters Elizabeth, Ann, and Mary Pipe walk up behind them, pull back the cocks of three flintlock rifles aimed at the back of their heads and simultaneously pull the triggers.

Crazy with anger, Oswald continued to bellow for a few seconds even after his head left his body in a cloud of heavy smoke and bounced into the wood yard.

Feeling a sense of calm, comfort, and accomplishment with the Pipe men's bodies buried and their guests' heads blown off, the women went about planning a visit to Magistrate Crockett Dick. If not all of it, they were all quite sure that Dick had been behind at least some of the night's horror.

As far as the Pipe sisters were concerned, the trip from Chelsington to Salem pretty much sucked. The restaurants and horse filling stations along the 25-mile journey were nothing special, except for one Massachuset Indian shop that advertised itself as "the low overhead leader in pre-owned jewelry."

Its proprietor, Chief Running Tchotchke, the product of a mixed marriage between his Indian father, Sprinting Beagle, and Jewish mother, Sylvia Goldberg, kept his costs low by pulling the earrings, rings, and necklaces off of butchered settlers. Being practical, the Pipe girls really didn't have a problem with the origin of the merchandise as long as it sparkled and didn't have too much blood on it. A hairpin that still had some scalp attached to it was more than okay for Mary, whose personal hygiene habits left a lot to be desired. Elizabeth, who had a bad attitude about almost everything, actually smiled over a lovely pair of earrings the sales squaw told her were knock-offs of a pair worn by Anne Boleyn on the day she was executed.

Eventually entering Salem on Chestnut Street, they stopped to ask directions.

"We are seeking Magistrate Dick and Master Palomino," Ann asked an old man with a mucous-heavy cough. The old man hocked up a large ball of phlegm and spat it on a passing sheep.

"You want Dick, you say?" the old man asked, squinting as if saying the name caused him actual physical pain.

"He's a hard man with a mind of his own. He has only one eye. You may find him at a table in the Old Mouse and Buzzard on Derby Street. If he is not there, make inquiries at the Old Bedbug and Crow. He may be upstairs joining giblets with the wife of Master Palomino."

⋏

In the shadows of the backroom of the Old Mouse and Buzzard, Crockett Dick and DeJon Palomino sat hunched over a piece of parchment and a candle with a dancing flame. Across the table were Arthur Wainscot and Ichabod Wormler. Not surprisingly, the meeting was less than friendly. In fact, it was so less than friendly that Palomino kept going over in his mind how beautiful it would be if all three of the assholes he was sitting with were torn in half by wolves. If he didn't like the fact that Wainscot and Wormler were going to cost him money, he definitely didn't like the fact that Dick was exchanging bodily fluids with his stacked 22-year-old wife, Bambi. Thirty years his junior, Bambi had only married him for his fast, low-mileage horses and unusual access to meat so fresh that it was still throbbing when it was brought into the kitchen.

"When will you provide the money to repay the company's account?" Wainscot asked Dick, clearing his throat and trying to act tough.

"We have decided that you will pay," Dick said. Wainscot laughed while cold sweat poured off of Wormler's shrinking testicles.

"What? You are an absurd little man," Wainscot said.

Dick looked at Palomino.

"You will pay all of it, pith bucket," Palomino lisped.

"We will pay nothing," Wainscot said defiantly to Palomino, pounding his fist on the table.

Palomino's face turned red.

"Why the hell are we debating this?" Dick thundered, looking at Palomino with anger in his eyes. "Let's just kill them."

With that, Wainscot lost control of his bowels. Wormler broke into tears first and then wet himself.

Palomino knew that he and Dick couldn't get away with public assassinations anymore. It wasn't like the good old days when you could just murder whoever you wanted to.

"I would juth ath well kill you both thith minute on thith very spot," Palomino sprayed on the accountants.

"But we will let you consider your decision," Dick said. "Pay and we will let you live. *Pay not and you will die!* You have until the morrow."

Dick stood up and walked out of the tavern with Palomino at his heels. They left Wainscot and Wormler alone to ponder their fates. Unfortunately for Wainscot, Wormler was of no help. He had moved well beyond rational thought and into the fetal position.

"We'll simply run and never come back," Wainscot said, trying to cheer Wormler up. "We'll go to New York and open a Hawaiian-Russian Fusion restaurant. No one will ever find us." Wormler smiled.

🜊

Because the sign hanging over the Old Mouse and Buzzard had been broken by vandals and now bore a close resemblance to the sign above the Old Chipmunk and Pigeon, it took the Pipe girls more than an hour to get to the right place. The delay wasn't because Salem was big. It was because many of the men inside the Old Chipmunk and Pigeon had never been around women, even ugly ones, and insisted on buying the girls drinks. Mary finally had to bring it to an end by stabbing one of her more passionate admirers through the wrist and thigh in one swift, forceful stroke.

With that as a fairly major buzz kill, the girls moved on towards the Old Mouse and Buzzard. They arrived just as two well-dressed gentlemen emerged from the front door.

"Where might we find Magistrate Dick and Master Palomino?" Mary asked, holding her flintlock rifle in clear sight.

Palomino recognized a few of the women from Steed-O-Rama City. They had come in with their husbands to buy a few of the low-end plow horses he sold with a worm-free, money back guarantee. He whispered the name "Pipe" in Dick's ear. Dick's eyes popped wide open.

"They are in there," Dick said, pointing at the tavern door. Considering how they were armed, whatever the women wanted didn't portend well for Dick and Palomino. "They are sitting at a table in the rear. You cannot mistake them, Mistresses. Dick is wearing a red scarf and Palomino is wearing a blue vest."

Mary smiled at the men and thanked them for their courtesy. Dick and Palomino tipped their hats and walked away as fast as their chubby little legs would carry them. They hid in a doorway to watch the looming disaster.

Strangely, but fortunately for Dick and Palomino, none of the Pipes asked a single question about the identity of anyone inside the tavern before all nine flintlocks exploded in unison, killing Wainscot, Wormler, and a guy molesting a chicken under the next table. The only good that came from the whole affair was the oddly attractive design the bullets made on the tavern wall. After the dead men were identified, the decorative pattern eventually became known as "Wainscoting."

There were two groups facing big problems in the aftermath of the killings.

The first, of course, was the Pipes who had just committed a triple homicide in front of some thirty witnesses. Rather than simply shooting the observers, they fled Salem, rode north, and bought a bank-owned co-op in Canada. Leaving their past behind them, the women lived under assumed names for decades and operated a farm with more than 100,000 head of Grade A Fancy rats. Flaked, formed and packaged under the name "Pilgrim Puffies," they became such popular appetizers in taverns that beer and Pilgrim Puffies became as much of a duo as cookies and milk and wine and cheese.

The other party with a big-ass problem was Dick and Palomino. On one hand there was good news: the embezzlement mess died in the same hail of musket balls that killed Wainscot and Wormler. On the other, Dick and Palomino had been overheard threatening the accountants only minutes before they died.

When the constable brought the witnesses from the Old Mouse and Buzzard together, several speculated that Dick and Palomino were somehow connected to the women who fired the shots. A few others said they saw Palomino reach for his knife shortly before the murders. Yet others speculated that Dick and Palomino had changed into dresses to fool everyone before they shot the men.

One observer was only interested in some "alone time" with the now-available chicken.

With so many fingers pointed at them, Dick and Palomino would have ordinarily squealed on the Pipes and washed their hands of the whole matter. In this case, unfortunately, there were more than a few complications to address.

First, revealing the women's identities might raise questions from the Constable that Dick, in particular, didn't want to answer. It didn't take a brain surgeon to figure out that the Pipes had come to find him and Palomino for a reason and, considering what they did to the accountants, it wasn't to check on their health.

Second, they had no idea where the Pipes were, and Dick didn't exactly want the law to see whatever Oswald had done, or didn't do, at the squirrel farm.

Last but not least was a very simple matter of life and death: once the women realized that they'd killed the wrong men, they might decide to correct their mistake.

Later that day after a few tankards of Cock-Ale, a lively blend of wine, ale, and chicken broth, Dick told Palomino that he had an idea to shift attention for the murders far away from them. With witchcraft hysteria in every corner of Salem, the question of who would make a good scapegoat looked like a no-brainer. In the meantime, they agreed that hanging out in Dick's well-hidden cottage in the woods for a while wouldn't be a bad idea.

The year 1692 was not a good one for women who could hold their breath underwater.

Three years earlier in 1689, Cotton Mather published his first mega-blockbuster, *Memorable Providences Relating to Witchcrafts and Possessions*, which rocketed to the top of the Massachusetts Bay Colony bestseller list almost overnight. A real page-turner, Mather's book educated readers to the existence of fugly, malevolent witches and terrifying demons that were eager to snatch wayward souls of all ages.

Sort of *The Exorcist* of its day, *Memorable Providences Relating to Witchcrafts and Possessions* scared the good citizens of the Colony so badly that many took out witchery and demonic possession insurance sold by Mather's Second Church of Boston. The ten-year term policies promised to protect the insured from persistent projectile vomiting, head spinning, floating above the bed, and loss of their immortal soul for the current-day equivalent of $100 a month per adult and $200 per child under 18.

No dummy, Mather understood that the more witches there were, the more policies his people could sell. Consequently, he did everything possible to make it easy to accuse people of being a witch and impossible for the accused to disprove it.

One of his more popular trials utilized something called a dunking stool, a chair lashed to a long wooden arm and suspended over deep water. For the accused, it was the ultimate in lose-lose situations. If the authorities strapped a woman to the chair, held her under water for five minutes and she lived, she was deemed guilty because the "purity" of God's water had rejected her. In that case, the next step was to drag her up to Gallows Hill and hang her by the neck.

Ironically, it was much less complicated for the accused to prove her innocence: all she had to do was drown.

Despite these shortcomings there was a remarkable silver lining. Because the accused couldn't wear anything more than a thin, white cotton smock, the Massachusetts Bay Colony inadvertently became the first place in America to sponsor wet T-shirt contests.

Although the dunking stool was clearly a crowd pleaser, the ever-inventive Mather came up with a new test that expanded his witch trial income. In this investigation, good-looking female contestants under the age of 30 were tied to a pole and stripped naked in public to see if they had a "witches' mark" on their bodies. Conveniently for the accusers, the mark could be anything from a mole to a patch of acne, depending on whether or not they wanted to find the woman guilty.

Witch stripping not only became wildly popular with Salem's male residents but eventually evolved into what we know today as pole dancing. In exchange for a guarantee of at least one stripping event for 16 consecutive weeks plus "strip-offs" to crown a winner in a "Miss Nude Witchcraft of the Year" contest, entrepreneurs paid the Second Church of Boston a hefty licensing fee for the rights to sell season tickets, cold ale, oysters, hot raccoon legs, and buttered possum platters to hungry fans.

Not surprisingly, the crowds were freaking massive.

When Miss Priscilla Norbertson's fresh, young 36DD's were put on display, the crowd was so large and heavy from devouring buttered possum that one of the viewing stands collapsed, killing three pre-teen boys who had snuck in and were hiding underneath it.

The promoters threatened to move the witch stripping to another city unless the stands were rebuilt immediately. As a result, hundreds of seats were added and corporate boxes were installed, all at the taxpayers' expense. Although there were critically important roads to be fixed and bridges to be erected in Salem, the city pushed everything out of the way and made the venue its top construction priority.

Two centuries later, pro sports team owners in America could look back with pride on these trailblazers, the first to force a city to build a new stadium that was entirely unnecessary.

Tick, Tock. Saturday, 3:37 a.m.

Her first nightmare took her inside a deep well where she was faced with either balancing herself on a mound of razor-sharp thorns or being torn apart by an angry horde of burqa-clad optometrists with shingles.

Her mother, BritNee, and the smoldering old fucker from the trailer park were motioning to her to jump onto a dangerously narrow ledge. Every time Constance Anne got ready to leap, a tattered, hideously ugly puppet with a single, bloody tooth would reach out to grab her. The good news was that there was a large woman with knee-length boobs, a porkpie hat, and a hockey stick between Constance Anne and the puppet. Whenever the puppet made a move, she would knock the shit out of it with the stick. Off in the distance, a huge man with an ass that looked like two bags of rats inappropriately bent over to show off the tiny thong he was wearing.

In the background, Frickey Dickie, Spruce Faller, Tiny Earl, and Sister Juan were all riding sheep and eating pork rinds.

She was naked in the dream that followed, locked inside a big wooden box with scant light and too little air. Somewhere outside the box a storm was battering the earth with thick rain and dazzling lightning strikes.

In the corner to her right, something that smelled foul and dirty was hissing and thumping something heavy on the floor.

Constance Anne could feel her heart pound in her throat. She wanted to run like hell, but banging again and again on the walls of the box did nothing more than streak her hands with blood. In one quick burst of lightning she saw that it was a komodo dragon, a vicious 8-foot, 190-pound lizard with a long, yellow forked tongue and a palate for meat. The monster rushed towards her in the dark, its tongue flicking in and out, grimly licking its way up her left thigh to the bottom of her bare back.

Constance Anne woke up in a cold sweat, but not until she had endured the creature goring her with one of its claws and tearing at her neck with rows of serrated teeth. She could feel its jaws throb.

She screamed until she simply couldn't scream any more.

Chapter 10

*"They stole two dented horses that were decorated with fringed
Puerto Rican flags from valet parking, shouted 'Come with us!' and
galloped down Essex Street."*

Living only a few miles away in Swampscott were identical twin sisters who were so ugly that bags refused to go over their heads.

Born a week apart, Helga and Elga Frigg were a handful for their impoverished parents from the get-go. They ate non-stop, screamed in between mouthfuls and overflowed the diaper they were forced to share throughout the day and night.

Their double-humped noses, massive nostrils, wart-covered faces, and bulging neck goiters were arresting to say the least, and made a remarkable addition to the thick, curly bunches of hair covering their craniums. One genetic quirk had sent pubic hair to their heads and thick, straight red hair between their thighs. Another had made them so buck-toothed that they could eat an apple from a foot away.

By the age of two, they had unintentionally scared the family dog into a permanent loss of bladder control. By the time they were five, they dressed out at nearly 150 pounds apiece and had to be careful not to be mistaken for wild boars.

Nonetheless, despite all of the sadness, complications, and disappointments they faced in life, the twins were exceptionally friendly and kind. They baked bread for the poor, scrubbed their church from top to bottom on Saturday mornings, and staged free puppet shows for children on Saturday afternoons. In fact, they would do anything to help anyone in need as long as they didn't have to show their faces. They had also been valued employees of Edward Gein & Sons Fur and Fillet Emporium, a local tannery and disembowelment plant, for more than 15 years. Since launching their careers at the age of six, they had been named the company's "Organ Sorters of the Year" nine times.

Regrettably, the girls' stellar career success alone failed to make them completely happy, and in 1692 they turned to witchcraft in hopes of finding a spell that would turn them into attractive marriage candidates. Although the odds of success looked about as good as teaching a hyena to waltz, they read a grimoire, a book of black magic, with rapt attention to learn how to devise the right incantations. Their work, sadly, was littered with misfires. After mangling one particular enchantment, they turned Elga's nose upside down, making it hard for her to shower without drowning. They turned a horseshoe into a smart-ass toilet seat that liked to shout things like *"Push, you fuckin' bitch! I don't have all freakin' day!"* to make people think their stool was disrespectful.

Yet another boo-boo changed their dachshund's feet into tiny hamsters with minds of their own that sent the poor dog racing right-left-backwards-forwards non-stop until it collapsed.

In between, however, they had successes that gave them the confidence to press on.

The sisters triumphantly turned Elga's nose back the right way. They whipped up a spell to make their shoes feel as soft as clouds no matter how many hours a day they wore them and another to give themselves an unlimited selection of designer purses and cute tote bags.

Unfortunately, their biggest mistake was right around the corner.

The sisters dearly loved the kind man who collected the monthly rent for the charming two-bedroom, one-quarter-bath cabin they lived in. For his birthday, they designed an incantation to turn all of his dilapidated wooden cups, mugs, spoons, and dishes into pewter. Rather than the last line of their spell coming out as "Give him the beauty of gorgeous pewter," however, mispronunciations caused it to come out as "Give him the cruelty of a conscious neuter."

There was simply no apology big enough to cover that.

Ever.

At the end of the 17th Century, Massachusetts Bay was not big enough for anyone to expect anonymity. That went at least twice for the Frigg sisters. As if they didn't already have enough shit in their lives, Crockett Dick not only knew who the Frigg girls were but had become well-acquainted with them over the years. Although few knew it, Dick had a variety of unusual interests starting with nasophilia, an intense sexual attraction to noses, dendrophilia, a sexual attraction to trees, and agalmatophilia, an appetite for sex with objects like mannequins and statues. He topped it off with oculolinctus, a form of dangerous, disease-spreading sexual gratification from licking a lover's eyeballs.

Dick had frequently offered the girls colossal sums of money to let him roger them in their nostrils and lick their corneas while they remained perfectly still under a blanket of tree bark. Ever proper and respectful, Helga and Elga politely declined Dick's offers so many times that he developed a mild depressive disorder. After that, Magistrate Dick spent his days plotting how he could have the girls put behind bars and held until he'd had all the eye-licking he wanted. He was even daydreaming about it the day he and Palomino arrived at his hideout.

Crockett Dick's log cabin sat deep in the woods 15 or so miles north of Salem near Ipswich. Ramshackle, cold, and gently kissed by the aroma of deer urine, its inaccessibility made it Dick's favorite place to do things that society found offensive, including doing a line of coke right before fucking a bee hive. The cabin was in a part of the forest that had such dense vegetation that horses were too big to navigate the narrow paths and low tree branches. To get there, visitors had to ride the last three miles bareback on merino wool sheep.

If they didn't have burning hot loins when they got on, they surely did when they got off.

Dazed from eating Dick's dinner of brined porcupine and kidney shavings, DeJon Palomino was wobbling on the edges of both acute dyspepsia and a nervous breakdown.

Besides his diet, Palomino's problem was that he was crazy with worry. Murder was a lot different from swindling people in the used horse game. He didn't have a problem selling horses that had been totaled or had bowel diseases. He didn't care that there were so many exclusions in his sales contracts that a customer couldn't even get their money back if their new horse died before it trotted off the lot. Murder, however, was a horse of a different color. As an accessory to both the Pipe and Wainscot-Wormler killings, he faced the possibility of going to the gallows.

"Whath your plan?" Palomino asked Dick with a generous spray of saliva as he reached for his sixth bottle of stepony, a raisin wine that only went well with lima beans and organ meat.

"We're going to tell everyone that the Frigg sisters are witches," Dick said, coughing up an unwieldy hairball he'd inhaled from the nine docile Persian cats he used as blankets. Palomino turned his head. He'd seen the hairballs before and wondered how the man could breathe with so much fur in his lungs. It was amazing that he didn't even wheeze.

"You see, my good man," Dick said, pacing back and forth and making up the story as he went along, "it happened like this: the sisters fell desperately in love with Wainscot and Wormler and eventually worked up the courage to express their feelings to them. Sadly, the men's response was unnecessarily cruel, an unusual thing since few accountants even have personalities. They made the poor sisters so sad that they cried their eyes out for days."

"How am I doing?" Dick asked. Palomino nodded in approval. He rubbed his index finger under his right eye as if he was about to start weeping himself.

Dick cleared his throat and finished his sales pitch. It sounded okay to Palomino, although he doubted that it would convince anyone that the Friggs practiced sorcery. A wave of panic washed over him. He felt his hands start to tremble.

"Thith had better work, ath monkey becauth if thith only workth ath well ath raiding that thitbag thquirrel farm we're thurley going to hang," Palomino sprayed.

Reacting to the enormous stress he felt, savagely inflamed hives began to break out all over his body until he looked like a horse apple with a triple chin. If DeJon Palomino thought his ride in on the sheep was uncomfortable, the ride out was going to take things up a notch or two. He was going to feel like someone set his crotch on fire and shoved a spear up his ass sideways. And that was the good news.

Dick picked the perfect time and place to whip Salem into a frenzy over the Friggs. The next Sunday promised to be a particularly exciting one for witch stripping devotees. There had been considerable pressure on Cotton Mather and the promoters to bring in witch candidates that were better-looking and had markedly larger jugs. That's not to say that they hadn't been doing their best to find hot, well-endowed girls; frankly, they had moved more meat around than elephants on a circus train. But without 21st-century growth hormones in food and super-sized fries to push up young women's bra sizes, they had to settle for what nature manufactured.

They had recently found Miss Brilliana Gundry, a 19-year-old blonde with a dazzling below-the-waist package and a mind-boggling pair of clean, low-mileage 42DD nose cones. The promoters gave her the nickname "Boom-Boom." With the promise of that kind of quality on display, it didn't take much for the promoters to sell every seat twice which they did as quickly as possible.

When the big day arrived, the crowds showed up drunk and obnoxious two hours before the show started. Thick gray clouds of a Nipmuc Indian drug called Crazy Bark traveled through the crowd making everyone shit-faced. Behind the bleachers, a man was selling nail clippings purportedly from the toes of Pilgrim Hall of Famers John and Priscilla Alden, Myles Standish and Governor William "Pooty" Bradford.

By the time Dick and Palomino slid into their first row center box seats, reverberations from shouts of "*We Want Boom-Boom!*" were shaking the stands. The opening act, a female contortionist, had one of her fake legs fall off and was pulled off the stage with a sheep's crook. The next one, a German woman who could make the cellulite on her ass ripple like an ocean wave, was taken into protective custody after spectators fired shots at her head.

When it was time for the main event, the announcer, Ambrose Clicket, walked to the front of the stage, let loose a raspy-sounding grunt and made ears on top of his head with the palms of his hands. Then he hopped around like a rabbit with stimulant psychosis to get everyone's attention.

"Good Day, Ladies and Germs," he shouted at the top of his lungs with shtick that was a few hundred years ahead of its time. "I am your humble host, Ambrose Clicket. I just galloped in from Plymouth and, boy, are my legs tired!"

Laughter erupted from the audience, although not because of the joke. "Clicket" was an old term for shtupping.

"We are here today to perform the somber duty of examining a woman for a witches' mark," he continued, winking and getting another tidal wave of laughter from the masses. Another explosion of cheers, whistles and drunken howls followed as "Boom-Boom" was escorted on stage by two armed men and tied to the stripping pole.

"Please welcome today's contestant, Miss Brilliana Gundry of Chelsington. Miss Gundry was seen near ..." said Clicket, who was cut off in mid-sentence by the out-of-control crowd bellowing *"Free her boobies!"*

As Clicket raised his hands in a plea for quiet, Dick and Palomino rose out of their seats and climbed on the stage. Palomino used the butt of his musket to move Clicket aside. The hoots and hollers from the stands turned to boos and hisses and shouts of *"Fuck you, Palomino!"* and *"You suck, Dick!"* The jeers were followed by wave after wave of airborne corn cobs that were so greasy that they turned the stage into an ice rink. Palomino raised his gun and fired it in the air to make sure the audience paid attention.

"Shut your damn mouths and listen carefully," Magistrate Dick said, ogling Boom-Boom's boom-booms extensively before purposely blocking everyone else's view. "I'm going to tell you who killed the men at the Old Mouse and Buzzard."

"Pull off her shirt! Take off her fucking shirt!" a shitfaced member of the Young Puritan's Club shouted, wobbling back and forth in the stands. Annoyed, the town sociopath walked over to the kid and jammed his eyeballs all the way to the back of his head.

"Who was it, Magistrate? We desperately want to know!" said Cosmord Smythe, a city sewage crawler and Salem's foremost ass-kisser. He was so smarmy that even Dick got sick of him sometimes.

"It was the Frigg sisters," Dick said. *"They are witches! They are real fucking witches!"* He let the words 'real,' 'fucking' and 'witches' roll off his tongue slowly to heighten the drama.

The crowd took a very deep, collective breath. Smythe put down his curried possum plate and raised a crucifix. With the audience firmly in his grasp, Dick began an animated account of how the sisters conspired to have Wainscot and Wormler murdered.

He explained that Helga and Elga both had the witches' mark and that they had fallen in love with the men after spotting them at a puppet show. He detailed how the accountants responded cruelly to the sisters' advances and described how Helga and Elga plotted revenge, using black magic to turn a pack of rats into angry women with a thirst for murder. In his finale, Dick told the crowd how the Friggs turned the women back into rats after their torrent of musket fire had reduced the bodies of Wainscot, Wormler, and the oft-forgotten chicken molester to beef jerky.

With their business complete, the rats left Salem in adorable little smocks and hats for parts unknown. Dick was going to mention that they also had little shoes, but he didn't want to sound ridiculous.

"Let us rise to face this danger together!" Dick cried, confident that his oratory would move the crowd to follow him. *"Let us kill the witches!"*

With that, two radiant white horses imported all the way across the ocean from Rome were brought on the stage by Steed-O-Rama City handlers who had painted "EZ Financing" and "You Got a Job? You Got a Horse!" on their flanks. As the handlers sliced the air with their swords while the horses reared their front legs, Dick felt he had channeled the spirit of Alexander the Great. When Palomino told him that he wanted to be Alexander the Great,

Dick said that he'd already called it and that Palomino could be Genghis Khan if he wanted to.

"*Charge!*" Dick said as he rode off with an unhappy Genghis Khan literally on his tail.

Much to Palomino's astonishment, the crowd was actually buying Dick's bullshit, and he fully expected that they would follow him to the Friggs' house. For that reason it was particularly amusing that Dick and Palomino proceeded to ride their horses over the edge of the five-foot-high stage, rather than down an adjacent, clearly-marked ramp. Instead of glory, there was a thunderous pile-up on the ground of man and equine as the horses and riders crashed on top of one another. Dick nearly suffocated beneath 1,000 pounds of Italian stallion. Palomino found the right side of his face lodged in the moist anus of Dick's mount.

Considering that both men should have died from the fall, it was all the more amazing that they climbed out of the chaos with their goal still in sight and ready to go. They stole two dented horses that were decorated with fringed Puerto Rican flags from valet parking, shouted "*Come with us!*" and galloped down Essex Street.

Everyone moved quickly, although not in Dick's and Palomino's direction. All of the ticketholders hurried back to their seats to see Brilliana Gundry undressed, laughing their asses off about the horse catastrophe every step of the way. The good news was that the hundreds of spectators moved in an orderly manner despite being uniformly bombed out of their minds; the bad news, however, was that when they looked at the stage, they saw that the stripping poll was Boom-Boomless. Miss Gundry had somehow slipped her bindings and run while the onlookers were distracted.

In its wisdom, the crowd rightly pinned its blistering anger on Dick and Palomino instead of Miss Gundry. Rather than follow Dick and Palomino to punish the Friggs, they formed a heavily-armed posse to go to the Frigg's house to punish Dick and Palomino.

Had the men of Salem cared half as much about the Friggs' alleged association with Satan as they did seeing Boom-Boom's sweater puppies, the sisters would have already been burned at the stake and had their ashes tossed in with the grain at the grist mill.

Beyond the view of the crowd, a season ticket holder in a black hooded cloak rented a horse with points earned from his Platinum Pilgrim card.

Known to other fans only as "the guy in the hoodie," his seat was so close to the stage that he could taste the accused's sweat, and did whenever there was an opportunity. In fact, he had nearly been arrested three weeks earlier for climbing on stage and licking the perspiration off of a witch's knee-cap. Dick's threats were alarming, and "the guy in the hoodie" immediately became concerned about the Friggs. He decided to warn them, and as soon as the rental attendants had washed a small Appaloosa and topped it off with a quarter bag of oats, he sped off for the girls' house in a cloud of dust.

To avoid Dick and Palomino, he took a shortcut through a field fertilized with rotting herring that opened his sinuses faster than anything ever had before.

Back in Swampscott, Helga and Elga dutifully practiced their magic spells, even as their dreams continued to slip away. They tried everything they could think of. Pissed off about the whole thing and feeling a little bloated one Saturday morning, Elga picked up a copy of a new book, *Get Out of the Cauldron! The Witch's Guide to Losing 20 Pounds in 20 Minutes.*

Different from mainstream sorcery weight loss programs, *Get Out of the Cauldron!* didn't start with the typical emphasis on cutting carbohydrates and disposing of "less critical" internal organs like a kidney or parts of the intestines. Rather, *Get Out of the Cauldron!* put the accent on the quality of the magical invocations and casting the spells with resolve and enthusiasm. After reading the entire book together, the girls decided to try its suggestions the next day. There were some big changes.

Previously, they'd stood on either side of a small metal pot of boiling water and said:

> Ear of frog, and bat's wool warm
> Now's the time we should transform!
> Lips of penguin and huge hog booties
> Make us into a pair of beauties!

Now, standing hand-in-hand at the helm of a giant, bubbling cauldron filled with magical potions, they excitedly repeated:

Eye of newt and wing of bat
We fed 'em both to our big black cat.
Round and round it ran all night
Nuthin' 'bout it seemed quite right.

Nose of wolf and tail of horse
Kittens and lambs we'll always endorse.
Give us a break and make us hot
Cuz the way shit's goin' we're quite distraught.

Eye of snake and feet of crow
We really think our faces blow.
Make us cool and damn good lookin'
Cuz these two chicks wanna be cookin'.

Boom-Shaka-Laka! Abracadabra!
We want hot guys, not cadavers!

Thirty minutes later absolutely nothing had happened, an oddity because even the lousiest spells usually made a few cups and saucers fly across the room.

By the time an hour had elapsed, the twins were quiet and feeling defeated.

After two hours, they were descending into deep emotional pain and sobbing in perfect sync even though Helga was inside the house and Elga was outside. Elga, in fact, was crying and digging a hole for a new outhouse at the same time. The enchanted toilet seat had complained loudly about the unspeakable smell around him and made it clear that he would whine about it day and night until there was a fresh hole. For good measure, he threatened to give the girls a nasty staph infection if they didn't get off their asses, so to speak.

Three hours later, there was a knock at the door.

"Helga? Elga?" said a man with a deep voice.

Helga slowly opened the door, careful as always to conceal most of her face in the shadows. To her surprise, the visitor was Reverend Samuel Willard, the preacher whose church she and Elga cleaned every week. A dignified member of the clergy, he was known to take a judicious approach to the witch issue, even though he'd voted in favor of a dozen or so dunkings. Confusion and alarm stretched across his face from the tip of his chin to a large, angry-looking ringworm scar in the middle of his forehead.

"I *must* see Helga and Elga," Willard said, sticking his head inside the door as one of the sisters' unusually large male goats ran out of the house.

"But I *am* Helga, Reverend," Helga said. Her feelings were hurt and she was bursting with anxiety. Now she was going to have to show him her entire face.

"That's very mean, young woman," Reverend Willard said. Helga was now confused and alarmed herself.

"Must I bring my face into the light?" she said, her eyes welling up with tears from a mixture of fear and the stench of herring on the Reverend's clothing.

"No, I can see you from here." Willard said. *"Step aside, woman, their lives are in danger!"*

Possessing an unjustifiably large ego and a flair for the dramatic, Willard rushed into the tiny cabin without waiting for his eyes adjust to the darkness inside. As a result, the Reverend tripped over his black hooded cloak, ran face first into the wall where the girls hung their puppets, and slid limply to floor. Hearing the uproar, Elga dropped her shovel and rushed to the front of the house. Helga rushed to the backyard to find Elga. Halfway in between they collided and fell to pieces in each other's arms, trembling with fear.

Helga didn't know what Willard meant by saying that their lives were in danger, and Elga didn't know what the hell was going on at all. As they held one another, Helga looked down over Elga's shoulder and noticed that the hem of her sister's ankle-length black skirt was uncharacteristically dragging on the ground. Elga was customarily as neat as a pin. Looking closer, she could see that it wasn't just the hem that was on the ground: it was nearly a third of the dress.

Helga stepped back to look at her sister. Then she stopped breathing.

Regrettably, like most people of the time, the girls were victims of a hodgepodge of superstitions that ranged from "step on a crack, break your mother's back" to holding your breath in a graveyard to avoid breathing in a wayward soul. While every superstition was forbidding, the one that scared the sisters most claimed that anyone who broke a mirror would suffer seven years' of bad luck. To guarantee that they would never break a mirror, Helga and Elga simply decided not to own one. Had the girls owned even a tiny mirror, they may have spared themselves an afternoon of heart-pounding, sphincter-clenching bewilderment.

Looking at her sister, it occurred to Elga that everything about her was in its place, but little of it seemed right.

Helga's stiff, black leather boots were fine. Her regular, "I'm-not-going-out-of-the-cabin-today" blue wool stockings were concealed under her skirt, which was perfectly normal. Her white apron was on top of her black skirt, and her violet petticoat was on top of that as it should be.

The only thing distinctive was that all three pieces of clothing looked as if they had come loose from where they were tied and gathered. In fact, they looked like they were barely hanging on and were about to slide off her waist. Her waistcoat was also unusual. It looked as if it had tripled in size just since breakfast. Her shift, which had been snug around her neck a few hours earlier, now had enough room for a small family.

Helga's hair was a different color, too. It was hanging down and covering her face, an oddity since she had been sporting her usual gauzy-looking orangey red Mohawk all day. Elga took a step forward and gently touched her sister's arm.

"What happened to you, darling?" Elga asked. Helga looked back at her, seemingly confused.

"*Me? What happened to you?*" Helga asked, struggling for air and barely able to form the words. Her voice was shaking, and tears were streaming down her face.

Literally up to her knees in the work of digging a new latrine, Elga hadn't paid attention to anything other than getting the sweaty, foul job finished.

She hadn't noticed that her clothes were sliding off.

She didn't know that her wispy red hair had become thick and blonde or that she'd lost more than half of herself and what was left had been drastically reorganized.

She was clueless that she'd been transformed into the kind of first-class hottie that made young Miss Gundry look like partially-digested meatloaf.

She had no idea that her beloved twin sister was now her twin in a hot new body and face, too.

Overcome with a head-spinning mixture of sheer joy and mind-blowing disbelief, Helga and Elga had to sit down before they both collapsed from emotional stress. As each other's only mirror, it wasn't surprising that they couldn't take their eyes off one another, turning every which way to make sure that one was exactly as beautiful as the other down to the dimples in their butt cheeks. At a point, it actually became all too much: too much beauty and too much change all too fast. It was as if they'd transformed from frogs to peacocks in the blink of an eye without a chance to catch their breath.

Unfortunately, the girls had little time to enjoy their new situation. No more than 30 feet away, Reverend Willard was regaining consciousness after hitting the wall full force with the left side of his face. It was so badly swollen that he couldn't open his left eye. To add to his problems, the vision in his right eye had been blurry for years, the result of a fellatio mishap that left his Indian girlfriend toothless and hard of hearing.

Helga and Elga rushed to the Reverend's side and sat him upright. Helga's heart skipped a beat when she remembered that Willard still had potentially frightening news to deliver. He was "droobling", a popular term in the day for drooling and wobbling at the same time.

"Why are Elga and I in danger?" she asked. Willard tried to focus on her face but couldn't see anything more than a fuzzy outline.

"Dick," he said. Helga thought his answer was wholly inappropriate and told him so. She wasn't about to whip his little pilgrim into a frenzy when their lives were at risk.

RIGORMORTIE

"*No, no!*" Willard said, shaking his head. His voice was thick and scary-sounding. "*He and Palomino are coming here to kill you! Kill you both!*"

"Because we wouldn't lick his eyeballs?" Helga asked, shocked that Dick could be pissed off enough about that to commit murder. Even through his massive swelling, she could tell that the Reverend was giving her a funny look. He didn't quite know how to respond other than to just keep talking.

"There I was at the witch show preaching the gospel to the crowds of idolaters and fornicators," he replied. "And the next thing I knew, Dick was loudly proclaiming that you two are witches. He said that you had two men murdered by rats. And that they were wearing women's clothing."

"Who was wearing women's clothing? The men?" asked Helga.

"*No! No!*" said the Reverend. "*The rats!* And they had little hats, too!"

"I see," Helga said, scanning the area to make sure that Willard couldn't reach anything sharp. Elga leaned forward and sniffed his breath for alcohol. The stench flowing from his pie hole was horrible beyond belief, vaguely like fresh sewage with a pinch of gangrene; however, it didn't seem to have even a hint of rum, wine, or Crazy Bark in it. She was afraid that the Reverend was sober.

She motioned for her sister to follow her out of Willard's earshot.

"Could he be telling the truth? I mean, could Dick really have said that?" Elga whispered.

"I don't know," Helga said. The thought made her shudder. She was growing more anxious by the minute.

"*This is excellent!*" Elga said.

"*Excellent?*" Helga asked, looking at her sister as if she had lost her mind. "*There are men coming to kill us! And the poor Reverend! He's in such terrible pain!*"

"*Kill him! Kill them all!*" Elga said. Her voice dropped so low when she said "all" that it must have come from a very dark place inside her. Helga was visibly taken aback. She'd never heard Elga say anything pricklier than "Oh, Bunny Buns!"

"No, no, dear!" Elga said, trying to comfort her sister. "It's excellent because we can leave! We can leave this hellhole and that stupid outhouse seat behind and start our lives all over again. And we can go anywhere we want!"

183

"No one even knows what we look like now. Not even this nackle-assed lobcock," she continued, pointing at Willard. Helga felt like she had the wind knocked out of her again. She was shocked that her sister would call him a run-down, lifeless dick. Helga didn't think he was boring at all.

"Don't you understand what's happened?" she said. "We're real fucking witches. On top of that, we're hotter than sheep in a fucking sauna. I mean, look at these fucking bodies!"

"*They can all eat it and beat it, baby!*" Elga added in a voice that was as excited as it was emphatically horny.

"Well ..." Helga said softly after taking a hard breath. "I guess we can't stay here. But where will we go? What will we do?"

"*Let's go to New York!*" Elga replied, shocking the hell out of Helga who had never dreamed of traveling so far from home.

"Oh, Helga, dear! We're free!" she said as she twirled around like a princess at a royal ball. "I want to party!"

"What do *you* want, dear?" Elga asked her sister. The love in her voice was palpable.

"I don't want my stool to *ever* speak to me that way again," replied Helga who had lower expectations from life than her twin. "It was *very* demanding and I was *very* embarrassed."

"You'll never have to take any crap from that shit again, darling. *I guarantee it!*" Elga said.

She put her arm around Helga's shoulders and gave her a hug.

"I need your help with something," Elga said, brushing Helga's thick blonde hair from her brow. Elga stooped slightly to look into her twin's downcast eyes.

"It has to do with Dick and Palomino. It'll cheer you up!" she added in a playful, sing-songy tone.

"What's that?" Helga asked in a voice so small that it was barely above a whisper.

Tick, Tock. Saturday, 5:02 a.m.
The wooden bed frame cracked again.

This time a splinter the size of a man's leg fired into Mortie's left flank like a rocket and lanced his gut like a shish kabob. Filth flew onto everything from the clothes Constance Anne had left on the floor to the dirty, rust-stained wall below the window air conditioning unit.

Having done an excellent job of holding herself together for quite some time, she finally started to lose it. She kicked her feet and bowed her back in a fast, savage attempt to free herself from underneath him. When it was clear that she was only expending what little energy she had left and was probably making her situation worse, she burst into tears of anger, frustration, and unadulterated terror.

Constance Anne realized that she was going to die.

If she could have seen herself in a mirror, people would have been able to hear her screams for miles. She was the color of pewter. Her lips were death-like and badly cracked from dehydration, and her hair, which had turned stiff from a mixture of anonymous bodily fluids, looked like greasy rags. Just to top it off, she desperately needed something to cool the fiery redness in her right eye, the likely result of a hemorrhage or two from violent blood pressure spikes.

The condition of the rest of her was anybody's guess. The shooting pains that felt like jolts of electricity through her legs had begun to wane sometime earlier and were now a dull ache. Her arms had tingling sensations that didn't get any better but mercifully didn't get any worse. She didn't know if that was good news or bad, although it really didn't matter. She wasn't expecting to use her body very much anyway, at least until she'd spent some quality time in an intensive care unit.

When a passing car's headlights momentarily injected light into the room, she was able to see the grayish-blue outline of the gantry and its shiny hardware. It was lying on its side, partly catty-corner across the lower part of the bed and partly on the floor where it had toppled over after a violent shaking.

She had a tiny smile of satisfaction on her face over the mere fact that she could remember it. Things were coming back to her, albeit slowly.

A little later, she found herself getting hungry. That was just too fucking crazy to deal with.

CHAPTER 11

*"Dick's scream was the first and the loudest, at least by default,
because Palomino was unable to make a sound."*

Elga hurried to the house to get the grimoire.

As she reached the front door, she had to take a large step over Willard whose incessant moaning had become terribly annoying. Instead of her foot coming down on the far side of the Reverend's left leg, it hit his knee cap and broke it.

Unmoved by what she had done, Elga continued through the door, even as his moans turned into blood-curdling screams.

Elga and Helga whipped through the pages of the book of spells until Elga found one nasty enough to suit her. Pointing to the ingredients required for the incantation, she told Helga that they would have to wait until they saw Dick and Palomino in the flesh. Elga also found another spell she thought might come in handy with their guests.

While they waited, the girls hid the still-unconscious Reverend Willard in the sheep pen and put a white rug over his head to help him blend in. Two hours passed before Dick and Palomino galloped into the girls' front yard. Palomino's horse had one of its hooves blow out on the road, and the men had to wait for the rental company to replace the horse with a loaner. Unfortunately, the only thing they had on the lot was a Shetland pony.

"Well, well, well!" Dick said as he dismounted. "Who are you ladies?" His eyes bugged out. He had never seen two such beautiful women in his life.

"My dickth getting hard," Palomino whispered to Dick, leaving drops of saliva on the Magistrate's earlobe. Dick bristled whenever anyone used his name to refer to their skin flute.

"We're the new occupants of this house," Elga said, making the story up as she went along.

"Where are the Frigg sisters?" Dick asked.

"The who?" asked Helga.

"Nathty looking twinth," Palomino interjected, spreading his saliva in a seven-foot radius.

"Sorry, no," Elga said as she ran her fingers through her thick blonde hair. "The place was empty when we got here. Can we do something for you gentlemen?"

"No," said Dick, taking in every inch of their sumptuous bodies. "Our business is with them."

Elga licked her lips so slowly that Palomino's balls nearly detonated. She purposely dropped her handkerchief and bent over far enough to make sure they could see the sexy crimson ribbons that held up her white knee-high hose.

"Wouldn't you rather do business with us?" Helga asked in a voice dripping with sensuality.

At this juncture, most men with sense would pause to make sure they weren't walking into a con. Not Dick and Palomino. Having already turned control of his life over to his dick, Dick dropped the urgency of murdering the Friggs the moment he saw the twins.

As creepy as they come, Palomino yelled "Mommy" and put both of his hands on Helga's rich bosoms.

"Let's play a game," Elga said.

"I love gameth!" said Palomino.

"Me too!" said Dick.

"You'll really like this one," Elga said, chuckling to herself about what tools they were. "First, though, we have to get naked!"

In the blink of an eye, Dick and Palomino pulled off every stitch of clothing, including their boots and stockings. Elga and Helga stripped, too, but much slower in order to wring out every last drop of anticipation. Unlike the men, however, the girls kept their boots and stockings on.

"The game is called Face Charades," Elga said. "We stand behind you and you have to guess the expressions on our faces. If you get them right, we'll go inside the house and make love all night."

"What if we don't geth right?" Palomino asked.

"Then we'll keep playing until you do!" said Helga, who decided to chirp in. Palomino smiled and released a narrow, high-pitched fart that sounded like a little song.

Helga took Palomino's hand and positioned him in front of her while Elga did the same with Dick. Once that was done, the women rolled their hips slowly and intensely against the men's buttocks. When Elga was sure that Dick and Palomino were defenseless, she gave Helga a nod. The girls reached into their boots for scissors and cut hanks of the men's hair. Then, they stuffed the awful-smelling locks in their stockings.

Hypnotized by the rhythm of the women's hips, neither man noticed that Elga put her hands over her eyes and whispered the spell from the grimoire she thought might come in handy:

> Light as day and dark as night,
> Make a memory with no delight.
> Make them panicked, make them shudder,
> A taste of hell for them to discover.
> Black turns white and white turns black,
> Give them both a heart attack.

With that Elga said, "Okay you handsome devils, it's time to guess our expressions!"

"Happineth!" shouted Palomino.

"No," said Elga with a giggle.

"Sadness!" said Dick.

"No!" replied Helga, laughing.

"Okay! Turn around!" said Elga.

For a long moment, the invisible gears that move the world ground to a stop. Everything became still and quiet, so much so that Dick later swore he could see and hear a flower slowly open each of its petals. He remembered Elga extending her hand and saying that she had her eye on him.

Dick's scream was the first and the loudest, at least by default, because Palomino was unable to make a sound.

The girls stood directly in front of the men with their right hands open.

In their palms were their eyeballs and where their eyeballs should have been were deep black holes.

It was hard to tell if both men had suffered heart attacks, brutal psychological trauma, or both. Either way, whatever hit them was devastating. It took more than a day for them to regain consciousness and several months before either man could complete a coherent sentence. Palomino's lisp expanded from just the letter "s" to "a", "e", "i", "o," and "u." A sentence like "She sells sea shells at the sea shore" was nothing more than an unintelligible saliva shower.

Elga loved it when a spell came together. *"This eyeball shit be killa!"* she said to Helga.

The Frigg sisters were quite something to see atop their snow-white stallions as they galloped into the City of New York with their sexy blonde tresses and half-buttoned blouses blowing in the wind. Once they settled into the The Old Boot and Bunion, a chic waterside resort that accepted reservations by carrier pigeon, the sisters opened the grimoire to the book's "Design-A-Curse" chapter.

Still spitting with anger, Elga demanded that her sister join her in not only putting a death hex on Dick and Palomino, but on every first-born male in their families until the end of time.

After putting the men's hair in a box together with some bright green thread, a hammer, and a blunt fashioned in the shape of a man, they cast a hex that would cause future generations to die by their own hands in a manner of speaking:

"A curse on Palominos,
A blight upon the Dicks,
Cruel and foul and mean they are,
Nasty fucking pricks!
This curse to kill each first-born male
And remove them from the world,
When they reach the age of two score years,
Let the flag of death unfurl!
Dispatch a fitting puppet
By enchanted means at night,
One whose look and nature
Drives each man's passions to ignite!
Let them bump and grind their puppets,
Rub inside them hard and long!
Let them love each and all the moments,
Such sweet comfort to their schlongs!
On a day they don't see coming,
An hour they don't expect,
Let them exercise their puppets,
While something evil breaks their necks!
Here's the hair of evil bastards,
Reefer, hammer, emerald thread!
Cast this plague for once and ever,
Speed them to the rotting dead!"

With that, Elga and Helga finished their incantation by kicking the shit out of the box and tossing it into their suite's roaring fireplace. Then they lit up the doobie. Eventually, the girls stopped giggling long enough to remember that they'd left Reverend Willard in the sheep pen. That started them giggling all over again. Either sister could have freed him with a little magic, but no sooner had they'd begun laughing than neither could remember what they'd been laughing about.

𝄞

Three hundred and twenty-odd years later, Constance Anne O'Leary stood on the very spot where the Pipe sisters had gunned down Wainscot and Wormler. Constance Anne didn't know anything about that, of course. All she knew was that she was hot and tired and anxious to go home. With a promise from Tiny Earl the day before to pick her up in Dickie's "Rolling Wheels of Death" van as soon as he finished with Faller's remains, she'd left the funeral and walked to 6th and Allison. There, she caught the bus to Salem to visit Frickey Dickie's grave.

Dickie had been wonderful to her at the car washes, and she had been very sad that Sister Juan hadn't allowed her to attend his services. As far as the good Sister was concerned, there were simply going to be too many cops, middle school teachers, and other car wash customers there that day, and she didn't want her girls exposed. Moreover, Sister Juan thought it was very strange that Dickie was being interred in Salem when his family was from Chelsington. Some people started a rumor that it was an FBI sting, which reduced the number of mourners by nearly 90%.

With Tiny Earl's help, Constance Anne was eventually able to put together enough money to afford the bus fare to Salem; however, she had to lie to Mitzi Jo about where she was going. Mitzi Jo considered her husband's grave sour ground and had personally defiled his headstone by inscribing "Stump Pumper" on it 26 times in different colors of spray paint. She let the wet, sticky blacks, greens, and reds drip down the granite in patterns that were dead-ringers for bloody, gangrened fingers.

After the bus ride, it took Constance Anne almost an hour to walk to the cemetery and another 20 minutes of wandering through tightly-packed graves until she spotted the headstone.

Along with the utter creepiness of the graffiti, the marker had a terrible error on it. The birth and death dates were right, and the photo of the deceased etched on the stone was clearly Frickey Dickie, even though the look on his face wasn't as excited as she was used to seeing. The problem was the name. It said "Frickman Cuthbert Dick." Constance Anne thought that the engraver had run out of room for the last two letters until she noticed that she was standing in a huge field of Dicks.

She was as confused as a blind lesbian in a tuna cannery.

As Constance Anne would eventually discover, the shocking backstory was that Frickey Dickie was a direct descendant of the despicable Magistrate Crockett Cuthbert Dick, also known as the "Plague of Plymouth," the "Bastard of Boston," and the "Stool of Salem."

When Dick died suddenly at the age of 39, his relatives scrambled to bury their connections to the bastard, including changing the family name.

Considering the kind of dick Dick was, he died a fitting death. Looking out the second story window of his opulent home on Andover Street one January afternoon, Magistrate Dick spotted an old woman with a cane struggling to walk down the ice-covered street below him. Feeling himself in high asshole gear, he opened the window, stuck out his head, and started screaming at her just for laughs.

"*Come on you old fuckwagon!*" Dick yelled, smiling as he watched her almost lose her footing. "*I hope you fall down and break your fucking hip!*"

Terrified, hard of hearing, and desperately trying to keep her footing, the old woman thankfully never heard a word out of Dick's filthy mouth.

Hanging from the sill of a window two stories above Dick were seven long, sharply-pointed icicles that had loosened as a result of an uptick in the temperature. At the same moment Dick leaned a little farther forward, four of the icicles came loose, one by one.

The first missed the top of his head by a hundredth of an inch.

The second, which followed in a flash, cut through the back of his head and exited through his mouth.

The third and fourth also entered the back of his head although at higher points, punching his eyes out of their sockets. They landed on the ground side by side.

When the Constable found them an hour later, the eyeballs were staring at each other.

Barely smarter than socks, the Magistrate's family found it hard to choose a name that would hide their identities as Dicks. After rejecting Smith because it was too hard to spell, they eventually agreed to add two letters to make what they thought was a "ballsy" change to Dickie. The new Dickie clan also decided to start a family business, a necessity since their odds of getting hired for anything beyond shaving cat genitals were about zero.

After considering their options, they chose to hitch their wagons to the star of the burgeoning outhouse industry as aftermarket shithole diggers.

Working with shovels was their only marketable talent, and they were surprisingly good at digging the square, 15-foot-deep holes that most families preferred for their decomposing sewer trouts. The Dickies' flair for moving dirt eventually led them to expand into America's growing funeral trade.

Learning the finer points of fraud as they went along, Dickie's Outhouse Excavation and Funeral Emporium erected a huge sign with the slogan, "Where there's a hole, there's a Dickie in it!" Then they opened its doors with a colossal "Meet and Meat" open house. It featured free pony rides, semi-clear drinking water, stewed pork intestines, and marshmallow possum skewers that were available only after guests listened to a brief marketing pitch. The event was the talk of the town for months.

It also paid off handsomely in sales of their innovative "Don't Ask, Don't Tell" special. Cost-conscious consumers could save big bucks by having Dickie's dig a single, extra-deep hole for use as both a cesspool and a grave. Stressing that "The dead won't know the difference, but your pocketbook will!" and giving the buyer the choice of what the hole was used for first, Dickie's salespeople racked up hundreds of orders within weeks. Unfortunately for the fledgling company, most of the specials were bought by men whose wives were horrified by the prospect of burying a loved one under a pile of shit. Almost 90% of the deals were cancelled before the first shovel was picked up.

Although Crockett Dick died before the curse could kill him, DeJon Palomino got more than his share of the whammy on the afternoon of his fortieth birthday.

Alone in the stifling hot Steed-O-Rama City garage, Palomino stretched out under a large female Appaloosa, whipped out a greased horse puppet, and ran it up and down his furlong. Just as he was coming down the stretch, 1,200 pounds of equine collapsed from heatstroke and broke his neck.

Bambi Palomino, his pregnant wife, immediately took control of the company. Over time, she made a fortune by adding predatory loans for indentured servants and "nostril-to-tail" warranties that promised "total horse protection" but barely covered horseshoes, much less expensive parts like legs. The dental coverage sucked, too.

Tick, Tock. Saturday, 6:49 a.m.

Trying to shut out the horror, Constance Anne found the memories of funny stories her mother shared more comforting than she ever imagined. BritNee had turned many of her exploits as a sex worker into bedtime stories for her then-four-year-old daughter.

Constance Anne's favorite was about the time her mommy needed a fast ace and went to the flea market to shake her ass.

Dressed in blue metallic hot pants and a paper-thin tee that showcased her gold nipple rings, BritNee found that she had mutual interests with a horny 70-year-old with a lazy left eye and a taste for electric-powered S&M. The old guy said he'd pay her what she wanted if he could "juice her nips," something she'd never experienced but was certainly willing to try for enough coin.

Twenty minutes later, BritNee found herself naked in his living room in her not quite white, not quite knee-high, patent leather boots. He was outside and she waited for him to come back in for what seemed like forever. The old guy lived in a grimy trailer that straddled a stream in a wooded area along the Northeast Expressway. Littered inside and out with roaches, rats, carrion flowers, and plastic chairs from a Death Row yard sale, the place was a horror show even by her low standards. Not even the hole he had cut in the floor for a water view/indoor toilet combo helped. With hundreds of plastic grocery bags shoved into gaping holes in the walls and ceilings, you could almost hear the place plead for gasoline and a lit match.

Eventually, the geezer walked in the front door with his engorged penis hanging down like a limp rag doll through the right leg of his stained cotton boxers. Curiously, he was holding a set of very long jumper cables attached to the battery of his absurdly oversized truck.

"I want to clamp these gators on your rings," he said, making them spark while coughing up a wad of phlegm onto one of the dancing pineapples that decorated his cheap Aloha shirt.

"Then I'll give my Caddy a lube and take a drive downtown."

"*Really*? And just *how* are you going to get your schlong up?"

She loved to say "schlong," a word she learned from Rabbi Goldenbaum who had a standing appointment with her every Monday. He was uncircumcised and liked her to play "hide the weasel" with his foreskin.

"You ain't seen nuthin' yet," the old man said as he disappeared into the bedroom.

He came back out with something that looked like a bicycle pump with a clear plastic chamber attached. He slid his sad-looking wang into the vagina-like opening in the chamber and pushed a red button. The machine immediately made a loud sucking sound and did something to make his meat twitch, jerking it upward in an unnatural way as if an invisible string was attached to it. In less than a minute, his eyes got misty, the head of his dick swelled up like it had been stung by a bee, and the shaft grew rigid.

"Thank God for Medicare," he said as he reached for the jumper cables. "Now bend over and grab your ankles, honey."

She leaned over, ready for him to clamp on the juice. But instead of feeling the electricity that would have likely killed her, she smelled something burning. Looking upside-down between her legs, she could see the old guy roasting like a turkey, the apparent victim of a short circuit involving the jumper cables that lit him up like a kid in a cupcake store.

As the man stood motionless, staring blankly into space with his Pedro in his hand and smoke rising from his brown velour slippers, she grabbed his money, her clothes, and a six-pack out of the refrigerator. Then she stole the old guy's truck and lived happily ever after until she ran out of Benjamin and had to find another John.

Even though the hellish trailer her mother described was in Massachusetts, Constance Anne thought that it was probably a lot like the seedy Florida motel where she was pretty sure she was going to die.

Originally named "The Lambskin Lodge," the three-story, 39-room, three-bathroom motel was built in 1963 by former Cosa Nostra hitman Ottavio Fartullo. Fartullo and his wife, Mindy, wanted to offer a warm, inviting home for Sicilian immigrants murdering their way to the top of the Florida orange juice industry. To make the construction project easier, Fartullo developed a close working relationship with the city's building inspector. The camaraderie allowed the inspector to keep breathing in exchange for ignoring codes governing the roof, walls, electrical, plumbing, windows, and floors.

To decorate the place, the Fartullos bought the entire stock of beautifully-crafted drapes, headboards, and linens from a super-low-priced clearance outlet. Because the store's inventory came from crime scene cleaners and was typically blood-soaked, they painted the headboards black and bleached the sheets, towels, and pillow cases until the stains turned to a sickly shade of pink. If anyone complained about the splotches, flecks, or the enduring smells of death, they were told that they'd have to leave a note about it for Al Capone. The Sicilians, who were unaware that the infamous American criminal had died in 1947, thought that was the coolest shit they'd ever heard.

In 1964, the entire Lambskin Lodge suddenly collapsed during a light rain, killing seven registered guests, a janitor, and nine unidentified ferrets that were in the bridal suite. Fartullo, who had only insured the hotel against arson, hurriedly left the country.

The Lodge stood in ratshit-covered ruins until 1991. Late that year, Belvin Beech bought the land to fulfill his dream of founding a White Christian motor hotel. Beech wanted a piece of the lucrative Jesus-centered, Old Testament-oriented, hellfire-and-brimstone and sacrificial lamb-focused Florida tour bus vacation market. To attract his target customers, he planned to name it "The Cowonojimbag," an anagram for Christian-only, White-only, No Jews, Indians, Mexicans, Blacks, Asians, or Gays. Moreover, he wanted to promote it with the catchy slogan, "Where Would Jesus Stay? The Cowonojimbag, for Christ's Sake!"

Had Beech been a religious man himself, things might have gone better. Easily influenced by deep, bouncy cleavage, he made bad decisions from the start. Before even breaking ground, Belvin spent half of his construction loan on lush carpeting and marble bathroom tiles at the urging of steamy Carpet and Tile Planet sales rep Crystal Snoorplowski. A go-getter who knew how to close a sale, she spent three hours whispering deliciously hot things in Beech's ear while gently stroking his Hiawatha. Instead of giving him a good "vacuum cleaning" immediately after the sale as he expected, the only immediate things 22-year-old Crystal did were collect her spectacular commission and take her boyfriend to Hawaii.

With few options available, Beech slashed the construction budget. He cut the number of rooms by half, sliced the size of each room by 40%, and had the pool dug only three feet deep. Rather than building the floors out of concrete, he used drywall, and instead of erecting a brightly-lit sign to promote the motel at night, he taped a flashlight to a tree and pointed it at the front door. Beech took the remaining $100,000 and, like Ottavio Fartullo before him, gave the building inspector a healthy incentive to look the other way.

Not surprisingly, the Cowonojimbag's first six months were bad and, as customer reviews went up on the internet, the next six months got worse. Despite adding in-room Communion, discounts for evangelicals on "Moses Mondays," and a gift shop that sold honey-covered locusts for "a real taste of the Bible," the motel's bottom-line kept sinking. Eventually, Beech had no choice other than to modify his business plan.

Contrary to his original path to success that kept people of certain races, creeds, and colors out, the new strategy let everybody in. Truly a man who had seen the light, he renamed the motel La Cama Cheapo and opened its doors to anyone and everyone attracted to perma-fried whores, hot railed crank, and all night PNPs. Altogether, the changes delivered 95% average occupancy and the kind of clientele that paid up-front in cash and didn't give a shit about the carpeting.

Within three months of changing direction, Belvin had made back every dime he had blown on not getting blown by Miss Snoorplowski and enough extra to add ten rooms exclusively for lunch hour clown sex.

After 20 years of "deferred maintenance," a euphemism for letting the motel go to hell, Belvin dumped the job of running La Cama Cheapo on his son, Mortie. A man with a complex personality that comprised equal shares of kindheartedness, self-loathing, and homicidal rage directed at his parents, he ran off every whore, junkie, and dealer and wrecked the business just to piss off his asshole mommy and daddy. It was amazing what one little fib could do. Best known as "J," Jorge Juan Jose Joaquin Jerico Javier Jaime Julian Jesus Jeronimo Julio Jacinto de Jackson held the uncontested title as the world's most vicious drug lord after crucifying the grandmother of a guy that owed him $100. An hour after Mortie posted signs that said, *"Welcome, J! Gracias for buying the motel!"* the place was a ghost town.

Mortie kept Room 209 for his private use, held a few others for ordinary customers, and rented out the rest to people who were down on their luck. Sometimes he would accidentally-on-purpose forget to collect their rent.

The 187 gallons of liquid expelled from the waterbed in Room 209 had thoroughly saturated every inch of the cheap drywall flooring beneath it. Squishy and foul, the floor was sagging inch-by-inch with the bed, Constance Anne, and Mortie all stacked up at the single weakest point.

On the ground floor of the motel directly below Constance Anne, 32-year-old Wayne Elmer Smeethe, Jr. was thinking about killing his wife. She had mortified him by wearing pink checkerboard shorts that made her look like a gay picnic table and deserved to die for it. Smeethe decided that he'd tell her to lean over and watch closely as he lowered a frozen turkey from a distance with a rod and reel into a boiling turkey fryer. Once the bird met the smoking-hot fryer, there would be a giant "kaboom" and then, "Bye-Bye, Bridie" as the explosion blew her head into the next week.

With darkly-stained teeth, filthy fingernails, and an odor like an un-flushed toilet, Smeethe was a textbook sociopath who had no conscience and felt no remorse or empathy. He was so cold, in fact, that his heartrate never rose a single beat even when he was beating the mailman over a misdelivered advertising circular. Smeethe was at La Cama Cheapo because it was Saturday. Every Saturday morning for the past six months he'd met blonde, 27-year-old Tiffany Hollandaise at the motel and rode her until his balls were dry. Despite their regular fuckfests, Smeethe didn't like the rail-thin, flat-chested, bowlegged woman's body and told her so to her face every week. If that wasn't enough of a confidence-booster, he regularly reminded her that she was nothing more than "chlamydia on legs."

Not surprisingly, the disgust was mutual.

Regrettably for Tiffany, Smeethe was her boss at Just Lance the Damn Thing!, a boutique medical practice that touted itself as "Florida's Economy Boil and Cyst Drainers." He made it clear that he'd fire her from her $7.25-an-hour position as a pus accumulator if she didn't do his bidding. With a small child and no one to rely on but herself, she desperately needed the healthcare coverage that came with the job. Despite the fact that benefits at Just Lance the Damn Thing! had been gutted when they were acquired by global behemoth American Boil & Cyst, what little remained was better than nothing. Even though very few things were covered, she slept better knowing that if she got cancer from a meteorite she was friggin' golden.

Although he didn't care for her physique, Smeethe actually liked having Tiffany as a fuck buddy because she seemed the least likely of the women he had authority over to fight back. He was right about that. He was also right that she would be the least likely to scream or laugh at him. Having been involved in a horrible penis accident at one time, Smeethe was prickly about his junk.

Several years earlier, Smeethe had been sexually harassed by JoJo Rackenmeyer, the company's human resources manager. An attractive woman, Rackenmeyer was so oddly turned on by unclean men with bad teeth that she was known to troll for sex in homeless shelters. When she was done fucking them, she kept their stained underwear as souvenirs. In Smeethe's case, Rackenmeyer threatened to accuse him of rape if he didn't comply with her demands. Among other things, she liked to be entered at high speed several times until she got down to serious fucking. That usually involved having her lover run across the room, leap into the air and, in one continuous move, faultlessly guide his Willy Weasel inside her quim. It was like a baseball player sliding headfirst into home plate.

After three amazingly successful plunges in a row, Smeethe missed and rammed his purple piccolo into her right thigh at full speed. The pain was so overpowering that he was convinced his longfellow had been snapped in half. After he begged Rackenmeyer for 30 minutes to take him to a doctor, she finally drove him to the Boring Memorial Hospital ER. Bent over and unable to take anything more than tiny steps, it took Smeethe an agonizing ten minutes to walk the 25 feet from the ER entrance to the registration desk. Rackenmeyer stayed with him, although only to find out when he'd be back in service.

"May I help you?" a young man in a tie asked from behind the desk. Sick of the never-ending parade of freaks, addicts, and black plague carriers that traipsed through the ER every day, he didn't even look at Smeethe.

"I need a doctor...," Smeethe whispered unintelligibly.

"What?" asked the admitting clerk. "You'll have to speak up if you want me to help you. What's wrong?"

"I think I broke my..." Smeethe said. The words dropped off in a garbled mess.

"*I can't hear you!*" the clerk shouted.

"I think I broke my penis," Smeethe said much louder than he wanted to.

"*You think you broke your dick?*" the clerk shouted at the top of his lungs. The crowded waiting room erupted in squeals of laughter.

A doctor just finishing with a chronic fish odor patient heard the commotion. After biting his tongue to stop snickering, he motioned Smeethe to come in. After ogling Rackenmeyer's magnificently-assembled body, he told her to come in, too.

"*You broke your dick?*" the doctor asked as loud as possible. The words attracted other medical professionals who knew that this was going to be a special career moment.

"Well, you can hurt it badly, but you really can't break it," the doctor said. "It's tissue, not a bone."

After examining it and determining that the injury wasn't serious, the doctor assigned the most junior nurse to inspect Smeethe's sausage at unnecessarily close range. Then, the doctor had an idea.

"We'll fix you up right here," he said.

Trying not to laugh like a hyena, the doctor reached into a drawer and took out two tongue depressors. He put one on top and one under Smeethe's trouser beast and wrapped it up with tape until it looked like an Egyptian mummy.

"Now go home, take two aspirins, and don't touch your junk for two weeks."

"She's good lookin'," the doctor said as Rackenmeyer paraded her tight ass and creamy cleavage out of the ER with Smeethe in tow, "but I wouldn't break my dick over her."

With the excitement over, the Boring Memorial staff went back to a regular day of pulling small plastics and white mice from elderly rectums. Two weeks later, JoJo Rackenmeyer dumped Smeethe and took up with a Buddhist bus driver with elephant skin disease and a constant erection.

Because Rackenmeyer demanded to ride Smeethe's hot dog right away, his penis never properly healed. His purple-headed warrior had an inch-high hump in the middle and swayed so far to the right that it looked like it was trying to make a U turn. For the rest of his life, he had to position himself at a 90-degree angle to piss in a urinal.

With a thang that resembled a roller-coaster, Smeethe's approach to sexual anything required time and concentration. Putting his beagle in the dog house through the back door, so to speak, could easily take 15 to 30 minutes of twisting and turning himself just to get in the right position. With that and dandruff so plentiful that roaches used his shoulders as a ski resort, it wasn't surprising that Smeethe didn't notice what seemed like snow falling on that sunny, hot Florida day.

"Come on, you worthless slut," Smeethe said while giving Tiffany what little he could muster from his sideways doggy-style position. He called Tiffany nasty names because she reminded him of Mrs. Crotchelm, his sixth grade teacher. He guessed that Tiffany might like being called a 'worthless slut' while they were fucking just like Mrs. Crotchelm did.

Flakes of plaster came down from the ceiling like a winter blizzard, followed by an ear-splitting *"Boom!"* that sounded like a very big bomb going off. Although Smeethe told Tiffany it was nothing, common sense told her otherwise.

As Tiffany scrambled for cover and her clothes, Smeethe felt something wet strike his cheek. He looked straight up to see waterlogged clumps of brown plaster hit his shoulder. Then there was a loud rumble as a refrigerator-size slab of dry rot, fiberglass insulation and human waste hit the floor and exploded into a thousand tiny fragments.

Stunned, Smeethe looked up again and opened his mouth in a silent scream. A thick, gooey ball of wet fungus roared past his front teeth and settled halfway down his throat. He might have screamed again when the late Mortie Beech and the air conditioner came down on top of him, but he had already choked to death.

Because first responders had been summoned to La Cama Cheapo so often over the years, calls about escaped goldfish had a higher 911 priority than emergencies at the motel. When the police, firefighters, and EMTs arrived later that morning, they saw that 90% of the building had been flattened like a pancake, and the rest was a disaster. Witnesses said that the entire structure literally came down in seconds. The question on everybody's mind wasn't if there was anyone alive, but how many were dead.

Across the street, two young women with blonde hair sat on the broken pieces of concrete that made up the curb. Glassy-eyed and disheveled, they held each other's hand so tightly that their flesh was colorless. When a police officer approached to ask them what they knew about the motel disaster, they said they hadn't seen a thing.

He believed them.

Other than an ungodly stench on the skimpy outfits they were wearing, there was nothing about the girls that was out of the ordinary. In that neighborhood, there were more half-naked kids with empty fucking stares than you could throw a stick at. Had the cop known that Tiffany had just put on her bra and shorts and loaned Constance Anne her shirt and panties, he might have looked at it differently.

Constance Anne felt a low, nervous laugh rise from deep inside her. She looked at Tiffany whose mouth and eyes were wide open with excitement like a five-year-old on Christmas morning.

Then they both started laughing, although neither knew completely why.

All they knew was that they had just met on top of a bathroom sink as everything fell to pieces.

Smiling, they walked off together in search of frozen yogurt.

CHAPTER 12

"His body was ... run over by at least 25 customers who were texting and paid no attention to the 'thump-thump' under their tires."

Constance Anne was worried sick.

It wasn't like Tiny Earl to blow her off and, after waiting almost three hours for him to pick her up in Salem, she found herself nervously pacing back and forth and wringing her hands. Considering that he was 250 pounds overweight and had veins with more sour cream in them than blood, she was terrified that he might have had a heart attack behind the wheel. For all she knew, Earl was lying in a ditch somewhere alone, frightened, and inching towards death. The very idea made her sob inconsolably.

Since Earl would have likely taken Western Avenue and Essex Street to meet her at the cemetery, Constance Anne decided to walk the 12 miles back to Chelsington along the same route. She prayed that Earl would suddenly drive up in the black Dickie's Funeral Home van muttering a million embarrassed apologies. She'd pretend not to accept them, of course, all the while feeling so happy and relieved that she was about to burst. She loved him like a father and, given the events of the last few days, needed his advice and counsel more than ever.

Even though Constance Anne didn't like to admit it, Spruce Faller's death was a godsend. Naively, she had hoped that his demise might also put the brakes on the rest of the school's sexual predators. It didn't, of course, and the morning after Faller stopped breathing, the remaining Chomo Club members hunted her down like Bambi on the first day of deer season.

English teacher Lilac Rosselli, the "Horny Hunchback of Notre Blough," tracked Constance Anne to a stall in the school ladies' room and wriggled under the door head first until her face was squarely in Constance Anne's naked crotch. Probably less surprised by this development than the average person sitting on a toilet, Constance Anne lost no time grabbing Rosselli by the neck, plunging her head under the dark, motionless commode water, and holding it there. Then she flushed the bowl every 20 seconds while she hummed the theme from *Titanic* seventeen times. By the sixth flush, Rosselli knew that she'd never be able to look at a toilet the same way again. By the twelfth, she was too psychologically damaged to ever use one again.

Not to be outdone, Licker Store Clark broke into Constance Anne's school locker one night and transformed the dull gray interior into something very special. No more than five minutes after Constance Anne opened the door the following morning, half of the student body and all of the faculty had heard her scream and rushed to her locker. There was a collective gasp as they shoved each other out of the way to shoot something epic like Eloni Running Bear Johnson-Gonzalez's Faller video. Inside was a collection of porno photos so indecent that they were later used in hospitals to test how much weird stuff medical students could handle. Each photo had a cutout of Constance Anne's face glued on one of the happy, smiling participants and Clark's face on one or more sex toys the smiling, happy participants were using. Although she did a nice job of gluing her portrait on pictures of rabbits and anal plugs, Clark clearly did her best work on the huge heads of lifelike mega-dildos.

As horrible as that was, the next day's events were actually worse.

Assuming that Constance Anne would be the first one to open the locker before the first period bell rang in the morning, Clark stuffed herself inside it like a Jack-in-the Box. She waited until she heard the dial on the combination lock turn and, when the door opened, sprang out in nothing but a big red bow and a twisted smile. Mr. Diaz, the janitor, who unbolted the locker because he sniffed something "muy mal" inside it, freaked and drew the aerosol can of roach spray he carried on his belt like a pistol. With a trigger finger that had sent more than one varmint to its grave, he fired. The insecticide exploded out of the nozzle and soaked every inch of Clark's stringy grey hair and shriveled, ankle-length boobs. Then he beat her with his shoe.

Regardless of what Rosselli, Clark, and creepy Percy Flagroot, who begged her to "pull his wee wee" did, Constance Anne thought that Blough's principal was actually the worst of the lot.

An arrogant, 64-year-old ex-pothole filler with wispy tufts of black ear hair and an unanchored left eye, Otho "Scoop" Beck had made it clear that he wanted Constance Anne to bear his children. To make sure she got the picture, Beck described everything about it out loud every day as he followed her home from school. At one time, in fact, he walked so closely behind her that she got a buzz from his bourbon-drenched breath. Now, thanks to a restraining order, all Beck could do was stand on the sidewalk outside of Dickie's, pray to catch a glimpse of Constance Anne through a window, and wait for his hollow-eyed, abused wife to pick him up near dawn. This happened every day, Monday through Saturday. On Sundays, he was busy with church.

After slugging down a fifth of 190-proof grain alcohol one Thursday night, Beck left his spot on the sidewalk, puked his guts out, and crept under Constance Anne's bedroom window. He meowed like a kitten in distress, irrationally hoping that he could kidnap Constance Anne when she opened the window to investigate the noise. Very fucked up, Beck forgot which window was which and accidentally woke up Mitzi Jo Dickie's "baby", a dog with a lot of unresolved anger towards cats. "Morgue," a 30-inch-high, 219-pound, drooling and perpetually horny English Mastiff, went ham over the kitty noises, sprinted out the back door of the building, and turned his immense, hairy body and huge jaws into a panting, slobbering love train aimed at Beck's crotch. Somewhere down the street, the dog could be heard growling and barking loudly. Witnesses heard only moans out of Beck.

Although Constance Anne couldn't have known it at the time, the end of the sexual harassment festival wasn't all that far away.

Traumatized by the constant flushing, Rosselli developed intensely painful constipation and died six months later at the hands of a jalapeno pepper that wedged itself in her colon. Several months after that, Licker Store passed away from vaginal mold, a grave condition that she refused to treat because she delighted in the itch and bleu cheese-like aroma. Beck, Flagroot, and Morgue entered into a committed, three-way relationship, moved to Vermont the next year, and opened a discreet adult dog breeding resort. They were never heard from again.

⅄

About two miles into her walk, Constance Anne heard one of her favorite electro tunes pulsing from somewhere over the hill behind her and, as the music came closer, looked over her shoulder to investigate the source. Coming down the hill a few hundred feet away was the coolest sports car she'd ever seen. An ice-blue convertible with a thick white racing stripe down the center, it was so expertly polished that Constance Anne found it practically hypnotizing, laughing to herself that it clearly wasn't the product of a St. Woody's car wash. Compact and close to the ground, the two-seater had hood-mounted, bug-eyed headlights, and a shiny, half-moon-shaped grille that made the front look just like a pair of eyes, a nose, and a smile.

At about a hundred feet away, she could see that the driver had dark hair. He or she was wearing sunglasses and a dark polo shirt with a popped collar.

At 50 feet, she could see that the car's tonneau cover was navy blue.

At 40 feet, she could see that the tires were so glossy you could probably see your reflection in them.

At 20 feet, her heart started pounding.

Slowing down to look at her was the closest thing Constance Anne had ever seen to a Greek god. His perfectly symmetrical face, sea-blue eyes, neatly trimmed black hair, chiseled features, and tanned, golden brown, clean-shaven skin made her lightheaded. As if his face alone wasn't enough to piss off every male on the planet, he had broad shoulders and a muscular upper body.

It was Jason Frosse.

He pulled over on the side of the road and pushed his sunglasses up on top of his head.

"Constance Anne!" Jason shouted excitedly. "It's so great to see you. What are you doing way out here?"

Constance Anne was smiling so broadly that she couldn't speak. She found him intoxicating. He was sweating a little, and she wanted to lick his face.

"Are you going to Chelsington?" he asked.

She nodded slowly in a dazed sort of way. She was staring at him so intently that she wasn't even blinking.

"Okay, come on. I'll give you a ride" he said, reaching over to open the door. Although Constance Anne didn't notice it at the time, the car didn't have outside door handles. Like its owner, the ride was way too cool for anything ordinary. When Jason Frosse was ready to roll, he didn't need no stinkin' door. He vaulted into the car like a secret agent.

Afraid that they may never see him again, all of the girls and some of the boys at Dickie's cried when Jason quit his job selling cremation urns. More than just splendidly handsome, Jason was unusually generous and compassionate. Even more, he had the stunning ability to sense if someone was sad just by looking at them and always knew the right thing to say or do to make them feel better. He was so popular, in fact, that people would mark their calendars to remember when he was scheduled to pay Mitzi Jo a visit. More than a few employees referred to him as "Tingle" because of the happy sensations he radiated like light.

Constance Anne had taken his leaving particularly hard. They had become friends, although Constance Anne wouldn't have wasted a second jumping his bones if he didn't think of her as a little sister. Partly because he wasn't trying to get in her pants like all the other men she'd met, she trusted him implicitly. Even more, they had one of those rare relationships in which the conversation never lags because the people involved are in absolute sync.

Faced with the prospect of having to club Mitzi Jo's old gray hamster every day for half the business he used to get, he took an exceptionally well-paying job driving an 80-foot passenger bus roundtrip between Boston and Oldmens.

He had literally just bought his shiny sports car in Salem and was driving home to Chelsington when he came across Constance Anne. Despite her big, goofy smile, Jason could tell that she was under a lot of strain. It wasn't surprising, then, that Constance Anne fired off every one of her worries about money, the Chomo Club, and her future for the next hour or so, both on the road and in a tattered red booth at the Pizza 'n Clam Trough restaurant on Route 107. She was scared that the scumbag Chomos would stop her from graduating. Even worse, she'd lose her job and home at Dickie's. She had a 'no excuses' deal with Mitzi Jo that required her to finish high school.

Crying and feeling a little queasy from a Shrimp and Chocolate Chip pizza with Gorgonzola cheese, Constance Anne said that she wished she could move away. Always ready to help, Jason told her that he'd see if the bus company was hiring. When they arrived in Chelsington, Constance Anne asked Jason to drop her off a block away from Dickie's so that Mitzi Jo, who still considered Jason's drumstick her personal property, wouldn't see them together.

Before she got out, she smiled and kissed him softly on his cheek. Then she put her hand on his thigh, pressed her lips against his ear, and whispered a breathy 'thank you'. She left him with a hot, tingling sensation that ran from his balls straight up through the top of his head and back down again. He was so happily incapacitated from it that he had to wait for his right leg to stop shaking involuntarily before he could drive off.

After three long days of checking her phone for a text every 30 seconds, Constance Anne finally heard from Jason again. When his number flashed on her phone, her heart raced in hopes that he wanted her body. Instead, his call was about a job opening at the bus company. If she played her cards right, he told her, she could enjoy a new career as what the HR department called a "Luxury Ideation Catalyst." The job posting described the position as "…a mission-critical interface with end-users that enhances customer delight and raises the company's return on invested capital." Although no one in HR could explain what the position actually involved or why it paid less than the minimum wage, Constance Anne applied for it anyway and kept the pen.

On her way out, she was pleasantly surprised to bump into her friend, Michael Spacchio. The Spaz worked there part-time as a "Conveyance Immaculator," removing chewing gum from under the bus seats. Despite that, he still wore a suit and tie every day. That made her smile. It was nice to know that some things never changed.

Massachusetts-based Lobstah Coach, LLC operated a fleet of a hundred long-haul, 350-passenger buses out of Boston on 80 routes across the United States, Canada, Mexico, and the Yucatan Peninsula. Thanks to increases in airline fares, 30% reductions in seat width, and carry-on charges of up to $100 for purses and briefcases, Lobstah Coach grew from an average of 50,000 passengers a year to more than a million in less than two years.

The trip from Boston to Oldmens was typical of the Lobstah Coach travel experience. It covered more than 1,400 miles, took 22 ass-breaking hours, and brazenly disregarded more than a dozen interstate transportation laws. To operate as cheaply as possible, the company used only one driver per round trip and carried two tack-welded 500-gallon gas tanks on the roof to avoid refueling. Once it left Boston, the bus didn't stop until it reached North Carolina and a 30-minute restroom break in the woods behind a Chinese-Armenian restaurant on I-95.

To make the trip more enjoyable, the company sold passengers huge bags of French fries, gigantic doughnuts, huge sodas, male enhancement pills, tissues, mixed drinks, beer, and deodorizers before they boarded. They also rented pajamas, slippers, lingerie, bedpans, travel urinals, pillows, blankets, and bondage kits. As it happened, the pillow guy had been caught buffing his clown on a feather-filled 12"x16" travel sizer in the company break room just the day before. Since he'd already received four written warnings about that particular hobby, Lobstah Coach let him go and deducted the cost of the defiled pillow from his last check.

Not convinced that Constance Anne could handle the stress of the job, the rentals supervisor hired her part-time on a trial basis. After a few days' experience, she realized that the pillow game was far trickier than she thought.

Despite an ad campaign that touted how clean the buses were, the truth was that the company rarely cleaned, washed, or replaced anything that wasn't putrefying. Management's thinking was simple: without restrooms on the bus, passengers were so distracted that they didn't give a damn if the stain they were sitting on was water or liver bile. Nevertheless, veteran rental reps stressed that it was critical to only show prospective customers, or "chumps" as they called them, the unstained portion of a pillow while convincing them to cough up a never-to-be-refunded $25 deposit and a $5 rental fee. As Constance Anne quickly discovered, it was far from easy to hide the stains since most were either so large or in so many layers that they'd covered the original white pillows and cases with a sickly, yellowish-green color.

The good part of the job was that it was easy to rent to men as long as she wore a tight tube top and kept licking her lips. Although she was paid a generous commission on the deposit, the downside was that she was occasionally docked for physical damage to the pillows. The Florida route could be pretty rough, and more than a few pillows were returned ripped, torn, gnawed, and partially eaten. One even came back with regurgitated foam tucked inside the pillowcase.

The great part of the job, though, was the company's sales incentive program. The rep with the most rentals would get a free one-way ticket to Oldmens.

Constance Anne intended to win that ticket if it killed her.

Despite her escalating fatigue from overwork, anxiety, depression, a urinary tract infection, a poor diet, and lack of sleep, the next several weeks passed happily enough. It might have continued that way had it not been for her missing breakfast and lunch one Thursday and a single event late that night that no one could have possibly imagined.

No sooner had Constance Anne pulled up her bed covers and nuzzled the stuffed sock she slept with in place of a teddy bear, than she felt the most severe, gnawing hunger pangs she'd ever known. She shot out of bed and into the Eternal Preservation Center to raid the narrow, seven-foot-high, three-shelf, triple-cadaver-capacity mini-fridge. Because the sous chef was only 4' 9", leftovers from the daily Mexican buffet were usually put on the bottom shelf. That night, however, they were on the top shelf. Although she couldn't see the food at that height, her nose told her that there were some rockin' chimichangas somewhere in the back. When Constance Anne tried to pull out the shelf, it stuck on something and she jerked it back and forth in frustration until the chimichangas and an open bowl of jalapeno sauce unluckily plopped onto the shelf beneath them. When she tried to pull that shelf out, it stuck, too.

So famished that she was losing her mind, she squeezed herself into the narrow space between the shelves and started to crawl to the back of the fridge. It wasn't until she started backing up with two sauce-drenched chimichangas in her hands that she noticed she was inching her way up the trunk of a sheet-covered corpse.

When Constance Anne got out, she was horrified to see that she'd left pools of oozy green dressing on the sheet. Scared of being yelled at by the embalmer, who didn't like his patrons smelling like Tijuana, she started to change the sheet.

When she lifted it, she saw the face of an elderly man.

She burst into tears.

Sitting on the floor, wiping her eyes with a tissue in one hand and a chimichanga in the other, her memories of the man she desperately wanted to have as her "Grampy" overwhelmed her. She had cried for weeks after losing him in the wake of their magical afternoon in his apartment, and she had held out hope that she'd find him again. Now, all hope was lost.

Constance Anne looked for information in Dickie's files about how and where Mr. Reeves died but didn't come up with much. His body was found in the 24-hour drive-thru lane of a "Beavers, Slugs 'N Suds" fast food franchise and had been run over by at least 25 customers who were texting and paid no attention to the "thump-thump" under their tires. Unfortunately, there wasn't anything to explain how he ended up in the drive-thru lane to begin with. The funeral had been pre-paid. Whoever wrote it down made a funny mistake. The invoice said it had been paid in 1901. They obviously meant 2001.

The services for Mr. Reeves were beautiful. The small chapel attached to Dickie's was filled with magnificent displays of white lilies, pink carnations, red tulips, and crimson roses. Poster-sized, black-and-white photos of Mr. Reeves as a younger man stood on evenly-spaced easels on either side of the entranceway. Next to the open casket was a horseshoe-shaped cactus arrangement with a card that read, "Wishing you all the pain in the world! Mistress Brandy and the gang at Testicles, Torture & More, LLC." An embarrassed delivery man came to retrieve it, mumbling an apology about confusing the funeral with the Wong-Whey wedding in the Pentecostal Church across the street.

Sobbing her eyes out in her little black dress, black heels, and a string of glass pearls, Constance Anne could have easily been mistaken for a grieving granddaughter. In fact, she didn't even look like herself. That day her usually windswept hair was tied back in a conservative knot at the nape of her neck, and her sad eyes replaced her casaba melons as her most prominent feature. Under the circumstances, it was understandable that Mr. Granville, one of Dickie's chilly-handed greeters, didn't recognize her when he entered the chapel. A small, pointy-headed man who was the spitting image of a garden gnome, Granville placed a 1980s-era boombox on the floor next to the casket, switched on a microphone, and asked "the family and friends of the deceased" to take a seat.

Without blinking an eye over the fact that there was only one mourner and Constance Anne was it, Granville punched the cassette "Play" button on the ghetto blaster and walked out. A pre-recorded funeral service with music, prayers, and readings from the Bible crackled out of the timeworn speakers. While this was tactless and mortifying all by itself, there was something even more appalling. Constance Anne later discovered that the recording was nothing more than a free, generic Christian service training tape for funeral directors. The cheap bastards she worked with didn't even bother to put Reeves' name in it. Every time the script referred to the deceased, a tedious voice on the tape simply said "Insert name here."

When the recording ended, Constance Anne walked to the casket and kissed Mr. Reeves on his cheek. Then, Narwood and Pappy came in, closed the casket, and hurriedly pushed it out to the hearse. They told her that they would take her to visit the grave site "later" and quickly left. With the corpse locked down in the back, they peeled out of the parking lot on their way to an outdoor "Porn & Poultry" festival near Lowell.

Constance Anne walked out of the chapel with tears still streaming down her face. It seemed as if everything had been falling apart recently. She was worried sick about the sudden, mysterious disappearance of Tiny Earl. Jason crushed her by saying she was too young for him, even though she reassured him that she was already developing bunions. The principal made her look at selfies of him spanking himself with rebar. Mrs. Dickie was bitchy because Jason's spoon wasn't stirring her cabbage anymore. And now "Grampy" was gone.

Although she always tried to keep a grateful heart, she had to admit that things pretty much sucked.

Standing outside of the chapel smoking a cigarette was a man in a wide-striped, green-and-white suit and dark green suede tassel loafers. Together with his gold shirt, silver tie, and neon-red pocket square, he looked like a Christmas tree designed by a Mongolian yak herder. If his outfit wasn't enough to make an average person's eyes water in pain, his curly combover mullet certainly was. Trying to look cool, Attorney Ray-Bob Clinton flicked his still-lit smoke into the air as soon as he saw Constance Anne. Not having his best day, Ray-Bob felt the cigarette tumble into the cuff of his pants and start a small fire that he couldn't put out until he hopped over to a water fountain, lifted his leg like a dog, and turned the handle.

Constance Anne suspected that he was an asshole.

"Miss O'Leary?" he asked in a voice that sounded like the guttural puking noise a cat makes when it's bringing up a hair ball. Constance Anne looked at him suspiciously. As far as she could recall, no one had ever called her "Miss" before.

"Miss *Constance Anne* O'Leary?" he asked more pointedly.

Not knowing what else to do, she nodded her head.

"Please step into my office," Ray-Bob said with a smile as he guided her to a steel patio set adjacent to Mitzi Jo's Memorable Memories. Before she could sit down, he had to shoo away a vulture scarfing down a rodent in the middle of the table. Confirming that he was an asshole, Ray-Bob didn't bother to clean up the revolting leftovers. Constance Anne wanted to strap him to the underside of a sex-starved moose and let nature take its course.

"I knew you'd be here," Ray-Bob said. "You and the old man must have been tight."

Constance Anne thought Clinton looked familiar but couldn't place him. Until she could figure it out, she planned to ask some questions but didn't intend to answer any.

"How well did you know him?" Ray-Bob asked.

"How well did *you* know him? And who the hell are *you*, anyway?" Constance Anne shot back. Her eyes narrowed into dark slits. She wasn't a fucking twit, and she wanted to be sure he knew that.

"You mean you don't recognize me?" Ray-Bob replied with the unearned arrogance of a complete jerk. He was convinced that he'd become a big celebrity by way of the Sister Juan trial. The thought that Constance Anne was clueless put him in a state of disbelief usually reserved for things like alien abductions or the Cubs winning the World Series.

Constance Anne eventually remembered that he was the moron who sent Sister Juan and Cracka to the slammer with the *"Don't know shit, must acquit!"* defense. The whole world had laughed its ass off over that line. When a North Korean comedian used it in his stand-up act, police hauled him off to prison in the middle of his show because the line was actually funny.

After a mind-numbing, ten-minute, narcissistic rant about what a fantastic everything he was, Ray-Bob finally ran out of bullshit. Considering that she found E.coli infections more entertaining, she felt like she'd just been released from Death Row.

"*What* do you want?" Constance Anne demanded in a voice that was growing angrier by the second.

"Mr. Reeves left you some things in his will," Ray-Bob said.

If there was any doubt that Ray-Bob Clinton and his brothers were among the 98% of lawyers that make the rest look bad, he was about to settle the matter.

After graduating at the bottom of their law school class, the Tri-Bobs focused on building a practice that would attract two kinds of clients: suckers *with* money and suckers who *could get* money. Although the Sister Juan case gained them almost as much infamy as if they'd blown chunks on the Pope, criminal law wasn't part of the Tri-Bobs' plan. The only reason they took the Sister Juan case, in fact, was because they wanted to sue the government for a trillion dollars.

The brothers had gained valuable knowledge about how to identify suckers one summer as college interns for one of the more accomplished Nigerian email inheritance fraud scammers. The best prospects were poorly educated and, because they didn't know any better, weren't suspicious of emails with horribly written sentences and misspelled words. They didn't question the notion that someone they didn't know had died in Africa and left them a million bucks. Even more, they had faith that the inheritance check would be on its way just as soon as they paid a few fees to people you couldn't even Google.

The icing on the cake for the Tri-Bobs was that you didn't even need the internet to run this scam. You could do it by mail, over the phone, and even face-to-face.

"What did he leave me?" Constance Anne asked. She was puzzled why Reeves would have left anything. She wasn't sure he even knew her whole name.

"Well, people normally leave money, jewelry, things like that," Ray-Bob replied, watching closely to see how she reacted. "Mr. Reeves had assets but no family. He willed everything he had to you."

"And I'm the attorney," he added, letting her assume whatever she wanted to assume.

Constance Anne was speechless.

"All you have to do," Ray-Bob added matter-of-factly, "is obey the law."

Doing his best to look relaxed, he leaned back in his patio chair. It made a painful-sounding creak under his weight. Another vulture stood nearby waiting to get at the rodent pie while Ray-Bob worked on Constance Anne.

"It's actually very easy," he said, doing his best imitation of an empathetic human being. Her confusion gave him a rush equal to a sweaty orgasm. To Ray-Bob, screwing people this way was deeper, more personal, and more intimate than sex. And it lasted longer, too.

"Let's start," he said. "The police expect that you won't do anything bad with the money like, say, buy drugs. Drugs sure are a big problem, aren't they?"

Ray-Bob was trying to get her to agree with him on as many things as possible. The more times she said 'yes', the easier it was to get her to say 'yes' again.

"Yes," Constance Anne replied. The mere mention of the cops began to inch her towards the "flight" side of a "fight-or-flight" response. Ray-Bob could tell because her pupils were dilating and she was perspiring. That meant her body was releasing adrenaline.

"Then, there's the issue of taxes. It's one of those stupid government things," he said with a little laugh. "But we can probably make this easy. Easy *is* best, isn't it?"

Ray-Bob shifted his body towards her in a sociable way, as if they were friends.

"Yes, it is," Constance Anne said. At this point, she was praying that he was going to show her the way out of this confusing mess. It was exactly what he wanted.

"I think because of your age … you're 18, aren't you?" he asked, although he already knew the answer. He also knew that she was one of the sad, penniless "Crotch Kids".

"Yes," she replied.

"Well, I think because of your age we can probably get this done for $5,000. I wouldn't charge you anything for my services, of course," he said. "That would bring it down to $4,000."

Ray-Bob enjoyed this part the most, because after making a cool 60 large doing this in just the past few months, he knew exactly what was next.

"I don't have that kind of money," Constance Anne said. She was getting paler by the minute.

"Oh, I guess I didn't tell you. Mr. Reeves' estate could be worth, well, maybe as much as $50,000. Would you like to know the *really* easy way to do this?" he said as he moved closer to her.

Not surprisingly, she emphatically shook her head 'yes'.

"Most people just borrow the money from their friends and then repay it when they get the money from the estate," he said. "It's sure better than having all of Mr. Reeves' things sold or thrown away."

Constance Anne immediately thought about the puppets. The anxiety over what might happen to them made her feel like someone was sitting on her chest.

He let her know that she had four days to get the money, all of which had to be in cash, and deliver it to a Sergeant Sufpher who would be waiting for her at the corner of Park and Tremont on the edge of Boston Common. Constance Anne said 'yes' to figuring out a way to come up with the money.

The cuff of Ray-Bob's shirt grazed the goopy sauce that the rodent had become in the afternoon sun as he handed her a business card with a colorful badge printed in the center and "Sergeant Victoria Sufpher" beneath it. He said that Victoria would take care of everything and, in turn, would give her what she needed to collect the inheritance.

Ray-Bob got into his shiny new sports car and drove away, leaving Constance Anne in tears and at her wit's end trying to figure out how to get the money.

In reality, Ray-Bob Clinton had never met Mr. Reeves and certainly wasn't his lawyer. Neither did the Boston Police have any expectations about what she would do with the money. He simply saw Reeves' death notice in the local paper and sent a temp to the County Clerk's office with a $45 money order to get a copy of his will. Then, after doing a little research about Constance Anne O'Leary, the executor and sole beneficiary, he showed up at the funeral to meet her. If all went well, he'd pick up a cool $3,500 after paying Sergeant Victoria Sufpher a $500 cut for being the bag man.

Not surprisingly, Sergeant Sufpher wasn't what she appeared to be either. Clearly not a member of the Boston Police department, Sergeant Vicki Torment, as she was known to her customers, was a local dominatrix whose performance as a surly police officer was worthy of an Oscar. Her business card even looked real as long as you didn't look at it too closely. In the center of the badge design were the words "Submission to Authority" and a pair of handcuffs.

Ray-Bob thought his mommy would be proud of him. Although he misled Constance Anne and took advantage of her naïveté, he never actually told her a lie. On top of that, the young lady would get "what she needed to collect the inheritance" as promised, albeit for several grand more than she needed to spend. Sergeant Sufpher would hand her a large envelope containing a copy of the late Mr. Reeves' Will and instructions about how to execute the Will in Massachusetts.

Ray-Bob enjoyed this part of his business and was going to miss it when he turned it over to his brother Bob-Bob.

Ray-Bob was going to build a new venture to help more families live the American Dream. For a generous fee, he'd help homeowners navigate the murky waters of defaulting on their mortgages, getting temporary eviction protection, and living in the house for free until the bank paid them to leave. For a piece of the action, he'd also provide ongoing advice about how to rent the same house to unsuspecting tenants, pocket the money, and squat in a nicer home that was also empty due to foreclosure.

As far as Ray-Bob was concerned, there was nothing but blue skies ahead for the Clinton triplets.

On their fortieth birthday, the Bobs were surprised to find three identical robin's-egg-blue boxes with white ribbon at the front door of the home they shared. When they opened them, the boys were delighted to find identical, brilliantly articulated, female hand puppets with super-sized booties made from $100 bills. After smacking their lips in unison, they retired to separate rooms. Although they did many things together, floggin' the dog wasn't one of them anymore.

The following day, the Tri-Bobs' bodies were found naked, acutely discolored, and oozing clear jelly in Adirondack chairs on a private beach in Maine. Each man was holding a badly burned puppet with a huge booty in his right hand. As a rule, the local authorities avoided conducting investigations that might inconvenience their wealthy citizens. After a complaint call from resident Ezra H. C. "Trip" Gravitas III, Prinharvia Class of '70, about the stench, the sanitation department quickly and quietly bagged up the Bobs and threw them away.

Gravitas would be damned if a triple homicide was going to screw up his morning swim and Cucumber Mint Gimlet.

Chapter 13

*"Unlike his siblings, whose teachers used words like 'terrifying,'
'creepy,' 'disturbed,' and 'unholy' to describe them in report cards,
Michael's teachers only had nice things to say."*

Nearing a nervous collapse, Constance Anne's thoughts drifted back to the lessons she learned at La Academy de Greatness, better known as LAG, the Crotch's on-campus school.

Although Sister Juan portrayed St. Woody's K-12 "experience" as one in which students learned the "wisdom of the ages," state education examiners would have likely disagreed. Despite the fact that the school raised hundreds of thousands of dollars each year to buy books, computers, and other educational resources, most students left St. Woody's believing gravity was something you put on mashed potatoes. Sadly for the students, a threatening phone call to the state's high school inspector followed by nine simultaneous vehicle explosions in front of his office guaranteed that Sister Juan could operate as she liked.

Like most of The Crotch's claims, there was usually just enough truth mixed in with all the half-truths and out-and-out lies to pass a cursory examination by an apathetic inspector.

It was true that students were encouraged to discover the wisdom of history's greatest minds; however, they could only do it on their own time and as long as they didn't get "all uppity" about it. It was also true that La Academy de Greatness inspired young scholars to explore the mysteries of science. What the school forgot to note was that their program didn't include expensive lab equipment or other academic tools unless they helped build LAG's nascent crank business. As Cracka crisply explained it to a new teacher, "Ain't poppin' no bands 'less it work chalk." Instead, science at La Academy de Greatness focused on low-to-no-cost alchemy, free leech-powered bloodletting methods from the Dark Ages, and a 12th-century medical course about illnesses brought on by "dwarves" and "ill humors" that came from the public library.

There was even extra fun for students with jobs. They could attend an annual "wisdom of the ages" lecture given by Priestess Carlistiara, the owner of a local occult and creepy shit store that sold amulets and talismans made by top-heavy virgins in Antarctica. The centerpiece of the speech was a limited-time offer to buy an enchanted plastic pen for $29.95. If you used the pen to study for a test and then used it when you took the test, she told the crowd, you'd always pass because the pen would remember the answers. Even J.J. "Thick" Porcapatato, the school's "dimwit-in-residence," was pretty sure her claim wasn't true but bought four pens anyway. He didn't think it really mattered that much if they weren't actually made by virgins.

More important than all of these put together, however, was the wisdom Sister Juan wanted to impart to her youngsters through the school's TITS program, an acronym for "Twelve Important Things" every student should remember. The Crotch's version of the Ten Commandments was drilled into their heads with flash cards. Sister Juan would frequently confront students in classrooms, hallways, and inside restroom stalls and order them to "flash," or recite, the 12 points:

1. Do unto others until they are unidentifiable.
2. If you bury anyone less than 16 feet deep, cadaver dogs can find them.
3. If somebody annoys you, force him into the sewage tank of a portable toilet. Then, put the seat down and turn off the light.
4. Use vinegar to clean up blood splatter in a jiff.

5. Always leave room in your tummy for evidence.
6. Never use a skidmarked thong to roll a doobie.
7. Tip your drug dealer at Christmas.
8. Plant the DNA of people you hate at crime scenes.
9. When you change apartments, take the copper pipes, electrical wiring, toilets, and appliances with you.
10. Disemboweling requires patience. Remember, intestines will spill out by themselves. There's no need to pull.
11. Most people suck.
12. Never trust a lawyer with a bag man.

As she did so often when she was worried or confused, Constance Anne flashed her TITS. When she got to Number 12, she felt an angry wave of anxiety wash over her. Ray-Bob Clinton was a lawyer and maybe Sergeant Sufpher was a bag man. Or a bag person.

With Sister Juan and Cracka in prison, Tiny Earl still missing, and Jason in her rearview mirror, Constance Anne had only one person to turn to.

She needed The Spaz.

From the moment they met, Constance Anne could tell that Michael Spacchio was a very intelligent guy. More importantly, she felt she could trust him. Unlike most other men she'd known, he was a gentleman, and the fact that he spoke to her face instead of her cleavage most of the time neither went unnoticed nor unappreciated. Even more unlike other people, the more she learned about him, the better she liked him. For a guy who reveled in rumors that he'd jerked out some dude's bowels with a vegetable peeler, he was remarkably kind and loving towards his family and the scant few people he let inside his world. She'd wondered more than once if The Spaz's trademark suit and briefcase were nothing more than psychological shields against all of the ugliness in the world. On the other hand, the briefcase may have simply been the easiest way to carry a fold-up assault rifle and a bologna sandwich.

Because she didn't own a cell phone, Constance Anne would have ordinarily used one of Dickie's land lines to call Michael. That was, at least, until Mitzi Jo announced that all calls in and out of the company were going to be monitored for quality assurance, the result of an incident in which a decedent's daughter was called by a new employee to report a delay in the viewing. "Yeah," said the Dickie's staffer, "yo' mama come in all bug-eyed and shit an' we hadda hamma down her eyeballs. Now, gotta shoot mo' 'balmin' juice in her 'cuz her ass so fat."

Since Mitzi Jo inexplicably put "Snooping Shirley" Schnauzman, a lumpy 67-year-old chain smoker with a strawberry nose the length of a hotdog, in charge, Constance Anne took the T to the Lobstah Coach offices to see Michael in person. Understandably, Constance Anne didn't want her personal business running around Dickie's like the roaches that scattered when she opened the door to the crematorium. If "Snooping Shirley" was known for anything, it was her love of cruel, insensitive gossip and willingness to stick her nose into other people's business anytime or anywhere. She was also in the habit of lifting up the front of her dress in public and vigorously scratching her crotch. When Constance Anne later learned that the crass, repulsive orangey-haired senior citizen and 40-something Bob-Bob Clinton were having an affair, it was weird and disturbing but strangely understandable. If that wasn't stomach-churning enough, the buzz about how they communicated their carnal desires to one another was worse. Shirley would clap her hands twice and shout "Peck-*er!*" Bob-Bob would prance naked into the bedroom with a Ku Klux Klan hood over his corn dog, whipping his ass while pretending to ride a horse.

Constance Anne found Michael lying on his back under the seats in Row 79 of the Boston to Steubenville Express bus. Although the aisles were thick with workers scraping handfuls of unspeakable, sticky, lumpy things off the seats and windows, Constance Anne found her boy in no time. The odds of anyone else on board wearing shiny black wingtips and cuffed trousers were as much a longshot as finding a Baptist Church with a liquor license. Constance Anne slid under the seats with The Spaz to help him dislodge what looked like a three-pound ham glued to the underside of an armrest. By the time they were done an hour later, Constance Anne had explained the whole situation to Michael in detail and they'd agreed to meet the next day at a place that was near and dear to Constance Anne's heart.

They also discovered, rather disturbingly, that the ham had a face.

▲

Constance Anne fell in love with the glitter and glam of dog racing on a kindergarten field trip to the track many years earlier. Painted completely in mint green, the Pissi-Tallaway Indian Track looked as if it was frozen in the 1960s, which also appeared to be the last time they cleaned the ladies' room. The infield, which was beautifully landscaped with thousands of plastic geraniums and lemon-yellow carnations, was also festooned with life-size, plastic blow-mold statues of pilgrims that lit up from the inside. Constance Anne found the track prettiest at sunrise, which was usually just before the first race. With morning "eye openers" that included 2-for-1 Bloody Marys, the track was an exceptionally relaxing place to visit before work or school. Clearly, the 32 elementary school teachers that came every day thought so. Usually, the racing day started with beagles or basset hounds and ended at midnight with the traditional "Groovy Dog Race," a special event featuring a field of one-year-old dachshunds in little doggie-size fedoras, dickies, and button-down collar shirts for a cool '60s vibe.

With his suit on and briefcase in hand, Michael was mistaken by the Pissi-Tallaway customer service staff for a high-roller and they escorted him, with Constance Anne in tow, to a trackside VIP table near the finish line. After being offered a lavish, free breakfast compliments of the management, Michael and Constance Anne toasted each other with weak orange juice to celebrate their exceptionally good luck. They were both starving and so broke they couldn't have paid cash for a day-old bagel.

Constance Anne leaned so far forward in her chair that her collarbone touched the table. She furrowed her brow and took a deep breath before launching into a rapid-fire reprise of everything she'd told Michael the night before. In fact, the deeper she got into the story, the faster she talked until Michael finally had to put his hands up in a timeout sign. Constance Anne looked at him quizzically until it dawned on her that she'd become a speeding freight train with a mouth. She covered her lips with the tips of her fingers and let her eyes communicate her embarrassment.

"All I can think about is those beautiful puppets," she said after settling down a little. "They were Mr. Reeves' life's work, his friends, maybe even the only family he ever had. I can't come up with that kind of money. And now they're going to be sold or thrown away or something worse. It's just not right."

She shook her head despondently.

"*I wanted him to be my Grampy!*" she said loudly with a catch in her voice. Her eyes were red, and tears were running down her face. Sorrier yet, the mascara she'd sponged off the mortuary cosmetologist was smearing. Clearly, the claim that it lasted for eternity was bullshit.

Constance Anne had rarely spoken to Michael about anything significant before and certainly nothing this big. While she was lying under the bus seat with Michael, she had talked and talked and talked and talked, almost without taking a breath until she saw the ham-like thing grin. Michael never said a word and, in fact, never even asked a question. Now, in the daylight, and without the discomforting sound of the ham-like thing smacking its lips, his silence really bothered her, and she began to wonder if she'd completely misjudged him. Maybe he was just plain weird and there was nothing inside his head except more weirdness. Maybe she'd romanticized that he'd be her knight in shining armor. Maybe she should just forget the whole damn thing.

Constance Anne felt her heart sink. She was feeling as out-of-sorts as a three-legged streetwalker with bunions.

Michael reached across the table to take her hand just as breakfast arrived, an icky, uncomfortable moment since the plates were soiled by bloodstains from a cut on the waiter's right thumb. Pissed off that the couple was so fussy that they demanded clean dishes, the server picked everything up, walked away with his nose up in the air, and never came back. As bugles blared "Call to the Post" for the start of the second race, a 3/8 of a mile turf contest for Boston terriers, Michael pulled his boxy, black briefcase out from under the table and clicked open the locks. He took out a large manila folder and laid it on the table. Then, he pulled out a fat, 64-ring cigar and lit it with a butane lighter hidden inside his wristwatch.

Michael turned sideways in his seat and crossed his legs knee over knee. The sun struck the diamond chip in one of his cufflinks and momentarily blinded her.

Constance Anne's head was spinning. She wanted to ask him who he was and what he had done with The Spaz.

"The lawyer lied to you," he said in the firm, yet annoying, nasally voice that was yet another one of his trademarks. In addition to frequent belching, wickedly bad breath, and exceptionally small feet, irritating sounds ran in his gene pool.

There wasn't a big enough word in the English language to describe Michael Spacchio's family.

His mother, Anna Maria Angelica Teresa Alessandra Calvina, a pallid, black-haired, 35-year-old gluten junkie, ran a successful numbers business in cooperation with the Cosa Nostra. As wonderful as the Spacchio family's lives looked from the outside, however, they were not always a bed of roses.

Sadly, due to what people in the mob community called a "self-administered" overdose of roofies in 2002, Anna Maria was unable to remember the first and last names of the four boys and four girls she had given birth to between 1996 and 2004. Uninterested in learning who they were, and not the least bit curious as to why they didn't even vaguely resemble one another, she called them all Jerome for the sake of simplicity. While that was accepted in some psychiatric circles as "no big deal," school mental health workers asserted that the Spacchio kids' lack of individual identity drove them to violence. That claim proved spot on when three of the Spacchio girls blew up the principal's home.

As in every family, some members reach greater heights than others. In the Spacchio home, the honor went to the baby of the family who was tried as an adult for a brutal assault with a deadly weapon when she was only six. No slouch in other endeavors, she was also a master shoplifter who could walk into a supermarket and emerge five minutes later with a six-course meal stuck to her thighs.

Michael's grandfather, who never gave his name to anyone including his late wife, also lived with the active brood. He spent his Golden Years sitting silently in the basement in a simple wooden chair, handguns strapped to both ankles, and his back to the wall. When he showered, he took a .38 Smith & Wesson with him. When he went to bed, he wore sunglasses so that no one could tell if he was awake or asleep.

Michael's suspected father, Delbono, lived up the street with a 25-year-old UFO groupie named Cricket. Cricket wore a red ceramic bowl on her head to keep "alien internet machines" from reaching her brain.

Despite their idiosyncrasies, however, everyone in the family was a sharp dresser.

"I broke into the Bookmobile last night and did some research about inheritances," Michael said, looking at Constance Anne with penetrating blue eyes she had never noticed before. "You don't have to pay him or the police a single cent. It's all bullshit. All we need is a copy of Mr. Reeves' Will and the name of the lawyer who drew it up."

Constance Anne was speechless.

"A copy of the Will costs 45 bucks. We can get it at the County Clerk's office," Michael said.

He saw her jaw tighten with the mention of money. The only thing she had in her pockets was lint.

"I've got this," he said quickly as he made a zipping motion across his lips. He didn't want her to say a word or ask any questions. Even though he didn't have any cash, the silencer his brother gave him for Christmas was in his briefcase. Silencers had become popular with people who wanted to accessorize their guns, and he doubted he'd have too much of a problem selling it. In fact, he unloaded it before they even left the track. As he came out of the restroom, an elderly woman walked up and, with a wink, asked him if he knew where she could get a "killer" gift for her grandson. When Michael told her that he had a silencer for sale, she smiled and started peeling off twenties. The fact that there was blood and tissue on the barrel didn't bug her a bit.

As soon as the County Clerk handed them the Last Will and Testament of John F. Reeves IV, Michael and Constance Anne sprinted down the street to Ammo, Ass & Avocados, a Park Street restaurant popular with politicians and members of the clergy, where the only thing waiters and waitresses wore were black heels and loaded handguns in thigh holsters. So hungry that they were on the verge of eating their own arms, the two of them went into a feeding frenzy on burgers, fries, clam rolls and onion rings. Once they finished the entire Boston cream pie they'd ordered for dessert, Constance Anne started reading the Will line-by-line, handing the pages to Michael as she finished. Although at times they needed a dictionary to figure out the legal language, the entire 12-page document all pretty much boiled down to three things: everything Reeves owned went to Constance Anne, it was all in a storage room somewhere in Florida, and the lawyer who prepared the Will was Shlomo D. Goldmetz, Esq.

An attachment to the Will said that Goldmetz and only Goldmetz knew the exact location of the storage room.

That obviously made him the man to see.

Fortunately, for two people who had just waddled out of a restaurant after powering down 5,000 calories apiece, Goldmetz's law office was only four blocks away in The Old Dribbler building. Erected in 1939 by wealthy Bostonian Orville Dribbler, the 16-story office building on Bromfield Street was built of alternating blocks of expensive Italian marble and cheap, unpainted concrete to achieve the architect's vision of urban sophistication fused with the country charm of a munitions bunker. Regrettably, as construction progressed, higher-than-expected concrete costs killed the plans for an elevator and forced the contractor to build the interior stairs from plywood and scaffolding. As more than 700 injury lawsuits against the Old Dribbler sharply illustrated, neither decision was a good one.

Exhausted after climbing 30 flights of stairs to Goldmetz's 15th floor office, Constance Anne and Michael were both angry and stunned to find it nearly empty. In the place of desks, furniture, and clients, there was a tall, gray file cabinet and an unhappy-looking young woman with pink hair, no eyebrows and a ferret tattoo on her neck. After introducing herself as a cleaner but refusing to give her name for "national security reasons," she explained in a bored, lifeless voice that made bus station announcers sound exciting, that Shlomo Goldmetz, Esq. was dead.

According to what she'd overheard in the ladies' room, Goldmetz had been killed while vacationing in Miami with his wife.

During the grand opening of a new mall, a women's shoe store put a decimal point in the wrong place and put an elite, legendary brand of sexy, spikey, strappy, "hot girl" shoes on sale for $58.60 instead of $586.00. As a result, thousands of wild-eyed, screaming women overran the store, including Goldmetz's wife, Muriel, who worshipped the shoes even though they were entirely too small for her size 13 feet. Dragging Shlomo and his credit card behind her and wielding a 2x4 with protruding nails to punch, hammer, and slash her way through the crowd, Muriel was able to tear six pairs of the shoes out of other women's hands and sprint to the checkout.

Soon after returning to Boston, Muriel received a phone call from the Miami police. Terrified that the authorities were going to tell her that she had to return the shoes, she felt a horrifying, almost paralyzing, surge of anxiety rip through her. When an officer told her that his call was to inform her that her husband had died, she immediately looked down at her new shoes and smiled.

Based on eyewitness accounts, Shlomo was simply in the wrong place at the wrong time as hundreds of empty shoeboxes stacked in a corner of the store toppled over from the aftershocks of some 2,000 women's feet pounding through the building. As he valiantly fought his way to the top of the pile, he fell victim to the unforgiving flesh of three hefty middle-aged women who fell on top of him as they struggled violently over a pair of red heels. Although his official report said that Shlomo had died of "accidental smothering," the coroner later told his golfing buddies that the women's dangerous overuse of cheap, heavy perfumes may have killed him before their asses did.

Muriel was so excited about the shoes that didn't fit her that she never noticed that her husband was missing until the cops called. Despite the deep sense of loss she felt, she picked up her purse, made sure Shlomo's credit card was still there, and went shopping.

"But we have important business with Mr. Goldmetz," Michael said to the young woman. "What are we supposed to do?"

"Do I look like fuckin' Google to you?" Miss Pink Hair responded acidly while raising her missing eye brows and pointing to her ferret art.

Constance Anne nearly fell on the floor laughing.

Appreciative of Constance Anne's support, Miss Pink Hair handed her some coffee-stained papers she'd found in the trash that listed Goldmetz's cases and the lawyers that had agreed to take them on. Considering the way her life had gone since birth, Constance Anne wasn't all that surprised to see Ray-Bob Clinton's name right next to "Will of John F. Reeves IV". According to the date scribbled on the same line, Clinton had only gotten his hands on the Reeves file the day before.

Although Constance Anne was understandably disheartened, Michael tried to keep up her spirits by remaining optimistic, or at least outwardly so. Sitting together on a bench, Constance Anne tapped her right foot nervously on the pavement while Michael chewed on his bottom lip so vigorously that it bled. Desperate to come up with an idea that would save the day, something unusual caught his attention just as he was losing all hope.

Some 50 yards away, a man with a large knife and a black nylon stocking pulled over his head was chasing a guy in a dark suit and tie across a stretch of grass. When the man with the knife caught the guy in the suit, he stabbed him 17 times. Then he took the suit guy's briefcase, wallet, and watch and simply disappeared into the crowd. Two smiling girls strolled by the scene arm-in-arm. They stepped over the suit guy as he struggled to take his last breath.

It gave Michael Emmanuel Spacchio exactly the inspiration he was praying for.

Even as a small child, Michael was known for his intelligence, imagination, and kindness to others. Unlike his siblings, whose teachers used words like "terrifying," "creepy," "disturbed," and "unholy" to describe them in report cards, Michael's teachers only had nice things to say. As his second grade teacher wrote, "Michael is going to go places in life other than prison. It's refreshing to meet a young man who knows exactly what he wants to be when he grows up and has the personal strength and discipline to achieve it." Had the teacher not confused Michael's goal of becoming a "Made Man" in the Cosa Nostra with the term "Self-Made Man," she might have revised her comments.

With so many good things inside his head and heart, it wasn't surprising that Michael took the bull by the horns to help Constance Anne succeed. He more than adored everything about her. The very look of her soft top lip gave him such a hard-on that it drained all the blood out of his head, chest and arms. His dreams of becoming an organized crime executive aside, Michael was the kind of guy who stood up for people in need, and particularly those who were getting fucked by someone or something evil. With a big smile and a mind bursting with ideas, he got up off the bench, told her that he'd be back in 15 or 20 minutes and walked to a thrift store two blocks away.

If there was anything Michael and Constance Anne understood exceptionally well, it was that they lived "no option, no tomorrow" lives.

English teacher Claudia Fireburn, commonly regarded as the only Blough High faculty member who was educated, used that term one day to describe Joe, a character in a novel who "was so poor that he could never enjoy the luxuries of failure or squandered time." With no family to back him up with either love or money, Joe had no option other than to become an overachiever at work and school. Being average was as bad as being a failure, and a failure was as disposable to society as a plastic water bottle. Even if he was the best at everything in his little world, he had to remember that few opportunities for anything good were going to come his way. If and when something did, he had to jump on it immediately. There was nothing he could afford to put off until tomorrow.

Constance Anne and Michael unquestionably identified with Joe better than perhaps anyone else in school. Constance Anne knew that she had to work day and night to move beyond a life where dinner was served on an embalming table that, frankly, wasn't cleaned off all that well. Michael knew that the Cosa Nostra entrance exam was much harder and radically different than it was back in the day. To get in, he not only had to be willing to serve the ruling Globzola crime family by committing murder, robbery, and extortion, but had to have a 3.9 GPA and an excellent assortment of extracurricular activities.

Michael came back from his mysterious mission right when he said he would and sat back down on the bench next to Constance Anne. He had two large plastic bags with him. Rather than show her what he'd bought, he posed a question.

"Remember Joe from Miss Firebrand's class?" he said.

Constance Anne smiled and flicked her head back, effortlessly tossing her long, thick blonde hair over her shoulders.

"What do you think he'd do in this situation?" he asked.

"I think he'd do whatever the hell he had to do," she said.

The Cotton Mather Memorial Office Towers and White People's Condominium Complex in downtown Boston was 779 feet tall, had 42 floors, 34 elevators, 1,100 parking spaces, and 448 security cameras. Due to expense cuts to fund the general manager's bonus, the security staff was reduced from 25 burly young men to one 62-year-old narcoleptic with plantar fasciitis. The building held a special significance to Michael. The 3,000-seat cafeteria on the ground floor was a huge money-laundering operation for secondary market meat dealers who sold metric tons of uninspected, expired, and Grade D sides of beef for cash. Michael had visited the "Cash Cow," as it was called, on a "Catholic Youth in Crime" field trip in seventh grade and dreamed of working there one day. Cotton Mather Towers was now even more important to him, but for a different reason.

Suite 1305, located on the 13th floor near an elevator, a custodian's closet, and a painting of Mather's insane third wife, Lydia Wasda Mather, was the headquarters of Tri-Bobs Law.

Hungry again, Michael and Constance Anne swung into Beaks, Gills, and Tongues, a Bulgarian restaurant chain that had recently opened its first American location. Although their signature dishes, Tarator, a cold soup made of cucumbers, garlic, olive oil, water, and yogurt, and Kebab with Rice were phenomenal, no one understood their badly translated advertising slogan, "Food Good on your Knees!" Since most passersby assumed that there was something kinky involved, business was always bad unless there were BDSM or fellatio conventions in town. Ironically, the only translation they got right was *"Fuck You!"*, which they wrote on the front door in red spray paint when they went out of business.

As he and Constance Anne threw themselves into grilled lamb livers served over prune yogurt and sardines, Michael made a case for breaking into the Tri-Bobs' offices that night. He was pretty sure that the brothers had the address of Reeves' storage room in their files and very sure that he and Constance Anne needed to get to it before the Bobs did. Constance Anne wholeheartedly agreed.

The first thing they had to do, however, was access the "Murky Web," a highly secret place on the internet often used by criminals, perverts, health insurance companies, and other terrorists. Constance Anne and Michael needed to connect with www.insecuritynow.com, a site that was among the worst of the worst.

Among thousands of sites hidden in the shadows of the Worldwide Web, insecuritynow.com contained precise details about the physical security weaknesses of office buildings, banks, water supplies, power grids and other critical infrastructure around the globe. As potentially damaging as the information was, it paled in comparison to how it was collected. Nearly all of the intelligence about the facilities came from the very people in charge of protecting them.

At one o'clock in the morning in each world time zone, bored, dejected security guards living the high life on minimum wage could log on to www.bottomlessdepression.com, the world's largest and kinkiest sex site. The site gave guards free web cam access to thousands of hot, young Russian women and men ready to do anything that could be done with or to a penis, vagina or other moist hole in the human body. They also worked with inanimate objects. All the guards had to do to make their dreams come true was supply information about how to disable alarms, steal or destroy important things, and escape undetected.

As an incentive, the guard who provided the week's most useful information won an all-expenses paid weekend of "free sex and hijinks" with their favorite web cam performer or object at Cleveland's trendy Carnivore Motor Hotel. Although one guy spent the weekend with an uncooked leg of lamb and nine rubber bands without incident, "free sex and hijinks" usually meant blackmail, "gettin' the mouth herps" or both.

After spending an hour exploring insecuritynow.com at a dingy whiskey and doughnuts place popular with Murky Web-ers, Michael and Constance Anne thought they had a good feel for the building's security flaws. They felt confident that they could go deep inside Cotton Mather through the back door.

Michael reached into one of the bags he brought from the store. He took out two very dark gray, breathable stretchy spandex suits made to completely cover their bodies, including their faces, from head to foot.

"We need to put these on," Michael said, tearing open a package and pressing a suit in her hand.

Constance Anne didn't respond. She just looked at him, wondering if the olive oil he put in his hair every day had leaked into his brain.

"You don't want anyone to see us, do you? With these we'll be nearly invisible," he said. "Just go into the ladies' room, take off your clothes, and put it on. I'll do the same. Give me your clothes when you're done and I'll put them in my briefcase. Trust me."

Not surprisingly, she'd heard the phrases "take off your clothes" and "trust me" in the same sentence before.

Michael could feel his heart beating in his neck. He was excited, but not about the crime they were about to commit. Michael was convinced that God had put a lot of extra time and effort into making Constance Anne, and just being near her overwhelmed his senses. He had to keep his hands in his pockets to cover the perpetual erection he couldn't shrink even by thinking about his grandmother doing the reverse cowgirl with the pope.

Confused but still trusting, Constance Anne did exactly as he asked. After she put on the suit, she walked out of the restroom and into the joint's dark, grimy back hallway.

If not for the meager light from an exit sign covered with dead bugs, she wouldn't have been able to see Michael at all. He was right. They simply blended into the shadows. A bald guy with harsh-smelling shoulder-length hair that sprouted from his sideburns walked right past Michael without a clue that he was there.

"There's one more thing," he told her. "Bend over a little."

Constance Anne had heard that before, too.

She felt him pull something over her head and shoulders.

"What on earth are you doing?" Constance Anne asked, laughing. She could only see when she looked down. Something floppy was hanging over her eyes and blocking part of her vision.

"We have to get on the bus. It's too far to walk," Michael replied with an answer to a different question. His mind was several steps ahead of their conversation.

Constance Anne put her hand up like a stop sign.

"What is this?" she asked firmly. She wasn't about to wear anything sight unseen even if she couldn't be seen in it.

"It's a hoodie," Michael told her as she pushed her left arm through the sleeve. "A really big one actually. An 8XL. I got it at the thrift store. We can both fit into it. I guess it will be pretty snuggly, though. There's only one hood and two sleeves."

Saying 'snuggly' to her made him blush. It was just as well that Constance Anne couldn't see his face.

Michael brought the hoodie closer so that she could see the color. It was dirty green, the fugliest color in the universe next to puce, which was the fugliest color in the universe next to chrome yellow.

"A lot of girls buy these, actually, particularly girls who worry about their boyfriends wandering off," he said, repeating what the sales clerk told him. "And conjoined twins. Very big with conjoined twins."

Constance Anne was at a complete loss for words, particularly when she saw that the hoodie was nearly long enough to reach her ankles.

"This really isn't as crazy as it seems," Michael explained, guessing correctly that she was growing less supportive by the second. "We can't walk down the street with blacked-out faces. Somebody will call the cops for sure. In fact, we don't want anyone to remember seeing us at all."

Michael reached into the bag again and took out two pairs of gigantic, bright red novelty sunglasses.

"What we do want them to remember, though, is a four-eyed, dancing Avocado."

He held off telling her that he'd also bought a child-size hoodie in the same color. As smart and original as he thought he was, he wasn't sure how she'd take knowing that it was for his briefcase.

CHAPTER 14

"If that was bad, it was worse that he'd been using his septic tank like an ATM. The tank was leaching, tens and twenties were floating to the top, and his cash was no longer welcome at the supermarket."

At precisely one o'clock in the morning, security guard "Icky" Schanazello entered the virtually vacant, 2,000 square foot security complex inside Cotton Mather Towers.

As he did every day unless he suddenly fell asleep, Schanazello settled into a cheap secretarial chair held together with tape and a serpentine belt from a junked Chevy. Within minutes of connecting with bottomlessdepression.com on one of the complex's computers, he was happily holding his wilted, 62-year-old Johnson in his hand, moving it back and forth to the throbbing beat of salsa music. Klementina, his much loved cam girl, used salsa as her personal "theme" music. Although "Icky" liked everything about her, what really turned him on were the ankle monitors she wore on both legs, one for the New York Department of Corrections and the other for a football team in Florida.

Had "Icky" been paying attention to the security cameras rather than the double nipple on Klementina's right snuggle puppy, he'd have seen a 5'10" thing that looked a lot more like a phlegm ball than an avocado cross the rear of the dimly lit lobby.

He would have also seen it walk into the men's restroom.

More importantly, he might have noticed that the phlegm ball never came out.

Michael and Constance Anne's trip to the Cotton Mather building had been surprisingly uneventful given their disguise. Boston transit workers are known to be a pretty cool, calm bunch and the bus driver didn't even blink when they boarded sideways one slow, sure step at a time like a 95-year-old grandmother. It may have been that the driver had seen enough weirdness over the years at 12:45 a.m. that Michael and Constance Anne were no big deal in comparison. It may also have been because there were already three white-hooded Ku Klux Klan members on the bus, along with a family with oversized turtleneck sweaters pulled over their heads so that their faces were hidden at the ends of long, wooly tunnels.

When Michael and Constance Anne got off the bus, they walked to the back of the Mather building where, just as insecuritynow.com had reported, a $250,000 bank vault-like security door was left propped open with a piece of cardboard to let smokers on the night crew go in and out. Then they went directly into the men's room adjacent to the front lobby, took off the hoodie and their sunglasses, and walked out into the shadows.

As he closed the men's room door, Michael noticed that there was a lawyer's office weirdly situated directly between the men's and women's restrooms. He could only imagine what it was like working in there, particularly on Tex-Mex Day in the cafeteria. Being wedged in between the stench of bowel-defiled refried beans and the roar of flushing toilets had to be special.

The Cotton Mather was an ugly mishmash of old and new construction designed by T. Archibald Fawlen, better known as "Wobbly," the cheapest and most careless architect in New England. After opening a 32-gauge steel security door with a biometric lock by rattling the handle, Michael and Constance Anne walked up the stairs to the third floor and boarded a dark, late 19th-century cage-styled elevator in the rear annex overlooking an air shaft. The old, creaky lift took them to the sixth floor where they got on a modern elevator with no security cameras and minimal lighting. Then they rode up to the 13th floor and hid inside a large electrical closet. Michael and Constance Anne stayed there until the cleaning crew finished at 2:30 a.m. and turned off the lights, laughing hysterically about how all of them had just tapped their kidneys in the coffee creamer cartons in every office refrigerator.

It took Michael and Constance Anne less than 15 seconds to reach Suite 1305 where a coffee-stained piece of paper with "Bob, Bob and Bob" scrawled on it was taped to the door. The door, which was made of cheap pine and worn with grease and peeling gray paint, oddly sported an antique rose porcelain knob. It also had a deadbolt lock every eight inches from the top to the bottom and, even stranger, three deadbolts across the top. Fortunately, Michael had more than enough tools in his briefcase to meet the challenge, including a lock pick set his grandmother gave him for his first Holy Communion. He also had a high-speed metal saw, three bricks of military grade C4, detonators, a thermite grenade, a roll of duct tape, and two egg salad sandwiches.

After spending 45 frustrating minutes devising a brilliant way to open all of the locks simultaneously with duct tape, Michael asked Constance Anne if she'd like to share a sandwich while he showed her what he'd cooked up. As he prepared to demonstrate how smart and cool he was, as she sat next to him on the floor, Constance Anne leaned over to run her index finger over the beautiful doorknob.

The "Bob, Bob and Bob" sign slid off and, as it wafted to the ground, the door opened. The cleaners had had so much fun pissing in refrigerated cartons of coffee creamer that they had forgotten to lock it.

Whatever Michael and Constance Anne had expected the Tri-Bobs' offices to look like, what they saw surely wasn't it. In the place of standard furniture and decorations in the waiting room was an aluminum picnic table and a taxidermied fox with its feet nailed to the ceiling. Of the three offices in the suite, one had nothing in it but a folding chair. Another was empty except for a dirty blanket that stunk of microwave burritos. The third office had six floor-to-ceiling metal file cabinets that were empty except for dust, a few dead roaches, and a handful of paperclips. The manila file folders that should have been in the drawers were haphazardly piled on the floor.

As Michael and Constance Anne soon discovered, the files weren't arranged alphabetically by client or even by broad areas of the law like taxes or divorce.

Instead, they were organized by crimes the Tri-Bobs were committing.

In fact, each corner of the office had its own crime category. Extortion was immediately to the left of the door, embezzlement was to the right, and blackmail was on the left in the rear. The corner of the room designated for fraud was overflowing with hundreds of files divided into sections for health insurance fraud, identity fraud, towing fraud, charity fraud, fraud in the inducement, bond fraud, and investment fraud.

Two hours into digging through mountains of current and future felonies, Constance Anne came across a folder covered with pale smiley face stickers.

It was simply labeled "Sgt. V."

She opened it.

Inside were notes about erotic sexual denial written with a shaky hand along with Christmas party photos of Sergeant Vicki in a black, cupless bustier bullwhipping an elf's balls. Nearly last, but not least, was Mr. Reeves' Will and a business card with the address of the storage room. Behind it was a much-abused 8"x10" print of Sergeant Vicki's exposed, silicone-enhanced baby buffets.

It was almost five o'clock. Michael and Constance Anne placed the papers in Michael's bag, closed the door behind them and disappeared into the shadows. Michael's plan had worked brilliantly. Beyond a few seconds' worth of a phlegm ball walking into a restroom, the security cameras hadn't recorded anything more than indistinct shadows and reflections from the briefcase's shiny metal locks.

A few months later, Schanazello sold the security footage for $200 and six stolen credit cards to *Paranormal Padres*, a TV ghost show that followed the adventures of six defrocked Catholic priests who interviewed celebrity ghosts in bars, hot tubs with bars, and massage parlors with bars. No stranger to fraud himself, "Icky" claimed that the video showed genuine, luggage-carrying 'shadow people,' a term for spirits that materialize as dark, human-like silhouettes. Desperate for a large audience, *Paranormal Padres* aired a three-hour special featuring "spiritual fashion counselors" who chatted about the attaché cases, purses, totes, and clutches available to souls in the sweet hereafter. All, of course, were available for purchase for a limited time from the show's "exclusive sponsor on both sides of the River Styx," Mitzi Jo's Mausoleum. Despite massive publicity, the segment, "Briefcases and Bags from Beyond: Luggage in the Afterlife," came in second in the ratings to a botched exorcism of the city of Detroit.

With their identities still protected by the dark, Michael and Constance Anne changed back into their street clothes behind the pinsetters in a 24-hour clothes-optional bowling alley. Then they walked down Washington Street to the Common and reclaimed the bench they had been sitting on hours earlier.

In the shadows made by a nearby streetlight, Constance Anne suddenly saw Michael differently. Instead of a neurotic with permanent fashion damage, she realized that he was really a genius with misguided taste. He was also the single most devoted friend she could possibly imagine. As Michael opened his case to take out the Will, she noticed the cute way his usually slicked-back hair had tumbled on his forehead and the sexy smell of the "Beefy Man" cologne he wore entirely too much of.

Then, without a hint or warning, she kissed him on the cheek.

Speechless and stunned, he handed her the Will while he tried to get his pork tower under control. It was on the verge of ripping through his zipper like Pinocchio's nose on steroids.

A minute or so went by as Constance Anne looked over the documents. When she was done, tears began to run down her cheeks.

The good news was that Ray-Bob had told her the truth about being Reeves' sole heir.

The horrible news was that the storage room was in Florida.

Constance Anne was completely crestfallen. For a girl so broke that she couldn't rub two nickels together, the storage room might as well have been as far away as Mars. On top of that, she was certain that her dream of winning the trip to Oldmens was already dead, too. Veteran pillow renter Shasta

Melatonin was already so far ahead of everyone else that it was impossible to catch up.

Far worse than anything else, though, she felt guilty about having taken up so much of Michael's time and money for absolutely nothing.

Constance Anne slumped against Michael's shoulder, apologizing profusely for what she had put him through. He put his arm around her and told her that there was nothing to apologize for. Then he offered her his life savings for the bus fare.

Even as she smiled and politely told him 'no,' she realized that Michael Spacchio was someone she could certainly fall in love with.

Shortly thereafter, they parted with a light hug. With more than half of his body's blood supply now throbbing inside his dangerously ballooned meat scepter, Michael appreciated the brief embrace more than she could have known. Another kiss might trigger an explosion that would leave him with nothing but a stump.

Constance Anne made it back to Dickie's at sunrise, just in time to sign for the regular weekly delivery of embalming fluid. She hated their vendor, New England Corpse, Inc. Not only did she despise the company's motto, "We're Never Dead on Arrival!" but their mondo-creepy delivery guy looked like a walking case of sepsis. Despite a lack of sleep and feeling sure that this wasn't going to be her day, she hauled herself into the shower only to find that the water had been turned off. With no better second choice, she stretched out on the embalming table in the nude and bathed herself with the hose used to clean new arrivals in the Eternal Preservation Center. Freezing because the water never even got warm, Constance Anne quickly dried herself off and put on her threadbare, almost white, third-hand bathrobe. Then she pulled the tightest knit shirt she had over her head and the superbly erect nipples on her large, bouncy Hindenburgs and walked out the door.

It was a wildly busy morning at Lobstah Coach. Hundreds of passengers of all shapes, sizes, and persuasions were lined up for four city blocks waiting to board a flotilla of buses bound for Oldmens. Constance Anne was more than a little surprised. While the town was always a popular destination, it was insanely so at the moment, as she learned, because of an unusual festival being held there. Marketed across the country as "Fluffstock," the event presented rock bands, native cuisine, Florida Union Collegiate University t-shirts, under-18 pole dancing, an all-male "hide the zucchini" contest, a "name that mole" showcase, and all-day, naked senior citizen volleyball, all in a family-friendly, damp atmosphere. Most importantly, it featured 25 intensively-trained fluffy hamsters piloting model airplanes from World War II-era P-51 Mustangs to modern F-18s that would have otherwise been flown by remote control. Dressed in tiny flight suits and helmets and equipped with parachutes in the event of in-flight mechanical failure, the hamsters raced the five foot wingspan aircraft from downtown Oldmens to the waters of the Gulf of Mexico and back as a crowd of some 50,000 watched them on Jumbotrons.

No sooner than Constance Anne took a seat behind her pillow rental stand, a 40-something South American man with at least two obviously severe gum diseases, a deeply creased face, a man bun, and feral-like movements leaned across the desk and started sniffing her cleavage. Justifiably fed up, the man's wife violently depantsed him, rammed a nail ring she wore on her right middle finger up his ass, and vigorously wiggled the sharp claw at the end until she had his rapt attention. After giving Constance Anne a nearly incomprehensible, although sincere, apology in broken English, the woman started asking questions about the pillows. Despite the fact that much of the conversation was conducted with hand signs, facial expressions and an odd rubbing motion that the wife kept making on her belly, it became clear to Constance Anne that the wife didn't want to rent just one pillow. She wanted an incredible 17, one for herself, one for her husband and one for each of their 15 children. For Constance Anne, this was the single largest order she'd ever had and she had to run around the terminal to get enough pillows. The six dollar commission she was going to earn convinced her to feel that it was well worth the effort.

Constance Anne helped the happy family board the bus. As she waved goodbye, they all made the same strange rubbing motion on their tummies.

Unfortunately for the family, they misunderstood the word pillow for armadillo, a staple of their diet in Bolivia, which they planned to sauté and serve over rice on the bus. Oddly, they couldn't understand why they didn't see the little critters when they looked inside the pillow cases. Finally, they concluded that the armadillos were wrapped inside the spongy bread inside the pillow case. Four of the hungriest members of the family died of foam-ingestion within a few hours. Six more exploded after drinking water on a foam-filled stomach as the bus crossed the Georgia state line.

The last bus to leave the East Boston terminal that night was "The City of Utica," the pride of the Lobstah Coach fleet. Headed west on a 24-hour, non-stop trip to Omaha, its freshly-washed exterior and ginormous hood ornament, a six-foot carving of Arianrhod, the Celtic goddess of fertility, sparkled in the moonlight. Despite the fact that the goddess was hollowed out to smuggle desperately needed control top pantyhose into Nebraska, it made Constance Anne think of the decorative figureheads on the hulls of majestic 17th-century sailing ships that were used to ward off evil spirits. Apparently, there were scarier things along I-80 W than the food.

With the seats more than 40 percent oversold and strangers of both sexes sitting in each other's laps, most females and most guys sitting on top of other guys were eager to rent pillows to avoid unwelcome genital mischief. The overcrowding was a huge boon for the company's pillow, adult diaper and hand sanitizer rental divisions; so much so, in fact, that those customers pushed pillow rentals over the company's sales goal for the one-way ticket incentive program.

As "The City of Utica" pulled out onto the street and passengers threw a terrified child who lost her ticket off the bus, Supreme Rental Director Placenta Gettleman, called "Blisters" behind her back because of her fondness for cooking bacon in the nude, convened a meeting of the company's pillow team. Gettleman told the crowd of six that she was going to announce the contest winner. Sadly unable to remember the winner's name, she searched for her notes in the folds of her relaxed, husky-size polyester skort and eventually found them in her right pocket next to a melted wad of unwrapped cough drops.

"And the winner of the one-way ticket to Oldmens is …," Gettleman said, leaving the answer in suspense for unwelcome dramatic effect.

"For Christ's sake, bitch, spit it the fuck out!" screamed staffer Roy "Del" Krampo who was late for the weekly blindfolded scorpion fights his elderly mother ran to supplement her Social Security.

"Is …," Gettleman said. "Constance Anne Melatonin!"

Of course, as the other four members of the pillow team knew, there was a Constance Anne O'Leary and a Shasta Melatonin, but no Constance Anne Melatonin. With such low brain activity that it was surprising she could blink, Gettleman had thought it would be excessive to learn the names of *all* six people she managed.

"Oh, I'll just give it to the first girl," she said, impressed with herself for coming up with such a novel solution. "Constance Anne wins and Melatonin is second."

Constance Anne nearly fainted. The trip to Florida that had been so hopeless and impossibly distant was suddenly, literally in her grasp.

Knowing that whatever happened after that moment wasn't going to be good, Constance Anne grabbed the ticket out of Gettleman's hand and sprinted out of the terminal. It proved to be one of the best decisions she ever made. The ensuing fight between Shasta Melatonin and Placenta Gettleman was pitiless, animalistic and gruesome. By the time Shasta "opened up the dumb" inside Gettleman's head with a crow bar, Constance Anne was more than a mile away.

That night, Constance Anne barely slept as her mind dashed back and forth between glee and terror. She felt like she was on the edge of a crumbling cliff.

In the morning, just as soon as she hosed off the weird glueyness she always felt on her flesh after touching bus pillows, Constance Anne walked through the maze of Dickie's hallways that led to Mitzi Jo's office. Proper to a fault, Constance Anne wanted to personally thank Mitzi Jo for the wonderful opportunity to live and work at Dickie's and submit her two-week notice. Constance Anne arrived in front of the locked office and took a seat in the lobby at exactly eight o'clock. Mitzi Jo's assistant, Jimmy, arrived at 8:30. Four hours later, disheveled, wreaking of Scotch, barefoot, and wearing sunglasses, Mitzi Jo finally staggered in and vomited in Jimmy's wicker wastebasket.

Although few people knew it, Mitzi Jo had been coming in later and later every day, the unhappy result of excessive boozing and new "ho-grade" breast implants that were making her lightheaded.

Mitzi Jo had been drinking like a fish to push away the pain of horrific business pressures. She had been hit hard with losses from the *Luggage in the Afterlife* TV show. When purchasers realized that the bags were made in China, not Heaven as implied, they not only demanded their money back but sent a well-known Baptist lynch mob to her home. Dickie's was also losing customers to After Death Sports, Inc., a new company that helped sports aficionados continue to be part of the games they loved long after they'd turned to dust. After Death was a more exciting, albeit more expensive alternative to Dickie's own "value menu" that offered "below ground pricing" for ashes encased in commuter mugs, Christmas ornaments, and other kitsch. With After Death, the deceased could have portions of their remains sealed inside anything sports-related, from game-used football helmets and golf balls to baseball bats and scoreboards, in exchange for a hefty fee. Even more, they'd be publicly recognized for their support. For sponsoring the north end zone in the Florida Union Collegiate University stadium, for example, the school painted "Brought to you by Super Fan Donald Krebsackiwitz, 1945-2013" and a giant, full-color portrait of the deceased on the grass. Although the public didn't know it, Krebsackiwitz was a resident, too. For an additional charge, he found a final resting place six feet below the middle of the goal line. As Krebsackiwitz's family liked to joke, opposing teams literally had to score over his dead body.

In light of Mitzi Jo's indiscriminate vomiting, Constance Anne approached her cautiously. Slumped behind her desk with her sunglasses still on, Mitzi Jo only moved enough to fish a filthy dollar bill out of her bra.

She held it out to Constance Anne.

"Get the fuck out of here and take that goddamn dog with you," Mitzi Jo barked, pointing to her own leather purse.

Seeing Mrs. Dickie in that condition broke Constance Anne's heart. With tears in her eyes, she walked to her room, cleaned it from top to bottom, and packed the few things she had in a small bag. Then she said farewell to the guests in the Eternal Preservation Center, pulling down the sheets covering each of their faces to make her goodbyes as personal as possible.

Memories both good and bad swarmed into her head like locusts.

The next bus to Oldmens left in an hour. She opened the door to leave.

"Strike the set," she said. She'd read that Hollywood directors used to say that when they finished filming a movie.

Constance Anne walked out into the sunshine and closed the door firmly behind her.

No sooner than the lock clicked, the late Edwin Schmetz, a former Chelsington resident who had recently relocated to a slab in Dickie's Funeral Home, blew his bowels all over the wall.

Finding Michael was Constance Anne's first objective when she walked into the terminal. He'd already heard through the grapevine that she'd won the ticket and, although he was very happy for her, he was understandably sad for himself. He was afraid that the pain of missing Constance Anne might be more than he could bear.

When she found him, he was tossing away bags of used charcoal, ashes, and animal fat drippings from the onboard grills. More than once, Michael had been fascinated by what people thought was okay to burn inside a bus that carried two huge gasoline tanks on its roof. Until he saw something else, the charred remains of a pound of lard with two attached webbed feet was the winner in the clubhouse.

Constance Anne took Michael's hand as they walked to a place behind the terminal where they could have some privacy. Thankfully, none of the smokers or compulsive masturbators that crowded together under a tiny rusted tin overhang were there yet. To reduce the time people were away from work, the HR department launched a poster campaign called, "Smoke, Stroke, and Go!" to encourage employees to do both together. Unfortunately, it actually made things worse. Instead of smoking one cigarette, employees ended up smoking one before they buffed their machinery and then smoking another before they fell asleep at their work stations.

Having been through so much together, Michael and Constance Anne had built a remarkable bond that neither had ever experienced before.

Holding on to him for dear life with her arms around his neck and her body pulled close to his, Constance Anne told Michael how wonderful he was and how much she adored him. Sad and struggling to hold back a nervous ass whistle as his eyes filled with tears, he mumbled things back to her that were largely incoherent.

The clock was ticking and she needed to get on the bus.

Constance Anne told Michael how much she wished he could go with her.

Then she gave him the kind of deep, promising kiss a man never forgets.

Constance Anne handed her ticket to the driver and turned around to wave goodbye. Michael waved back with his left hand while he tried to calm his painfully enlarged, thumping Master of Ceremonies with his right. After maintaining the kind of erection legends are made of for four days, he finally threw in the towel and went to a urologist. The doctor diagnosed Michael's condition as Perpetuss Mentula Elephantus, also known by the acronym CLUB, for Constantly Large Unbearable Boner. He prescribed two hours on the internet viewing autopsy photos on top of 45 minutes' worth of male catheter TV commercials. By the time the catheter ads ended, his warrior king had returned to its normally flaccid 10 inches.

The driver, Mac Queso, congratulated Constance Anne for winning the ticket contest and suggested that she take a seat in the middle of the bus because it would hurt less when they "hit shit." Although the bus had an animal catcher on the front that usually filled-up pretty quickly with birds, squirrels, turtles, and possums, they also occasionally picked up something meaty like an alligator or a deer. During their single stop in North Carolina, passengers could bid on the road kill for a snack or a large meal.

Sometimes people even brought road kill and live animals with them. By the time they crossed into Connecticut, Constance Anne could hear the woman behind her break the neck of a chicken that she'd eventually bleed, pluck, dress right where she sat, and cook on a grill located under her seat cushion. The company's commitment to being "green" led them to power all of the grills with the bus's own burning-hot exhaust fumes.

Constance Anne curled up comfortably in a window seat and promptly fell asleep. Although the aisle seat next to her was unoccupied when she closed her eyes, she woke up in the company of a paper-thin woman on the muddy side of 50 with teal-colored hair and dinner plate-size earrings. The smell of burning chicken fat, scorched soy sauce and body odor was a great conversation starter, and the woman eventually shared that she was going to Florida to teach a college class called "The Many Shades of Blue," a survey of the uses of different shades of blue throughout world history. She had just finished a five-year stint at a Boston-area university teaching "The Many Shades of Red" and had taught similar courses around the country that, among other colors, covered green, orange, brown, yellow, purple, white, gray, lavender, and pink. Dressed in a very attractive Florida Union Collegiate University tee shirt, the professor said she could ride the bus to Oldmens and then take the university's triple-decker airboat some 250 miles through swamps to Florida Union's campus in the Everglades.

Trying to be polite, Constance Anne acted as if she was interested in the professor's life's work and inadvertently encouraged her to rant about red and blue for two hours. Although Constance Anne nodded off, a large man with angry nostrils sitting across the aisle from the professor became so angry with her nonstop yammering that he threatened to kill her. Dangerously self-absorbed, the professor ignored him and, at some point during the night, she simply disappeared. Although no one admitted to seeing what happened, everyone on the bus heard about it, and nearly every passenger filed by her vacant seat to see the tuft of blood-streaked teal hair caught in a wet piece of gum stuck to her tray table.

The mystery reminded Constance Anne of what happened to one of her mother's boyfriends, a sleazebag who worked as a school janitor and gave out stolen pencils stamped "Boston School System" as Christmas presents. He simply vanished one day, too, leaving behind nothing but the right side of his mustache floating in a bucket of soapy water.

No one who ever worked for Lobstah Coach would seriously suggest that the company's employees had all of their marbles. Among the people who were more than just a little off was Mac Queso himself who had desperately wanted to be an airline pilot. A washout in the Air Force because he frequently forgot that the 'N' on a compass stood for North, he poured his passions into ground transportation. All the same, the fact that he drove a bus didn't stop him from pretending that he was flying a 747.

When the bus was about 20 minutes outside of Oldmens, Queso switched on the scratchy public address system and coughed into the microphone to make sure it worked.

"Ladies and Gentlemen, this is your Captain speaking," Queso said in an unnaturally deep voice. "We've begun our descent into Oldmens International where the current weather is 80 degrees with bright sunshine. At this time, we ask that you put away all electronic devices. We'll be at the gate in about 20 minutes. Flight Attendants, please prepare the doors for arrival and cross-check."

Far from being amused, most of the passengers were terrified. Panicked by the announcement that they were flying, people climbed over one another to look out the windows and, not seeing wings, started screaming and praying.

When the bus finally stopped in Oldmens, more than a hundred passengers trampled over one another as they stampeded out the door, dropped to their hands and knees, and kissed the ground. After interviewing one man who identified himself as a "survivor," a local newspaper reported that the "captain" had flown into a thunderstorm that caused them to experience sudden updrafts and violent drops. The man, who limped on both legs, claimed that his extensive injuries were due to "flying negligence." His personal injury attorney made it clear that they would sue for "bazillions."

Despite all of the excitement, Constance Anne's arrival in Oldmens proved disappointing.

For some reason she had imagined the Oldmens bus terminal as a huge, gleaming structure made of glass and steel with a colossal fountain in the front and a meticulously clean, bright orange and aqua-colored interior.

The reality was somewhat different.

Oldmens "International" consisted of a badly-weathered park bench, a patch of dirt, and a single blue flip-flop that had clearly been gnawed if not also violently regurgitated. Twenty yards behind it was an incinerated convenience store that a hundred or more bus passengers were desperately racing towards to use as an open toilet. To the left of it was a combination Vietnamese nail salon and poultry shop and, to the right, a small building that looked like a good place to dump a body.

None of the passengers seemed to know how they were going to get to Fluffstock or anywhere else now that the bus trip was over. Some simply sat on the ground and others walked around trying to get the feeling back in their legs. At least one family threw down a blanket and continued to eat the wild turkey they had flash fried and sautéed in garlic and clotted hog fat on the bus the previous night.

Constance Anne decided to walk into the Vietnamese nail salon. She was starving and could smell poached chicken through the wall of acetone, formaldehyde, toluene, and dibutyl phthalate fumes pouring out of the place.

Started by refugees in 1976, "Poached Poultry & Pedi" became one of the town's most successful businesses by providing white women with the nearly spiritual joys of manicures, pedicures, and food they didn't have to make. Run in an almost military manner by a short, sweaty taskmaster with a pencil-thin mustache, the salon emitted a chorus of tiny Asian women screeching "Pick you coror!" "You need eyeblow?" and "Want hot lock pedi?" that swamped Constance Anne the moment she opened the door.

"Thank you. But I'd really just like some chicken," Constance Anne said politely.

"No *fucking* chicken!" the boss, whose name was Petie, screamed in her face in a high-pitched voice that put excessive emphasis on the word "fuck-ing." As Petie yelled, something gel-like sprayed from his lips. Whatever it was had been clotted on his gums.

"Mani, chicken? *Fuck* yes!"

"Pedi, chicken? *Fuck* yes!"

"Eyeblow, chicken? Yes!"

"Onry ploached chicken? No! No! *Fuck* no!"

Already famished and now overcome by the shrieking voices and unrelenting upsells, Constance Anne slumped into a giant, cream-colored, pleather recliner.

Saturated with God-knows-what in the way of body emissions, the chair had a worn-out massage mechanism that made a weird buzzing noise on one side and was hot to the touch on the other side even when its switch was turned off. At the base of the chair was a glass bowl with a rusty faucet set and drain inside it that was yellowed in ten little spots from a decade's worth of soaking toes. When not in use as a pedicure bath, it made a handy pot for poaching chicken. The herb-infused foot soak made a perfect meat tenderizer. Every morning, the women threw chicken parts in the vat, turned on the faucet, and rotated the dial to the "Super-Spa Pedicure" setting for two hours.

"Wa wong, gir?" a young lady named Anh asked.

Constance Anne felt so physically and emotionally exhausted that she could barely raise her head to answer.

Anh had very kind eyes and a compassionate smile and something about her made Constance Anne feel very safe. So safe, in fact, that Constance Anne's eyes welled up with tears. A good cry had been a long time coming, and Constance Anne added to it with a lengthy, disjointed, sniffle-filled, and mostly unintelligible recounting of her life that was appropriately met at points with cheers, laughter, and gagging noises from the people in the shop. Far from a nuisance, the customers found her stories exceptionally entertaining and started adding on other expensive services so that they could stay and listen. As the receipts got bigger and bigger, Petie, a colossal asshole but no dummy, gave Constance Anne all the chicken she could eat to keep her talking. By the time they closed their doors for the day, "Poached Poultry & Pedi" had made more money in eight hours than it usually made in a week.

Optimistic that her astounding success might at least get her a job as an acrylic sniffer, Constance Anne was shocked when Petie smiled and told her that his short answer was "*Fuck* no!" and his longer, more detailed answer was "*Fuck* no, *bitch*!"

He did, however, offer to let her stay with the "nail girls" for a few days as long as she promised never to come back to the salon again.

Ever.

Perplexed and hurt, but with no options, she took his offer.

Had Constance Anne known exactly how large of an asshole Petie was, she might not have felt so badly. For one thing, he didn't want anyone around who spoke English better than he did. The language barrier made ripping off the already overworked and underpaid nail girls nearly effortless. More than that, he'd convinced the owner, a married podiatrist who used the business to support three children his wife didn't know he had, that the company's profits were 30% lower than they actually were. Petie had been embezzling the difference for years and had stolen so much cash that he didn't know where to hide it anymore. The last thing he needed was somebody like Constance Anne who would produce even more.

As it was, he'd already stuffed 40,000 five dollar bills in his attic ceiling to insulate his waterfront McMansion.

If that was bad, it was worse that he'd been using his septic tank like an ATM. The tank was leaching, tens and twenties were floating to the top, and Petie and his cash were no longer welcome at the supermarket.

CHAPTER 15

"As soon as she was able to wash herself in the apartment's
quarter bath, a sink that served multiple purposes too disturbing to
contemplate, Constance Anne put on her tube top, short-shorts, and
heels and went off to find a job."

Petie was a liar, a misogynist and a thief. The only good news in that was that
he was consistent.

Because keeping the young nail girls illiterate, broke and exhausted was a
critical part of the salon's human resources program, Petie took his responsi-
bilities to educate the women about American life very seriously. More than
just explaining that no one in the U.S. made more than a dollar an hour, he
also made sure they knew that Vietnamese women could be put in prison if
they didn't walk to and from work every day. For the nail girls, that meant a
six-mile roundtrip, rain or shine, in high heels, very short, very tight skirts
and backless halter tops from their apartment to the salon 365 days a year.
According to Petie, the high heels and skimpy outfits were required by law,
too.

He said that it all had something to do with Americans still being pissed
about the Vietnam War, one of many reasons he gave them for never speaking to the police. In fact, Petie told them that if they ever were questioned
by the authorities, they were to say that they were from Arkansas where they
attended blow job school.

As if the poor women weren't terrified enough by Petie's America, they were also regularly mistaken for prostitutes. Although the lewd comments from drooling men driving by were helping them learn English, the cat calls became so frequent and scary that several nail girls literally inched down the street together every day, tightly packed like they were in a football huddle. Instead of toning down the vulgarity and making the women feel safer, "The Huddle" actually made things worse. The tiny steps they had to take to keep together added two hours to their daily travel and, with it, two more hours of insults from guys who couldn't get laid by a box of tissues.

Not surprisingly, hunger was a problem, too.

As Anh and Constance Anne walked to the apartment in the dark that night, Anh nearly tripped over a dead skunk on the sidewalk. Crouching down to sniff the carcass for freshness while Constance Anne tried not to puke, Anh broke into a broad smile. She was confident that if she threw the sweet, tender skunk meat in a crock pot with some pineapple chutney and soy sauce it would go a long way towards mending her relationship with her roommates. She'd hogged their only bath towel beyond the allotted five minutes every other day to get some wax out of her ear and everybody had gone nuts. At least one had accused her of being "a thug" and another refused to share her breaded iguana fingers with her.

With the dead skunk in tow, Anh and Constance Anne climbed 12 flights of wooden stairs to the apartment and opened the door.

It was good that very little surprised Constance Anne anymore. Where some people might have been shocked to find 11 women and a goat suspended in hammocks inside a tiny apartment with no windows, Constance Anne didn't fucking blink. Anh told Constance Anne that she'd make a group introduction in the morning. Individual introductions weren't necessary because everyone other than Anh and the goat was conveniently named Trang.

All the Trangs were as nice as they could be given that Constance Anne's addition reduced everybody's living space by three square feet, a big deal when they had under 45 square feet to begin with and even less when you threw in something for the goat.

Constance Anne was very grateful for her new friends' hospitality and their offer to let her stay as long as she needed to. Nevertheless, she was determined to get on her own two feet as quickly as possible. As soon as she was able to wash herself in the apartment's quarter bath, a sink that served multiple purposes too disturbing to contemplate, Constance Anne put on her tube top, short-shorts, and heels and went off to find a job.

Her optimism was genuine and exciting.

Five hours later, Constance Anne was ready to throw herself into an alligator pit. Everything that could have gone wrong did.

Florida's 90 degree heat and breath-robbing humidity had left her sweat-drenched; so much, in fact, that it looked like she was wearing a wet bikini. Constance Anne was also miserably uncomfortable and the steady drip of perspiration from the small of her back into her butt crack was terribly distracting. Moreover, the four interviews she'd had with HR managers so far that day weren't very productive. Although they all said that they had job openings, the meetings never went beyond sexually suggestive remarks, attempted lickings, and promises of jobs in exchange for sex right then and there under the desk. Always looking for a bright side, however, Constance Anne thought that her poor appearance and approach to finding a job so far that day had taught her two important lessons:

The first was to dress for success.
The second was not to interview with churches anymore.

Although she couldn't afford to dress for success right away, Constance Anne wasn't about to waste the rest of the day. She cleaned herself up in the ladies' room of a department store and tested some make-up and perfume at the cosmetics counter.

Then, she changed into her St. Woody's uniform, the only thing she had left that wasn't sweat-logged. She liked the fact that the white leather bustier, pleated, blue plaid skirtini that barely covered her thighs, white ankle socks, and black platform pumps with five-inch heels helped differentiate her from the rest of the crowd.

Luckily not immune to the luck of the Irish, Constance Anne turned to the right as she walked out of the store. Straight ahead of her on the second floor of a building on the other side of the street a man in a white coat was posting a Help Wanted sign in his office window. Constance Anne took off her high heels and ran into the building and up the stairs. There were four offices, occupied from left to right by three gynecologists and a urologist.

It occurred to her that the urologist might have had the idea of building his practice by giving husbands and boyfriends something to do while they waited. If that had been his plan, it hadn't worked. The waiting room was empty.

Nevertheless, 20 minutes after meeting Dr. Leo Shammerschmitz, the "Urologist to the Stars" as he liked to call himself for no apparent reason, Constance Anne had a real job that paid 50 cents more a day than the minimum wage.

On top of that, Dr. Shammerschmitz seemed to be a gentleman.

What Constance Anne didn't know, however, was that Shammerschmitz was also a man with a problem.

The doctor had operated a thriving practice for two decades until his nurse, Sydney, made a very bad decision. Unknown to Shammerschmitz, Sydney had idiotically started smoking PCP, a nightmarish, exceedingly dangerous drug that, among other things, can produce ferocious anger, paranoia, hallucinations and psychotic disorders virtually identical to schizophrenia.

One morning, patient Jacob Weissochowitz, an accountant on the third floor, staggered into the office in torturous pain from a completely full bladder that he couldn't empty. As Sydney prepared to insert a urinary catheter into his bladder via his meatus, the hole in the tip of the penis, and urethra, Weissochowitz complained that she wasn't working fast enough. Pissed off, Sydney became uncontrollably violent, picked up a razor-sharp, large-gauge hypodermic needle and jammed it through his meatus 29 times.

Sydney went to prison and, immediately after Mr. Weissochowitz's funeral, his widow sued the practice for $100 million. No sooner than the suit was filed, Mrs. Weissochowitz and her attorney held a press conference that included a photo presentation of her late husband's dead, perforated dude piston, Mr. Weissochowitz drinking the cup of coffee that pushed his bladder over the edge, social media postings of Sydney doing drugs, and unflattering close-ups of Dr. Shammerschmitz and his family. Needless to say, there was considerably more press about the tragedy than the doctor wanted.

While that was unspeakably horrible, the reaction of at least one of his fellow urologists was undeniably depraved. With the goal of cornering the lucrative failing bladder market, urologist Georgio Schentyve, M.D. started to run television commercials for his practice, Urology Cowboys, P.A. In his ads, Schentyve stood behind a medical exam table with a plastic penis in his left hand and an oversized hypodermic needle in his right and stabbed the "play dick" in the head with it again and again and again while fake blood spurted out and another man screamed in pain. Then, with a creepy smile plastered on his face Schentyve looked into the camera, put a ten-gallon hat on his head, mounted a life-size plastic horse and said, "Just say 'no' to urinary tract violence. And remember folks, at Urology Cowboys, we treat your urethra just like our own. Yee-haw!"

As offensive and stupid as the commercial was, it worked. Within a month, Dr. Shammerschmitz had lost nearly all of his patients to Urology Cowboys. He had to rebuild his practice and, as fate would have it, he and Constance Anne needed one another very badly.

Unaware that Shammerschmitz was an incredibly cheap bastard who let his office receptionist of 15 years go because she asked for a $1 a day raise, Constance Anne took over the job the next morning in her St. Woody's outfit.

Within a week, graffiti about "the hottie body in urology" was scrawled inside every stall in every men's room in the 19-story building.

Within two weeks, appointments for prostate exams were coming in day and night and the waiting room was nearly always full of the happiest male urology patients in the world. They even showed up early for appointments and encouraged the doctor to make them wait.

This was an entirely different experience for Constance Anne, and she was loving every minute of it.

The first Saturday after she got paid, Constance Anne hit the mass transit system in search of Mr. Reeves' storage room. Three hours, two bus transfers and four miles by foot later, she found herself outside of a one-story, concrete building so creepy and dilapidated that it would have made a toxic waste site look like a five-star hotel. Entire sections of the place were boarded up with waterlogged 4x8 plywood sheets that had unnatural-looking things growing out of them. Trash blew around everywhere, and when you looked up you could see that the roof was sagging like an old man's nut sack. The rusted barbed wire fence surrounding the whole mess had been violently twisted and torn in sections by something very large and pissed off. The capper was that the collapsed fence had let in a small community of wild animals and people, including a man who was diligently trying to his urinate his name on a green and black graffiti-strewn wall.

Constance Anne was pretty sure that he spelled out "Frank."

As strange as the entire landscape was, it was stranger yet that the facility was still in business. It even had a security guard who approached Constance Anne as she carefully tiptoed over a patch of barbwire. Wearing a black beret, a blue "I Eat Cheerleaders" T-shirt and extra-short shorts that were all incalculably bad ideas, he gave her directions to Unit 202. He proudly told her that he lived in one of the better storage units and invited her to stop by when she was done.

Constance Anne thought the man looked like a dating site for infectious diseases. She wasn't even going to shake his hand.

Anxious to get to the storage room and far away from a looming case of hemorrhagic fever, she said goodbye and walked as fast as she could towards Mr. Reeves' unit. Constance Anne could feel her excitement intensify with every door she passed.

When she reached Unit 202, she stopped and simply stared at it for a moment or two. Then she placed her head and the palms of her hands against the wide, roll-up door as if it was a religious shrine. Constance Anne had come a very long way to this place, and her success in overcoming so many odds to do so tasted remarkably sweet.

Eager to see what was inside, she gripped the handle and tried to pull up the door.

It didn't move.

Constance Anne looked around and found a padlock on the door. Curiously, a white envelope was attached to it. Inside the envelope was a bright pink card decorated with cute little bunnies that read:

Fuckface in 202:
U oe me $500 in back rint. If u dewnt pay me by thre weiks from twoday, Ill aukshin ur shit er kil u er both.
Kindist reegardz an Fuck u.
Sined,
Lonnie
Gy whooz gona oen ur shit er kil u er both if u dewnt pay.

Whomever or whatever Lonnie was, he had scrawled his name in crayon. That freaked Constance Anne out a little.

Based on the date the note was written, Constance Anne had ten days to come up with the cash. Her first reaction was that she was glad to know that there were people in the world who were worse spellers than she was. Her second was to take a deep breath and let the stress flow out of her. After twirling her hair about 50 times as she mulled over her options, she broke into a smile when she realized that all she needed was a small advance on her salary. That, together with what she saved from her last payday and $50 Sweet Michael had hidden in her bag, would be enough to cover the bill. She'd just have to stay with the nail girls a little longer. No one was pushing her out and, besides that, she was getting used to the goat that was now sleeping in the hammock directly above her.

Constance Anne reported to the doctor's office earlier than usual Monday morning. The appointment book for the day had patients scheduled every 30 minutes from eight to six, meaning that a lot of people were going to get double-parked. To try to avoid that and, most importantly, squeeze in enough time to speak with Dr. Shammerschmitz about her advance, she needed to make sure that he kept shoving whatever needed shoving into patients in a continuous flow. Ready or not, she opened the door at exactly eight and happily watched patients flood the waiting room. Within 15 minutes it was bursting at the seams like a diabetic foot stuffed into a stiletto.

Constance Anne could handle it all except for one thing.

Dr. Shammerschmitz wasn't there. To make things worse, wary of another "incident," Shammerschmitz had never hired another nurse.

Constance Anne was all alone.

She bravely stood up, asked for everyone's attention, and lied through her teeth. She announced that the doctor was stuck in traffic. The female patients, all of whom were rational and understanding, had no problem with it. Aggravated and cranky, the men were a whole different kettle of fish. Constance Anne eventually got them to calm down, but it took exposing another full inch of her cleavage to do it.

Terrified, she started dialing the doctor's cell phone, his wife's cell and their home phone every ten minutes to no avail. At noon, she called the police and asked them to make a welfare check at the house. The officer reported that he couldn't find a single Shammerschmitz anywhere.

By two o'clock, she could barely keep the morning crowd in their seats by walking to the front of her desk, hopping up on the edge and slowly crossing and uncrossing her long, toned legs. By four, the room was empty except for the patients that came in for their appointments, only to be told that the doctor wasn't there.

One angry man said he was going to take his "urinary incontinence back to Urology Cowboys where it belongs."

At a little after six, Constance Anne decided to throw in the towel and go home. As she restored her cleavage to its regular position, the door swung open.

Standing in the doorway like a giant sloth with stringy, Dijon mustard-colored hair was "Big Jeanne" Shammerschmitz, the Doctor's wife, who, at 6'4" and a strapping 285, more than lived up to her billing. She was holding the hand of her seven-year-old son, Sammy Shammerschmitz, whose name and pronounced lisp were a union made in hell.

"Who the fuck are *you*?" "Big Jeanne" asked Constance Anne in a voice that was unusually deep even for a man.

Constance Anne introduced herself politely, but succinctly. She desperately wanted to know what happened to the doctor.

"You can go home now, whatever-your-name-is," "Big Jeanne" said, rudely dismissing Constance Anne without offering any further information.

"But what happened to Dr. Shammerschmitz?" Constance Anne begged as she followed "Big Jeanne" to the door of the doctor's private office.

"Big Jeanne" looked annoyed. She looked down at her feet, looked back up at Constance Anne indignantly and took a deep, irritated-sounding breath.

"He's dead and you're fired," she said as she collected papers from the doctor's desk and put them in her purse. She also picked up the doctor's collection of plastic, life-size urinary tract models he kept on his credenza.

"Here," she said to Constance Anne as she tossed her a couple of penises, kidneys and a bladder. "They're souvenirs. Knock yourself out."

Sentimental to the core, Constance Anne put them in a plastic bag with the prostate gland-shaped hard candies Dr. Shammerschmitz's pharmaceutical rep gave him. Then she closed the door and whispered "strike the set."

Then she started to cry.

It would take several days for the police to piece together exactly how the "Urologist to the Stars" died. When the report was finally issued, the local community was stunned.

According to investigators, Shammerschmitz spent his final hours at The Pubic Bone, a gritty local nightclub frequented by urologists, podiatrists and veterinarians. After settling into a plush couch with three Romanian honeybuns in the VIP Champagne Room, Shammerschmitz, who insisted that the "Bone" staff call him "The Barbarian," spent the next five hours under the thumping, thrusting anatomy of steamy, all-nude, full-touch lap dancers. He also threw back ten or so Swamp Missiles, a spunky mix of raw egg yolks, jalapeno peppers, cilantro and 80 proof tequila.

At approximately 11 o'clock, one of the Romanian goddesses lit a cigarette. A hot ash fell on "The Barbarian's" tequila-sprinkled shirt and set him on fire. As the crowd inside the club quickly abandoned him, a spark ignited the rest of his clothing and, eventually, his body fat. Too drunk to move because of a .73 blood alcohol level, he combusted and was cremated in his seat.

The coroner had little to work with other than ashes, some oily residue on one of the sofa cushions, and a finger that had fallen off.

Not unexpectedly, Constance Anne was beside herself with grief and anxiety. Sad to lose such a nice boss and a job she liked, she was also terribly worried about how she was going to support herself and pay the $500 storage room fee.

Sitting on the floor of the apartment eating a Vietnamese dish consisting of noodles and thoroughly cooked land snails, she talked about her problems with her roommates, most of whom seemed to have an emotional, if not linguistic, understanding of what was going on. Every once in a while, the girls would blurt out "Oh, shit!" or "Eat me!" in English for no particular reason just to feel like they were part of the conversation.

After they all shared too much of the snake wine they made by immersing venomous snakes in grain alcohol and letting it soak for months, one of the Trangs stood up to speak.

Wobbly, with way too much snake vino in her bloodstream, Trang stood up, raised her hand, and read from a small piece of paper that she pulled from under the goat's collar.

"Kirr Petie! Serr his kidneys! Kirr Petie! Serr his kidneys! Kirr Petie! Serr his kidneys!" she shouted as she danced around in a tiny circle with her arms in the air. The rest of the girls and the goat cheered her on while another Trang offered her opinion by shrieking "Fuck fol it!"

A little lit herself, Constance Anne wondered how the goat learned English.

While everyone else slept, Constance Anne tossed and turned in her hammock as she thought about Mr. Reeves. She had no idea what she was going to do to come up with the money she needed, but she certainly wasn't going to kill Petie and sell his internal organs.

And she sure as hell wasn't going to sell her body for it.

That night, her dreams took her to a dark place.

Constance Anne was back at Blough High, walking the hallways to spread the news that Faller was dead. Try as she might to get everybody's attention, the kids simply ignored her. They were busy laughing at a man dressed in wet, badly stained clothes standing by the school trophy case. Constance Anne saw the man slowly turn his head towards her and felt her heart skip a beat. He smiled and beckoned her with a bruised, ragged-edged finger that he was holding in the palm of his hand. When she realized that the man waving somebody else's finger was Faller, she screamed louder than she had ever screamed before.

Constance Anne ran into a long, smoky tunnel littered with broken glass where the goat was sitting on a suitcase trying to thumb a ride. When she stopped, he threw his front legs around her neck and held on for dear life as Constance Anne hurriedly picked up speed again. She was twice as terrified now. Something was chasing them and closing in so fast that they could feel its saliva shower them every time it snapped its jaws.

Constance Anne could see light at the end of the tunnel until Mrs. Rivera, the neighbor who sold dust blunt at the bus stop when she was little, stepped in front of it and said something only the goat understood. They laughed, but stopped when Mrs. Rivera's jaw came off its hinges and her mouth fell open in a toothless black yawn.

Images of people, places and things were now dancing wildly around Constance Anne like reflections from a disco ball. In the twinkling of an eye, Mr. Reeves was in front of her, shimmering against a backdrop of bright light, with one eyebrow raised and hand puppets lined up behind him as far as the eye could see.

"Help us," Mr. Reeves said. "Please help us. Please, dear. Help us."

"Help us now! Get us out of this shit!" the puppets shrieked. They were advancing on Constance Anne with clubs in their hands. She could see that some of them were smoking unfiltered cigarettes, which was very strange.

Constance Anne woke up from her hellish nightmare with her arms wrapped around the goat. She was drenched in sweat and unknown goat fluids, and it was obvious that the goat didn't want to talk about any of it.

The next morning, Constance Anne got up with the rest of her roommates and helped them prepare for "The Huddle." After they left, she had a cup of Jasmine tea, a bite of leftover chicken lung, and sat down on the floor.

She had a knife in one hand and platform pumps with five inch heels in the other.

She looked at one and then the other, back and forth, as she weighed her options. Tears ran down her cheeks.

Then she tightened her grip on the knife and made a decision.

⋏

Less than a week later, an unmarked police car made a discreet U-turn into bumper-to-bumper northbound traffic on a four-lane highway during afternoon rush hour. The driver, a tough veteran cop who'd seen it all and then some, wanted a closer look at a woman on the other side of the road. Her very long legs and impossibly tight tube top loosely fit the description of the person the department was looking for. He was particularly concerned about the large backpack she was wearing and the unusually large, box-shaped bulge in the back of it. The top of the backpack was only half-zipped.

As he slowly steered his high-powered, dark blue Dodge Charger Pursuit in her direction, he had every intent of catching her by surprise. The last thing he wanted to do in 92 degree heat and 85% humidity was chase her on foot.

New details came into focus every time the Charger's wheels rolled forward.

First, it was definitely her. She was about 5'7", 125 pounds, with light blue eyes, and shoulder-length dirty blonde hair with a long sweep bang. And, as one of the more expressive guys at the station had pointed out, she had an ass like "a hot cinnamon bun." Assuming that his description meant that the back of her bus was like a sweet roll and not just sticky, that checked out, too.

Second, she was holding something with a pink handle grip and a black top that made him just as wary as the backpack did. For the life of him, he couldn't tell what it was.

Dressed in plain clothes, he slowly got out of his car. As he walked towards her, he ran his fingers over the handles of his gun and Taser.

Just in case.

He had to be careful. Anybody could be a threat these days.

Constance Anne turned towards him.

As they locked eyes, she raised the pink and black thing. He tensed up.

A crackle, like the kind you'd hear from an old vinyl record, cut through the air.

"Bl ...?" she said into the microphone that was attached to the square, battery-operated kid's karaoke machine in her backpack that acted like a PA system. He cut her off mid-word when he flashed his badge.

"Are you going to arrest me?" Constance Anne asked, lowering the mike so that she didn't broadcast her business to every Tom, Dick and Harry on Earth.

"Not this time," he said. "But we *are* going to have a serious talk."

Constance Anne had just started her work day and needed this like a hole in the head. As it was, she'd already been busted once for solicitation and gotten a ticket for loitering. Her bid to make money in the "personal services" industry was sinking like the Titanic. In fact, she had become the laughing stock of the local prostitution trade because she hadn't made a dime. Her first customer turned out to be an undercover cop. The rest she walked away from, she told the other ladies of the evening, because all of the "Johns" she'd met had infected cysts, warts, carbuncles, mouth ulcers, cold sores, boils or a combination of them all on their faces. Although all of them made her queasy, she really drew a line when it came to pus.

She also swore that one guy had diaper rash.

On his lips.

More truthfully, she had convinced herself to hold out until she met a man with a nice smile, nice clothes, and a nice car.

"Honey, them men ain't lookin' for no crack-ass street whore," said "Dream-Crusher," a white girl who sold her body a few nights a week to pay the interest on her college loan. "They the creepiest ones. They lookin' for sumptin' to bury."

Obviously, Constance Anne had decided to take a pass on selling Petie's lungs, although she had to admit that she wasn't unfamiliar with the idea. There had been rumors more than once around St. Woody's about janitors, cafeteria workers, and gardeners being hired and never being seen anywhere or by anyone again. There was also an incident at Florida Union Collegiate

University she'd read about. Twenty school security guards had been murdered there in the span of ten days. Although the university president said the deaths were due to "drug-related violence" committed by meth-selling alligators, the police questioned why each man's kidneys, liver, corneas, and lungs, each worth tens, if not hundreds, of thousands of dollars apiece on the black market, had been surgically removed before they died.

A few weeks later, the investigation was terminated when the lead detective, his wife and their families, including parents, aunts, uncles, nieces and nephews, suddenly disappeared.

⋏

Alone in the apartment the morning after her nightmare, Constance Anne put the knife away and put her mind to work on launching a career in prostitution, or what she preferred to call "short-term leasing." Since there weren't any Small Business Administration booklets about sexual entrepreneurship, she picked up a book about running a business at the library and decided to turn to her roommates for more personal advice. Constance Anne spent the day drawing pictures on the walls and practicing hand gestures to overcome the language obstacle. If this worked, she thought to herself, it would be because women understood things faster and more intuitively than men could ever hope to.

It got off to a rough start.

When Constance Anne introduced the topic to Anh and the Trangs by jabbing the first finger of her right hand back and forth through a circle she made with the thumb and first finger of her left, there was immediate confusion. Although the roomies generally understood what Constance Anne was trying to say, they thought she was telling them that she wanted to fuck people. That, of course, led them to the natural assumption that she wanted to be a politician. The tallest Trang stood up and pretended to stab another girl in the back while robbing her blind. The crowd applauded in agreement. That was exactly what all politicians did.

When Constance Anne shook her head 'no,' there was a collective sigh of disappointment.

No sooner than Constance Anne got the gang's attention again, another Trang, who suffered from near-legendary meat sweats, laid down on her back with her legs spread open and brutally strangled an imaginary figure lying on top of her. For some reason, she thought Constance Anne wanted to murder a man during sex and was more than happy to demonstrate a few deadly moves. Although it was met with a polite 'no' too, the rest of the Trangs felt that they had just gotten to know "Trang the Sweater" at a much deeper, more soulful level. It appeared that killing dudes while they were glazing her donut was part of her skill set. That took icy cold balls and it was good to know that they had somebody like that around.

Not to be outdone, the Trang who'd suggested selling Petie a la carte bellowed "*No! No! Kirr Petie! Kirr Petie! Serr his kidneys!*" again. This time she added emphasis by burying a hatchet in a hog's head. The goat, who was rightfully concerned that he might be next, moved as far away from her as possible.

Seeing nothing but upside in that for everyone but Petie, the roommates unanimously urged Constance Anne to kill him.

She was now frustrated to the point of tears.

According to the business book, Constance Anne needed to collect market research. To do that, she decided to ask the "Huddle" girls to tell her what men shouted at them every morning and night. That, hopefully, would give her an idea of what customers wanted and how much they were willing to pay. Although the Trangs didn't necessarily understand what was being yelled at them, they had heard the same crap from the same guys so many times that they could imitate the men down to very small voice inflections.

"Hey, wanna gimme a blow job real quick, eh? Ten bucks, ya know? Meet me at the stop 'n go light!" one of the girls said with an accent that had Wisconsin written all over it.

"Hey! You reckon' you wanna fuck? I got me a fuckin' ten with your name on it, baby! Come git in mah truck. It's slicker than pig snot on a radiator!" another girl said, perfectly mimicking a redneck who drove a gargantuan white truck probably because he had a tiny gearshift.

The "Huddle" team went on for 20 minutes without repeating a single sex act.

Constance Anne was flabbergasted.

The good news was that there were a lot of opportunities. The bad news was that the going rate for most everything she could do in a car was ten bucks. That meant that she'd have to have to have some sort of sex with somebody about every half hour over the handful of nights she had left to raise the money. That seemed like a lot.

Nevertheless, she was happy to know that the only thing that stood between her and saving Mr. Reeves' legacy was 50 zippers and bottle of mouthwash.

Because the business book suggested that she make a list of the products and services she offered, she put together a "Menyou of Survisis" to give customers when she got in their cars. Anh gave her a working smart phone with a credit card reader that someone "lost" when Anh leaned over and took it from her purse during a pedicure. Another roomie came up with an idea that would help everybody hear exactly what Constance Anne was selling. The other girls chipped in a dollar apiece to help her out, and Constance Anne found a pink and black karaoke machine with a pink and black microphone in a thrift store the next day. It had cool flashing lights, too.

Constance Anne was deeply grateful for the way her roommates rallied around her. The ones that weren't ticking time bombs were incredibly good people.

A few years later, she would read a story about a group of Vietnamese girls who had been forced into virtual slavery by man named Mr. Petie. She'd also read how one of the young women, Anh, bought a lottery ticket and won $10 million the same day Mr. Petie suddenly and inexplicably disappeared. The girls retired to a waterfront McMansion they bought at a foreclosure auction which, as an incidental benefit, had tens of thousands of dollars in U.S. currency stuffed in the attic as insulation.

The story was next to an article about a hospital that mysteriously received a pair lifesaving lungs, kidneys, a heart, a liver, and corneas packed in ice inside a picnic cooler. The organs did a lot of good for a lot of people.

It was a shame that no one knew who to thank.

⅄

"You can't walk up and down the highway shouting 'Blow jobs, ten bucks' on a karaoke machine," the officer told her. He was a good man, an old school kind of guy who, when he could, far preferred to talk some sense into someone rather than throw them in jail.

"There are children in those cars, for God's sake," he said pointing at traffic that was backed up for a mile. "What you're doing isn't just illegal. It's stupid. Really stupid."

Then he really hammered her.

He talked about how dangerous the men who wanted to "lease" her were and how easily she could catch a horrible disease or even die. She tried to explain about Mr. Reeves and his puppets and how badly she needed $500 to pay the back rent on his storage room.

He told her that whatever she was trying to save wasn't worth it if she had to sell her body for it. He told her that if he saw her selling herself on the street again that he'd throw her in jail.

She broke down and cried. She looked like she'd been hit by a car that stopped, backed up, and ran over her again.

He reached into his pocket and gave her a $10 bill so she could get something to eat.

As an afterthought, he handed her a half-off coupon for Uncle Deng's All You Can Eat (Not Sit on Your Fat Ass and Eat 4Ever) Chinese Super Buffet.

CHAPTER 16

*"The branch in the family tree ... had been replaced with a crude
drawing of small male genitals. The head of the little guy pointed to
Palomino's wife, Bambi. It simply said 'Dicked.'"*

Two blocks away from the devastation of La Camo Cheapo, Constance Anne
and Tiffany sat under a big red umbrella at Curdles and Clots with sugar
cones filled to overflowing with chocolate frozen yogurt. Even though it was
2-for-1 Sausage and Egg-flavored Ice Cream Day at the store, they pretty
much had the place to themselves.

Although the emotional outbursts, anger, and denial that normally mark
psychological trauma were right around the corner, the initial shock of what
had just happened hadn't really hit them yet. Not only had they miraculously
escaped death by the width of an eyelash, Constance Anne walked out of the
rubble with nothing more than minor scratches. Tiffany wasn't injured at all.
Putting aside occasional trembles in Constance Anne's hands and the fact
that Tiffany was as white as a sheet, they acted like any other young women
out for a little fun. The dessert was Tiffany's treat and, even though she
wasn't very talkative, Constance Anne could see relief beautifying her friend's
face. She was going home.

On the flip side, Constance Anne was so animated and talking so quickly
that most people on the receiving end would have felt compelled to suffocate
her. Surprisingly, Constance Anne's exhausting, anxiety-ridden babble about
everything from St. Woody's to Mr. Reeves' storage room didn't seem to

bother Tiffany a bit. Far from it, she smiled empathetically and even seemed to be listening.

There was no doubt that Tiffany was cool. If Constance Anne was amazed by that, she was about to be rendered speechless.

When they finished eating, Tiffany offered to drive Constance Anne to the storage room in her, pastel blue "Rice Edition" Magua, so named because it was cheap and sticky.

As they pulled up to the facility, Constance Anne noticed that something had been added to the landscape since her first visit. Clustered near the entrance were 20 immense dumpsters. As she later learned, the owner of the storage facility had started a chain of "deep discount" medical waste facilities. Their business plan opened the way for a host of different medical providers to get rid of things like needles, scalpels, blood products, secretions and "leftovers" like kidney stones, appendixes, arms, and legs at half the cost of companies that complied with State and Federal laws. When the dumpster was full, the company planned to put the infectious "merchandise" in pickup trucks and dump it on golf courses, school playgrounds, and country club tennis courts during the night. That way, they could ensure that it would be properly disposed of at someone else's expense.

Moving along as fast as the sputtering Magua would carry them, Constance Anne and Tiffany reached Mr. Reeves' space without a moment to spare. Standing in profile in front of Unit 202 was a man with a sledgehammer getting ready to knock the bejesus out of the combination lock. She quickly deduced that he was Lonnie because somebody had scrawled "Loonie" on the front of his T-shirt in black marker.

Concerned that he might be as dangerous as he was creepy, Constance Anne approached him carefully.

He turned to face her. There were three things she noticed about him immediately:

He was only about 14 years old.
He was barely five feet tall.
He was mostly head.

Despite having a properly proportioned body and face, he had a forehead that was about 12 inches wide. Constance Anne felt badly for him. She could only imagine how hard it had to be to buy a hat.

On the other hand, she quickly discovered that he was an obnoxious, pizza-faced pipsqueak. He told Constance Anne that he'd "think about letting her pay the bill" on the storage room if she pinky-swore that she'd sext with him. He wanted to see her boobs, and he told her that she would definitely want to see his junk.

Anxious to get into the room, she reluctantly agreed to his middle school brand of extortion as long as he would agree to go first. Shocked that she was going to do it, his teeny-bopper voice cracked when he said 'yes'.

An appallingly bad speller or not, one thing 14-year-old Lonnie knew how to do was use phone apps. That made it easy for Constance Anne to transfer the $500 balance to the company and be finished with the matter. When that was done, the little weasel demanded her phone number.

Since she was just borrowing the phone Anh stole and really didn't have a number, she responded with the next best thing.

"Don't keep me waiting, baby," Constance Anne said in her breathiest Marilyn Monroe-style voice, letting him get just close enough to her chest to hear the blood pumping behind his eyes. "Send me pictures of your big, stiff Moby Dick, baby. Send me a lot of pictures. All night long."

Then she blew softly in his ear and, as he staggered off on three legs, handed him the private number of "Big Jeanne" Shammerschmitz.

Tiffany took a careful look at the lock and went to the trunk of her car. She came right back with a huge pair of bolt cutters, heavy gloves, and safety goggles. Before Constance Anne could even turn around, the lock was no more. It was a good thing she had thought to bring a replacement lock.

Constance Anne gripped the handle of the 8' wide door, pulled upward and felt it start to rise.

The next thing she saw was a room that was all but pitch black.

She felt around for a light switch, found it, and a split second later, the 10' x 15' unit with a 9' ceiling was filled with surprisingly bright fluorescent light.

The place looked like it had been designed by someone with OCD.

Perfectly spotless medium-size cardboard boxes were arranged in nine rows that were four high and six deep. Every box was numbered sequentially from right to left. They were so tightly packed that counting them required taking out parts of rows in order to see all the way down to the floor and to an aluminum wall in the very back. A tenth row, on the far left of the room, was four high but only five boxes deep. It seemed odd that whoever stacked the boxes chose to leave a spot open in the very back rather than the front.

Being pretty organized herself, Constance Anne thought it would be a good idea to inventory all of the contents as soon as possible. Tiffany didn't raise an objection, and one by one the boxes were relocated to the asphalt in front of the storage unit door.

As they moved from box to box, there weren't any big surprises, at least not as far as Constance Anne was concerned. There were puppets on top of puppets. Some, like Clark Gable, Marilyn Monroe, Joan of Arc, and Marie Antoinette, she recognized. Others, particularly the morbidly obese Santa Claus who stabbed her with scissors, were impossible to even look at. Tiffany, on the other hand, was literally speechless. Constance Anne thought her friend might freak a little when she noticed that none of the puppets had a single brush stroke or visible seam anywhere on them.

Constance Anne certainly had. She was convinced that they were alive.

The rest of the work went smoothly, and within a few hours all but four boxes had been investigated. They stood stacked on top of one another in the row with the odd open spot.

Constance Anne couldn't deal with another box. She sat down on the floor to rest. There were 647 hand puppets so far with more to go and she had absolutely no clue what she was going to do with any of them.

Her heart started pounding. She was having an anxiety attack and her thoughts were running wild.

"I don't even have a place to live," Constance Anne told herself.

Something was squeezing the breath out of her.

"What the fuck am I going to do now?" she roared, this time out loud. "I almost died twice. Reeves shouldn't have done this to me. Why did he have to make these fucking puppets anyway? Oh, God! Did I kill Mortie?"

She was crying and couldn't stop. She didn't even remember starting to cry.

"I want to go home. I want Michael," she whispered.

Her mind was stuck in a dark corner and she couldn't get it out.

"Fuck this!" she shouted.

Anger was pouring out of her. Anxiety and grief were right behind. She wanted to kill something.

"Fuck *all* of this!" she said in a low, raspy voice that would have terrified anyone who heard it.

She screamed bloody murder.

She screamed when she kicked the bottom box so hard that all the boxes flew into the wall.

She screamed when the boxes vomited puppets all over the place.

She screamed while she tore one box apart so violently that her fingers bled.

It wasn't surprising that it took Constance Anne a while to stop crying, much less pull herself together. When she eventually got to her feet, a quick look around was more than enough to verify that she'd gone postal. The room was littered with puppet crap. She was a little surprised that Tiffany and her Magua were nowhere to be found.

Then again, maybe it wasn't so surprising after all.

Constance Anne started cleaning up the debris field, apologizing to each puppet for having gone psycho and promising not to do it again, at least not when they were around. In the left corner of the unit, one of the boxes had overturned and thrown eight or nine puppets into a twisted pile that looked like a bad car crash before there were seatbelts.

She picked up each one carefully and gently re-wrapped them. As she approached the bottom of the pile, she saw a piece of badly-worn aqua blue plaid cloth sticking out. It reminded her of her mother's filthy bathrobe. If only because the color brought back bad memories, she picked it up between her thumb and forefinger the same way she would have handled a dead rat.

It turned out to be pretty much the same thing.

The threadbare puppet was the spitting image of her mother.

Constance Anne's rage was immediate. There was nothing but white hot anger towards the woman who threw her away when she was five, dumping her at St. Woody's with nothing but an onion in a paper bag.

She ripped her mother's head off and threw it down on the concrete. Then she tossed the rest of the body next to it.

"Fucking bitch," Constance Anne said uncharacteristically as the corpse bounced on the floor. Her advancing acute stress disorder wasn't only directing her fury anymore. It was speaking for her, too.

Something very white was sticking out from what had been her mommy's neck. Constance Anne leaned over and pulled it out of the puppet's chest cavity. Handwritten on a white slip of paper were the words, "Look in the bottom of Box 19."

Constance Anne threw up her hands. She was pretty sure by now that Reeves was nothing more than a nasty bastard who liked to fuck with people. God only knew why he picked her as the fuckee. She was confident that he watching all of this from Hell and laughing his ass off.

Right then and there she decided to burn all of his shit and go back to Chelsington.

Alone now, Constance Anne started to literally throw the boxes she and Tiffany had put on the driveway back into the storage room. Since they were going to be the only guests at her barbeque, their condition didn't exactly matter.

Box 19 began to stare at her. Constance Anne told it to fuck off and promised herself that when she got to it, she was going to chuck it in the room just like the others.

She didn't last five minutes. She climbed over 15 other boxes to get to it, opened it up, and dug for the bottom. There was nothing but the same puppets and packing materials that were there before.

Then she felt something thick and cylindrical that reminded her of the fun coffee mug-shaped dildos that were very "in" with caffeine junkies. Now she was really furious with herself for falling for such a stupid joke.

Constance Anne pulled out a large book with a lock on it and two 8 ½" x 11" envelopes that had been rolled up and kept together with a rubber band.

One envelope was very thick and the other very thin. Damned if she knew why she missed them the first time through.

Her name was handwritten on the outside of both envelopes.

She opened the thick one first and found several $100 bills. Fifty of them, actually. They looked real.

Constance Anne opened the thin one. It contained a single piece of light brown paper written in black ink in a very old style of cursive penmanship. It looked like a poem.

"My dearest Constance Anne," it began.

"This letter will explain in verse
The story of an ancient curse
Made in anger that was right
To render judgment black and white
That some must die because of birth
Their ancestors built a hell on Earth.

Each of these puppets have been given to you
To make your future bright and true
No longer to walk a slippery ledge
If what I ask you truly pledge.
I have died and you must take
Careful control of three families' fates.

This story started long ago
When a Dick hurt a Frigg and wouldn't let go.
You are a Frigg, a descendant of witches,
For that you inherit remarkable riches.
A spell of revenge was cast in fire one night
One filled with anger a legacy of spite.

Now each first male Dick as you will hear
Must lay upon a funeral bier.
So must the first boy of another
For Palomino served as brother.
At forty years old they must all kick the bucket
The causes of death contained in their puppet.

Now open the book that lists each descendant
Whether rich man or wise man or no more than a peasant.
By taking their puppets and tweaking their meat
As long as they die you'll get five grand a week.
But fail to succeed and you'll pay quite a price
So just do the work and heed my advice.

You'll find things to help you if you will just look.
Most important of all is the ancestry book.
And when you're confused and problems accrue,
Look in the boxes, they hold answers, too.
Just never forget that men think with their penis
And that success in this job doesn't require a genius.

Your grandfather,
John Frigg Reeves IV"

Utterly overwhelmed, Constance Anne wasn't able to absorb anything any-more. In fact, a lot of things started to leak out of her head.

She gingerly straightened up the boxes, gave each one a kiss, collected the envelopes and the book, closed the door, and put on the new combination lock. Then, she took the bus home.

It took her two days to remember that Tiffany had run away.

It took her three days to remember that she had five large in cash.

A week later, Constance Anne had her own spacious three-bedroom, two-bath apartment in one of Oldmens' prettiest complexes and, a few days after that, had furnished it from top to bottom. She arranged the place to accommodate cots for at least half of the Trang gang every night. After hogging the bathroom way too many times, however, the goat wasn't invited back. Frankly, it was for her own safety. In the aftermath of one of the goat's notorious 20-minute showers with the door locked, several girls measured her and started whispering about new gloves.

For the next three weeks, Constance Anne devoted her days to hanging out with the puppets, studying about Dicks and Palominos and spending her newly acquired wealth wisely. She bought a clean, used SUV, clothes at thrift shops, and things the Trangs desperately needed which, of course, included everything. Constance Anne was thrilled that she could help her friends and swore that as long as she was around, they would never have to make soup from deer placentas again. Try as she might, though, she couldn't get them to quit their jobs and let her take care of them.

Not that she would have ever had a reason to think about it before, but Constance Anne was astounded to learn how many Dicks and Palominos there were in the United States alone. What didn't surprise her was that a large percentage of them were in state and federal correctional institutions. If there was one thing that the book her grandfather gave her made clear it was that crime played an important role in both families. As the Dicks in particular were fond of saying, "The family that betrays together stays together."

Constance Anne was making a list of the first-born males who were nearing their 40th birthdays state-by-state when a lightbulb went off in her head. She could have sworn that Mortie said that he was related to the Palominos.

She quickly flipped to the Florida section and ran her finger down the list. Looking back at her was the name "Morton Wayne Beech." But when she traced his ancestors back to Massachusetts, it didn't look right. The branch in the family tree that would have connected him to DeJon Palomino had been replaced with a crude drawing of small male genitals. The head of the little guy pointed to Palomino's wife, Bambi. It simply said "Dicked." Constance

Anne figured out what that meant. Bambi had "buried the broomstick" with the Magistrate and had given birth to his child after her husband died.

Constance Anne flipped more pages. Tiny Earl was a Palomino. Frickey Dickie was a Dick. Spruce Faller was a Dick. Mitzi Jo Dickie was a Dick by marriage. She didn't know if that counted or not, but she had turned into a dick anyway.

She had to face the truth. Her life was filled with Dicks.

But by far the worst discovery, worst by a magnitude of a billion, was that Michael Spacchio was a Palomino.

Mulling that over in her mind literally kept Constance Anne awake for several days. Insomnia was a terrible thing, and she felt badly for anyone who had it. She couldn't get comfortable and had a very hard time falling asleep. Even when she did, she would wake up after only a few hours and not be able to go back to sleep. She was sleepy all the time. She was so irritable that the only one who would agree to be around her was the goat, and that was only if she got to use the shower.

With her hand shaking one day, she accidentally cut her right index finger in the kitchen. The cut became infected and, in spite of the Trangs' offer to fix her up with a sharpened wolf bone and some nail polish remover, she decided to see a doctor.

The doctor's office was overly crowded, hot, and reminded her of a pork processing plant.

Constance Anne showed the crotchety old broad behind the check-in desk her infected finger and was promptly handed 15 pages of paperwork to fill out with a pen that some guy had just sneezed on. When she turned it in, a different crotchety old broad said that the doctor would see her in just a few minutes. Although she didn't care for all of the fresh, unrecognizable stains on the waiting room furniture, Constance Anne sat down anyway. Looking for something to occupy her, she studied a box of lost and found items. It contained the usual type of stuff like glasses and handkerchiefs. It also had a very large tooth and a blue prosthetic eyeball that rolled around whenever somebody bumped into the box.

Two hours later, a small woman who didn't speak English escorted her into an examining area, took her temperature, weighed her and gave her an instant blood test that only required a prick on her finger. The fact that the small woman pricked the finger that was infected didn't seem to bother anyone but Constance Anne. Then, the small woman slapped her own ass and squatted down. Although Constance Anne wasn't immediately sure if that meant that the small woman had to go to the bathroom or was about to go to the bathroom right there, she finally figured out that she was telling her to take a seat in the waiting room again.

The happiest news of the moment was that someone had turned on the TV. After nine consecutive car commercials, the local news came on and the anchor launched into an "eyewitness" story about an assisted living facility where a knife fight over a walker sent two men in their nineties to the hospital. After showing entirely too much footage of the drab exterior of the building and interviewing two residents who "sorta" knew the men and thought they were both assholes, the anchor rolled into the next story.

"Police now know the identities of the three people who died in the tragic La Cama Cheapo collapse," he said as he looked into the camera with an appropriately mournful expression that was being caused by a wedgie. "Here's more from Jane Jones at the scene. Jane?"

This had Constance Anne's full attention.

"Thanks, Huck. Police now know the identities of the three people who died in the tragic La Cama Cheapo collapse that took the city, and certainly the people who were flattened like tortillas, by surprise," the reporter said with a little smile.

To boost ratings, a number of stations had "gone inappropriate" recently. The most popular report so far had described a shootout by saying, "Police then put eight bullets through the gunman's head, spewing blood-soaked chunks of brain matter over two blocks."

"The dead are identified as Morton Wayne Beech, 40, of Oldmens, Wayne Elmer Smeethe, 32, of Balsa Wood Estates, and Tiffany Ann Hollandaise, 27, of West Toaster. As you'll recall, it's taken several weeks to make the identifications due to the conditions of the bodies. There's not a lot you can do when they're first identified as lasagna. Back to you, Huck."

"*What?*" Constance Anne said out loud.

The small woman tapped her on the shoulder, motioned for her to follow, and put her in an examining room about three steps ahead of the doctor.

"Constance Anne, it's nice to meet you," the doctor said, looking through her file absent-mindedly. "Let's take a look at that finger. Mommies can't have hurt fingers, can they?"

"*What?*" Constance Anne said.

"Oh, the instant blood test. We always do them because they're so easy. I thought you knew. You're pregnant."

Constance Anne slowly walked out of the doctor's office with her newly-bandaged finger, a prescription for an antibiotic, and a list of pre-natal vitamins she was supposed to take.

More than a little wobbly, she took the first chair she could find.

"*Oh my God!*" she said to the empty corridor.

"*I have a Dick in me!*"

Made in the USA
San Bernardino, CA
10 September 2016